A Portrait of Emily Price

Center Point
Large Print

Also by Katherine Reay and available from
Center Point Large Print:

Lizzy & Jane
Brontë Plot

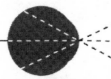

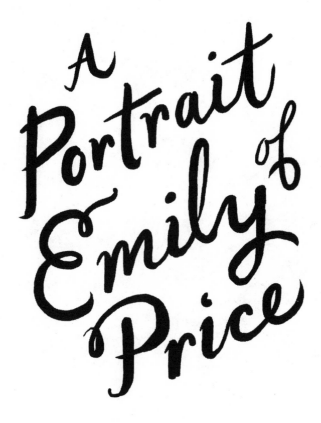

Katherine Reay

CENTER POINT LARGE PRINT
THORNDIKE, MAINE

This Center Point Large Print edition is published in the year 2017 by arrangement with Thomas Nelson.

This novel is a work of fiction. Names, characters, places, and incidents are either products of the author's imagination or used fictitiously. All characters are fictional, and any similarity to people living or dead is purely coincidental.

The text of this Large Print edition is unabridged. In other aspects, this book may vary from the original edition. Printed in the United States of America on permanent paper. Set in 16-point Times New Roman type.

ISBN: 978-1-68324-237-6

Library of Congress Cataloging-in-Publication Data

Names: Reay, Katherine, 1970– author.
Title: A portrait of Emily Price / Katherine Reay.
Description: Center Point Large Print edition. | Thorndike, Maine : Center Point Large Print, 2017.
Identifiers: LCCN 2016043683 | ISBN 9781683242376
    (hardcover : alk. paper)
Subjects: LCSH: Americans—Italy—Fiction. | Large type books. | GSAFD: Love stories. | Christian fiction.
Classification: LCC PS3618.E23 P67 2017 | DDC 813/.6—dc23
LC record available at https://lccn.loc.gov/2016043683

For MMR and the "MMR Club"
True seekers of Joy

All Joy reminds. It is never a possession, always a desire for something longer ago or further away or still "about to be."
—C. S. LEWIS, *Surprised by Joy*

❧ Chapter 1 ❧

Piccolo. The restaurant matched its name—a tiny and delicate white stucco building with a short, neat brick walk leading from its front door to the parking lot. Its wilted green awning and window boxes filled with equally droopy flowers made it look worn and comfortable—completely at odds with the man flashing his eyes between his watch and me.

I pulled a couple inches farther into the parking space, dabbed on lip gloss, and hurried to the restaurant's front door. Joseph had already pulled it open.

"Thank you for letting me follow you," I said. "Chicago is nothing like this; it's built on a grid system. I had no idea Atlanta had so many trees and hills and winding roads . . . But you didn't need to bring me to dinner. Not that I don't appreciate it." I pressed my lips shut. It was time to stop talking.

"It's your first night in town, and my aunt and uncle own this place. If you want to feel welcome in Atlanta, this is where you come."

I smiled. Despite the invitation, nothing about Joseph Vassallo felt welcoming. After knowing him for all of five minutes, I suspected it would take a good hair day, flawless makeup, and four-inch heels to comfortably stand next to this man. But today, after a thirteen-hour drive and only a Dairy Queen Blizzard as sustenance, I was the poker-playing-dog-set-on-velvet next to his Michelangelo, complete with lilting Italian accent.

He escorted me into the restaurant with a hand at the small of my back and imperious nods to the waitstaff. A petite, dark-haired woman darted across the dining room, and Joseph's mask dropped as his first genuine smile broke free.

"You didn't tell me you were coming tonight!"

He laughed, then bent and kissed her cheeks, one then the other in quick succession. "Surprise." He gestured to me. "Zia Maria, meet Emily Price. She's the insurance restorer from Chicago I told you about, renting studio space."

"Alone. So far to come." She clucked and bustled us to a table. "Sit. You need a good meal."

Joseph raised an *I told you so* eyebrow to me.

She soon settled us with water and a plastic carafe of wine, forbade us to order, promised us the chef's best, and left us. I looked around the restaurant, not knowing what to say and too worn to give it much thought. The silence stretched.

"Zia Maria said you had company."

My head spun back. To a man kneeling at the table. *Oh my . . . There are two of them.*

Fully aware I must look like a bobblehead, I couldn't help myself. Back and forth, and again, back and forth . . . There *were* two of them. Both tall. At least the one kneeling beside me looked as though he must be as tall as Joseph. His long fingers gripped the edge of the table. *Yes, tall.* And handsome. Just that same kind. The right kind— the dark, lean kind with a four o'clock shadow because five o'clock would be too de rigueur. The guy you watch walking down the plane aisle, hoping he'll sit next to you. Yet he never does. He sits right behind you—with his wife.

And what was even better, this guy had no clue how handsome he was. You could tell by his eyes. Eyes never hide and never lie. His danced with laughter and no awareness at all that I was melting right before him. But the other? I glanced over and studied his eyes a moment. Joseph knew.

"You must be brothers?" I asked them both.

Joseph lifted a single brow, but its meaning wasn't so clear this time. It felt almost as if the question required thought. "He's six years younger." His English was so smooth—all the right words and contractions, yet eking out the curves of his native Italian.

Joseph faced his brother. "Ben, meet Emily Price. Her insurance company is renting her a worktable in my studio for the next couple weeks." He glanced back to me. "House fire in Buckhead, yes?"

"Yes." I nodded and turned to Ben myself. "I do insurance restoration. This house has some damaged walls, a mural, and other pieces I'll put back together."

Ben's smile called out an answering one from me, except I could feel mine stretch too far from ear to ear. And his hands . . . One reached out and held mine. "We are both visitors. You at Joseph's and me here. I have the better deal. I get to play in a kitchen." The last part was lobbed to his brother.

"As long as you keep your play to the kitchen." Joseph's murmur killed my grin.

Ben's grip tightened as he shot his brother a look. I did the same.

"No. Not her." Joseph drew back, surprised. He flashed his gaze to me. "Not you. Sorry." He returned to Ben, who sported a *You stepped in that all by yourself* grin.

I was right. There were two of them.

Joseph continued, tilting toward his brother. "You should have said no. You say you know, but you don't. You're meddling in things you don't understand."

I thought of my sister, Amy, who often accused me of the same thing.

Ben's tone brought me back to the conversation. "Beppe, stop. Your Emily does not need to hear this."

Joseph's jaw flexed. What was already square became chiseled and pulsed right below his earlobes. "Joseph." To me he whispered, "*Beppe* is short for Giuseppe. And he won't stop using it."

Ben winked at me. "We start again. *Ciao*, I am Benito. Joseph is my brother." He emphasized the name, flattening out the vowels like an American. "And I'm Emily." I smiled all over again.

Still holding my hand, he addressed Joseph. *"Hai una bella ospite stasera."*

"It's not a date. I just told you. She's a restorer renting space. She arrived this afternoon and doesn't know anyone in town." Joseph thrust out his palm as if tempted to push his brother over. "Stop baiting me."

"I am sorry." Ben bounced up, withdrawing his hand from mine in the process, and leaned on the table. He flexed his fingers across the checked tablecloth as if he had something important to stay. "Let me recommend something special tonight for your non-date." He addressed me. *"Ho convinto zia Maria per pemettermi di fare zuppa di spinaci e ricotta."*

I worked the words through my head, knowing I was changing them, altering them, but praying I understood them.

Joseph waved his hand as if ridding us of a pest. "Fine. Two."

Ben's eyes stayed focused on mine, one brow reaching into his hairline.

"Yes, I'll have that too," I said, without fully grasping what we'd ordered. "Thanks."

He nodded and walked away.

The silence turned oppressive.

11

I looked around again, searching for a comment, and landed on, "Your aunt and uncle's restaurant is lovely."

Outside, the white stucco and faded awning had given a rumpled cottage look, almost as if it belonged in a small English village, but the inside was quintessential Italian—at least my impression of it. Dark green walls, red-and-white-checked cloths, red plastic votive holders with matching breadbaskets, and small bottles of vinegar and olive oil. Wine served in clear plastic carafes. It felt like family had to sit close, share dishes with their stories, and the garlic would linger on your clothes and in your hair as you carried home your leftovers.

"Hmm . . ." Joseph's eyes followed the trail mine had just completed. "Ben comes for a visit and they pounce on him, thinking because he works at our family's restaurant back in Italy he can help, he can make all this better." He rattled on, each word overlapping the next. "And Ben agreed. He didn't even know them before he arrived, and he agreed. He made all these plans to change everything, from the menu to the decor. It will end in disaster." He stopped and stared at me and, I suspected, remembered that we'd only just met.

"Why?"

"Why did they ask or why did he agree?" Joseph sighed. "Piccolo is slowing down. Look around—

even your first time here you must sense it. Vito and Maria are older now, tired. There is no *vita*, life, here anymore, and if they want to sell, it won't bring enough. It could, though. It's good space and in a good neighborhood. As for Ben . . . He's not the guy to do this kind of work. He's a chef, a dreamer. At least as a kid that's who he was. Always eager to help and jump aboard any sinking ship. But righting the ship takes another personality."

"But—" I clamped off my protest. Who was I to have an opinion at all? Just because a guy has a gorgeous smile and dancing eyes . . .

After a few moments the silence lay too heavy again, and I wondered why Joseph had invited me to dinner at all. He had no obligation. Covington Insurance had merely rented me a workstation at his studio for two weeks, nothing more. I had a job to do, a Residence Inn suite to sleep in, my books, my paintings, and a Netflix account to keep me occupied in the evenings . . . I had no need for awkward dinners with a surly Italian in the midst of a family feud.

I asked, "What did you order for us?"

Joseph's eyes took on a flash of alarm. "I'm sorry, he set me off and I assumed you understood. Soup with spinach and ricotta. He'll bring it with a salad and bread; it will be enough."

"Oddly, I'm not that hungry. You would think I would be, with only a Blizzard today."

"A blizzard?" His arch tone killed my enthusiasm and my explanation. I nodded, as if he had questioned my choice rather than my meaning.

The food soon arrived and *not the guy* pulled up a chair. I wasn't sure what kind of guy Ben was that precluded his ability to help his aunt and uncle, but he was a demonstrative guy, hands waving like a cyclone. He was a happy guy, eyes lit with laughter even when Joseph's tone—I couldn't catch many of the words—conveyed a reprimand. He was a kind guy, hands slowing and voice softening as he tried to draw me into the conversation while easing his brother's clear annoyance.

He was exactly what I had always envisioned my ideal *that guy* to be. Actually, the whole list, fully formed at age eight, started and ended with *Italian*—all the rest was icing.

I sat quietly and watched Ben's hands move. They were strong, with long fingers, not tapered, but blunt at the nails. And they flew, moving at the rate of his words. I tried to catch the gist of them, but his Italian eclipsed his English and I missed much of it. Something about pizza, the restaurant closing to paint, not closing to paint, and Papa.

I heard *irresponsabile* and *lavoro*, meaning "work," but was certain I'd missed the mark as *leprechaun* and *swirl* made no sense. Clearly checking out Rosetta Stone a few times from the library had not made me fluent.

The conversation drew to a quiet close as Ben's hands dropped to his lap. *"So che posso . . ."*

I know I can, I translated in my head . . . then, *"Aiuto,"* we whispered together. *Help. He knows he can help.*

I clamped my hand over my mouth; I hadn't meant to say it aloud.

Ben seized my hand. "You understand."

I could only nod. Yes, I understood. I got it—not all he'd said, but what he was trying to do. He wanted to give his aunt and uncle something more. A chance. A better life. Joy. I wasn't sure any of it was possible, but I appreciated that he believed it. It was so clear, so beautifully clear, that he believed it.

Ben nodded at me as if an entire conversation was passing between us and we sat in perfect agreement. He then turned back to his brother, perhaps not realizing he still held my hand captive beneath his. "I can help, Joseph. Let me do what I know."

Joseph looked between us as if stumbling upon something unexpected. He didn't reply.

Ben looked down at our hands. His eyes widened with embarrassment and he pulled his away so fast I felt an instant chill. *"Mi scusi."* He sat back, crossed his arms, and smiled slow and broad. "You speak Italian?"

"Un po." I tapped my fingers together. The whole moment flustered me, so I stood—and

knocked back my chair. Ben lunged to catch it. I added, "*Ho bisogno di usare il buco.*"

"You do speak *un po.*" Ben compressed a smile. "You mean *il bagno.* Bathroom."

"What did I say?"

"Hole."

I felt my face flame as I strode to the front of the restaurant. "Zia Maria" intercepted me with nods and a guiding hand on my arm, pointing to the ladies' room.

"*Grazie.*"

"You are welcome, my dear."

Moments later I pushed back through the door and into the small lobby to find Joseph waiting by the hostess stand.

"We can go now." He held open the front door. "We shouldn't have gotten into it with you here."

"It's all right. I didn't understand most of it."

"You caught enough, and I apologize." He stepped into the warm night, then away from me. "Welcome to Atlanta, Emily, and I'll see you at the studio tomorrow morning." He crossed to his car, and I stood next to my station wagon.

"Thank you for dinner," I called after him.

I stood by my car a few minutes, tempted to go back inside. There was something about *that guy*—not only what he wanted to do, but who he was and how he listened to his brother's rantings and insults with patience, with those bottomless brown eyes that didn't carry resentment or indignation, but instead, gold flecks, barely contained laughter, and even joy.

And although he seemed playful—sending a few winks my direction when Joseph got really heated—I somehow knew he wasn't flighty. He meant what he said. He wanted to help his aunt and uncle, and he would. It was that, that *drive* to fix what was broken, that resonated with me.

I finally dropped into my car with another ear-to-ear grin. *Welcome to Atlanta.*

❯❯❯ Chapter 2 ❮❮❮

My eyes ate up the empty studio. I hadn't stepped inside the day before, as Joseph had met me on the sidewalk and immediately invited me to dinner. But what a space . . .

Atlanta Conservation, Inc., was a dust-free conservator's Nirvana—the likes of which I'd never seen. Cement floor, thirty-foot ceilings, metal ducts, polished pipes—nothing soft, nothing that allowed a speck of dust to float, much less land. And each workstation outfitted with LED, ultraviolet, and infrared lighting capabilities, freestanding Leica F12 I microscopes, Decon FS500 vents on retractable arms, state-of-the-art carbon-handled tools, a heated suction table in the center, and some unknown and intimidating-looking machine poised against the far wall. And the solvents—vials of raw elements that required a chemistry background to pronounce, let alone mix in the tall glass beakers.

It was everything I dreamed restoration could be when we first met at age eight. My father took me to the Art Institute of Chicago's Caravaggio exhibit, and rather than look at the paintings, I spent the entire afternoon trailing a tour of grown-ups on a tour called "Maintaining the Masters." The leader, not a docent, but a graduate student with a passionate, melodic—and Italian—accent, mesmerized me. He didn't talk about the subjects of the paintings. Instead, he told the story behind them—the processes of preserving them, identifying everything that attacked them over time—moisture, age, microbes—and all he and his kind did to keep art safe. I hung on his every word, certain he held the secrets and the tools needed to fix things, make them whole, and keep them healthy.

It was the last outing I remembered with my dad before he moved out of our house. And no coincidence that I believed that man's dictums about paintings would serve as well as a manual for life. We could keep things together by putting all the pieces in place and gluing them there. If you worked hard enough and were diligent, anything could be fixed.

I began scouring garage sales in my neighborhood for trinkets. In high school, I read every book the library held on art criticism, restoration, and design. I even checked out the Rosetta Stone's Italian courses over and over—somehow knowing Caravaggio's Italy was the Asgard of art and if I knew its secrets all would be well. And I was good at it. My mind could see how the pieces fit, my fingers were nimble enough to get the minutest shard of porcelain back in a broken figurine, and I was creative enough to use anything that came my way to make the process more efficient, clean, and stable. In college I found it a great way to make extra money. Any other ideas I held or embellished about that man's looks and accent over the years were probably fed around this time by a steady diet of romantic comedies and art documentaries.

But this morning, when finally gaining entrance to my own Asgard, I made a less than stellar impression. I was so overwhelmed when Joseph ushered me inside that, looking across the room now, I couldn't remember who he said worked at each station. I did recall that his three con-servators held degrees from the country's best postgraduate programs; one was on site in San Francisco working on a Rembrandt, another was on sabbatical at the Vatican, and the third must be nearby. At one workstation there was a Cassatt propped on an easel and some wooden loveliness behind a Leica magnifying scope.

"Move any equipment you don't need out of

your way," Joseph said. "Don't you use superglue and acrylics and call it done?"

His accent threw me. It made the question sound sincere, and it took a second for me to find it insulting.

I offered a slightly less than bright smile and pretended the question was real. "You'd be surprised how useful superglue truly is. But you're right, I don't use most of this. And I bring my own tools since I usually work on the small stuff on site or at my hotel. Having Covington rent me studio space is rare."

After a few more moments of Joseph pointing out what I probably *would not need* and *need not touch,* he walked away. And I had to come to terms with the truth of all of it. While I might do a first-class professional job on Aunt Edna's wedding portrait damaged by a water leak, or the Lladró figurine shattered when Bobby pretended the umbrella was a light saber, there was no use pretending I knew anything about restoring a Cassatt—even a copy of one.

With a deep breath, I opened my toolbox and fingered the tools inside as if meeting old friends. I was reluctant to unpack them into ACI's shiny glass mason jars. My baby toothbrush for fine metal cleaning was going to look ridiculous next to the studio's bamboo brush with its fine horsehair bristles. I couldn't even imagine what Joseph might say about my purple plastic tongue scraper or my bright red gum depressor. Cheap and odd, dental tools did the job when it came to distressing wood and applying adhesives to tight spaces.

I dropped each into a jar, reminding myself with every *plink* that I did first-class work—the grown-up equivalent of *I think I can.*

My phone startled me with a loud rendition of Cyndi Lauper's "Girls Just Want to Have Fun," and I fumbled to answer it. I did not want Joseph to emerge from his office—especially on this note.

"I think I need a new song for your ringtone," I whispered.

"Oh, don't change Cyndi. I love that song."

I brushed aside my sister's protest. "What's up?"

"Are you there yet?"

"I got here yesterday. You knew that."

Amy sighed with great drama. "You must be exhausted."

I could hear chatter and laughter in the background. More noise than the accounting office at Covington Insurance generated in a year.

"Where are you?" I barked before I remembered the reason I'd been whispering.

The background sound lessened, and she ignored my question. "I was kinda hoping I'd get your voice mail."

Our twenty-two-month age difference instantly stretched to years as I took a deep breath. I released it slowly in an effort to keep calm. I knew what was coming next—what always came next with Amy.

She huffed a small sigh. "I wanted you to hear it from me . . ."

"You lost your job."

Silence.

"Amy, I asked the accounting department to hire you—as a favor. I helped you move to Chicago for it."

"I only missed one meeting . . . *one*. But that wasn't it, honest. They're making cuts. Three others got let go last week."

"I haven't heard about any cuts." I closed my eyes, sure she was lying. "Can you go back in and beg? I can't ask for any more favors."

"Forget it, Em." Amy's voice became strong and clear. "It wasn't right for me from the start. I hate filing, and I kept messing up the phone messages."

I closed my eyes and saw images of blond, bubbly Amy sliding little pink pieces of paper across the department's central desk. *Here, y'all. Come grab your messages. I'm not sure who's who yet, so y'all just sift through them.*

She'd flip her blond hair, bat her unnaturally long lashes—made more annoying by actually being natural—and draw upon those six short months we'd lived in Alabama. She was only seven years old at the time, but she'd quickly learned the power of a pretty face and a deep drawl.

I opened my eyes. "It was good money . . . and benefits. We have great health insurance."

"True, but it's also gone." She paused. "Look, you're in Atlanta and you don't need to deal with this. I'll handle it. Half our high school lives here; I've got tons of friends with leads."

"No, I'll start looking tonight. I saw some solid listings on Monster and ZipRecruiter last week."

"What were you doing on—"

"I'm always on those sites, Amy. How do you think I always know about these jobs? How do you think *you* get the good interviews? It's why—"

"Slow down."

"If you'd keep a job, I could slow down." I pressed my lips tight. After a thirteen-hour drive, an awkward "work dinner," and a hotel pillow made of Styrofoam, I was too tired for this conversation. "Did you tell Mom?"

"Why would I do that? It's as bad as telling you. She'll shed a few fake tears and send me money. It's like a pat on the head, only worse, and you go off—"

"Don't bite the hand that finds you the jobs, sis."

"Yeah . . . I know." Her voice dipped low. "I just didn't want someone from Covington contacting you before I did."

ACI's front door swung open.

"I gotta go. I'll send you ideas later." I tapped off my phone and switched it to silent as a woman stepped into the studio and stared at me.

"Company!" She threw her arm out as she crossed the studio. "You're the insurance restorer!" Her low heels made a staccato click across the floor. She looked about my age, but taller, darker, her black hair cut into a sleek bob that swung with every step.

I stood and met her in the studio's center, hand outstretched. "I'm Emily Price."

"Lily Crider."

I gestured to the empty worktables. "I think Mr. Vassallo said we three are the only ones here right now."

"Ugh . . . Don't call him that." She grinned and dropped her bag at her station. "Besides, you won't see much of Joseph out here. He has a workroom behind his office."

I touched her microscope with a light finger. "Your equipment is extraordinary."

"Isn't it? He spared no expense when setting up this place." She tapped the Decon's bright yellow hood. "You can stick (E)2-butene-1-thiol and 3-methyl-1-butanethiol under your nose with this on and not smell a thing. Cameron tried. He was fortunate it worked. Joseph would've fired him before he could've recapped the vial."

"Butan—?"

"The stinky elements in skunk."

I felt my fingers pinch my nose and dropped them. "Oh . . ."

"Yeah . . . It was a risk." Lily propped herself on her stool and rolled to her scope. "Come see this." She reached over and flipped the Leica's switch. A bright focused beam lit a one-inch circle on the triptych—a patch of deliciously green grass.

"Oh my . . ."

"I feel that way every day. This baby is part of the Rijksmuseum's collection. Fifteenth century. Oil on wood. It'll be here in the High Museum for a year once I'm finished. A full cleaning and restoration was part of the loan contract. I've got about a month of work left."

I leaned closer and fully absorbed the difference in our worlds. Lily was working inch by inch through a masterpiece. I focused on boxes full of stuff and wall space measured in feet, and kept my time commensurate with the insurance company's valuation of damages. But still . . . I loved it.

Lily gestured for me to peek through her scope. The inch expanded, and I could see the microscopic crackling as if I were kneeling in a mud puddle after the water evaporated. Each crack was huge and the edges clear and precise.

She'd restored about half of the area captured within the scope's field of vision, and her work was excellent. She hadn't erased or filled in the painting's natural evolution or signs of decay; she'd inpainted subtly through them with exquisite delicacy, allowing the piece to be its full and best self. The changes were now part of its story, but stabilized so as not to end the story.

I straightened up. "How do you get the paint in? It's so fine."

"I've developed an incredibly lean paint for this. Very low fat content."

"And the brush?"

She reached over to a cloth on which lay a dozen brushes. She raised one. Its head was as fine as a needle.

"It's so tiny."

She held it close. "I expect there aren't more than five hairs in there. Horse. Each tipped on the bias. I'd spread them and count, but that'd ruin the brush."

"No. Don't do that." I stepped back.

She twisted on her stool to face me. "So what brings you here?"

I liked Lily's expression, open without condescension. I liked *her*. "I'm the company's go-to girl for midlevel on-site restorations, but I only got the call for this one last week. An emergency." I made air quotes with my fingers.

"There can be emergencies."

I flicked a finger at her triptych. "For you, maybe. In my world, getting the fire out, clearing the water, bringing art, wood—anything organic —to a level of stasis, constitutes the emergency. And all that happens long before I get on site. I'm the girl who glues Auntie May's Precious Moments figurine back together."

"Okay, you win. But Auntie May might disagree."

"True . . . and this might be one of those times. It usually takes weeks, if not months, to schedule restoration work, but my boss got me down here within forty-eight hours of the claim's approval, and he sweetened the deal by renting me a spot here."

"Well, I'm happy to have you." She pointed across the room. "Cameron's in San Francisco, Will's at the Vatican, and it's too quiet. Do you like Pink Martini?"

"Is that a drink?"

"A band. They've been keeping me company lately, but feel free to stream your own playlist. Joseph's got the place wired on Sonos."

With that she rolled in front of her Leica scope and I returned to my table to finish sorting my dental tools.

⫸ Chapter 3 ⫷

That afternoon, after forty-five minutes and countless missed turns, I pulled into the driveway of a lovely white wood colonial in Buckhead and let my eyes trail over the house: clean black shutters, crisp white paint, plantings fresh and watered. Its perfection let me know I had the right house. In my six years of insurance work, I found no one keeps up on home repairs and maintenance until forced—usually by loss.

The insurance files reported that they'd caught the fire early and most of the interior damage came from smoke and water. I suspected the inside was entirely brand-new—insulation, drywall, fixtures, and even appliances—as fire travels fast and hot along electrical lines. And, covered or not, clearly the outside had gotten a significant lift as well.

I walked through the open front door and wandered the first floor, saying hello to workmen as I passed. It smelled new—plaster, woodwork, adhesives, and paint—with a fine coating of white construction dust everywhere. That was always my greatest challenge—keeping the ever-present dust out of drying varnish.

The contractor's quick use of several desiccant dryers had saved the dining room. Painted in the 1930s, the walls' delicate brushwork and burnished blue glaze gave the room depth and the illusion of light and movement running over the walls. There was distinct water damage near the baseboards and smoke discoloration, but nothing that a thorough cleaning, a little inpainting, and some fresh varnish couldn't fix. It'd be a good project, a soothing project.

"Are you Covington's restorationist?"

I turned and found a middle-aged woman, several inches above my five foot five, assessing me, arms crossed. In art and life, that gesture ran two ways: aggression or protection.

"Restorer. But yes, I'm Emily Price."

She dropped her arms. *Protection.* "Restorer, restorationist, restorationer, restorist . . . I wasn't sure what to call you."

"No one ever is." I took a quick catalog of what I saw. Rachel Peterson looked like a soccer mom who lunched, highlighted her blond hair, and changed her lipstick and nail color with trends and seasons. On the whole, good clients, efficient, knew what they wanted and recognized a job well done.

But she didn't quite fit the mold at present. Her eyes were lined and tired, skin dry; roots dark and threaded with gray; and her chapped lower lip slightly swollen on one side as she dragged it through her teeth. There was a wariness about her, as if she'd learned something new and didn't know what to do with the information.

I ran my hand over the wall's stippled surface. "These are dry and sound. They look great."

"Can you save them?" Her voice wavered at the end of the question.

My hand stilled. Listening, not looking, I recognized that too. She wasn't talking about the walls.

After Dad left, Mom's clock kept breaking and

Amy's toys needed constant gluing or mending. *Emily, can you fix this?* Money was tight, so if I couldn't fix it, we lost it. Over and over . . . Suddenly I had a purpose, a job, and everything else made sense. Objects carried weight, and in fixing those, I found one could mend so much more.

"Yes, I can. It'll take a couple weeks, but they'll be gorgeous."

Rachel shifted her weight and gestured to the stairs. "Have you seen my daughter's room? It's bad, but . . . more important."

I followed her, recalling my notes. Originally the upstairs mural was to be cut out with the rest of the damaged drywall. But after the claim was filed, it was added to the list with a note. *No expense spared. Cost covered by client.*

We turned into an upstairs room void of furniture and painted a bleached cotton white. The bathroom was equally bright with new white tile and curving chrome fixtures set on a white marble countertop.

"All this in two months?"

"The contractor has been wonderful. He flooded the house with his team. They say we can move back in a few weeks."

"That's remarkable. I've seen situations in which it took a year to get this far." I offered encouragement, but Rachel's face fell.

"I don't know how people survive that," she

whispered, then started, as if she hadn't meant to say the words aloud. "The mural's over here."

We walked deeper into the L-shaped room and faced a square mural, pink and dingy, starkly dirty against the white walls. Deep grooves around it made it look more like a scab than a treasure.

"We were going to take it out with the drywall. You can see the cut into the picture here." She ran her finger along a jagged line in the picture severing the young girl's shoe as she reached high into the sky on a swing. "But my daughter, Brooke, lost it. The contractor said it's safe to keep."

I pressed my palm against the wall and dragged it between the new and old drywall. "It is."

"You can tell by touching?"

"After a while you can feel it. There's no change in temperature, humidity, or strength. No sponginess or disintegration. Listen." I drummed my fingers over the two surfaces. "The same."

"It's worse than downstairs."

"It took on a lot more water." I stepped back to take in the full scene. A little blond girl, about three years old, swinging up, her face looking up in wonder as if she could touch the sky. Brown shoes, brown swing, brown bark on the tree behind her. Water had discolored many of the colors—the browns were tinged to orange in some places, the sky's blue was pocked, the pinks of the girl's dress and face carried slight puce tones.

"I can make it lovely. I promise."

Rachel released a breath that sounded like it'd been held for months. She touched her fingers to her lips and hurried from the room as she called back, "I'll leave you to it."

I was standing in the room where the fire started. A curling iron left on and a tissue too close. What a burden for a fourteen-year-old.

I'd seen pictures of the room in the insurance file. The girl who lived here had felt popular and carefree—I could tell by examining the details: posters pinned across the walls, pictures of friends on a huge bulletin board, clothes and makeup scattered, food wrappers crumpled under the desk. Her mother had taken the photographs in an effort to convince her daughter to clean her room. Instead, they proved invaluable for the insurance claim.

They also revealed how the mural had survived at all. It had been hidden behind a huge framed One Direction poster.

I got out my notebook and studied the picture, determining what to do. I wanted to give that girl a little of her childhood back, but mature it somehow, redeem it. I decided to employ a faux framing technique to give the picture distinction and a little sophistication. There was also a sallowness about the drawing, beyond the damage,

that I could massage away. *Blame it on smoke.*
There was a look in her eyes that was clouded. It
could be cleared. *Blame it on water.* A restorer's
job was never to enhance, simply reveal. And
yet . . . I felt confident no one would call me out
on it.

I shoved my notebook back in my bag and
propped myself on the window ledge to check
e-mails on my phone.

Human Resources? I tapped the e-mail.

To: Emily Price
Fr: Covington Insurance, Human Resources
Re: Employment Termination

Dear Ms. Price,

As you've been informed, Covington
Insurance will dissolve its restoration
department as of May 19th. Please be
advised that this e-mail constitutes a
formal release agreement and employment will be terminated on that date. All
details or ancillary terms will be outlined
within your department.

Thank you.
J. Cummings

I slid down the wall and tapped my boss's
number.

"I'm fired?"

Henry groaned. "You weren't supposed to get that e-mail until next week."

"But I was supposed to get it?" I pressed my fingers against my forehead. It felt ready to explode.

"It's why I sent you to Atlanta. I was buying you time."

"But I'm still fired? Then I need to be in Chicago. How can I find a job stuck down here?"

"I'm sorry, but by sending you down there I got another couple weeks' pay for you. Randy and Bonnie have already transitioned to customer service. Yesterday. I was trying—"

"Yesterday? How long have you known about this, Henry?"

"A month . . ." He paused, as if expecting me to explode, then rushed on when I didn't. "I can get you a job in customer service."

"No . . ." The warmth of panic washed over me. "I like what I do. I'm good at it." Joseph's dig came to mind, and my defense shot out before I could stop it. "It's more than acrylics and glue!"

"I know that."

I heard a soft chuckle, which only bothered me more. "Don't, please. Don't laugh about this."

"I'm not. That's why I classified this one as an emergency. It'll buy you another week or two and give you time to look for a job. That studio I found? The owner, Vassallo, had an online query for a conservator a few months back. He pulled the posting but never filled it. I thought perhaps . . ." Henry let his words drift.

"I wondered why you found me such swanky digs, but I'm not in their class. It's a conservation studio. Master's degrees and masterpieces."

"A gifted restorer like you fits anywhere she wants."

I didn't want a pep talk. "Are you going to customer service too?"

Henry gave a soft snort. "They offered me a severance package and a watch. No one keeps workers my age, not if they can help it."

"I'm sorry."

"Me too. I've been here forty-five years, and it's been good. It'll never love you back, though. Remember that."

"Yeah . . ." The warmth left in exchange for a sudden chill. I crossed my arms.

Henry continued. "Look, I know it's not Chicago, but I couldn't find anything here. They've already outsourced all the work. But out-of-town gives you that great expense account —at least for now."

"Thanks. You've always looked out for me."

"Call if you need anything, okay? Now that HR has reached out, you'll get a flurry of e-mails. Let me know if something doesn't make sense."

"I will." A noise drew my eyes to the door and I quickly said good-bye.

A young boy with tousled brown hair stood above me.

"Are you the mural lady?"

I smiled, loving the title and hoping to remain one, and not cry on this small child. "I am. I'm Emily. Who are you?"

"Parker." He held out a plastic horse with two legs. "This is Patches."

I touched the horse's nose. "Nice to meet you, Patches. I think you must have trouble running."

Parker pulled the horse back. "He lost his legs." He reached into his pocket and drew out a small plastic leg about the size of my pinky and handed it to me.

I fingered its sharp edges. "The fire didn't do this."

"Brooke stomped on him. She was mad."

I tapped the leg against the body, then handed it back to him. "I may be able to fix that. Think he could run with three legs?"

"Maybe stand too."

"Standing's good." I waited for Parker to hand me the horse. I wanted him to know he had a choice. He stretched both parts to me.

"You're sure it's okay if I borrow him?"

"Can you fix him?"

"I believe so." I pushed up against the wall to stand. "Can you take me to the garage? I understand there's a box out there with more stuff I need to fix." I slid the horse and his leg into my bag and followed Parker out the door, wondering how I was going to fix everything else that was crashing around me.

I drove out of Buckhead in a daze, trying to make sense of Henry's phone call and wondering how I could possibly find jobs for Amy and myself and stay focused on the task before me. Did I take a wrong turn, or did some part of my brain deliberately guide me onto this street and past a strip mall I'd seen before? That white stucco building. That short brick walk to the restaurant's door. Twenty-eight years old and I felt like a teenager driving by a crush's house or waiting outside the school's front doors to watch him emerge when the bell rang.

With a sharp right turn, I landed in a parking spot directly in front of Piccolo. I sat there for five minutes, telling myself to throw the car into reverse and get back to ACI. Part of me knew this was crazy. I didn't know this guy or his family. And yet I couldn't help myself. My sister . . . Henry's call . . . I felt adrift, and somehow Piccolo, Ben, all his plans for the restaurant, and those crinkly brown-gold eyes felt like a gift . . . They felt like joy.

I vacillated for several more minutes before I forced my knuckles to the glass door.

A young man answered. "We're not—"

"I know you're not open, but is Ben Vassallo in?"

"Wait here."

He left me by the hostess stand and strode through the dining room and into the kitchen. Not even a beat later, dressed in a white jacket and looking . . . perfect . . . Ben emerged.

His stride hit a snag when he recognized me. "Emily?"

"Yes, I . . ." *What? I want to help? You make me smile? I think I . . .* I tried again. "Last night . . . Your plans to help here, fix it up . . . I've run teams for restoration projects, I know paints, scheduling, fixing all sorts of stuff . . . I'm kind of a compulsive planner . . ." I stopped in a confused mixture of embarrassment, humiliation, and unexpected longing. I turned to leave.

"You want to help me?" His tone spun me around. It held an eager anticipation that matched my own.

"Yes!"

"*Bene.*" He laughed. "I need you. Beppe—Joseph—is afraid I misled Maria and Vito. That I will hurt them by trying to slay their dragon."

I looked around. "He might be right about the dragon part. There's a lot of work to be done if what Joseph mentioned at dinner is true. What are your plans?"

"Come. We talk." He waved his hand back to the kitchen and I followed.

I dropped my bag inside a gray-toned kitchen with stainless steel counters and the biggest stove

I'd ever seen. Ben walked straight to it and started stirring something with a large wooden spoon—a tangy mix of tomatoes, garlic, anchovies, and something I couldn't name wafted on the steam rising from the pot.

He pointed to a stool.

I grabbed my notebook and a pen and sat down. "Tell me all you're thinking."

He smiled, then began to talk . . . He'd wanted to find his brother again, after many years, wanted to leave home to develop a pizza recipe he couldn't perfect at his family's restaurant due to family ties, tensions, and expectations. Although his words were halting, stumbling over unfamiliar English translations, I understood them, understood what was behind them.

About twenty minutes in, his tone changed. It softened as he told about meeting his aunt and uncle for the first time. He'd not known they lived in Atlanta, or that they even existed, until Joseph introduced them. They were wonderful and already he loved them. They'd welcomed him and needed his help—and he wanted to give it to them, leave them happier and more whole for having been with him, having trusted him.

His monologue left me with more questions than answers, but I didn't interrupt. He wasn't sharing a list or a plan, as I often did; he was sharing himself. And it was . . . mesmerizing.

Somewhere along the way his "I" morphed

to "we," and my hearted melted a little more.

Forty-five minutes and three pages later, Ben stepped behind me to read my notes. His hand rested on my shoulder. "You picked all that out? Is it too much?"

"It's a lot, but it sounds beautiful too." I looked up and found my face inches from his.

"You have green eyes," he whispered.

"You don't."

Ben's eyes crinkled in reply. "I do not," he agreed and brushed a strand of hair behind my ear.

He grazed my cheek with a quick kiss before he straightened and stepped away.

I was thankful he turned back to his sauce, as a blush warmed my face. I took a deep, silent breath.

"Joseph is angry. He feels protective of them and I understand, but they asked me," he continued, "and if they are to retire, they need more from this place."

"I only have a little over two weeks here, so if you want my help, we should start soon."

"That is all I have left too. Can you come to the supply store with me tomorrow?"

I quickly assessed my next two weeks of work. The Peterson house was going to take significant time . . . finding Amy a job . . . finding me a job . . . "Four o'clock?"

"Three thirty?" he countered with a smile.

"Three thirty." *Note to self: Cut out all sleep.*

He twisted fully from the stove and watched

me, a smile settling on his lips, as if I were something fine and delicious—not merely ready help in a time of need.

"Come." He crooked a finger at me, then reached across me for a small spoon. "Taste." He dipped it into the bubbling sauce, dark and thick, and held it out to me.

I touched it to my lips, surprised by the intensity. *"Bistecca alla Pizzaiola.* You might say *la bistecca della moglie del pizzaiolo* to be precise."

"The beef of the pizza mole?"

He chuckled. "The steak of the pizza maker's wife. It is a nationally favorite recipe from Napoli, with sauce so thick it stands—a winter dish, warm and intimate. Not for summer, but it was on my mind today." He glanced back at me. "I cannot tell you how glad I am that you are here, that you came today."

"Because you need so much help?"

"Because, I think, I need you."

⧽⧽ Chapter 4 ⧼⧼

True to my word, I cut out sleep. After a night of futile Internet searches and, at best, minutes of sketchy sleep, I tried to let the job hunts go. Maybe Amy could find her own job. *Not likely.* Maybe Joseph would hire me at ACI. *Not likely.*

As I lay in the dark, a line from a book read

long ago ran on repeat through my mind: *An ever increasing craving for an ever diminishing pleasure* . . . The author had been striving to understand vice, sin, and addiction. I lay there grasping for peace and yearning for something more.

I threw the sheets off before dawn, made mediocre coffee in the hotel suite's mini machine, and headed to ACI. Too early to arrive at the Petersons', it was time to attack their box of knickknacks and see what could be done about Patches.

Lily had already arrived and was poised over the Leica scope.

"Hey," I called softly.

She bounced up. "Hello. How was your first day?"

I gave the standard answer. "Very good. How are you?"

"Okay so far. Moving inch by inch." She drifted back to her scope as if her mind hadn't left it.

I set down the box from the Petersons' garage and cataloged it—five porcelain figurines broken in the chaos, three picture frames stained and warped, and some random odds and ends that meant too much to throw away—including one plastic horse. Small fun projects to fill early mornings and a few evenings. I smiled because I now had Piccolo to do that too.

Rather than dig in, however, I drew out the

small bundle of wood supports I lugged to each job and tapped finishing nails into the corners to create frames. I then pulled out five rolled canvases from a box I'd shoved under the table the day before. These were where my heart and dreams lay, and despite their inadequacies I carried them everywhere I went.

I glanced around—Lily was absorbed at her desk and the rest of the studio was empty—then unrolled the first canvas. This was private stuff. Paintings even Amy had never seen. I usually worked on them in my apartment or in hotel rooms on the road. But the lighting and equipment here were too tempting. Maybe what was missing wasn't something I lacked, but some external element I could find here and now.

I pulled smooth the painting of a couple boys on a slide and fastened it into the supports. Next came the poppies, then the churning waves at Chicago's Oak Street Beach, the old man watching his dog, and, my favorite, the young girl peeking through the leaves at a park in Evanston. After framing the last one, I propped it on the easel and stared at it.

I'd come across her last fall as I was snapping pictures of the changing leaves along the lake-front. She was a surprise—her young face open and expressive—and I didn't even see her looking out through the gold and red until I clicked the shutter. Brown eyes, big and almost perfectly round, a pointed chin within a heart-shaped face and curling dark hair.

She hadn't seen me either. She was in a fairy world, her eyes gazing through the branches unfocused and dreamlike. That was the challenge —I was desperate to capture that moment in my painting, that soft, innocent, wondering look.

But I had failed. Over and over again.

I lowered myself on my stool and held the photograph up to the painting. My girl's eyes were too *aware,* and the resulting image was dull and calculated, not innocent and young. On my last attempt they'd become two-dimensional black dots.

"Your problem lies in layering."

I snatched the painting from the easel and spun around. Joseph stood next to me staring down at the picture now hanging by my side.

"Put it back. It was good."

"It's . . . only a hobby."

"Please." He gestured to the easel.

I obeyed, and Joseph stepped toward the painting. I rolled away.

The silence grew oppressive.

"It's a mess," I blurted. "Humans need eyes. I've tried to paint people without them, turning the faces, but it comes off staged and creepy. So there she is, a five-year-old with black Modigliani dots for eyes in a face that needs . . . I don't even know what."

He smiled. "You know your Italians. Very good."

I shrugged.

"You're right, they don't work." He nodded in agreement. "But your technique is outstanding. Your brushwork. Exquisite detail." He offered another crooked smile. "Your style is more classic. Luini. That's why you need eyes. They are the windows to the soul."

Luini. I was stunned. Comparison to an Italian master—false and exaggerated as it was—was still lovely. I could tell by his expression that Joseph knew it too—he'd gone over the top deliberately.

But I didn't care. It was offered in understanding, jest, or camaraderie, one artist to another, and I accepted it.

He propped himself on the worktable. "If eyes are such a problem, paint landscapes or stills."

"I have, but they're no better. Here." Joseph's attempt at a compliment had given me courage. Or I was simply desperate enough to ask for help.

I pulled out the field of flowers. Bright colors, a mix of poppies with daffodils sprinkled into the edges. I'd seen it along the highway during an assignment in Iowa the previous summer.

Again, it revealed good brushwork and even a sense of movement. You could almost catch the wind working to bend the stems. *Almost* because the stems didn't yield, wouldn't yield, no matter how strong the wind. Rather, they strained against snapping.

Joseph's eyes flashed from the flowers to the little girl and back again. I knew he caught it too. So much of the girl radiated warmth. There was a dewy softness in her cheek, an animated rose to her mouth, and a suppleness in the curve of her hand grabbing the branch above her head. She was alive and warm, and yet . . . There was an excitement or an anticipation that was missing from my hand and therefore from her—an animation that should play out in my soul and translate to her eyes. *Windows to the soul.*

"These are all yours?" He flipped through the other three unfinished canvases.

"All mine."

He scrubbed at his chin, then nodded. "Stick to portraiture."

I snickered. It was meant to sound light and lively, but disappointment and self-derision twisted it.

Joseph's eyes softened. "Your people are alive, *piena di vita,* and powerful. I can see that your heart is in them, not in the flowers. That's why I say portraiture. Chase life."

I liked that and quickly committed it to memory. *Chase life.*

He pushed off the table. "Ben told me you stopped by Piccolo yesterday afternoon."

My breath caught. *Brothers.* Of course they

talked. Ben was probably staying with him. Joseph wasn't my boss, and yet I felt as if I'd stepped into something sticky.

"At dinner I got the impression he was going to go ahead with his plans, so when I found myself driving by Piccolo yesterday, I stopped by to see if I could help." I heard my voice trail up with each word. I hoped I had stopped before he caught those final pleading notes.

"Why would you do that? You have your job."

I gestured to my paintings. "This isn't enough to keep me busy between drying times at the Petersons'. And I like projects. I'm very organized. And if this can help your family . . ."

Joseph tilted his head. "That's the problem. Ben is under the same misapprehension. You can dress up Piccolo, make it ready to sell, but that won't help the family. Not the way he thinks."

Not the way he thinks . . .

Joseph's comment struck me. It felt like he was saying that helping Maria and Vito retire was not Ben's primary goal. Then what was? And why couldn't he achieve it?

As Joseph walked away, I put away the paintings and picked up Patches. His leg required fast-drying adhesive and a dab of joining compound to soften the break lines. I then moved on to a Bing & Grøndahl figurine, a nineteen-inch-high shepherdess—the porcelain so thick it had broken only into a few dozen pieces rather than shattering into thousands. A couple coffees and a few hours later, I was satisfied with both.

It was time to head to the Peterson house to wash Brooke's mural. Cleaning a painting or a mural brought out its true colors—like a rainbow after a storm—and made it feel new and bright. It made *me* feel new and bright. It was my favorite part of my job.

Two more coffees and I was moving apace across the top third, relishing the colors revealed, when a high-pitched scream stopped me.

"What are you doing? You're ruining it!"

I spun around and found myself two feet from and eye-to-eye with a very angry girl—blond hair, close to the tone of my own, pale skin, and the most anguish-filled blue eyes I'd ever seen. Brooke.

I held up my hands. "No, no. I'm cleaning it, to fix it. Look."

She dropped her backpack with a massive *thud*.

"See?" I pointed to the top of the mural. "I've already cleaned this section. It's a slow process, but I can get all the smoke damage, dirt, everything that's corrupted it for the past decade off without damaging the paint underneath. See how much brighter the sky looks. Then I'll fix any damage I find . . ." I shot her a quick glance. "Then reseal and varnish it."

"She's not even pretty."

She. The tone. The pronoun. Both made me sad.

"It's a beautiful mural, and I think the girl is lovely." I resumed working.

"Can I help?" She spoke so quietly I barely caught her question.

"Of course. Take this and dab only within a couple inches. When you see a lift in color—a brightness—stop and blot, don't rub, with this damp rag." I modeled the procedure for her, then handed her a clean linen rag.

We stood like that for over an hour, silently dabbing, blotting, dabbing again until two-thirds of the mural was clean.

"What will you do about this?" She ran her finger along the fissure through the little girl's brown shoe.

"I'll fill it in, then touch it up with paint. You'll soon forget it was ever there."

"I doubt that."

"I had another idea."

She looked at me, her eyes no longer pinched and tight, but round with curiosity.

"What do you think about taking this whole area and framing it? I could apply a wood frame if you'd like, to give it dimensionality—like a painting you hang on the wall. Or I could paint you a frame, which would give you the option of covering it with another poster."

She studied the mural. "I don't want to cover it."

I waited.

"Can you put a real frame on it?"

"Of course. I was thinking because your room is so white now, we could frame it in a color that either matches the room, like if you have a dark color you're putting on your bed, or we can pull one from the picture itself. What about polished wood, a deep brown, maybe a mahogany that matches the brown of the swing?"

"I like that." She looked around the empty room. "It was all ruined. All my pillows. Everything."

"Soft things never give up the smoke, no matter how much you wash them. I'm sorry about that. Have you decided how you want to decorate?"

She shook her head.

"It'll all come together. Everything can be fixed—it just takes time."

My words stopped me. I said them to myself, to my sister, to friends. I said them to clients. I'd said them to Ben and Joseph during dinner—like I was some midcentury peddler selling a cure-all elixir —and again to Ben yesterday. They suddenly sounded empty, floating between me and this hurt girl.

Usually by the time I arrived on the scene, the major devastation had been cleared away and reparation was in full swing. The words didn't feel useless and trite, especially when said to adults who were ready to move on and get the workers out of their offices or homes.

But this time I'd been wrong to fling my words so quickly, so carelessly. Brooke didn't love the mural for the mural's sake—she loved what it represented: a happy time, a happy childhood, a happy home. And standing in this empty house, every surface new but tenaciously holding a lingering whiff of smoke and that tang of burning tar paper that takes months to fade, who was I to offer such assurances?

≫ Chapter 5 ≪

"Are you sure you have time?" Ben leaned into my car window.

I'd pulled up to Piccolo a few minutes before four o'clock and found him sitting on the small bench outside the restaurant's front door.

"I do and I'm sorry I'm late. I needed to finish washing a mural."

"Joseph called to remind me this was my mess. He said I am imposing on you." Ben hopped into the car.

"You aren't. I came to you. Remember?" I looked over at him as I pulled onto the road.

"Tell me about your mural."

"Really?"

"*Sì*. Tell me what you do."

As I talked, I put my finger on something that had intrigued me about him—not everything, but one thing. His stillness.

During dinner that first night he was fire and

action, squeezing himself into our small table and quarreling with Joseph. But yesterday he'd been slow and thoughtful, his wrist, stirring the sauce, providing the only movement. Then he turned and looked at me and not a muscle moved. I liked that. It felt as if he understood the proper speed of things, the proper weight of life, and it didn't intimidate him. He didn't need to fill it up with clutter.

After describing Brooke and the mural, I trailed on, hardly thinking where I was going until "I was fired yesterday" popped out. I glanced over to catch his eyes widen, but he didn't speak. "My company is closing its restoration department and outsourcing the work, so this is a good distraction. Keeps thinking about the inevitable at bay."

"I am sorry."

"I'll be okay." I shrugged off his concern.

"Work is important. It is an extension of who we are."

His words settled between us.

"I came here as a last effort to get my head around work too." He said it as if sharing a piece of his soul with me.

"You did?"

"Back home in Montevello, my family owns a restaurant, Coccocino. Four generations have worked there. I will be the fifth. My papa was chef for years, then Mama took over—he's much older —and now she has quit to be with him. I have worked as sous chef for years, but she controlled the kitchen. And change is hard. She . . ." Ben searched for a word. "She barks . . . balks . . . at my changes, so Papa suggested I go and work on them. Master them. Away from Coccocino."

He nodded at me as if it all made sense between us. And it did.

"So here I am, to see my brother after so many years, and to get to the place where I take over Coccocino, without becoming lost."

I turned into the supply shop's parking lot.

"You have the list?" Ben hopped out.

"I do." I grabbed my bag and chased after him.

By the time I reached the door, I knew that stillness was gone. Ben was ready to roll and had secured a cart. The restaurant supply store was a warehouse the size of a Costco, overflowing with every item a restaurateur could need—from light fixtures to appliances, from lemon peelers and napkin rings to the tiny umbrellas bartenders fling into drinks. I grabbed a second broad, flat cart and rolled after him.

We stacked boxes of antiqued wire bread-baskets, cut-glass votive holders, inexpensive picture frames that I could enhance with a little mottled silver appliqué, and slim glass carafes onto one of the carts before I figured out what was niggling at me. The glimpse in the car wasn't enough. Everything about him fascinated me.

"Joseph said you didn't know about your aunt and uncle? That you'd never met them? Aren't you all close? Living together? Big families and all?"

Ben's lips quirked up on one side.

"That didn't sound right. I didn't think it was like some *Godfather* movie, I just meant . . ." I took a breath and started over. "You hadn't met your aunt and uncle before?"

Ben reached for a stack of menu holders and laid them on the cart. "Mama never talks about her family. I knew nothing before Joseph introduced me to Maria. She is Mama's older sister. And there is a brother, too, Antonio, back in Italy. He is in Rubano, near Venice. Two hours away and I never knew him either. Joseph said he chose Atlanta at first because he knew they were here." He lifted a package of dark table linens. "Yes?"

"I wouldn't. White will stay fresher longer with a little Oxy Clean, bleach, and a vinegar rinse every now and then. Besides, lighter will give that linen feel you're going for with your wall color. Remember, Piccolo is a small space."

"White." He grabbed three wrapped stacks of white linens.

"How long has Joseph lived here?"

"Ten years."

"Ten years and he never told you he lived near family? That you had an aunt and uncle?"

Ben smiled. "I do not blame him. Mama does

not talk to him either. And she could have told me thirty years ago, yes? That is family, how it works."

I pushed ahead, thinking that when it came to family dysfunction, our experiences weren't so far apart after all.

We moved on to pans, and he selected a couple forty-gallon stockpots and a stack of pizza stones. I tapped one. "Pizza isn't on Piccolo's menu. Are you adding it?"

"Against Maria's wishes." Ben grinned. "She may not talk to Mama, but they are very alike. Mama dislikes pizza too. But Piccolo *and* Coccocino need it. I almost have the dough perfect."

"You don't know how to make a pizza?"

His laugh held the same disappointment and self-derision mine had held that morning when discussing my paintings with Joseph.

"I was kidding."

"I was not." Ben stopped. "Coccocino is a beautiful place, three times the size of Piccolo, and it swells in the summer with tourists. It has an impeccable reputation, and I wanted to give it something special. Mine. Tourists expect pizza, and Italy offers the world's best. I want to offer the best, so I brought a suitcase of flour to my brother's to work on it away from prying eyes and tongues." He tilted his head. "I sound like a fool. Perfection is not possible."

"You don't sound like a fool, except for the suitcase of flour." I looked down and regretted my last words. I had tried to offer a joke, but he gripped the handle of the cart so tight his nail bases had blued. I reached out, then just as quickly withdrew my hand. "I'm sorry. I was trying to make you smile."

He shrugged off my concern. "Flour is unique. The grains are different, textures different, and what you learn with one does not pass . . . translate? . . . and the yeast is an always changing variable. I needed the flour to be a constant so I brought my own." He dropped his head and continued to himself, as if working out a problem, before he looked up at me. "Bread is life in Italy. Papa makes it. All kinds. And Mama makes pasta so light it rises to your mouth. Pizza is the form of bread left for me—a way to make the restaurant different, mine, and prove my hands are good." He shook his head. "No, that sounds wrong. I—"

"You mean that it's in good hands." I reached again and laid my hand on top of his.

He stared at it and continued. "Yes. They can trust me. I am close, but . . . I will go home soon. Maybe with nothing to show." He brought his gaze up and traced a finger from his free hand along my cheek.

"Let's at least give something to Maria and Vito."

We finished our shopping and packed my station wagon so tight Ben was buried in the passenger seat.

"Thank you, Emily," he called.

I smiled at the disembodied voice and the way he pronounced my name, as if the first and last syllables rolled with an extra *e* or two, or three.

"You're welcome," I called back.

"Will you come to Piccolo tonight? I will not be out of the kitchen until about ten, but could you come?"

The voice sounded more vulnerable this time. It quickened my heartbeat. I looked over and was confronted with a wall of cardboard.

"Are you there?" it called again.

"Of course I am. It's just strange talking to a box."

"It is worse than squishing by one." He waited. "So?"

"Yes. I'll be there."

"*Bene*. I will have a surprise for you. Something special."

We pulled around back to the service entrance of Piccolo, and a couple guys emerged from the kitchen to help us unload the car. We stacked everything into a back closet with great efficiency and few words—until Maria found us.

"Look. Look what you've done!" She oohed and aahed over everything in a lovely Italian Southern drawl. "It's going to be *bellissimo*." She grabbed us one after the other into hugs and kisses between loads from the car.

After the last trip, I left Maria digging through the storage closet and found my hand captured within Ben's as I passed him, heading toward my car. He made tiny circles in my palm with his thumb. "Tonight?"

Without thinking I stepped closer. Thinking, and glancing Maria's way, I stepped back. "I'll be here."

I walked into the restaurant around nine o'clock and stalled three steps inside the door. Joseph sat at the bar directly in front of me, his back to the door. I wavered and stepped back, but he spun, most likely catching my reflection in the mirror facing him. He smiled and tapped the next stool.

"Hello, Emily. I should have known you'd be here tonight."

"Ben asked me to come."

"Yes . . . I heard you had an exciting afternoon."

I slid onto the stool. "I know you're against it, and I hardly know either of you, but it's a good plan, Joseph. It can work. And Ben—"

"My brother is very compelling." Joseph turned back to his plate. "I also know you underpromise and overdeliver, not the other way around. I called your boss."

"You did?"

"You're a good worker. Good at your job.

Creative. Organized. On time. And your results always exceed expectations. You are more than you appear."

Again . . . *Insult or compliment?* I waffled. "And?"

"And I'm out." He held up his hands. "I don't see my brother much. In fact, I haven't seen him more than a handful of times in eighteen years. But I know he was a good kid and now he's a good man, and Maria and Vito asked for his help. I learned today that any skills he may lack, you have in spades." Joseph twisted his stool toward me. "So I guess I'm asking you to take his plans seriously now too."

"I . . . Of course." My head spun.

He laughed, lighter than I expected, and raised his glass to me. "I expect you'll have fun too."

That settled, Joseph's manner quickly warmed. We sat and chatted about art—paintings he'd seen in person and I'd studied in books. We talked about new restoration techniques; again, he was employing them and I was only reading about them. We were on equal ground, however, with the discovery that we both loved mystery novels.

"You should try Iain Pears. His Jonathan Argyll mysteries always feature good art."

He reached around the bar to grab another glass and share his wine. "And you, Donna Leon."

"Of course I've read her. She's Italian. I have a weakness for . . ." I stalled, warming.

"American, actually, living in Venice. After twenty-five years, we've begun to claim her." Joseph smiled with a seventy-thirty mix of delight and condescension.

"Fine. I'll recommend Daniel Silva. American writer, who lives in America, with a former Israeli secret agent turned art restorer protagonist. And they're excellent."

After about an hour, Joseph stretched and looked around. "It's almost empty. Whatever Ben wants with us, he'd better get to it quick. I've got an early appointment tomorrow."

As if cued, Ben pushed through the kitchen door. I caught his eye as he wove through the tables and received an electric grin. I tapped Joseph, who turned around.

He then looked back to me with too many questions in his eyes.

"Bella! Beppe! It is time."

Ben stepped behind the bar and immediately picked up Joseph's wine bottle and topped off our glasses. He then reached his hand behind my head and pulled me forward, laying a quick but firm kiss on my mouth.

I sat back, eyes wide. Only Joseph noted my surprise with a wry smile. Ben had already gestured to the waiter who stood next to him. "Please." He spread his arm to the bar.

The waiter laid four broad white plates before us. Each was topped with a different pizza. The bit of crust I could see on the edges was light and airy, and the toppings stunning: one with arugula and prosciutto; another, figs and mascarpone; a third, sausage, duck eggs, and pecorino? And the last, all green with who knows what. And the smell? We were enveloped in Italy.

"You inspired me this afternoon. After you left . . . it was time. No more fear." He darted a glance to his brother, who stared at him.

Emotions flew across Joseph's face—wonder, jealousy and its slight variant, envy, pride, and . . . respect.

The artist in me wanted to capture each. The human in me wanted to ask a lot of questions.

"Congratulations." Joseph said the word softly. Sincerely.

"*Finalmente.*" Ben nodded to him.

Joseph turned to me. "Ben's been chasing this forever, so he tells me. The perfect crust, found metaphorically somewhere between Rome and Naples." He slid a teasing glance to his brother. "It's a heavy burden, perfection." He paused. "Our father believes bread is as close to the divine as we get on earth. An element of life, made holy by its relation to God. And Mama . . . She may not agree, but she runs the show. Rigid lines, never to be crossed. She makes the pasta. So with a family restaurant, we sons must find our place. In or out." He picked up a knife and fork and took a good-sized bite.

Ben released his breath and came around to our side of the bar. He dropped onto the vacant stool on my right, sandwiching me between the brothers. I shifted back a little so they could see each other, but that didn't stop Ben from resting his arm on the back of my stool and leaning across me. Somehow, I didn't mind.

"Well done, little brother. It's everything you've wanted."

Ben's eyes rounded in surprise at Joseph's blessing. In spite of his strong jaw and chin, his deep-set, dark eyes—the defined, cut face of a man—I saw a boy. A boy young enough to need his older brother.

We sampled the pizzas in silence for several minutes, then Joseph put down his fork and stood. "I'll see you at home, Ben. This was outstanding." He tapped my shoulder. "Tomorrow, Emily."

Ben jumped up and crossed behind me to pull Joseph into a hug. Then, as his brother walked out the door, he dropped down and let out a deep breath.

"Are you okay?"

"Were they good?" Ben leaned close.

"Completely delicious, and more importantly, Joseph thought so. He knows you, he knows what you're after, and . . ." I scrunched my nose. "I don't get the impression your brother doles out compliments carelessly."

Ben chuckled. "He never did."

As the tables cleared, we moved to the restaurant's one booth. And curled into the back corner, we talked—about everything and nothing. We talked through the last customer's departure and through the staff's cleanup and Uncle Vito's mischievous good-bye: "Be sure to turn the ovens on at four for the bread."

Without breaking his story, Ben waved off his uncle and continued to tell about his family, the names rolling off his tongue, and his life back home. Among all the richness of his tale, I noted he didn't answer my many unasked questions. Why hadn't Joseph seen him in eighteen years? How had he not known about his aunt and uncle? The intimacy of a back booth in the dark almost gave me the courage to pepper him, but I held back. After all, I suspected, there'd be time.

Soon we moved on to food, art, books, more about my work, and our plans for Piccolo . . . and his delight that both our countries drive on the right side of the road.

Finally I stretched and looked beyond our entwined hands, resting on the table. "I thought your uncle was joking."

"What?"

"Look." I pointed to the front windows. The light outside was changing. I could see gray creeping into the black.

"I need to let you sleep." Ben trailed a finger up my wrist.

"You too. But first, I suspect we need to turn on his ovens." I leaned back and glanced around the empty dining room. "Do you start the bread too? You won't get any sleep."

"I will steal a few hours, then come in early this afternoon to prep. Vito makes his own bread." Ben sat back as well. "Thank you for coming with me today, yesterday, to the store. For this too." He pulled my hand to help me scoot from the booth.

We walked outside, dawn creeping fast from gray to hints of pink. I stopped by my car to dig around for my keys—secretly pleased that older cars don't open automatically when you approach. My fumbling gave me time to figure out how to handle the moment.

I pulled the keys from my bag before I found a solution. "Got 'em."

Ben wrapped his hand around them, lowering both my keys and my hand to my side.

"I am going to kiss you now. Again."

"Oh . . ."

He moved in so slowly that I reached up to close the last few inches. Clearly he understood stillness better than I did.

He drew me closer, enfolding me in his arms as I dipped in response to his touch. Some time later, but still too soon, he pulled away. "I think you like Italian art?"

"Yes."

"Do you know Francesco Hayez? *Il bacio*?"

I shook my head, trying to think coherently.

"Look it up." He touched his lips to mine again. "This was that moment."

⫸ Chapter 6 ⫷

The next day began a three-day rinse, wash, and repeat cycle: early morning at the studio working my way through the Petersons' box, late morning to early afternoon washing the Petersons' dining room walls, afternoon to evening moving upstairs to work beside Brooke on her mural.

And then came the evenings . . . three delicious evenings sitting at Piccolo's long wooden bar catching glimpses of Ben and snacking on anything yummy he sent from the kitchen. And when the kitchen closed, he would collect me from the front of the restaurant and settle beside me in the back booth. Time stopped at night— time spent in the booth talking and kissing, and in the kitchen cooking, baking, and . . . as nonsensical as it sounded, falling for him, fast.

"I looked up that picture. *Il bacio*?"

"And?" Ben leaned forward. No blinking.

"Quite a picture. Quite a kiss. I have one for you now . . . by Gustav Klimt."

"Another beautiful kiss."

"You know it?" I deflated.

"Bella, it's one of the most famous paintings ever."

"Maybe, but ninety-nine out of a hundred Americans wouldn't be able to identify it."

"Not all had Joseph for a brother. Besides—"

"Don't give me that. It's not because you're Italian. It's not in your water. You all don't absorb art by osmosis." I laughed.

He'd spent the last two nights regaling me with his country's superiority: *migliore* cheese, *migliore* wine, *migliore* art, *migliore* sports. Better, better, better . . . Actually, we called a tie on sports because he refused to discuss "soccer" at all.

"Okay, leaving that behind, here, I found a picture of what I want to do with those frames we bought." I handed him my phone. "See, I'll put a silver wash on them and it'll lighten up the whole aesthetic, then we'll hang them in the hall on the way to the restroom."

"Perfect." He looked at me like he wasn't talking about the frames at all. He tapped my phone and started to hand it to me, then pulled it back.

I grabbed for it. "No."

He grinned. "Bella." He said the word softly while staring at the phone rather than me. *Il bacio*, Hayez's, not Klimt's, was my home screen.

The weekend arrived—with little sleep, delicious food, and a grin I couldn't pull down if I tried.

I packed up the Petersons' now completed box of treasures and examined my work on Patches' leg.

"Are you going to make him a new one?" Lily called from her worktable.

"I'm about to paint over the filler on this one. It's dry." I held him high. "How could I make a new one?"

She flicked her finger the opposite direction. "Program the 3D printer. That's what it's there for."

"You've got a 3D printer?" I jumped off my stool. "I've never seen one. I wondered what that thing was."

"I'll help you program it. I need a break anyway." Lily rolled her stool away from her triptych to a computer. "Joseph upgraded our CAD program a few months ago. He used to it create molds for detail work on a Fabergé egg. You should ask to see the pictures; it was the best work I've ever seen."

I grabbed my stool and rolled next to her, and we measured, designed, and programmed the fourth leg.

"I could learn this."

She looked at me, puzzled. "Of course you could."

"No, I mean . . ." I paused. It felt like begging, but I loved my field, my small field in which jobs were competitive and scarce, and I wanted to stay in it. "Covington is shutting down their restoration department. Come next month, I'm out of a job." I rolled a few inches away. "Do you think learning something like this could help me land another? . . . Maybe here, helping you all?"

"There's plenty to do here." She glanced over to my workstation. "I hope you don't mind, I examined your work on the porcelain figurines yesterday. It's really good. Exceptional, really. And the frame . . . I wouldn't have thought of taking wood from the inner edge to build the supports, but it makes perfect sense. It's already tempered to structure and will conform in perfect harmony."

"Exactly." I grinned.

"You should talk to Joseph. He took on an estate being prepped for auction last month, and we could use the help."

"I will." I looked to Joseph's office door. *As soon as I finish a stellar job at Piccolo.*

The leg was soon programmed, and Lily showed me how to thread the gray filament into the printer. It sprang to life and started pulling the filament into itself with a high-pitched whirl.

"Done." She wiped her hands together. "It'll take about four hours to crank that baby out, but Patches will have a new leg soon."

"Thank you."

She returned to her current inch of green loveliness, and I tapped on Joseph's door.

"Other than a little work on the walls, I've finished the repairs for this Covington job and I have some spare time. Do you have anything I can help with?"

"Piccolo." Joseph's tone was sharp.

I pulled back from the door.

"Emily, wait," he called.

I put my head back in.

"Here." He grabbed a box off a side table and carried it out to my worktable. "I could use your help with these. I saw the figurines you repaired. You did an excellent job. These I want to paint myself, but could you handle the reconstruction?"

"Let me look."

While he went back to his office to grab the second box, I peeked inside. It was a late Ming Dynasty bell jar broken into several large pieces—clean breaks, as if it had fallen onto a carpeted floor rather than wood or stone. The edges held little shearing. With careful layering, tucking pieces behind each other, I was certain they'd fit perfectly with almost invisible crack lines. There were a few chips, but filler and paint would deal with those.

Joseph stood beside me as I moved piece after piece into place, working out the puzzle.

"I suggest a non-yellowing clear epoxy, one with no less than a five-minute drying time as there's some layering to do in the porcelain."

"I agree." He unpacked the final pieces on the

table's corner. "Can you finish them by early next week? I'd like to start the painting midweek."

I nodded.

"Thank you, and I'm sorry about what I said before. It was unfair. I said I was staying out of it." He flicked me a glance as he walked away. "And get some sleep. Ben's wandering around like the living dead, and you look no better."

There was no use replying; he was gone. I noted Lily hadn't moved a muscle. She was either too focused on her work to hear us or too polite to comment.

I laid out each piece of the blue-and-white vase into a grid system on the table for later, then headed for the Petersons' for a couple hours on Brooke's mural.

Painting was one of my favorite aspects of my work. Second to washing. Unlike my own attempts at painting or portraiture, restoration work was like a sophisticated paint-by-numbers exercise. Great skill meant you stayed in the lines and matched your colors, textures, and viscosity to perfection.

And the melding of rote action to creative expression allowed my mind to roam, dream, and solve problems. Usually I worked out how to fix some mess, work or otherwise. But for the last few days, every dream circled around and through Ben—every dip of his voice, touch, quirk of a brow, or the fact that he could make one side of his mouth move independently of the other when annoyed or amused. And his kisses—

"It looks really good." Brooke crashed into the dream.

I didn't turn around. I'd learned something else in the last four days. If I didn't pay attention to her, she relaxed more. So I simply continued to apply dabs of color with my homemade Q-tip. The texture it produced matched the wall perfectly. "Just you wait."

She stepped beside me. "Can I help again today?"

I'd hoped for that, prepared for it. Brooke had joined me each afternoon, and yesterday she'd begun talking. But even before that point, I had listened. I had been still. I had waited. That was new for me—another thing I attributed to Ben. I pushed my thoughts back onto Brooke.

Her body language told me all I needed to know about her. Stiff and jarring at first, it had softened with each day and each cotton ball. It almost made me wonder if I'd gotten it all wrong. Perhaps fixing things wasn't about the end product—it was, oftentimes, about the process.

I waved my Q-tip toward the brushes standing in a small mason jar, borrowed from ACI. "If you'd grab the pink solvent in the box and wipe those brushes with a little of it, I'd really appreciate it. Wipe only *with* the bristle, not against." There were a few of ACI's gorgeous brushes in the jar with mine, and I did not want to ruin them.

I heard her drop to the floor and the brushes tinkle about in the jar as she removed one. She soon began to talk about her room. What she liked before, what she'd chosen to replace it, and how she might, maybe, like the new choices better.

She also talked about the hotel they were staying at, how it was far from school and her friends, and how she hated sleeping in the same room as Parker, who apparently snored. She even admitted to purposely stomping Patches.

"He said you're fixing him."

"As best I can. I can glue the leg on, but the jury's out about more." I didn't want to reveal the possible new leg until it was adhered and painted.

"I shouldn't have done that."

A hitch in her voice made me turn. "We all do things we regret. Living in a hotel . . . and all this . . . It's stressful."

She reached for another brush, and I rolled another cotton swab. I then used it to mix a dollop of umber within three greens. Time to start on the tree.

"Mom says it's all fine, but that only makes it worse."

"Worse?"

"Like admitting it's awful would only make me feel guilty, so she doesn't. But pretending that it's no big deal, that everything's fine, that just makes it worse. Like really it's so bad we can't even talk about it."

"Have you told her that?"

Brooke snorted. "That *would* make it worse."

"You do realize that made no sense."

She shrugged and rubbed the soap against the bristles.

Since it was my brush, I stifled my cringe and returned to the wall. "What's your dad say?"

No answer.

I painted on.

"He's gone."

I closed my eyes briefly. Her voice carried a weight I knew. I flicked her a quick glance. If she'd been me, she would have continued cleaning the brushes and never stopped. There was always a new brush. I was surprised and oddly relieved to find her sitting perfectly still, legs crossed, staring at me.

Insurance files include everything—I mean everything. So I knew her parents weren't divorced. Same address. Joint policy. I also knew this was sacred ground and I needed to tread carefully.

"Gone gone? Trip gone? Work gone?" There are many types of gone.

"Work gone?" She said it like a question.

"Done." I nodded to the tree. Then I dropped next to her to pull out a new plastic palette to mix two browns, one for the swing, one for the shoes. It was also time to attack that fissure across the bottom, which I'd sealed the day before.

I sat facing her. "People deal with stress in a lot of ways. This is stress." I dabbled the brush in the air as if coloring over said stress. "I think you should probably tell your mom how you feel. She may not know you need to talk about it, so you can't blame her for wanting to protect you." I squeezed a dime-size dollop of raw sienna onto my pearl drop of Venetian brown.

Brooke shrugged. "I told her what you said, about everything getting fixed."

"And?"

"She says some things can't be fixed. We just have to endure them."

≫ Chapter 7 ≪

I left the Petersons' house at noon. After all, it was the weekend. And Ben had invited me on an adventure. Only seven hours apart and I already missed him . . . It amazed me how, sitting in that back booth or standing side by side in the kitchen, we hadn't run out of things to say, stories to tell, or dreams to share.

"Why don't you ever wait inside?" I pulled up to find him, once again, waiting on Piccolo's front bench. "It's cooler."

"I get to see you sooner." He stepped to the driver's door and kissed me through the open window before circling the car, dropping into the passenger seat, and kissing me all over again. "We have a lot to do today."

It was the first time I'd heard nerves, even fear, in his voice.

"Not really. Piccolo's still open for business tonight. Once we close tomorrow, it'll get crazy and stay that way for several days. Think of this as the calm before the storm."

"Joseph was right. I poked a dragon."

I twisted in my seat. "Do you want to pull back? Nothing is set in stone, and Maria and Vito will be pleased with anything we do. New linens alone will be a good lift."

"I trust you. All your lists. You have this planned." Ben reached for my hand. "I trust us. The menu changes over the past month are making a difference already. We can do this, and I want it for them." He kissed my palm. "I am only getting nervous. *Terrified* is the best word, I think."

"It'll be work, but it's doable. Very doable."

He directed me first to a coffee shop. Dripworks. It was a small place with metal counters, industrial stools, and a hipster vibe that would thrive in Seattle or Chicago's Old Town. We sat up front and I pulled out my notebook, which Ben gently grabbed and shoved back into my bag, laying a light kiss on my lips. "You said we were fine. Today is about fun."

"I . . ."

"Fun."

I smiled and took a bite of my croissant, promptly forgetting about my notebook. "This is amazing."

"Just you wait."

He then led me to a farmers market in the small neighborhood behind the shop.

"How do you know about all these places? You've been here, what, a month? It's like you live here."

"Joseph thinks I do nothing with my mornings, but this is research and, yes, this is life. Piccolo needs fresh produce, and the way you get the best is changing. They can order direct and get fresher goods at better prices. Farmers like it, too, because they have a committed buyer. So now I know these farmers, share with them, and now I will set up orders. Come on, I will introduce you."

Ben did just that. I met a couple farmers who came to the markets on the weekends but were thrilled to make scheduled deliveries at Piccolo. The butcher even remarked that after meeting Ben he'd approached a few other restaurants directly and had increased his "secured" weekly revenue by over 50 percent. That comment erupted into a moment of firm hand pumping and back-slapping. Ben was as delighted as the butcher.

After a second market, we passed down a side street and found ourselves in a small block of artisan shops and galleries.

"The coffee shop is around the corner." Ben slid his hand down my arm and captured my own.

"Another?" I wasn't sure how much more caffeine I could take.

He pushed open a worn green wood door and we found ourselves in a small workroom-cum-shop.

"A coffee*maker* shop?"

"What did I say?"

"A coffee shop. Which I guess is right. I just expected another cappuccino and tasty treat."

"This is better. Come see." He walked across the small room to a large stainless-steel La Marzocco machine sitting on a high wood countertop. "It has digital display, dual boilers, and pulls three shots at once. Maybe one more than Piccolo needs, but it will set the tone at the bar and make beautiful espresso."

He was right. It was gorgeous and would definitely make a statement. I lifted the tag. There were two prices. One extraordinary. One astronomical. "Do you get to pick your price?"

"*Sì.*" Ben smiled as if about to share a secret. "One if I want them to refurbish it; the other if I do the work. Costly, but this is the best and coffee is popular. Piccolo cannot skimp."

"Can you refurbish it?"

The smile dropped. "No. Piccolo must pay the higher price."

I studied the machine. "I'd have to open it up to look inside, but after years of restoring lamps, clocks, radios, even a model steam engine, I bet, with the schematics, I could do it."

Ben raised a brow.

"Fixing can't mean too much more than valve work and getting this electrical panel functional."

"Are you sure?" At my nod, he grinned and pulled me into a hug. He pushed me back, holding me by the shoulders. "You don't need to do this. Are you very sure?"

"I hope so." My matching grin faltered; I wanted so much to be all he saw in me. I ducked my head before he could see any doubt.

"*Bene.*" He squeezed me again, then called for the salesman. The two of them soon carried the La Marzocco to my wagon. Ben's second trip brought all its extra parts and another machine.

"What's that?"

"A La Pavoni with a matching knock box. He gave them to me."

The machine was rusted, the glass on the gauge broken. "I can see why."

"It is for you."

My head bounced up.

"I tasted your coffee yesterday when you came o Piccolo, remember? Cold drip is not coffee,

Bella." His last word rolled off in an anguished breath.

"It's not that bad."

"It is."

Machines safely ensconced in the car, we walked on, hand in hand, in and out of the shops and galleries. We found an antique plate rack. Ben envisioned replacing the plastic flowers on Piccolo's long interior wall with Italian plates. We found cut crystal bulb holders to be used alongside the votives at the larger tables. We even found a couple old prints in pristine condition for the small front lobby area. I could build the frames easily.

Then we found lunch—an amazing place with rough-hewn tables flanking a long communal table that seated at least fifty and stretched the length of the restaurant. The ceiling was high, with antique brass pipes and vent work, clean and shiny, adding a touch of industrial class.

"Ammazza." I picked up the menu.

"*Ammazza,*" Ben corrected me, and the word sounded completely different and infinitely lovelier.

"Didn't I say that?"

"Not close." He smiled and scanned the menu. "Do you mind if we order pizza? I brought you on purpose. They serve Neapolitan style, first rate and all the flavors I choose. They know pizza."

"Are we checking out the competition?"

"Much can be learned from the competition." Ben's face softened. "Did I not tell you that I did not learn to cook at Coccocino?" He looked around. "And this is not competition for Piccolo. This is the heart of the city's young; they make their own mozzarella, cure their meats on site. Maria and Vito cannot do this, and I would not ask them to try. They feed families. But this has good excitement, I think."

"So this is what we're trying to create. *Vita.* Life." I looked around. "Then we have our work cut out for us. I may need to pull out my little notebook."

"Come here instead." He wagged a finger, and I leaned over the small table. He laid a light kiss on me and smiled. "Thank you for believing in this—in me."

As I rocked back on the bench, a new and disconcerting thought threaded through me. When I returned to Piccolo that first day, I never imagined that it was for anyone but me. It never occurred to me that someone could find a sense of wonder, a sense of wholeness or delight in me—that I could be someone's great surprise. But if it was true and I was or could be—what did that mean?

⇒ Chapter 8 ⇐

Sunday started too early.

I met Ben at Piccolo at five thirty and we spread tarps over the equipment in the kitchen, stacked the tables to the center of the dining room, and began to tarp them as well before the painters arrived.

By noon we had finished prep, eaten Maria and Vito's amazing lunch, and begun painting. With a small army of painters busy at work, Piccolo transformed before my eyes. What was a dark, kitschy, small space opened and widened as the walls were coated in starched white primer, then, by late evening, in a linen white.

Joseph's studio and Ammazza had inspired me to make a last-minute change to our plans. I changed the trim color from white to a deep brown and spent the early-morning hours mixing an inert cleaning solution to brighten the exposed copper piping and brass metalwork. The resulting gold and red tones added a splash of warmth and light against the white. I also suggested we paint the ceiling a complementary deep brown to further the effect. Ben agreed, and by late afternoon the first swipe of brown stretched across the ceiling above our booth.

Maria loved the changes as well and, despite

my protests, climbed a tall ladder and led the charge to clean the pipes.

I reached up to tap her knee. "Please let me do that."

"You may grab another ladder beside me." She looked down and smiled. "And you should. Wiping this across the pipes is like discovering a sunrise."

"Thank you." I grinned, warmed by her praise. "I will."

Hours later, we both climbed down. Ben was instantly at my side.

"It is beautiful." He swung an arm around my shoulders and tucked me close. "We did so much. Maybe I was wrong to ask they close for the week."

"Don't say it." I laughed, circling my arms around his waist. "There's still a ton to do. Next Friday will be here before you know it."

"We must stop or we will tire out. It's already much too late." Maria waved her hands at the painters and waitstaff scattered around the dining room.

As she circled the room with thanks and good-byes, shooing everyone out the door, Ben drew me to the kitchen.

As soon as the door shut behind us, he pulled me close and kissed me. "It is more than I thought. We did this."

"We did." I smiled. *We.* My work was usually so

solitary. This was new, and the joy of it bubbled within me. "You might want to include Maria and Vito."

"Not at this moment." Ben kissed me again. "They can lock up. Let us go too."

I grabbed my bag from a kitchen cubby and, while he returned to the dining room to say our good-byes, checked my phone. Three missed calls and a voice mail from Amy.

Ems, it's me. Surprise! Where are you? I'm at your hotel, but they won't let me into your rooms. Call me back.

Ben swung the door to the kitchen back open. "Where shall we go? I know a couple more places I think you will love."

I shook my head. "First things first; I need a shower."

"Good idea." He smiled.

I held up my hand. "You're going to Joseph's, me to my hotel. Call me in an hour?"

Ben tilted his head. I knew my tone caught him; it was strident, angry, but I couldn't explain. Maybe I'd misunderstood the message. "Do you want a ride to Joseph's?"

"He lives only a few blocks away. The walk will feel good. Are you sure you are well?"

I rushed out the back door. "I'm fine. Call me soon?"

Ben followed and I drove away with him standing still, watching me. My heart folded in; I had hurt him. But what if I had heard correctly? *Amy? Here?*

I walked into the lobby of the Residence Inn and stalled. I felt her. She was here . . . somewhere.

"Ems!"

I heard her before I saw her. I hadn't noticed her waiting by the door, and now she bounced into my arms. In so many ways it was like seeing myself fly at me—we were about the same height, though highlighting gave her more varied and blonder tones; we had the same eyes, though hers were a deeper green; and we . . . I took in her short skirt and tight tank top . . . We did not dress alike.

People often mistook us for twins. But looking at her, I instantly felt stretched thin and dried out.

I stepped back and tucked a chunk of hair behind my ear. Ben had flicked paint on me, but the moment, and the fun, was gone, and only embarrassing and sticky white paint remained. "How'd you get here? And why? You've got interviews this week."

"It's good to see you too."

"It is good to see you, but . . ." I closed my eyes. This was not the time or the place to get into it. "Come on up." I headed to the elevators.

She picked up her bag and followed me. "Before you freak out, I called both those companies and neither minded pushing the interviews back."

"That doesn't mean they won't fill the positions

before you get there." I jabbed at the elevator button.

"Then they weren't the jobs for me." She grinned and reached for something on my head. "What did you do to your hair?"

I groaned and pulled the clump of paint from her fingers. "That's not how it works. *You* want the job, not them. *You* work on *their* schedule." I pushed my way into the suite, the door sticking in the humidity.

Amy spun around. "This is great. You have a little living room, even a kitchen."

"They do a good job here." I pointed to the couch. "That's a pullout. You can sleep there."

"Thanks." Amy dropped her small suitcase and plopped down on it. "What do you want to do?"

Go out with Ben. "I kinda had plans."

"You did? Tell me." Amy's face brightened.

"Let me start with a shower first." I didn't want to talk about Ben. I didn't want to share him. Every sweater, every coat, every guy. They met me, then their eyes followed her.

"Great. You do that and—" She opened the kitchen's small refrigerator. "What have you been living on?"

"Italian food," I called on my way to the bedroom.

"Pricey," she yelled back.

"Free, actually. Those are my plans tonight. Dinner with the chef of an Italian restaurant." *There. That's all I'm going to share.*

"Ooohh . . . You shower, and I'm going to grab something at the little grocery across the street. I'm starving, but I want to hear the whole story. Can I take a key?"

"Grab one off the counter."

I heard the door slam right before I turned on the water.

I had finally combed out the last of the paint when a firm knock on the door rattled the entire suite. *She forgot the key!* I crossed the living room with a groan and yanked the doorknob, forgetting how thin and light hollow doors are. It careened into me and sent me stumbling backward, wet hair whipping me in the eyes.

Ben caught my arm.

"What are you doing here?"

His face was inches from mine. "You were tired and something was wrong . . . I brought dinner. Besides, I was at a lost myself."

"At a *loss*."

He smiled down and released me. "That too."

Righting myself, I stepped aside. "Come in. My sister showed up today."

"That is what that was about?"

"I'm sorry I didn't tell you. I got the message as we left Piccolo."

"You know my brother. Can I meet your sister?" Ben smiled as if this was a "meeting the family" moment.

No. Yes. No. While I mentally cycled through a

variety of answers, he shoved a green cloth bag into my hands. It was heavy.

"I borrowed Joseph's car and bought us dinner. Take this to your kitchen."

"What is this?" I looked in and found produce, pasta, oil—groceries. "Are you cooking for us? Me? Us?"

"No." He cut off my words with a solid kiss. "*We* are cooking for *us*. Sister, too, now."

"Speaking of . . . Where is she?" I balanced the bag to reach for my phone. Amy had texted while I was in the shower. "It may be only us. She's met some guy in the lobby . . ." I laid down the phone, unwilling to read the rest of her message.

Ben pulled the teetering bag from my arms and set it on the counter.

"You don't have to do this." I stepped into the tiny kitchen behind him. "But what are we making?"

He smiled back at me. "I want to try something new. With you." He passed me a bottle of olive oil and a large sauté pan. "You be in charge of the shrimp."

I poured in the oil and twisted the burner knob to medium, then unwrapped the brown paper package.

"You said you never cook." He raised a brow. "You knew to heat it first."

I winked, that feeling from the morning returning —the light and free feeling that ended in sticky white hair and a swipe of paint across his cheek. "You never get a reaction without a little heat."

"Ah . . ." He stole another kiss, and we spent the next few minutes with me sautéing the shrimp and him washing, dicing, and splicing a variety of vegetables. Over the past several nights, we'd perfected this dance—moving around a kitchen together, talking, tasting, and me cleaning rather than cooking. This was my first cooking assignment. I snuck a glance at Ben, oddly delighted to be trusted with shrimp.

He didn't notice and continued to chop his vegetables. I didn't comment and continued to sauté the shrimp. We didn't speak, and I savored the silence. It lay softly with Ben, light, warm, and beautiful. Until I thought of Amy . . .

He nudged my shoulder. "You make a terrible face when you concentrate. Those?" He ran his thumb across the space between my eyebrows. "They come right together. In here."

"Never tell a girl she looks terrible."

"Not you." He pinched his face tight. "That expression."

I narrowed my eyes, working not to laugh. "Still . . ."

"I should flatter you?" Ben pulled my shoulder until I faced him. "We are past that."

"We are? When did that happen? We've known each other about a week."

He closed the tiny distance between us as if

prepared to stare me down. I had to tilt my head back to keep eye contact. "The moment we met."

"Really?" I whispered. "I like that."

The click of the key card broke the moment.

I heard Amy push open the door. "I got us . . . Hello?" She froze, staring at Ben.

I trailed her gaze to absorb what she must see—tall, lithe, short dark hair, stubble from having started the day so early, and flecks of paint here and there that the shower hadn't washed away but only made him more adorable. I couldn't blame Amy for the unabashed interest that flashed through her eyes.

Wait until he speaks.

I flapped my arm between the two. "Amy, Ben. Ben, my sister, Amy. Ben's brother is Joseph, who owns the studio I'm at. He's a chef and . . ." *Get it over with.* "He's Italian." I clamped my mouth shut.

Ben sent me an amused glance.

"Hi." Amy didn't stumble like I might have. Instead, she floated the three steps as her single word became a monosyllabic greeting with a decisively Southern drawl.

I rolled my eyes.

Ben was no better. His accent thickened with every word as he welcomed her and told her that we had dinner under control.

"Wonderful. I'll just perch here and let you two cook." She poured herself a glass of wine and climbed onto one of the high stools at the counter.

Ben and I continued cooking. Me, silent. Him, keeping up a charming prattle, laced with way too much flattery.

Soon he tossed his vegetables, my shrimp, and the pasta together and carried the three dishes to the small dining table. I still hadn't spoken a word since the introductions.

After a few bites I relented and tapped his bowl with my fork. We'd made a shell pasta dish full of fresh vegetables and sautéed shrimp and bound it all in a creamed basil pesto with smoked chilies. "Not bad."

"How can you say that? It's delicious." Amy raised her glass. "To the chef. Cheers."

Ben mimicked her motion and laid his other hand on my shoulder. "Chefs." He smiled at me as I, too, raised my glass. "It is not delicious enough." He leaned back, still watching me. "Think on it. What are we missing?"

I almost laughed. Amy and I grew up on Kraft Mac and Cheese or Annie's, if we had enough to splurge. I shot her a glance and knew she was in the same predicament. Neither of us had a clue as to what might be missing.

I poked my fork around what was left and found an opinion. "Smoke the shrimp? Can you grill them or sear them to get that flavor?"

"Yes . . ." He nodded for me to continue.

"It needs depth, but without any spice that might

overpower all your vegetables and the basil. You've already got chilies in the sauce, so you need something else, not more of the same."

"Hmm . . ." He stabbed a shrimp and chewed it slowly, considering my suggestion. "Again, you said you never cook."

"This feels like a good painting. It's layering, flavors rather than color, and tasting rather than seeing."

"I feel that way. This is my art."

"You two," Amy cut in. "No wonder you're friends." Her last word lifted in question, and I knew what she was asking.

I ignored her.

She tried a different tack. "Have you been here before, Ben?" She poked her fork around the room.

I worked hard not to narrow my eyes at her or show any emotion at all.

"No. I am staying with—"

Something caught his eye and he reached to the sofa's side table, only feet away in the tiny place.

"Vasari?" He lifted the heavy book. "You know Vasari?"

"Of course. He's basically the founder of art history and criticism, and his writings form the basis for restoration . . . He's Italian too. But of course you knew that. He was no big fan of Caravaggio, who is kind of my favorite painter, but I've forgiven him for that."

Ben's eyes warmed, and I forgot every uncharitable thought I'd been sending Amy's way.

"You should see some of Caravaggio's work."

"I have, years ago at the Art Institute in Chicago."

Ben laid his hand on the book. "No. In the churches. In the original places. In Rome, you walk into Santa Maria del Popolo or San Luigi dei Francesi and he's there. His works are all around you."

I sighed. "I wish." I was no longer talking, or thinking, about Caravaggio. And from the look in his eyes, Ben wasn't either.

"I think you could also add more parsley." Amy tapped her fork on her bowl. "To the pasta."

Ben's eyes widened as if he'd forgotten Amy sat across from him. He swallowed and said, "I can tell you a story about parsley . . ."

The next hour was filled with Ben's story of his Nonna, her garden, and the year her parsley overran all the other vegetables. And by the end, I couldn't blame Amy for any crush she might have on him.

As Ben had drifted back into his childhood, his face softened, his hands moved more fluidly, his accent tripped across octaves, and Italian sprinkled his English like jimmies on a sundae— each utterly delicious.

The spell broke only when I stood to clear the table.

"Do you mind if I go hop in the shower?"

I smiled at Amy's timing—just as the dishes needed to be washed. "Not at all. There's only one shower, through my room."

Amy grabbed her bag and disappeared while Ben picked up the glasses and followed me the few steps to the kitchen.

"And you said you don't flatter," I gently teased.

Ben glanced toward my closed bedroom door. "Is that not what she expects? One always says lovely things to a *girasole*."

"A what?"

"You call them sunflowers. They turn all through the day, following the sun. They cover the fields this time of year at home."

"Oh."

He touched my chin, lifting my face to his. "It is nothing to say lovely things to someone who expects them, needs them. The beauty is when one who does *not* expect them comes to believe them—that only happens when the compliments and the love behind them are sincere."

Love?

Before the question could hit my eyes, I tamped it down with a "Harrumph . . ."

Only Ben could make *not* giving compliments sound like a compliment.

"My own *girasole*." He laughed. "Please, Bella, only turn toward me."

The comment was so suggestive and enticing it

startled me. It was also alluring—that sense that the warmth and electricity between us weren't fleeting, but could last and spread through my bones, warming me for life. I wasn't sure if we were having a language issue, an amazing flirtation . . . or what would happen next week.

He waited a beat more before continuing, a teasing light in his eyes. "Were you jealous?"

"Not at—"

He closed the distance between us. All words stopped. All thought stopped.

"I am here for you." He tugged my hips closer and kissed me.

It took me a few moments to catch my breath and whisper, "What will you do when Piccolo's ready? You've done what you came to do, right? The pizza. The restaurant."

Ben leaned back against the counter, pulling me with him. "*Sì*. But you complicate things."

I bit my lip.

"I need to go home, Bella. For you, I would stay if I could. Already I know that. But Papa is not well, and I stole all the time I can. Saturday, I go."

"We have less than a week."

"Every moment of a week." He captured my lips and kissed me again and again.

After a few moments I heard the bathroom door open. "Amy," I whispered.

"Her timing is good."

"It is?"

"As you said, you never get a reaction without a little heat. That is plenty of heat for now. Besides—"

He stopped as Amy opened the bedroom door, straight across the small living room.

"Hey." Her voice dipped to a purr. "Hey . . ." She glanced between us, confusion skittering through her eyes. "Am I interrupting something?"

"Dishes." Ben winked at me and grabbed a rag to wipe the counters.

⁂ Chapter 9 ⁂

Monday started too early as well—or maybe Sunday had ended too late. It was dark. I was sore from wiping the copper pipes above my head. And upon entering my tiny living room, I stumbled into the couch. *Amy.*

"Ouch!"

"What time is it?" she mumbled into the dark.

"Five a.m. I'm turning on a light."

"Are you kidding me? What are you doing up?"

I heard her punch the pillows and moan as I flipped the switch in the kitchen. "I've got a lot of work today and I want to get to Piccolo by midafternoon."

"He's adorable," she sighed into her pillow.

Rather than comment, I scooped the coffee into the machine, remembering his comment about my bad coffee and remembering the two machines on my worktable. I wanted to finish those as well. A surprise.

"Make me a cup. I'm coming with you." Amy appeared beside me.

"You can't come with me."

"Then drop me off at Piccolo. I'll keep Ben company."

Oh no . . . My heart constricted. All those guys in high school . . . guys who dated me, then met my sister. Guys who dated me to meet my sister. Guys who didn't look at me, but only at my sister. We looked alike, but she had that some-thing more—*vita*. If I was Piccolo before Ben and I started to transform it, then she was Piccolo after. She shone brighter, laughed with lovely intonation, questioned with rapt expression and wide eyes, and drew people to her. It was Amy's great gift—she galvanized everyone around her into a happy band of devotees.

And yet the reality was—she was here and wasn't going to sit in my tiny hotel suite all day. So, knowing at least Maria would be at the restaurant so early, I dropped her off at Piccolo on my way to the studio.

Lily was already there, coffee on her work-table, eye in her scope. "Good morning." She glanced up as I slammed through the door.

"We'll see . . ." Something caught my eye. A painting was propped on my easel. I'd seen the style. I paused for a moment to form my own impressions. Russian realism. Mid-nineteenth century. "What's this?"

"Joseph left you a note." She waved at my worktable and returned to her scope.

It was a letter really, written in a neat up-down script.

Emily,
    I'd like to see what you'd do with this. Nikolai Yaroshenko. Girl Student. 1883. It's a commission from the Van Geld estate and needs to be completed quickly, as the estate goes to auction at the end of the month. Assess the damage, make a report, and estimate the cost for restoration—based on your own metrics. Then, if all is well, I want you to handle the work.

Joseph

A Yaroshenko? That meant the painting valued near thirty thousand dollars. "He wants me to restore it."

"Don't you want to?" Lily looked up.

"Yes. But—" Doubt crept in—on all fronts.

"This is what you wanted. Start. If you get in a jam anywhere, give a shout."

I laid the note down and started deconstructing and polishing the La Marzocco, giving my hands something to do as I studied the painting. I jotted a few notes, then put it under the Leica.

There was so much to see. The damage was minimal—dryness about the eyes, some scaling within the woman's shawl. I laid it on the worktable and carefully removed the framing to examine the stretcher. Oxidation had left a yellow tinge only visible when taken in contrast to the clear borders. In the end, it required nothing more than a cleaning, minimal inpainting, and a new coat of varnish.

Joseph knew all this.

By midmorning I'd finished cleaning both coffee machines and left them readied for their new parts, e-mailed Joseph my report on the Yaroshenko, and headed to the Petersons'. As I drove by Piccolo, it took all my willpower not to turn off the street and into its parking lot.

After applying the varnish to Brooke's mural, I stood back and studied it, making sure I'd done all it needed. Set within the applied faux frame, it was certainly a more sophisticated treatment— if not a little sad. The formality of its framing reinforced that the little girl, and perhaps her joy, was gone.

But that was reality. The girl in the picture *was* gone. I pulled the photos out of my folder and compared them to the mural as it appeared now. There was no doubt I'd enhanced it. But what was I to do? With Brooke sitting right beside me, was I to squeeze out fawn and ochre colors and say, "Isn't this nice?"

They weren't. They were dull and sallow colors. And if adding a little life and liveliness to her mural made it better in some way . . . it was worth it.

"Jeremy hired a painter to create that from a photo I took the day we moved in. There was a swing out back. It felt like the most romantic thing ever."

I capped the bottle of varnish. "It was. And it's beautiful. Good as new."

"Better than, I think . . ." Rachel's voice drifted away. She leaned against Brooke's windowsill. "You've been a good friend to the kids this past week. And that? It's definitely better than the original." Rachel struggled with a smile.

"Please don't say that. Don't even think it." I laughed. "I'm supposed to restore, never enhance."

"I won't blow your cover, but you . . . you made her face happier. I always thought the picture made her look sallow, and she thought she looked like a brat. Now she loves it."

"She's fourteen. She'll change her mind tomorrow."

"Wouldn't that be nice? If we could all go back . . ." Rachel looked away. I noticed her grip on the windowsill. Nail tips white, bases purple. "Brooke was sitting with you the other day."

"She did that all last week. She did a good job cleaning the mural, then I moved her onto brush duty."

"Did she . . . She doesn't talk to me, but I

noticed . . ." She let her unasked questions drift between us.

Rachel and I hadn't talked the previous week beyond logistics. Anything I'd picked up, beyond Brooke, had sifted onto me like dust.

"I think doing things with your hands, like painting or cleaning brushes, helps. The physical activity allows the mind to wander. It doesn't feel so scary to talk." I shrugged, knowing I'd probably revealed a deep truth about myself and how I coped with things rather than anything she didn't already know about her daughter.

"Should I buy a bunch of brushes?"

I laughed. "If Parker plans to paint, yes, but I offered to let Brooke paint and she only wanted to clean. It might be weird if they start showing up after I've gone."

"We're all fine—alive and well—and the house, it's standing better than ever. We've got freshly painted rooms, a new roof, a new kitchen, and two new bathrooms. And yet it tore us apart. How strong I thought we were. How naive I was." Rachel let go of the windowsill and crossed her arms. "Did she tell you how it started?"

"I read the insurance report." I shrugged. "It helps me to know what's happened to the pieces I restore."

"Ah . . . She blames herself."

"I can understand that." I didn't know what else to say. "How's Parker?"

Rachel quirked a small smile. "He's okay. He misses that silly horse. Jeremy gave it to him."

I reached into my bag. "Look."

Rachel's eyes filled. "You found another?"

"This is Patches. Parker had saved the one leg, and I made another." I handed it to her. "It was a nice clean break, so I filed the edges after gluing it back and then filled any gaps with a light caulking compound. And then I learned how to use a 3D printer. Have you ever seen one?"

Rachel looked up at me.

"I'm babbling. You couldn't care less about the process."

"Not really." She burst out a sobby laugh. "But I'm so thankful. It's such a stupid horse."

"You should give it to him."

Rachel shoved Patches back to me. "You did all the work."

I bent and threw all my equipment into my small crate. "If you don't mind, I have to get going." I lifted the box, arms now full. "Tomorrow?"

"Tomorrow." She jiggled the horse in her hand. "Thank you."

Piccolo. Part of me wanted to be there more than anything, and the other part wanted to hop on I-75 and head home to Chicago. Ben had been a dream that lasted one week. And for that one week, I was the Amy—the light and shining one. Side by side, I could never compete. It wasn't even that I wanted to compete; it was that I couldn't be "that girl" in front of her. She knew me, and I wasn't me right now. I was brighter with Ben—like those copper pipes that turned to sunrise with a simple swipe of solvent. And I loved it. Would she notice a change and ask? *Why are you trying to be someone you aren't?* Would I have the courage to ask back? *What if I'm trying to be someone I can be?*

I pulled into Piccolo's parking lot completely shaken—until I saw Ben through the window. He was helping a painter remount the small lobby's lighting fixture. He noticed me and jumped from the ladder, pushed through the door, and reached the car in a few strides.

"You are here."

"I am here." I climbed out to be pulled into a hug.

"Come see."

He led me inside, and the place was unrecognizable. They'd finished the painting and were cleaning and mopping, careful to stay clear of the walls. My solution had worked, and the copper pipes glowed warm from the ceiling. Amy was leaning over the bar rubbing a paste wax I'd bought, a beeswax and carnauba mixture, into the wood. Half the bar glowed so bright you could see an accurate reflection of the lightbulbs from the ceiling above.

"You did this on purpose," she threw out with a

huff and a smile. "What ever happened to a simple furniture spray?"

"It doesn't work. Bad for the wood too. Think how shapely your upper arms will be."

"They already are." She lowered her head and kept buffing.

A few hours later found the last survivors slumped at a table over food Joseph brought from his apartment.

Amy wiggled in her seat and looked around the room. Her large blue eyes widened in wonder. Not real wonder, just the image of it. It was a look I knew well and suspected she practiced in the mirror. Doe-eyed, glowing, innocent. "This is adorable. It's going to be such a hit."

Joseph leaned forward, mesmerized. Their eyes met and held, and I almost rolled mine. But as Amy looked away to further absorb Piccolo's "adorableness," Joseph shifted his gaze to mine and winked.

You snake! I held back my laugh. I was quickly learning that despite many icy features, Joseph was a warm guy. He simply forgot how to melt most days.

He schooled his expression and addressed Amy. "Ben's always been a busy one. As a kid, he was into everything, wanted to share in every experience. Aunt Maria fell in love with him the moment he arrived and threw all this at him."

"But you had to help. Ems says you're the artist."

"Conservator," I interjected.

Joseph's eyes clouded, then cleared. "Ben doesn't need my help. Your sister helped quite a bit, though. You should ask her about it."

Amy continued as if she hadn't heard, popping a sage leaf–wrapped anchovy into her mouth. A quick "yummy" distracted her before she put her hand over her mouth and kept talking. "You two sound extraordinary."

"You don't know us yet," Joseph challenged.

"That'll be my top priority this week." She dabbed her napkin at the corners of her mouth and smiled.

This time I did roll my eyes.

"Sounds delightful." Joseph locked eyes on me and smirked.

"I think we should head home, Ames. It's late."

Amy preempted my move and jumped from her seat. "I need the ladies' room. You stay here." She dragged her eyes across the table. "Don't let her leave, y'all."

As she sashayed away, Ben reached for my hand. "She *is* good."

I slid him a look. "You noticed."

"Everyone did. She had every worker today falling over himself to help her." He smiled and kissed my temple.

I held still, enjoying being near him for just that

moment. The sense of relief, or understanding, or acceptance—I honestly couldn't name it— flooded over me.

"Thank you," I whispered.

"No grazie necessari."

Joseph stood and narrowed his eyes at me. "I'm going to do you two a favor."

"You are?" I sat straight.

"I'm taking your sister back to your hotel. It'll cost me twenty minutes, but if it'll get you two to stop looking like you're missing out on dessert, it'll be worth it."

"Beppe!" Ben grinned.

"Save your thanks, little brother, and stop calling me that." He softened the command with a crooked half smile. He turned on Amy as she emerged from the ladies' room. "These two have work to do, so you're coming with me. I'll take you back to Emily's hotel." His tone left no room for discussion.

Amy glanced to me in momentary confusion, then followed.

"I think my brother . . ." Ben paused, searching for a word. "He outmaneuvered your sister."

I grinned. "Isn't it wonderful?"

≫ Chapter 10 ≪

Joseph's shoes squealed across the cement floor. "You've begun?"

I paused, leaned back from the scope, and held the brush away from the Yaroshenko. "I got here early this morning."

He'd kept leaving me notes and tasks. Between these and the Petersons' work, I found myself stretched to reach Piccolo by midafternoon each day. But I didn't begrudge him any of it—each night he drove Amy home.

He stepped closer. "The cleaning looks good. You've eradicated the ill effects of that poor restoration job. I suspect it occurred sometime in the sixties."

"I wondered how long it'd been." I rolled away. "You did your own analysis first, didn't you?"

He smiled. "Of course."

"And the eyes?" I gestured to the scope.

As he pressed his eye to the viewfinder, I took in the whole painting. It was a portrait of a young woman, dressed for the rain and walking toward the artist, eyes locked. She was luminescent in the morning light—her skin translucent and her wool shawl so soft you could roll it between your fingers.

"I've never known anyone as hungry as you."

Joseph backed away. "Or as naturally talented. That work's exceptional." Before I could respond, he continued. "How can you achieve it in this, but not in your own work? Every emotion is in those eyes."

"Down at its core, this is a sophisticated paint-by-number," I managed. "Yaroshenko did all the hard work; mine's not a creative decision. I simply stay true to what's there—and the closer I get, the better." I tapped the Leica scope. "This is unbelievable. Maybe that's where my talent lies; I'm a master imposter."

"Ben says you have the soul of an artist. One can't fake that. You've captured what Yaroshenko expressed. Don't diminish it." He tilted his head to the crate under my worktable. "You should try that girl's eyes now. You've gained something new."

Gained something new? Hope bubbled up within me. Part of me wanted to call after him, *What have I gained?* I rolled back to the scope. Joseph was right; I had stayed true to the artist's intent. The woman's focus and hesitant innocence endured. She was on the cusp of something new. Perhaps I was too . . .

Joseph was also right about seeing something new within my work; there was a lightness to my touch that I'd never felt before. And it felt visible. It wasn't a paint-by-number. I had entered into Yaroshenko's vision and emotion to convey it, and not cover or diminish it.

"She's almost finished."

I looked up hours later to find Lily studying my *Girl Student* as well. "A few more hours today, a day or two to set, and I'll varnish her."

Lily glanced back to Joseph's office. "Has he offered you a job yet?"

"No, but he's sending a lot of work my way. If he doesn't, I may have to start charging him."

"He will. You're becoming valuable around here." She patted my shoulder and crossed to her station.

A loud *"Buongiorno,* Emily. *Ciao,* Lily" boomed across the room.

I rolled clear of the painting. "What are you doing here?"

Ben crossed over and kissed me. "I came to see my coffeemakers." He tugged at my hair.

"What?"

He leaned down and whispered, "You've got paint in your hair."

My hand shot up and found a clump underneath in the back. My hair had been pulled into a ponytail last night. Or was it early this morning when Ben had flicked his paintbrush in my direction and I'd retaliated?

"How did I miss that?"

Ben gently tugged it again. "I will always love that shade of linen."

I giggled, then turned it into a cough and cleared

my throat. "Coffeemakers." I pointed to the far end of the worktable. "They're almost done. I'm waiting on the parts you ordered."

"I had them sent to Joseph. Let me go check."

Ben loped across the studio, and I cleaned up my scattered tubes of paint. When both men emerged, Ben carried a small box. "I have the gasket and the valves."

He handed me the box as Joseph examined the machines. "I hardly recognize them. You did this?"

I nodded.

"Then I have a question for you. Olivia Barton asked me to make supports for a client's mixed media piece. She's trying to suspend it from fishing lines. Wait." He walked back to his office.

I looked at Ben and mouthed, *Olivia Barton*, but he only raised his brows in reply.

Joseph returned with a sketch and photograph. "Here. What do you think?"

The piece looked several feet long, a mix of wires, paper, sheet metal, and . . . rock? "How much does it weigh?"

"Twenty pounds, maybe slightly more."

"I guess I'd say to use aluminum and put two supports in, crossing, from this fold to here and here." I pointed to two spots on the picture where the piece appeared to have the most strength.

"Could you build them?"

I laid down the pictures. "I'd need to see it and make measurements."

"I'll text her you're on your way. Her gallery is near Piccolo." Joseph walked away, the matter decided.

"Is he always like that?" I flicked my finger at his retreating figure.

"He likes you. He knows you want to prove yourself."

"I do?"

Ben raised an eyebrow.

"Stop that. Fine. I do." Without waiting for a reply, I continued. "Do you know who Olivia Barton is?"

"No."

"She's this gallery owner, been featured in *Art Papers* constantly, but that's Atlanta-based so that's no surprise. But she's in practically every other art publication too. She's edgy, critical, has a perfect eye, and owns a small gallery with an impeccable reputation for launching new artists —maybe not the blockbusters, but the award winners." I finally drew a breath.

"And?"

"I'm kind of a fan girl."

Ben chuckled. I wasn't sure he knew what a fan girl was, but I couldn't explain. I followed Barton's critiques and essays in *ARTnews*, and secretly her gallery was my dream. I knew exactly where it was; I glanced at it every time I passed and had even walked through it one day. But I hadn't spoken to her. Quite the opposite—when she caught up to me near the back ogling a stunning gold appliquéd woman on Tahitian paper and asked if I had any questions, I had fled. Mumbled a quick "No thanks" and beelined it out the door. I hoped she couldn't recall that moment.

I grabbed my bag and toolbox. "Do you want a ride back to Piccolo?"

"I need one. I brought back Joseph's car." Ben glanced over to my portrait of my girl, not Yaroshenko's. After Joseph's comment, I'd set them side by side. "You've changed her."

"I've been playing with her." I stilled, realizing that although I'd been working on her, I hadn't really stepped back and taken her in. While painting, I had felt something soft and light come through the brush, but I hadn't wanted to analyze it or dwell on it too much. Staying in the moment had been a new experience—almost a laying down of self—and I wasn't ready to look, even now.

Ben raced a few steps to catch up. "You are not going to tell me about it?"

"I can't. If I do, I might lose it. I didn't think about her, I felt her." I shook my head. "I can't explain it any other way."

Ben opened my car door for me. "There is no need to."

In a few minutes we were at the gallery. How did one approach an Olivia Barton? I'd already failed to talk to her once, but now I had a reason to be there. A reason behind an introduction. This was my chance.

I stalled just inside the front door. It was freezing. Next I noticed white. Nothing but white —a polar-bear-sitting-on-an-ice-cap kind of white. When I'd visited just days before, I'd been intrigued by her use of grays. The color had played against the gold within the pieces perfectly. Now the floor, ceiling, every wall and hanging space between them, was flat white. The effect was to make the structure completely disappear. There was nothing to compete with the bold chaos of the art, as she'd also removed all tables, benches, and chairs. You had to leave the gallery to find any seating. Crossing the room to look out the side windows, I saw she'd set up several high tables, stools, and a bar on her bricked patio.

"Startling, isn't it? I lowered the temperature to clear the paint fumes, then felt it complemented the show's aesthetic."

I spun around to find Olivia Barton walking toward me, hand outstretched. Her wrist dropped down as if it was too much effort to hold it out straight. She looked exactly as she had the other day, tall with raven hair, tightly coiffed and glinting red-toned under the lights. She wore a white cotton A-line dress. "Olivia Barton."

"Emily Price. Joseph Vassallo sent me."

Without a beat of recognition she faced Ben and narrowed her eyes. "Have we met?"

"I am Ben Vassallo. Joseph's brother."

She held his hand loosely within her own. "I had no idea. Where's he been hiding you?"

Ben smiled. "I am visiting for a couple months. I return home next week."

"To Montevello?"

Ben nodded.

"Lovely. I visited there, years ago." She dragged her eyes from him back to me. "Joseph says you can fix my little problem."

"I have some ideas."

Without more words, she led us through a maze-like series of faux walls to the back. On the floor rested the mixed media piece, and as I expected, it was about six feet by eighteen inches.

"He said you want to use fishing lines?"

"If possible. Vaughn sent it with bars for hanging. Can you imagine? It would look like a beached whale or a dead animal, legs straight up. It needs to float."

I knelt to measure it and test its strength. "We can make it float."

"I'll leave you to it then." She strode away on her four-inch heels, and I got to work.

Ben crouched next to me. "What can I do?"

"Write down these numbers for me." I handed him my notebook and measured each dimension, lifted it to feel for bend and flex, then marked the piece for soldering points. "All done. I'll make these at the studio, then fuse them here. I'm sure she has a back room." I looked up at the ceiling. "I'll also paint them white rather than the gray of this metalwork. That way the supports will disappear into the ceiling rather than become part of the piece."

Ben whispered, "Go talk to her. Tell her."

"About what?" *How does he know?*

"Your work."

"I can't." I felt like a kid whispering behind the teacher's back.

"Go." He reached for my tools and shooed me away.

I wove my way through the maze and found Olivia in a small alcove.

"Ms. Barton? I've got all the measurements and can have the supports here to solder tomorrow. I don't think you'll need more than three thirty-pound braided lines to hang them."

"Perfect. Joseph said you had talent." She dragged her gaze from my head to my toes. "As an artist too."

"He did?"

"Send me pictures of your work. I never promise, but I am intrigued by anything Joseph finds interesting."

"Thank you." Stunned, I made my way back to Ben. "Your brother made the entire introduction for me."

"I told you. He likes you."

"Who knew?"

As we made our way out, Olivia nowhere in sight, a painting caught my eye. It was bold, a cross between Picasso and Pollock, but like neither too. It had fine brushstrokes at the very center, reminiscent of seventeenth-century classical work, but the geometric designs surrounding it and washing over it at the corners made it feel jarring and random, beyond postmodern. Then the edges—pure chaos.

Exactly how I felt.

⫸ Chapter 11 ⫷

I spent the entire day applying the final coat of varnish to the Petersons' dining room walls, pondering the painting I'd seen at the gallery. All my life I'd studied art criticism, restoration, the rules and the procedures, and I worked to master the technique. I didn't stretch boundaries; I worked within them. A master imposter. I shook my head. Not an imposter. An imitator.

And in restoration it worked. It was a field based on the finite nature of any work—a work already in existence. But that painting? It was as if it and I were bursting out of that central focal point together. It was something new. A surprise. If I let myself go, forgot the boundaries, forgot the rules

I myself fashioned and imposed, what could happen?

"You've worked hard today."

Rachel's voice startled me, and I accidentally dropped the brush I was wiping back into the jar of soap.

"Sorry. I was somewhere else. That's the beauty of laying down varnish and even cleaning up. You get to escape."

"I knit."

"I've never tried that." I waved my hand to encompass the three walls before us. "These weren't bad at all. Tiny water damage and a light layer of smoke soot. Once this dries, forty-eight hours, you can hang art and move back in here."

I stepped back to stand next to her. The blue walls glistened like lapis lazuli with threads of gold catching in the sun.

"I find this room peaceful."

"It feels like water. Working on it, I felt like I was on the tip of something wonderful. That it was going to rise up on a wave and crash into me." I glanced at her. "In a good way."

Her eyes took on a gleam I hadn't seen before. "I don't think you needed these waves for that." Before I could form a reply, she stepped toward the kitchen. "Would you like a cup of coffee?"

"You have coffee?" The last time I noted the kitchen, yesterday, it'd been empty.

116

"I do. Thanks to Jeremy."

She hadn't mentioned her husband much. I knelt by my crate and grabbed another rag to re-wipe the soapy brush. "Let me box this up and I'll be right in."

I walked into the kitchen a moment later to find Rachel next to a La Pavoni coffeemaker exactly like the one Ben acquired for me.

"You have one of these? I just refurbished one."

"Jeremy and I bought this years ago—actually, we bought two, one for home and one for his office. He's a total coffee snob." She looked around the kitchen. "He brought this one from his office. Now it's beginning to feel like home again."

"Can you show me how to use it? I tested mine out this morning, and the results were horrid." The idea of surprising Ben pleased me.

"Sure." Rachel ground the beans, weighed the coffee, tamped it down, pulled the shot, steamed the milk . . . all the while explaining each step.

"I'll never remember all this. My . . ." I stalled. *What do I call him?* "My boyfriend. He's visiting here, like me really, and we're fixing up a machine . . . a whole restaurant, really, and—"

"Oh my gosh, you're blushing." Rachel squeezed my arm. "You're adorable. I mean . . . That sounds so condescending, but you are. You're adorable. Now you have to tell me. Please."

I felt heat flood my face. I hadn't told anyone. I only knew Lily and Joseph, and there was no way I could talk to them. I didn't want to call friends at home. They didn't know Ben, hadn't seen him, wouldn't understand. And, although Amy asked countless questions each morning when I woke her and each early dawn when I tried to sneak back into the hotel room, I didn't want to share— not a single moment, not with her. But I knew I was about to spill everything and there was no way to stop myself.

"I just met him. He's here from Italy, some tiny town I guess, visiting his brother, but his aunt and uncle live here too. They're the ones who own the restaurant. His brother owns the studio I'm working in and that's how we met . . . but I'm helping him refurbish his aunt's place and that's how we really met. I go each night, and we talk and we work on stuff and he's been teaching me to cook and . . . We've only got a couple days left and I've got paint in my hair all the time. I can't get it out and I can't imagine not being with him, not getting to share every thought. At first I just wanted to help because I love projects, but now I love—" I stopped, fully aware of where I was headed.

Rachel caught it too. "Was that a surprise?"

I flapped my hand, trying to cycle through the days. "I've hardly slept. I'm sure it's because . . . It's been seven days? Eight? I probably just need sleep. But . . . do you think? No, I've known him a week."

"I'm sure it's just lack of sleep." Her eyes danced.

"Of course, but . . ." A horrid giggle burst out. I bit my lip to stop it. "What if it's not? What if he goes home and I go home and I never see him again? I mean, it could be more, right? He's different. He sees things completely the opposite of me. Not completely, but creatively. He shares, like he wants to be a part of your world and you his. That's what helping his aunt and uncle was about. And he speaks perfect English with this beautiful accent, but no contractions. He can't figure them out, or doesn't want to. Do you have any idea how adorable no contractions are?"

"No." Rachel shook her head, eyes still dancing. "I have no idea how adorable no contractions are."

"Sorry. That was pretty bad." I wrapped my hands around the cappuccino she handed me. "I'm going to stop now. That was so much more than you needed to know."

"I asked. And I think it's nice. When you get to be my age . . ." She threw me a glance, a challenge, as if daring me to protest our twentyish-year age difference. "You sometimes forget. But marriage should be like that too. Sure, you might get more sleep, but you can feel just that alive every day—as long as you don't forget. After all, you get to be with that one guy—for you, the adorable no-contractions guy—who lights up your world and shares it with you. For me, he makes good coffee and sings to me. At least he used to . . ." She took a sip of her coffee, too, remembering. "Enjoy it. Hang on to it."

I settled back on firm ground. "Mine's just a blip. He's going home and . . . Chicago's a long way from Italy."

"Ah . . . 'Summer lovin', had me a blast; summer lovin', happened so fast . . .' " Her voice rose and dipped in song. "No? You don't know *Grease*?"

"Oh . . . I've seen that."

"*Phew.* For a minute there I was going to worry about your generation."

I studied the brightly painted mug in my hands. "This really is delicious."

"Then don't be so eager to let it go." Rachel winked and started singing again.

⋙ Chapter 12 ⋘

I pulled open Piccolo's front door. The tables were still grouped in the center of the room, but everything around them was unrecognizable now that the ladders and drop cloths were gone. The space felt huge. It was light and bright, with the white linen playing against the dark wood accents.

They had already hung the plate rack we'd found and it was filled with hand-painted Italian plates, bringing character and color to the space. Ben had also laid out the templates I'd given him, and Amy was perched high on a ladder stenciling a delicate design within the center panels of the back wall.

"You're doing a beautiful job," I called up to her.

"Hey." She leaned back.

"Careful." I reached up my arms.

"I'm fine. It is looking good, isn't it? Your design is super cool."

"Thank you." Her compliment surprised me. "Where is everybody?"

"Ben cleared everyone out a few minutes ago. He said they had all worked hard and deserved a break." She stepped down the ladder. "Can we talk a minute?"

As she took the last steps down, I realized that although we'd shared the same space for several days, we'd barely had a conversation. I knew I'd set it up that way, by arriving home long after she'd crashed on the sleeper sofa and only waking her each morning in time to head out the door, but now it felt like a small way to treat my sister.

"Sure." I dropped my bag and pulled over a chair. She leaned against the ladder.

"I wanted to talk to you about those interviews you set up."

"You didn't cancel, right? They're still next week?" I reached into my bag. "I was checking this morning, and there are a few more postings at—"

"Stop." She laid her palm over my notebook. "I don't want to take them. I want to find this next job on my own."

"That's fine to say, but who gets called when you get fired? Me. You call me. Mom calls me. You even asked, 'What's next?' last time, so I called Covington."

"I know, but when I told you and Mom what I wanted to do from the first, neither of you would let me. You forced me into that accounting firm. I hated it, and then it was just easier to quit arguing."

"That's a little dramatic."

"Not really. You wouldn't know; you do what you love." She held up her hands. "Look, I know what I want to do. That's what I came here to tell you, if you'd only talk to me. I've got a lead on a party planner job right in Lincoln Park, so I can stay in Chicago."

"You know nothing about party planning. It's not like being a professional guest; you don't actually *go* to the parties."

"That's so patronizing, Emily. And mean."

I slumped in the chair. "I'm not trying to be mean, but—"

"Thanks for the vote of confidence." She

climbed back up the ladder. "I've got work to do."

"Amy," I called up to her. "That was nasty of me. I'm sorry."

She narrowed her eyes. "Seriously?"

"Seriously. I'm sorry." I didn't want to say any more. I didn't know what *to* say. I gave a last nod and headed to the kitchen.

I found Ben cleaning away dust.

"It looks wonderful out there."

"Thank Amy. She is a hard worker." Ben grabbed a white bag and handed it to me. "I bought you a gift. There is a bookstore across the parking lot." He couldn't wait for me to open it. "It is a book. *Acqua Alta*. That is a true phenomenon in Venice—the tide can rise and flood the city—but this is a mystery novel by an Italian writer. You said you love mysteries. Her detective, Guido Brunetti, solves mysteries in Italy. This one is about art."

"Art *and* a puzzle." I smiled.

"You like it?"

"I love it."

"Good. I also cleared everyone out for another surprise. As soon as Joseph gets back, we will begin. He will bring us food and bread too. Lots of bread."

"What are we doing?"

"We must rebuild the wine list. I will keep all they have, but they need to add younger bottles. Americans like tighter, younger reds." Ben crossed the kitchen and lifted a box. He proceeded to pull the corks on six bottles.

"All of them?"

"These are the ones I question. Good price points, but I wonder if too young, which is why the good price points."

"I don't know that much about wine."

"I do," Joseph called from the doorway.

Amy pushed through behind him. "Ems, can I take your car? I'm tired and think I'll head back to the hotel." She turned to Joseph and asked in an arch tone, "Can you give *her* a ride home tonight?"

Joseph chuckled. "Of course."

I passed him and followed Amy back into the dining room. "We're having a serious wine tasting. Don't you want to stay?"

"Not tonight. I'll grab something at the grocery across the street and . . . I need to talk to my contact, find out more about that job."

"Amy . . ."

"I'm okay. Please."

"I feel like you think I've been squishing you."

"Not squishing. But somewhere along the way you didn't notice that I grew up too. I don't need you to fix everything. I don't want you to anymore."

"Ouch."

"Sorry." She shrugged and flung her arms around me in a tight hug. "I still love you, though."

"Thanks." I eked a laugh out of compressed lungs, then handed her my keys.

Joseph and Ben made up plates, and soon the three of us were seated at a table in the center of the dining room surrounded by glasses, bottles, and bags of takeout.

"Grab your notebook, Bella."

I took a sip and poised pen over page. "This one has mellow aspects of cranberry and cinnamon in a bed of fine, mossy dirt."

"You're making that up and it sounds ridiculous," Joseph said.

"Of course I am. It tastes like wine."

Joseph swirled his glass. "No. It tastes like gravel underlying chocolate. It hails from a Piedmont property and the ground gives up the elements reluctantly, making the Nebbiolo grapes work for those deep notes."

"Well then . . ." I scribbled down each word. We ate and sipped, and I listened and recorded everything the brothers said about each wine—mostly Joseph, I observed.

"You're really good at this," I said.

Joseph smiled and said, "It was my job, long ago."

Ben sat back. "You cannot just leave it at that."

I looked between the brothers. "What?"

"When Joseph was a teenager, it *was* his job. He chose Coccocino's wine and wrote the menu. He did such a good job Michel put him in charge of Osteria Acquacheta's too. He has a gift."

"You all really do believe in helping the competition." I laughed.

"In fact, one time I brought us food from Osteria while we tasted. Michel was teaching me sauces that summer, and we . . ." Ben's voice trailed away.

Confusion skittered through his eyes, and Joseph's face darkened. We fell silent as if something chilly had come upon us.

Joseph looked up. "I remember that night."

Ben was silent, and I could see in his eyes that he was returning in time, figuring out a puzzle of his own.

"I had not realized," he said. "That was the night—"

"Not now, Benito."

"When?"

"Never?"

For a moment I saw the same expression Ben had worn when asking Joseph about the pizza—except it was Joseph now who looked young, who needed something from his brother.

The eyes are the windows to the soul. Joseph had pegged that one. They convey every emotion, cloud to hide you behind an impenetrable wall, or strip you bare and leave you fully exposed.

Joseph blinked, and the vulnerability was gone. Ben accepted it with a nod and reached for another bottle, pulling himself back to the present. "Try this one. No cranberry, no cinnamon, but see if you can taste plum notes."

I smiled and went with the change in conversation.

After a few more sips, Joseph pushed his chair away. "I need to go. I've got an early day tomorrow. I'll walk so you can drive Emily home later." He wagged his finger to the wine bottles. "Will you be okay? Forget it, I know you two; you won't be taking her back for hours."

Ben stood and gripped his brother's shoulder before Joseph ducked away and walked out the front door.

Ben and I cleared the containers, moved to our favorite booth, and sat with a last sip of wine.

"I'm about to pry." I leaned back and let him absorb my warning.

"I would too." He shrugged. "But I have no answers. We were all at Coccocino that night. I was fourteen, and it was my first year to share in selecting the wines. It was a good time. But that night something happened. Joseph left Coccocino and went on what you would call a bout of . . ." He sat thinking. "Vandalism. It is near the same word for us too. Don Pietro, our priest, is the one who kept Joseph from jail. He took responsibility for him and gave Joseph a whole summer's worth of jobs in reparation. But Papa sent me away to my cousin Anne's family, and when I got back,

Joseph was off to university in Naples. Gone."

"How far was Naples?"

"Distance is not only physical."

"True." When I graduated high school, I, too, left home. College was only a few miles away, but it might as well have been around the world for all the care, attention, or time I gave Mom and Amy. I never went back, not really. Not in the ways that mattered.

Hours later, the sky was graying with morning as we stepped outside and locked the door. Ben walked me to Joseph's fancy car.

I rested my hand on his chest. "Joseph's place is just around the corner. If you trust me with this beauty, I'll drive myself home. You can be asleep in five minutes and I'll bring this back here later in the morning. Amy can follow in my car."

"Are you sure?"

"Yes. It makes the most sense." I reached up and kissed him. "Sleep well."

Ben pulled me close and with a much better and lingering kiss, he left me with a *"Buona notte, cara mia"* pressed against my cheek.

As I pulled out of the parking lot, I watched him walk across the lot and around the corner—his long legs eating up the pavement and his shoulders rounded with exhaustion.

Everyone talked about Piccolo's transformation and all our hard work. Each day things changed faster than I could absorb them, and it was all good and right. You could see the obvious delight, relief, and joy in Maria and Vito's faces.

And the nights . . . I knew Ben savored them as much as I did. But tonight revealed something new. Something I hadn't known. Ben hadn't come to Atlanta to visit his brother—he came to chase him.

≫ Chapter 13 ≪

Amy was awake before me and banging around with my new coffee machine.

"What are you doing?"

"Trying to make coffee with this thing. Where'd it come from?"

"Ben and I found it last week, and I restored it. Here, let me show you . . . It makes the best coffee you'll ever taste."

I poured water into the La Pavoni's reservoir, measured the beans Ben had ground for me at Piccolo, and went through every step Rachel showed me, counting down the time and tamping the beans with what I hoped was the right pressure.

I pulled Amy a shot, steamed the milk, and handed her the small porcelain cup we'd also found that Saturday. "Here."

She held the delicate cup high, her face full of questions. I nodded and twisted free the portafilter, slamming it against the knock box to release the grounds and make myself a cup.

In my periphery I saw her lower it and touch the rim to her lips. "Umm . . ."

"Delicious, right?"

She stretched the cup to me, offering me a sip. "It's horrid!"

"I wondered . . ."

I wiggled the machine. "I don't understand."

"Maybe it takes practice."

"It wasn't supposed to be hard. It's coffee—a morning basic. You should've seen Rachel, Mrs. Peterson; she flew through it. Why is nothing fun and easy? You think one moment, maybe, and then . . ." I flopped on the couch. "Hey, you made your bed."

"It wasn't hard."

I looked at her. "Why do I feel like you're handling all this better than I am?"

She smiled, small and without humor. It was odd to see myself in her. "Hey . . . What happened? This isn't like you."

"What?"

She dropped next to me with a smile. "I mean, not like you this week."

I tilted my head back, looking for answers on the ceiling. "I think I remembered last night that life is hard. No one gets off easy." There was a water spot on the ceiling. "Ben's leaving soon, and he didn't get what he wanted from Joseph.

I'm leaving soon, and I didn't get Ben or a job. Not that I was going to get to keep Ben—life's not that good . . . I just thought Joseph would give me a job, and though I know Ben will move on with some gorgeous Italian girl, it'd be like being close to him too."

"In a very weird way . . ."

"I hadn't thought that one through. Basically, I need to get a job and let all this go."

"Would you move here?" She nudged me, and I stopped studying the water spot.

"Yes. No. If Joseph gave me a job, I'd be a fool not to take it. Restoration isn't a huge field."

"Office jobs are much more secure." Her voice mimicked mine to perfection.

"Yes. Good benefits too. And health care," I droned in my *big sister knows best* voice, cringing as I found it uncomfortably close to my normal one.

"Always a must." She tipped into me.

"We make quite a pair, don't we?" I looped my arm around her shoulder.

Amy twisted out from under my arm and looked at me straight on.

"What?" I said.

"That's the nicest thing you've said to me in years."

I pulled into my now usual spot at Piccolo. Amy opened her door.

"Aren't you coming in?"

"I have a surprise at the studio I need to pick up. Will you tell Ben I'll be here soon?"

She dropped back into her seat. "He talks about you, you know. While we work. He talks about you constantly. His eyes light up."

"It's a fun flirtation. Amazing one, really, but he'll go back to Italy, and I, hopefully, will stay here."

Amy got out of the car, then leaned in and looked at me. "I've never seen anyone like Ben with you. If a guy looked at me that way, I'd . . . well, I'd do anything."

"You mean if a guy simply looked that way."

Amy laughed. "That too." She shut the door and waved behind her back as she headed into the restaurant.

I drove back to ACI to fetch the surprise I had for Maria and Vito, and for Ben. I'd taken a few family photos out of the storage closet, restored them digitally, then reprinted and reframed them in a larger format so they'd fill the space in the short hallway to the restrooms and tell their story of family and food.

As I was stacking them in a crate, a shadow fell over me. I looked up at Joseph. "How do you do that?"

He leaned against my stool and lifted a soft leather driving loafer. "Partly good shoes. Partly skill. While growing up, you did not want Nonna to catch you sneaking past the kitchen. If she did, you cooked for hours."

I laid down the picture. Joseph never talked of family or home. Anything I'd learned came from Ben. *He* talked of family all the time, and they sounded pretty ideal—boisterous, but ideal. Ben used warm words like *laughter, love, teasing,* and *hugs.* Words that tasted sweet and coated you. Joseph, if he did have anything to say, used words from my lexicon: *obligation, work, duty, challenge.* Hard words I could tap with my small finishing hammer. I suspected Joseph and I had both spent years tapping at those words.

"Ben makes me miss home." Joseph reached forward and fingered some tubes of color on my tray. "Is it hard having your sister here?"

"In some ways. It was a complete surprise, but it's not turning out quite like I imagined."

"Do things ever?" Joseph took a deep breath and held it.

Silence fell, and I didn't know where to go \next. *Family.* That was how he'd started.

"Ben said your father isn't well?"

"Papa's older. Twenty years older than Mama. He's . . . over eighty now." Joseph rubbed his chin as if the math surprised him. "In my mind, he's still what he was when I left. Ben was, too, until he showed up." He shook his head. "I can't imagine now. My father came a few years ago, but I don't even remember how he looked. My mother has called me three times this month. That's enough to worry me."

"Can you go visit?" I asked softly, suspecting after last night that this was dangerous ground.

"Once the High opens the Muniz exhibit, I could. I've got three pieces for it, and I want to be at the opening." He looked around the room, then fixed his gaze on me. "Lily told me about Covington's downsizing."

"I figured she did, and all your 'favors' were tests."

Joseph had the grace to chuckle. "And you passed each with colors flying, as Ben would say." I smiled at the twisted colloquialism. "The supports for the Vaughn piece worked perfectly. Three thirty-pound braided lines, as you said. It soared. Olivia thanks you."

"I sent her pictures of my paintings, by the \way. Thank you for that."

Joseph squirmed. He seemed as uncomfortable with thanks as I did. He continued. "And you were spot on with the Harnett."

The Harnett, a small landscape, was another of Joseph's tests.

"The Connor job too," he added.

"I liked that one. It feels like the integrity of the piece is maintained, doesn't it?" I propped myself on the worktable, enjoying this discussion. Enjoying my work. "Not that adding new supports would be bad."

"It wouldn't be bad . . . but you were right. The canvas was so delicate . . . And your placement, Mrs. Connor will appreciate that. She was nervous that the supports would be intrusive. She likes to display it freestanding on a table." He was back to fiddling with my paint tubes. "I hope you'll consider staying. Here are terms." He handed me a cream linen envelope.

I tapped the envelope against my hand. It looked so formal, elegant linen paper, sealed. Like something in a movie. "Am I to open it now?"

"Look through it later and let me know. If you accept, I know you'll need to find a place here and get settled. I've included allowances for that."

"Thank you, Joseph." I knew there was more to say, but like him, I wasn't good at that stuff either.

He saved me from it as he pushed himself off the stool, nodded to me, and turned back toward his office.

I tore open the envelope. It was detailed— expectations, salary, hours, vacation time. He even gave me two weeks up front, paid, to get settled. Lily was right when she'd said they needed a "fix-it girl among their gilded lilies." I'd laughed at her, but this outlined that exact role—a support role, a prep role, an organizational role— all meant to facilitate the conservators' work.

Part of me wanted to be offended. I'd worked years and in many ways knew more about the

135

nuts and bolts of fixing basic things than they did. But it was also perfect, for I could do those things and still learn more, be a part of more. The Yaroshenko had been a thrill. Building the supports for the Vaughn, exciting. Figuring out the Connor drawing, a stretch and a success. And my own art was changing daily. I was changing daily.

⫸ Chapter 14 ⫷

I backed my way through Piccolo's front door, clutching my box of photographs.

Aunt Maria was at the hostess stand putting all the details back in place. Vito was dusting the bar. Amy was laying out the linens and positioning the votives. Ben was nowhere in sight.

I smiled and greeted them all as I headed to the kitchen.

"*Ciao*. Ben?"

"Bella!" he called from behind the freezer door. "We start to prep. Tomorrow night!"

"I can't believe it." I waved him over. "Come see what I brought." I set down the box and pulled out the pictures, laying them across the stainless-steel counter to unwrap them one by one.

"You did this?" he exclaimed, then froze. "That is Mama." He pointed to a striking teenager with jet-black hair and wide, expressive eyes.

"That's your mom? She's gorgeous." I pointed to the girl next to her. "Is that Maria?"

"*Sì.*"

"Who's this one?"

Ben shook his head. "I do not know. I told you, Mama never mentions her family. I do not know of any of them, but I suspect that is older brother Antonio."

"Have you ever asked why they don't talk?"

"*Sì.* I have asked all my life. When I met Maria and Vito, I asked. I asked Joseph. No one will say," Ben said quietly. "Let us hang these tonight after they leave. They will love the surprise." He pulled me into a hug. "This is a beautiful gift, Emily. Thank you. Maria . . . She still loves Mama. They will appreciate this." He pushed me back to arm's length. "I love how you are such a romantic." With that he placed his palms on both my cheeks and pulled me in for another kiss.

I hadn't thought of restoring the pictures as "romantic," but I guess it was. Planning a surprise for no reason other than to bring another person delight was, in fact, romantic.

Ben and I spent the rest of the afternoon prepping for Friday's reopening. Rather, he prepped and I got in his way. He'd given me small tasks over the evenings, but unsupervised—as he now had to move more quickly—I was more hindrance than help. Cutting an onion into rings rather than chopping them for a Bolognese sauce was the last straw. I moved on to odd jobs around the kitchen—a loose pot handle, a wiggly light switch, a door not closing fully.

We also learned that I excelled at hanging pictures. That night we hung most of the photographs in the hallway, salon style, and the one of Maria and her sister by the hostess stand. All finished, we poured a glass of wine and relished our work from the corner booth. The tables were set with the new cut-glass votives and vases; the hand-painted plates set the right tone; and the AC was turned low to reduce the humidity and clear the paint smell.

"Joseph offered me a job today."

"Bella." He said it softly, and I couldn't tell if it was pleasure or regret that danced within the notes. "I told you he liked you." He sat silent for a moment. "Will you take it?"

"I need it, and I've liked it here. I've been . . . brighter." I took a sip of wine. "Of course that might be all you and disappear when you go home."

Ben didn't look at me. "It will be nice to know where you are, to be able to see you in my mind. You will not feel so far away."

"Will you be sad to go? To leave all this?" I gestured to the restaurant, but I meant me.

"It was never mine to keep." Ben shifted in his seat and caught my eyes. "But you? You I want to keep. Imagining where you are is not enough. Could never be enough."

When I didn't move, Ben leaned closer still. "I need to be clear, Bella. I do not mean a visit; I mean a life. I know you have one here. But I love you. Please. Come. With. Me." He articulated each word clearly, as if they alone could create a bridge across the Atlantic.

He reached for my hands and held them between us, elbows resting on his knees. "I have loved you since the moment we met. Right here." He pointed to the back table, and I remembered that first night. Trying to understand him and missing almost every word, but understanding his heart. *Aiuto.* The word we'd spoken together. Had we been apart in any sense since? I doubted it, but then again, I'd worked hard not to analyze it. I'd worked hard, as weird as that sounded, to simply enjoy it.

He tucked a strand of hair behind my ear as if the action would heighten my hearing, my presence. "Please. Marry me?"

Marry you? The question caught me as the biggest surprise, then again as the most logical step. The very idea tasted rich and delicious on my tongue, and I waited for logic to sour it.

It didn't. Nothing did. Instead, it was there— that excitement or anticipation that what had been missing from my head and my heart was right before me, and that to reach out, while scary, was also right because such a possibility didn't come often, if ever again, and to let it go would be devastating.

If Ben thought my silence was odd, I had to give him credit. He said nothing. He merely held my hands and watched my eyes go through . . . who knows what. I'm certain every hope, dream —dashed or not—fear, and uncertainty flittered through. Finally I felt my vision and my heart still. Everything stilled—into perfect clarity.

"Yes."

⫸ Chapter 15 ⫷

Amy was still asleep when I snuck through the room, careful to keep my shin from knocking on her sofa.

I left her a note and gently shut the door behind me. I didn't want to share, not yet. And I didn't want to defend my decision.

Ben was already at Piccolo—again waiting on the front bench.

He was at my car, opening the door, before I'd turned off the engine. "Bella." He pulled me to him as I stepped out, and with a quick, firm kiss he asked, "Are you ready?"

"Absolutely."

"First coffee." He reopened my car door and we headed to Dripworks, the coffee shop he'd taken me to the week before. We sat at the high counter and I pulled out my phone.

"Have you looked any of this up? I mean, we can't actually get married today, you know. We'd have to go to Vegas for that. Most states have waiting periods." I searched for the rules and regulations in Georgia.

"Italy. Illinois. In my home and yours, you must wait, but not in Georgia. Today is the day."

My head shot up. "You looked it up?"

"Of course. Last week."

"Last week?"

He grinned. "This is not a spur in the moment."

I hiked a brow at him, knowing I couldn't create the same arch look he and Joseph achieved.

"Maybe *un po*," he conceded with a soft smile. "But I had hoped."

I stared at him, again waiting for that voice of reason to step in, and found myself shaking my head back and forth. "You're the romantic."

"Come on. Oh . . ." He twisted one hand within mine to hold it and used the other to reach for my chocolate croissant. "You cannot leave this behind."

"Where are we going?"

"Fulton County Probate Office at 136 Pryor Street," he recited, looking at his phone.

Within a half hour we'd found chairs in a large lobby area surrounded by booths, much like Chicago's Department of Motor Vehicles, and Ben filled out his section of the form.

"We meet all the requirements. In person. Over eighteen. And my passport has a certified English translation."

"How do you have that?" I leaned over his shoulder.

"I needed it to work at Piccolo, even as an unpaid nephew, in case the health board visited."

He handed me the clipboard to begin my section and settled back into his plastic chair. "It is what I hoped for them. It will sell better now, when they are ready."

I sat back too. "It's beautiful, but it makes me sad too. All our hard work, and a new owner will probably rip it out and put in a frozen yogurt shop or a Build A Bear."

"A what?"

"You know, you build a stuffed bear and put in a little heart . . . Oh, never mind."

Ben tapped the clipboard, drawing my attention back to the blanks. "I love that you defend me, us. But it was a gift for them. That is what you do for family. They have no family here."

"There's Joseph." I wasn't sure why I needed to offer him up. Ben didn't need reminding, but in some way I felt as if Joseph was getting left behind. In the months to come, he'd be left driving by that Build A Bear alone.

I dropped the clipboard into my lap. "Well, I'm going to miss how the bar gleams, and the woodwork and those pipes. It's some of my best work."

"You can redo Coccocino if you like."

"It's probably already perfect." I filled in another blank. "Even Joseph thinks that."

"He does?"

"You know he does." Despite Joseph's imposed isolation, he thought about family as often as Ben did. It wasn't hard to figure that out.

Ben peered over my shoulder and tapped a line at the bottom of the page. "If we had decided this earlier, we could save money with 'premarital education.' Forty dollars."

"And how much earlier could we have decided this?" I smiled as a booming "Number 47" filled the room.

"The moment we met." He winked and reached for my hand. "Our number."

He wrapped his arm around me as I laid the clipboard on the counter. A broad woman pulled it to her and, without looking up, ticked off a series of boxes while examining Ben's passport and my driver's license. She finally glanced up and droned the same words she'd probably said a million times before.

"If you're marryin' here in Fulton County, that'll be fifty-six dollars."

Three minutes later we held a marriage license and a sheet of paper with the names and phone numbers of area judges.

I tapped the third down the list. "Call that one."

"Why?"

"His name's Ben."

Ben dialed the number and listened. "Voice mail."

I picked another. After a short conversation, ending with a series of "Yes . . . Yes . . . We can find it . . . Yes . . . Thank you," he hung up and grinned. "Judge Briggs and his wife are near Capital Gateway Park. We are to meet them there in fifteen minutes."

"Fifteen minutes?" I looked down at my white T-shirt and floral print skirt. "This isn't exactly what every girl dreams of for her wedding dress. I should've at least worn heels, maybe a blouse."

"You look beautiful."

I spent the drive fidgeting with my hair. Up. Down. Low ponytail. High bun. I finally settled on leaving it down, as I was the only woman *ever* who liked what humidity did to her hair—a little wave was a good thing.

We found parking and walked down a broad sidewalk to a central fountain. People milled about, but no one looked like they were preparing for a wedding.

"Doesn't it feel strange? Like there should be flowers or something? Gaudy dresses, boutonnieres, drunk relatives?"

Ben stopped. "We should plan something."

"I think we did, and it starts in about five minutes." I nodded toward an approaching elderly couple.

The man fit my mental idea of a judge. He and his wife were almost the same height, about mine, and she had her hand in the crook of his elbow. He had little hair; she was a perfectly coiffed and frosted blonde. He wore glasses and squinted in the morning sun. She wore large sunglasses and had smooth pale skin. Southern skin—only found on women who have long understood the power of shade and sun hats.

Ben pulled my hand back as if logic had kicked in for him. "We should wait."

"You aren't sure?"

"You should have a dress, anything you want. I only want you."

"And this is the most romantic thing in the world. Better than I could ever imagine."

He pulled me close, and his eyes trailed over every inch of my face. "*Ti amo.* I love you."

I felt my lips part. "I caught that one."

"Mr. Vassallo?"

I smiled. The judge pronounced Ben's last name "Vass-aloe" like a variant of Vaseline ointment.

Ben spun. "*Sì* . . . that is, yes."

The man thrust out his hand and seized Ben's between his own. "No need to be nervous, son. This is an excitin' day. We don't need witnesses here'n Georgia, but I'm with my wife, so do y'all mind if she stays?" His voice was slow and gentle.

"Not at all." I stepped forward. I'd had too much coffee for this pace and my nerves were ramping up. "I'm Emily Price . . . The bride, I guess."

"You don't know?" Judge Briggs now folded my hand within both of his. They were soft and cool.

"I do." I nodded with determination. "I'm the bride."

"Well now, that's settled. Come on over here. I love this grove of trees for a city settin' on a day like this." He looked up at the sky while he walked. "In another couple hours this would'a been too hot and I'd ask y'all to go to another favorite spot. But that's about an hour away and I don't have that kinda time right now. You would'na believe how busy you can get once ya retire."

Ben and I smiled at each other over the rambling and followed the judge and his wife into a small courtyard surrounded by cherry trees. Mrs. Briggs laid her handbag on a nearby bench, then came to stand next to her husband.

"All righty then." Judge Briggs looked around with satisfaction. "This is just right. Now, I charge $250 for the ceremony, and y'all can pay me with a check or cash."

I looked to Ben and widened my eyes. I hadn't thought about money.

"I have cash."

"You do?" I blurted.

Ben unfolded two hundred-dollar bills, a fifty, and the marriage license.

"You *are* prepared," I whispered to him. He held a finger to his lips.

Judge Briggs had not heard me. "Thank you. I'll sign this and mail it in."

Ben nodded. I followed suit.

"All righty then," the judge repeated as he stood straight and held the marriage license in front of him. "Let's begin." He looked each of us in the eyes, then nodded. "We are gathered here to join Benito Vassallo and Emily Price in a civil union as allowed by law and United States Supreme Court decisions. This is not a religious ceremony and I have no religious authority. You have presented a marriage license issued by the Probate Court of Fulton County on the nineteenth day of May, 2016." He then folded the license and passed it to his wife.

"Now let's be clear," he continued, "that each of you affirms to me that you have not gotten counsel about these matters from me, and you have thought about these matters on your own or y'all have gotten counsel on the issues related to a civil union from competent professionals and/or personal acquaintances. Is that correct?" He paused, then added, "You say yes or no."

"Yes," I whispered.

Ben said his yes more clearly and calmly.

The judge glanced to his wife with a *Here we go* look and continued. "Do you understand that you are givin' up considerable rights and freedoms in exchange for the benefits, liabilities, and duties imposed and granted under Georgia and United States laws and regulations?"

Giving up? I had felt as if I were chasing something good and right. His words cracked open doubt, and I missed the next part.

". . . understand and agree to the exchange? This answer is an 'I do.' "

Ben spoke immediately. "I do."

I paused, trying to track this thought to its end. "I do."

"The US Supreme Court recently identified a number of benefits. These aspects include taxation, inheritance and property rights, rule of intestate succession, spouse privilege in the law of evidence, hospital access, mediate decision-makin' authority, adoption rights, the rights and benefits of survivors, birth and death certificates, professional ethics rules, campaign finance restrictions, workers' compensation benefits, health insurance, and child custody, support, and visitation rules." Judge Briggs's eyes danced as if this were his favorite stuff to discuss. "And there are some important nonlegal duties and benefits as well: attentiveness to each other, tolerance, care, love, and affection. Do y'all understand these matters and freely and voluntarily commit to them?"

Before he could tell us the proper answer, Ben declared, "I do."

The judge smiled at me.

"I do too."

"Do each of you commit to the other your life, your property, your loyalty, and your faithfulness in wealth and poverty, in sickness and health, and in sorrow and joy?"

This time we spoke together. Two "I do's" sounding as one.

"I don't expect you have rings." Judge Briggs waited.

"I do. Right here." Ben dug into his pocket.

"You do?" the judge and I called out together. He was surprised. I was impressed.

The judge beamed. "That's so nice, son. They're optional, and so many couples don't bring 'em anymore. Now I can say a good bit about the outward and visible sign of your promise. These rings . . ." He fingered the small gold bands. "They are powerful symbols of deep, abidin', and eternal love. And now, with these rings, I pronounce you to be, as of this moment, a couple united under civil law. And I present to you, dear"—he flapped his hand at his wife—"since you're the only one present today, Benito Vasallo and Emily Price as a married couple. You may kiss . . ."

A married couple? I looked to Ben and felt that first flicker of doubt swell. What if I'm not *that girl?* What if I hadn't realized, hadn't known that I was trying to be someone I couldn't be, but was only pretending . . . What if he saw through me . . .

His voice tunneled and I couldn't find him.

One . . . Two . . .

The world morphed to blue.

⇒ Chapter 16 ⇐

Everything was cloudy and heavy, without form. Shadow. Then light.

My hand hit something solid. My head flew back. My eyes stung and my nose throbbed.

"No . . . Oh . . . Bella," Ben called gently through the haze. His hand, warm and solid, folded around the back of my neck.

My vision cleared. Judge Briggs's wife was no longer wearing sunglasses. She had cold blue eyes and a red cheek. She held a small vial in one hand as she lifted the other to her face.

Ben knelt beside me. "Are you okay? You fainted and dropped hard."

"I didn't faint."

"Is that not the word?" He looked up at Mrs. Briggs.

"Oh no, darlin', you fainted." She shook her head. "And you have a mean left hook, young lady," she added dryly.

I struggled to sit up. "I hit you? I'm so sorry. That's horrible." A wave of blue threatened to break, and I leaned back into Ben's arm. "Was I out long?"

"A few seconds." Mrs. Briggs capped her vial. The judge stood silently next to her. They shared a quick wordless exchange before she tapped Ben's shoulder. "Take her to the hospital, young man. In her condition, you can't be too safe." Her voice oozed with Southern gentility and blatant condescension.

"Her condition?" Ben looked down at me, his dark eyes wide with concern.

"She thinks I'm pregnant." I struggled to stand.

He lifted me to my feet. "Why would she think that?"

"You're kidding, right? Everyone will think that. Why else would someone get a license and marry within a moment? This is standard shotgun wedding procedure." I faced Mrs. Briggs and continued. "But ours isn't one, actually. No pregnancy. No shotgun. Just a croissant and too much coffee." I swayed.

"I'm glad to hear that." Mrs. Briggs looked to her husband. "We'll leave you in privacy then."

A weak "Okay" was all I could muster.

The judge stepped forward and shook Ben's only available hand. "You'll receive your certificate from the probate court's office within three weeks."

"Thank you." Ben nodded as Judge Briggs and his wife headed to the gravel path. He lifted a hand to the back of my head. "You have a large bump."

I stretched my back and felt around his fingers. "I whacked it, didn't I?"

"I almost caught you. Almost. I think she is right. We need a hospital."

"I'm clearly not pregnant, Ben."

"But you might have a . . . *sbattimento*. Brain bruise."

"A concussion." I couldn't deny the possibility, so after a little debate, recognizing it as our first marital skirmish, we settled on a MinuteClinic at the corner Walgreens.

Twenty minutes, a pack of Skittles, a Diet Coke, and no concussion later, we exited the double doors.

"Now what, husband dear?" I looped my arm through Ben's and looked around the parking lot, scattered with cars, and wondered what came next.

Ben followed my gaze. "Lunch?"

"Yes. Lunch."

He tucked me safely into the passenger seat and, after another twenty minutes, I dropped into a booth at Farm Burger Buckhead and sighed. "This feels good. That park was warm. That Walgreens was warm. On the whole, Atlanta is warm. Is Montevello?"

"At this time of year, yes. And no air-conditioning."

"You couldn't have told me this before?"

Ben reached over and touched my hand. "Are you sure you are okay?"

"I'd had little to eat, stood in the heat, probably locked my knees, and got married. I'm surprised I only fainted." I took a bite of my burger to end further questions. One more query and I'd probably start blabbing all that was spinning through my brain.

But Ben didn't notice—he was focused on sending and receiving a flurry of texts. I asked about them repeatedly, but only got cryptic answers.

"Prep questions at Piccolo. The ovens . . . The menu . . . Do you mind if we drop by this afternoon?"

"It's reopening tonight. We can't miss it."

Ben laid down his phone. "We can if you want to; this is your night."

"True . . ." I leaned back and thought through the implications of that sentence.

Ben smiled. "Do not think too much. Your eyes are getting big again. Like the painting of the girl you called 'freaky.' "

I smiled at the way his accent made the word sound like a compliment. "That's for the eyes I paint, not mine."

"It is for your eyes too." He smiled. "Eat your burger. Enjoy the day."

So we did. We sat in that booth and chatted

for several hours. After finishing the burgers, he bought us shakes. Slurping down a thick chocolate shake, infused with spicy honey, I learned more about his family—my family now. Francesca, his little sister, was going to be thrilled with his news. Lucio, his father, he wasn't sure about. Donata, his mother, he was sure about—she'd be furious.

"What about your family?"

I shrugged. "We'll tell Amy today, but no one else is going to care that much. Mom's been married a few times and kinda checked out on us awhile ago . . . I'm not sure about my dad."

Dad was my wild card. He either wouldn't care at all or would read me the riot act. As long as I kept adding to my 401K, paid my taxes on time, locked my doors, and carried pepper spray, I wasn't lectured often.

"Joseph?

Ben mirrored my shrug. "He is like Mama. He likes things very controlled, in order and on time, but I think he will be happy. Though he loses an employee." Ben shifted in his seat. "This time has been good with him. It felt like old times here and there."

"Old times before that night? His last at Coccocino?"

Ben's eyes clouded. "His last as my brother."

"What happened, Ben?"

"I wish I knew. You ask and I ask and no one

talks. Maybe, in Italy, you ask Mama." Ben grinned with his challenge.

"Sure . . ." I nodded with an exaggerated motion, noting the pain at the back of my head. "I think that'd be a great way to start our relationship."

We talked on until the restaurant reached that quiet moment between lunch and dinner, and Ben scooted out of the booth. "Let us go check on Piccolo."

I scooted out, too, dropped my hand in his, and he pulled me through the door and toward the car. "Will you be sad to leave Joseph?"

"It is time to go home, and I am taking you with me. How can I be sad?"

"Flattery will get you everything."

He raised an eyebrow and pulled me close, and my jaw dropped as I recognized the emotion in his eyes.

Ben kissed me lightly once, twice, then lingered . . . He leaned away and smiled. "Get in the car before you faint again."

Ben pulled into the restaurant's parking lot, and I was surprised by the number of cars. "Piccolo doesn't open until six. What's going on?"

"Come on."

Amy stood just inside the door and pounced on me as I crossed the threshold. "Ben texted me to get here. He said you have a surprise. Is it for me?"

"No, I . . ."

Ben pulled up behind me and grabbed me around the waist. I looked up at him, then trailed his gaze deeper into the restaurant. The entire waitstaff stood there . . . waiting.

A shout of "Surprise" mixed with "Congratulations" hit us as we stepped from the lobby into the dining room.

"We married!" Ben announced.

Joseph strode forward. "You mean you're *getting* married."

Ben shook his head and lifted our hands. The gold bands glowed. "We *are* married."

The room fell silent.

Chaos broke out—as much as can be created by about fourteen people—as everyone moved forward en masse for hugs and handshakes.

Amy yanked me aside. "This is a joke, right?"

"No."

"You planned this? You and Ben?"

"No. Yes." I glanced back to Ben. "He asked me last night."

"And you him married today? Without telling me?" She dropped my arm.

I expected her eyes to be fighting and hard. We were often in that place. But they weren't. They were sad, hurt, and they struck me. They reminded me of our childhood—each time we packed to move to a new apartment, each time she leaned on me to sort out the details and make our new room feel like home. They reminded me of myself just yesterday when I leaned against her on the couch and asked why everything had to be so hard.

"Oh, Amy. I'm sorry."

"As long as you're happy . . ." She turned away, then spun back. "No, forget that. This is supposed to mean something. Despite Mom. Despite Dad. We always said it was supposed to be for life. That when we married, it'd be forever."

"I still believe that." My head felt fuzzy again. "What makes you think this won't be forever?"

"You barely know this guy. Two weeks and you're married? That's not for life, that's for lust."

"Hey—"

"Also, if it was for real, you would've told me. I'm your sister; I was supposed to stand beside you." Her voice cracked.

"Amy." I drew her back into a hug, but she didn't lift her arms. "It is real and I should've told you this morning when I left. I guess I didn't want to lose courage. I wanted to be *that girl.* That girl who could do something like this, knowing it was right, and not fear the jump. You're like that. You would've done it."

"I would've told you."

"You're right, but you always did have more courage." As she stepped away, I tugged her back. "You should have been there. You would've gotten a kick out of the judge. He talked like

Willie Nelson and had a whole bunch of legalese and thought it was the most interesting stuff in the whole world. And I punched his wife when she shoved smelling salts under my nose. She thought I was pregnant. She said that after I fainted and—"

"You fainted?" Amy pushed out of my arms.

"Fell like a rock. Feel." I placed her fingers on the back of my head.

"Oh, Ems. I'm so sorry . . . Not really. I hope your head really hurts." She shoved her lower lip out in an exaggerated and well-practiced pout.

I could only laugh. "It does. And again, I'm sorry."

After a few bites of cake and a few sips of Prosecco, the staff resumed their preparations for the big night.

"We do not need to stay. We did what they wanted," Ben whispered.

I looked over at Maria and Vito. Maria had hugged me and cried happy tears over the family photos. Vito swelled with pride as he laid the new menus on the hostess stand and lit the candles within each glass votive. Ben was right. As they hurried their staff back to work, they'd clearly taken control of their restaurant again and were fidgety to open the doors—fidgety to move forward.

Ben slipped his hand into mine and pulled me to him. "We are not needed here, Bella. So where to? Your place? Joseph's? I did some more research . . . We can have a room at the Ritz."

I twisted toward him and considered his question. Amy would be on my sofa bed. But there was no way I could wake up to share morning coffee with Joseph. Yet neither of us had a ton of money. And I was unemployed . . . and not going to accept Joseph's offer . . . and . . . "My place, probably."

Ben smiled as if he'd followed my spiraling thoughts. "That is sweet, but it is the wrong answer. We are headed to the Ritz . . . It is our wedding night, Mrs. Vassallo, and that only comes once in our lifetime."

⨠ Chapter 17 ⨟

The next morning I awoke with Ben's arm draped around my waist. It lay heavy, solid, and infinitely comfortable. I snuggled deeper, savoring it, and marveling at this feeling of completion and wholeness—knowing it came from nothing I did or could control. It was simply us—and I couldn't see or feel a separation between his heart and mine. I finally rolled out from the covers to order us coffee.

I curled into the armchair across the room and watched him sleep. He now had one arm thrown above his head. I could only see his chin and the shadow created right beneath his lower lip—and the fact that his typical three-to-five o'clock shadow approached roguish status at seven in the morning.

I watched him a few seconds more, then reached to check my phone. I hadn't checked messages or e-mails in a couple days. One from Gallery Barton had arrived late in the night.

Dear Emily,

Again, I thank you for your work with Vaughn's *Pegasus 16*. It positively floated, and it sold within fifteen minutes of opening the doors. His show is proving to be a remarkable success and a profitable introduction for Vaughn to Atlanta and to American contemporary arts. That isn't always the case. While small galleries thrive on discovering and introducing new talent, it puts us in a vulnerable position when our gambles don't pay.

This leads me to the pictures you sent. Your work is intriguing. Your perspective is fresh, colors vibrant, and even from the photographs, I can discern a touch that is both precise and innovative. You play on the past, yet push to the future.

I've only seen a few artists employ both brush and palette work within a single piece. Your skill in this area reminds me of Jaline Pol.

Nevertheless, I can't offer a show at this time. I sense a restraint and confinement within your work. That said, consider me very interested if and when you cut loose.

All the best and I hope to see you at our opening for Stratton in August.

Olivia Barton

"What is it?"

I looked up to find Ben sitting in bed watching me, a smile curving his lips. It was intimate and for me. He tapped the space between his brows, indicating that I was not returning his lovely smile.

I scrunched all my facial muscles to release the tension as I crawled back onto the bed beside him and handed him the phone.

"Olivia Barton. She didn't like my work."

Ben read the e-mail. "She does not say that. She is saying the same as we thought. There is more changing in them now."

I tipped over sideways into his lap. "The fact that we already knew it doesn't make it better."

Ben laughed. "Yes it does." He trailed his fingers through my hair. "What if she found something you did not think? Or rejected it all?"

I pushed myself up. "It'd be great if she'd found something else. I might be able to fix that. This is the one thing I can't work on. I have to *not* work

161

to make it happen. Says so right there, *cut loose.* That is not one of my strengths." I looked at him, all those fears from our wedding flooding in. "You already know that, right? I'm not very much fun."

"I disagree." Ben's voice lifted.

I tipped over again, this time from embarrassment. "I'm not talking about that."

"I am. You are not a bunch of people. You are one whole and beautiful person." He chuckled and pulled me close. "Do not get discouraged. This does not require something new, just more you." He rested his lips on the top of my head. "Every day brings something new."

"True." I wrapped my arms around his waist. "Who'd have dreamt this?"

"Me." I felt his lips spread into a smile. "I have something to cheer you."

"What?"

"We need to buy you a ticket."

I was slow to catch on. "A ticket?" I pushed myself up.

Ben tucked my hair behind each ear. "It is Saturday, Bella." He shook his head. "I did not think this part through. I did not cancel my ticket. I fly home at six o'clock."

"You what? Tonight?"

He nodded. "I can try to change it." He reached for his phone.

I laid my hand over it. "Why? We've finished Piccolo and, with your dad sick, you don't have time right now to visit Chicago. Let's just go. It'll make for a busy day, but what else do we have to do?"

"Are you out of your mind?" Amy stood, hands on her hips, in my hotel bedroom. "Where's Ben?"

"I told you. He's packing, too, then going to say good-bye to Joseph . . . Of course I'm going, Amy. He's my husband. I love him. So help me pack, but no yelling. Not today." I pulled my neck back. She looked different somehow. "My goodness, you look and sound like me."

She rolled her eyes.

"Besides, I don't have much to pack, clothes-wise. Most of it will fit in a single suitcase, and you can drive the rest back to Chicago."

"All your books? All these little projects you've got lying around?" She palmed a miniature mantel clock and an eighteenth-century snuffbox in each fist.

"Awww . . . I haven't fixed that hinge yet." I stopped myself from reaching for it. "Doesn't matter. We'll box them all up."

"Your blankie?" She then picked up my copy of *The Way Things Work*—the binding barely holding together, the front cover disconnected at the top.

"Be careful with that." I reached for it and sat down on the bed to thumb through the pages. "I love this book."

She dropped next to me. "It's falling apart."

"It's twenty years old."

She scanned the room. "You carry around a lot of stuff, Ems. We'll never get through all this."

"There are several boxes in the living room closet. We'll pack it all, and you can take them to my apartment."

She gently pulled the book from my hands and carried it to the living room. "What about the magazines?" she called. "You've got like twenty copies of *Architectural Digest* here."

"Pack those. There's stuff in all of them I like. I get ideas for restoration and color from those. And don't even ask about the mystery novels. Pack them all."

She moaned but didn't complain further.

The two rooms were soon cleared of any sign of either of us.

"You sure you don't mind driving my car back alone?" I shoved the last box onto the kitchen counter.

"Not at all. I'll figure out where to park it. How long until the lease on your apartment is up?"

"Two months."

"Then I'll park it at your place and figure it out from there." Amy narrowed her eyes as if committing a checklist to memory.

"Take over my lease, if you want. It's a good building."

"I'll need a job first. That's been the great thing about living with four girls—low rent." She blinked as if a lightbulb turned on. "And if I don't take your apartment? What happens to your stuff?"

"Storage?"

"And I'm to handle that?"

"Please?" I bit my lip. "You can move it all to that facility on Dempster."

Amy crossed her arms and stared at me. "So this is what it feels like to be you." She shook her head. "And being you, I have to ask. Have you called Mom?"

I unscrewed the faucet cap, cleaned it, and replaced it.

She swatted my arm. "Stop fixing stuff. Did you call Mom?"

"I left a voice mail. She hasn't called back."

"Dad?" She perched herself between me and the kitchen faucet. The hot water handle was loose, and I hadn't gotten to it yet either.

"He laughed at me, then grew livid when he realized I was serious. I guess I can't blame him. You said it yourself, two weeks, then marriage must be for lust, not love."

"I'm sorry I ever said that. It's not true." Amy stepped away and let me get to the handle. "Besides, when do you listen to me?"

I shrugged. "But what do I know?" I slanted her a small smile. "He *is* Italian."

Amy burst out laughing. "Nice try. And with any other Italian I might give it to you, but I've never

ever seen anything like you two. Why don't you accept the reality that love, true love, can and does exist? And that you are *that girl*."

I felt my breath catch.

"The way he looks at you? It's pure magic." Amy crossed the room and rolled our suitcases to the door. "Hurry up and fix that handle so we can load the car. Your husband and Italy await, and I've got to get on the road."

⋙ Chapter 18 ⋘

Italy. I pressed my forehead against the window as the plane descended. Morning was breaking over the countryside and spilling gold onto the fields and villages. Rome approached, low and broad. It was gold, too, and the ground seemed to reach up and both absorb and reflect the light at once. It was everywhere and it was everything I had imagined and I hadn't even touched down yet.

It wasn't plotted in a grid like the Midwest; the lines curved and swept. I was already too close to discern the whole. I strained to see farther.

I jabbed Ben. "Aren't you excited?"

He leaned past me. "For you to see my home and meet my family, yes. But I enjoyed Atlanta too. It is good to get away at times."

"I've moved so much; I like the idea of roots and a home."

The plane touched down, and the passengers erupted in cheers.

"Why's everyone clapping?"

"Why don't you?" Ben laughed. "No one in America does."

I had no answer for that one, so I returned to the window. Rome's airport felt like an extension of the city, low and spread wide. Large sections were hidden behind scaffolding and bright yellow canopies. In the morning light, it, too, looked washed in a patina of gold.

"It's beautiful."

He poked his head past me. "It is yellow tarping." He grinned. "If you think the airport is beautiful, wait until you see the Sistine Chapel or St. Peter's Basilica or the light hitting the *duomo* in Florence. Or Montevello on a summer evening when the sun warms the stone walls or when the *girasoli* turn and stretch . . ."

"I didn't mean the airport . . . I meant everything."

When the plane was parked, Ben grabbed our bags from the overhead bin and I was ready to launch. But the exit line moved incredibly slowly, as if everyone was saying personal good-byes to the flight attendant. Even Ben paused. From a few people behind, I couldn't see or understand the holdup until I reached her myself. She handed me a large red foil heart.

"For me?"

"Thank you for flying with us and welcome to Rome." She smiled, poised and perfect, with a precise German accent.

"Thank you." I followed Ben, balancing my handbag and assorted junk that hadn't made it into my duffel, as I shoved the chocolate into my mouth. I looked up from chewing to find him pointing across the room to a sign, *Non EU Passports*.

"Someday we will not have to separate. You will be Italian."

Italian? Everything stopped. People pushed around me, as if in slow motion, and the whirlwind of the past two weeks crystallized into a single moment. I looked across the terminal. Nothing was familiar. Even the English spoken rolled in a different cadence and tone. *This is home.*

"Emily?" Ben rested his hand on the back of my neck.

I looked up at him. "I think it's all hitting me."

He squeezed my neck. "Take deep breaths. Planes go both ways. You have not dropped off the end of the earth."

"I know that." I shook myself awake.

He pointed to the line. "Then go get in line so we can go to Anne's."

Passport stamped, I caught up with him at baggage claim. "Where is this castle exactly?"

"It is fifteen kilometers away on the outskirts of the city. Vincenzo has oil and wine we need to get . . . And you can meet Anne."

"Got it. And she's what again?" I rolled my bag behind him, taking two steps to each of his.

"Papa's second cousin's daughter. She was my closest ally growing up."

"What does she do again? Is she the teacher?"

"That is my sister, Francesca. Anne's parents made their home into a small hotel, part of Relais & Châteaux, when she was young, and now she runs it. We will stay there tonight and then tomorrow, rested, we go to Montevello." He reached up and touched my hair.

"Are you trying to tell me something?"

Ben only smiled as I ran my fingers through my ponytail and cringed. It was tangled, I was rumpled, my teeth felt fuzzy, and my eyelids scraped like sandpaper. Not to mention that one broad smile would crack my dry face. But I didn't feel any paint.

I glanced up to assess him. Clearly I loved this man because, to me, he still looked perfect.

With a *harrumph* I dragged my bag alongside him to the car park, where we piled into an impossibly tiny car, smaller than a smart car, if any American could imagine that. Ben then dashed like a lunatic onto the Roman roads. Cars were everywhere, careening between lanes, zipping at high speeds down frightfully narrow streets, dodging trucks and pedestrians, and climbing hills in switchback turns.

Twenty harrowing minutes later he pulled onto a

gravel road and, not decelerating at all, dusted up a cloud behind us as pebbles pinged the car's underbelly, shooting to the end of a long drive. He stopped with a flourish and a skid at the front door of the most beautiful castle, the only castle, I'd ever seen. It was three stories, a mix of stone and brick, with a tower stretching two stories higher. All topped with terra-cotta tiles.

I unfolded myself from the car and stood staring. But only for a moment, as a woman launched herself from the front door, a cacophony of flowing color, light brown hair, and bright sandals, into Ben's arms.

"You rotter! How dare you marry without me!"

My mouth dropped.

She pushed him away and yanked me into a hug. "I'm Anne." She then whacked Ben in the chest. "You didn't tell her about me, did you? She was expecting Francesca. Lovely and demure—and Italian?"

Ben grinned.

I shook my head. "I just assumed."

"This family's like a good puzzle. Takes time, but the pieces all fit." She looked back to Ben. "Have you told her about Donata?"

"It is best to simply meet Mama." Ben cast me a glance before continuing. "We head home tomorrow."

"Oh . . . I'd love to be a fly on that wall." Anne looped her arm through mine. "Don't be scared.

You're going to love Ben's mum." A distinct note of sarcasm danced between us as she waved a hand back to Ben. "I reserved the Castelluccia Suite. And you're lucky it was available, considering you gave me one day's notice. Actually, it wasn't, so you'd better not tell Daddy I moved a Dutch couple."

"Is your dad Australian or your mom?"

Anne gripped my arm tighter. "Mum. She's a hoot, but she's out of town right now. My sister just had a baby in Paris, so she's doing the doting grandmama thing. But I'm sure she'll pop up to see you soon." She laughed. "And you really *will* love her. Everybody does."

We passed the lobby with an "I've got you all checked in" as she led us up a winding staircase. It wasn't broad and grand, but tight and narrow and only led to the second floor. It opened onto a series of hallways leading in four directions.

She walked toward the right and pointed out the window. "This'll be your view." She then called back to Ben. "It's the room your parents always stay in. Remember, we used to watch movies in it?"

"That one's too grand for us," Ben replied.

"Not for your honeymoon." Her voice arched with innuendo.

"*Grazie*, Anne."

She unlocked the door and led us in. "I'm not going through the spiel. You know where everything is. Sleep and come find me for dinner, or lunch in a couple hours if you want. Up to you. *Ciao, piccioncini!*"

The room was spectacular. Red tiled floor, cream plaster walls with a gold glaze, and gold brocade quilts with rich blue velvet pillows. The same deep fabric draped from the windows and covered the chairs and a small couch. Above the bed was a huge circular fresco, a lion's head painted in gold on a lapis-blue background.

"How old is this?" I climbed on the bed and reached toward it, touching it lightly with a finger. I noted a few points of restoration—excellent work. A section of the lion's mane had crumbled, but someone had filled it and then sealed it with a clear glaze. "It's amazing. He looks alive."

"I expect it is original—mid-twelfth century."

He flopped on the bed, shaking it. I lost my balance and landed on him.

"And you are right, it is very beautiful," he whispered, brushing my cheek with his thumb. "You tired?"

"No . . ."

"*Bene.* Me neither."

I slept. Really truly slept, probably for the first time in two weeks. And when I woke, the room, the fresco, everything was more beautiful than I remembered. I reached to the side of the bed to find it empty.

A quick shower, a linen skirt and T-shirt, and I was in the corridor, completely lost. I trailed down one hall, then another, and soon found myself following voices, hoping they'd lead me out and to Ben.

Eventually I landed in the lobby.

"Breakfast is in the dining room, miss."

"Thank you." I walked into a large room with three long tables. One was covered in cheeses, another in breads and salamis, and the third overflowed with beautiful fruits, a large bowl of hard-boiled eggs, and a variety of tarts and pastries. I stalled, tempted and hungry.

A young man was clearing a white linen-draped table under a matching sunshade beyond the dining room's doors. I stopped in front of him. "Could you . . . I'm sorry, I don't speak Italian."

"I speak English."

"Excellent. I'm looking for Ben Vassallo. He's Anne's cousin. Are they here?"

"Ah . . . They went to the cave." At my lost look, he continued. "Down the steps. They're loading wine into your car."

The side of the patio seemed to end into nothing, like one of those infinity pools you see in *Architectural Digest*. I crossed it and found steps leading from the terrace. Down. Down. Five flights of steps, cut from stone and worn by time and feet.

I hadn't realized the previous morning that the

castle was built into a hill. The back went down more stories than the front went up. Four flights later and one long flight from the bottom, I reached a grassy ledge with black openings into the hill. *Caves.*

I stepped into the shadow. It was instantly dank, dark, chilly, and quiet. It was an old, deep quiet, a listening quiet that seemed to promise something profound and powerful. Somehow it reminded me of the lion above our bed. He'd lurk in an old place such as this.

I stood at the edge absorbing it. I felt this way sometimes when working on a painting, when I became lost in the work and realized I didn't have control over it—that something large and powerful, intrinsically good, lay out there, out of reach and out of sight, and that only by stillness and surrender could I reach it. But as much as I relished those moments, I was also quick to retreat from them. I'd flip on the radio, take a break, or move on to another project.

True to form, I tapped my phone's flashlight on and the moment ended. I stepped forward, listening to the pebbles crunch under my feet and the sound echo off the walls around me. Soon I heard a noise and dashed beyond the stretch of my flashlight, sure it was Ben, Anne, and another way out.

When I slowed, I realized it was only water dripping over stone. I kept on a few minutes more, one passage leading to another, then spun around to find my way back and was confronted with three dark holes in the earth. I had no idea which one I'd come through.

"Hello!" I called. My voice didn't bounce back, as expected. It was absorbed into the wet darkness. "Brilliant, Emily. You'll die here." I picked one tunnel and followed it. There were shallow stairs leading down that I knew I hadn't walked up. I retreated.

"Ugh!" I wandered down another tunnel, but it didn't feel right so I again retraced my steps to the widening. *How is it possible they're all wrong?*

"Emily?" A voice thin and too far away called.

"Hey! I'm here. Where are you?"

I heard Ben's faint laugh. "Where are *you?*"

"If I knew, I wouldn't be here."

"Stay where you are. I will find you."

I pressed my back against the wall. It was damp and I imagined thousands of little creatures crawling down it. I jumped to the center of the widening and called again. "Are you still coming?"

"*Sì.*" His answer came back a little stronger, a little closer.

After what seemed an interminably long wait, a flashlight wavered through the second tunnel.

"Ah . . . You found the caves, Sleeping Beauty."

"I was told you were in here."

"Not these. Vincenzo cut into the hill beyond the pool and built a cellar. These haven't been used since . . . I do not know when." He waved his light around the cavern. "Anne and I found bones here when we were kids. Aunt Nell said they were pig bones, but I did not believe her." He clasped my hand and led me out. "I was sure they were human. Then there was treasure. But that was plastic and Aunt Nell planted it." He stopped. "You are shaking."

"It's cold and . . . I got a little nervous."

He stopped at the dim light of the entrance and pulled my hands together against his chest. "Those were good summers. I was too young to be scared. But when I was about twelve, I went missing too." He tilted his head back into the cave. "Papa found me; he followed the sound of sobbing. I was farther back than you were—it goes deeper to the south. When Papa found me he knelt down and said, 'I will always come for you.' I have never forgotten that."

"I can imagine."

Ben raised my fists and kissed the back of one hand, then the other, keeping his eyes trained on mine. "I will always come for you."

He drew me close and kissed me, moving his hands from mine to frame my face, as if sealing a promise, a covenant. We stood like that until we heard a throat clear nearby.

My vision felt fuzzy as I glanced out of the cave. It landed on Anne, her arms crossed, one hip jutting out. "Enough, you two."

Without another word, she headed up the stairs. Chuckling, Ben pulled me along in her wake, up to the dining room where he piled my plate with cured meats, cheeses, and fruit, and Anne regaled us with childhood stories of a boisterous Ben I had yet to meet.

And all was fun and right until Ben said, "I called home and told them we are finally coming today."

"Wasn't that always the plan?" I popped a melon ball into my mouth.

"Yesterday was the plan. You slept through it."

"You let me sleep through an entire day! How? Who does that?"

Ben merged onto the highway. "You were tired."

"What must your family think of me?"

"That you were tired," he offered again.

"This is bad. I wanted to make a good impression, and now . . ."

"I love you and you will be fine." Ben shot me a quick glance.

"Tell me who's who again. I need to at least get that right."

He shook his head, as I'd asked that question a few times on the plane, trying to solidify all the details within his many stories. But rather than clearing everything up, he started in with new details, new stories.

"Aunt Sophia is Romanian, which is funny

because she can be nasty to outsiders. She has completely forgotten she is one. She and Mama do not mix well some days. Francesca, you will like. I have told you all about her, but not that she is like Amy, bright and eager, but in a dark and quieter way. As you know, she is the teacher, and we have seven, no eight, young cousins in her school and . . ."

I kept my eyes trained out the window, listening to his words, but soon all the names jumbled and I found myself absorbed by the scenery.

It was filled with light and color and a texture completely foreign to me. The landscape rose and fell in gentle hills. And every now and then the highway cut through a mountain, rather than rising over it as they do in the US, and we emerged from the tunnel into sunlight on the edge of a valley dipping below us, bathed in green— often with a beautiful medieval walled village perched above. Cypress trees, pine trees, olive trees, vineyards, and pastures sloped all around us.

I noted the same rises and dips in Ben's voice s he trailed through his long list of relatives. I had thought he spoke English like an American fairly well—minus contractions, colloquialisms, and some intonation. But here his voice took on a new undulating tone, different syllables lengthening and catching.

"How many languages do you speak?" I interrupted him.

"Four. Italian, English, German, and French."

"I only speak one."

"American." He patted my knee as one does a small child.

"Hey . . . English."

"That is debatable. You use odd contractions and wrong pronunciations. You will love Francesca. She went to an American school in Florence. You will think her accent is flawless."

"Why didn't you go? Where'd you learn your English?"

"Joseph and I had a standard Italian curriculum, first in Montevello, then in Florence. But my father only spoke in English or German at home. He taught us first. Papa is like that; he was a good chef, but would have enjoyed teaching more, I think." Ben tapped his finger on his window. "*Girasoli.*"

I lifted up to see past him. "Sunflowers! They're amazing. I've never seen so many." A huge field of sunflowers stretched up a hillside. Thousands upon thousands of happy yellow petals with bold green stalks. "They're all facing away from us."

"As I told you, they follow the sun. This afternoon they will grace the road with their smiles, and you will never find a rebel. I know. I ran through a neighbor's field once and searched. I twisted a few and they snapped. They must turn on their own."

⫷ Chapter 19 ⫸

Ben pulled onto a single-track gravel road. Soon it became lined with trees and I realized it was a driveway ending right at the front door of a two-story stone-and-brick house. It was tall and symmetrical and fit into the countryside perfectly. The upstairs windows were swung wide as if letting the world in or as if there were no inside versus outside at all—it was all one.

But the massive front door, situated directly center and made of dark polished wood, at least eight feet tall and five feet wide, stood firmly shut.

"This is home?"

"Home." Ben climbed out of the car and stared at it with a warm smile. "It has been in Papa's family, on his mother's side, for at least eight generations. You must ask him. He loves to tell the story—monks in the sixteenth century sold it to his family." He lifted the door's huge iron knocker and let it drop.

"You're knocking?"

"Wait and see."

We heard an "*Un momento*" from inside just before the door swung open, yanked by a petite woman with black hair threaded with gray. Her eyes, so dark I couldn't find the irises, were harried and tight until she focused on the sight before her. In an instant her face and body became animated and years dropped away. The girl from the photo stood before me. Donata.

"Benito!" She pulled him by the shoulders until she'd engulfed as much as she could seize of his taller frame within her arms.

"*Mama. Non è così stretto.*" He then switched to English, whispering to me, "She hugs too tight." He untangled himself from her arms. "I have someone for you to meet." He pulled me forward, directly in front of his mother, and her eyes narrowed again. "Mama, this is Emily Price, now Vassallo. My wife."

"You were to come yesterday. It is only a few hours' drive." Her English was slow, hard, and precise.

I threw Ben a quick look. He watched her.

"Mama, we were tired. It is okay now. Meet Emily."

Another second passed before she pulled me into a small hug. "Welcome to *la famiglia*, Emily." She articulated my name slowly, pulling each syllable long, paying special attention to the center *mal.* It stretched forever. In Italian, I knew it meant "ache" or "evil," and I figured her emphasis was no coincidence.

I missed Ben's beautiful trail of *e*'s and instinctively stepped back—bumping into his chest. There was no retreat.

181

Ben's mother continued in the same clipped tone. "I am Donata. Benito's mama. It is a shame we meet after the marriage, rather than before."

"Mama," Ben gently warned. "I told you on the phone. We married at the right time and in the right way."

"Says who?"

"Mama." The sharpness softened to pleading.

"*Va bene.* You work to make it reasonable." She flapped her hands at him. "And Papa says I am to be quiet."

"That will be new," Ben teased and hugged her again.

"Do not start or I will forget this promise and give you that earful grandchildren will remember."

Their banter surprised me, and I stood tense, waiting for the "earful." It didn't come.

"Come inside. Come." She pulled us both through the door.

Ben headed to the back of the house, but I paused in the hallway. On the right, thick wood steps led to the second floor, supported by a wrought-iron railing sunk in stone. The floor was flagged stone, of a matching tone, but it turned to tile where Ben had entered what was clearly a kitchen. I caught sight of a huge basket filled with fruits.

To the left, a short hallway led to a room bursting with light. The door was wide open and

I could see books on a far shelf and yellow, a sense of bright, happy, sunflower yellow. I took a step in that direction before I caught myself and followed Ben to the kitchen. It stretched the entire back of the house with its double ovens, stainless counters, two sinks, multiple refrigerators, and three sets of double doors opening onto a stone patio. A huge butcher block formed an island in the center.

I stalled. "Wow . . ."

"Do not get used to this. No one in the history of kitchens has one so grand. Mama went crazy a couple years ago."

"*Noi cuciniamo*—" She stopped, hands midair, and pursed her lips as if tasting something sour. "We cook. The whole village comes here. Why not be comfortable?"

Ah . . . The English tastes sour.

Once the words were out, she followed Ben across the kitchen, pulling food out of the refrigerator and from the baskets. Her face smoothed. She clearly loved her son and her kitchen—and was preparing *him* a late lunch.

Ben kissed her cheek again. "Is Papa at the restaurant?"

Donata's expression fell. "He was not honest with you. He rests upstairs."

Her tone set off alarm bells. My eyes flew to Ben. He had said his father was ill, aging. But this felt different; it felt urgent.

183

"What?" Ben's stiff posture confirmed it.

"Wait!" Donata pulled at his arm. "Do not be angry. He wanted you to have your time, and I respected that wish."

"You have had to keep quiet a lot, I think." Ben touched her cheek and strode from the kitchen. He immediately ducked back in, arm outstretched. "Come. You will love my papa."

"Don't you want to see him alone first?" I stepped backward.

"I want him to see you first." With that, Ben overtook me in two steps and folded my hand within his.

At the top of the stairs, the house split. He pointed to a room. "That one is mine. Ours now." He was still talking, but all my thoughts had stopped at one word. *Ours.* Here? We were going to live here? How had I not known this?

Ben continued. "Papa was born in that room, too, but do not let him tell you that story."

"Do you mean we live . . ." My question stalled as he pulled me around to the front of the house and tapped on the doorjamb of the bedroom overlooking the drive.

Its windows were the ones I'd seen from below, open to the sunlight that spilled in and turned the wood floor to a golden blond. A huge wood bed stood in the corner, but my eyes quickly trailed to the seating area in front of the windows. There I found his father.

He was reading and didn't look up until we stood before him. When he did, his rheumy brown eyes brightened and he struggled to stand. "My pizza maker . . ." He beamed. Then he looked around Ben and pointed to me with a soft, joyful laugh. "And his wife!"

Ben dropped onto the ottoman in front of him and pulled him into a hug. "Don't get up."

I stood there as pieces clicked into place. A puzzle, as Anne had called it. *La bistecca della moglie del pizzaiolo.* Ben's favorite dish. An old recipe from Napoli. He had been making it when I'd arrived at Piccolo the day after we met. *The steak of the pizza maker's wife.* He said it was a winter dish but that he hadn't been able to get it off his mind. *Me.* He hadn't been able to get *me* off his mind. The thought made me smile anew, and I suspected he hadn't been exaggerating when he said he'd looked up Georgia marriage rules right after we'd met.

Ben's voice drew me back to the moment. "Why did you let me go? And six weeks? You could have told me. That was not honest, Papa." I could see the muscles in his arms tense, hugging his father tighter.

"You needed to be there and see Joseph." He held his hand to Ben's cheek. "You are here so much, and yet, you are like me. We need the outside world. You brought some home." He looked over Ben's shoulder and caught my eye.

"Move so I may welcome my new daughter."

Ben pulled away and leaned back so his father and I were face-to-face.

I leaned down and offered my hand. "I'm Emily. It's nice to meet you."

He swatted a thin hand at Ben. "Get up, son. I want to hug her."

Ben slipped away, and his father gathered me close. "Call me Lucio. Someday Papa, but Lucio will do for now. Ben says you are an artist and you like mysteries and can fix anything and you worked with Joseph."

"I . . . Yes, that's all true." I glanced at Ben, wondering what else he'd told his father.

"He is like you." Ben chuckled. "He asks lots of questions."

Ben's expression caught me. My Ben was deep, funny, creative, and even light—but before me stood a more boyish, exuberant, and free Ben. Lines I'd seen around his mouth and eyes seemed softened and lifted, despite his lack of sleep. Ben was most definitely home.

"I want to hear about the ceremony, short as it was." Lucio tapped my knee.

I glanced to Ben.

"You stepped into that one." Ben shook his head slightly. "I did not tell him."

"Tell me what?" Lucio glanced between us.

"I fainted. I said 'I do' and hit the ground like a stone."

Lucio laughed. "Oh . . . I hope he caught you!"

"I tried," Ben said.

Lucio chuckled again. "That is a story for the grandchildren."

"Within five minutes, you and Mama have both mentioned them." Ben dropped onto the ottoman next to me. "No more for now."

"Done," Lucio lied with a wink. He then moved his eyes out the window. "Since we must talk of something new, look out that window, Emily."

I smiled. He said my name the way Ben did, with all those lovely and welcoming e's. I stepped to the window.

"All the land to that hill has been in my family for over eight generations, through my mother's side. My father came from the north; he was accepted for her sake. That's how family works, and you are part of that now too. You are family. Close to the house, you see the olive trees. They are for oil, not eating. Make Ben tell you how he cracked a tooth, then was up all night vomiting after a dare to eat a tree full."

"Not a tree—"

"Hush, Benito, you're ruining my story. Then, Emily, look to the right, up the rise, and you see grapevines. Beyond that, Montevello. Has Ben taken you?"

"We came here first," Ben offered. "But there is wine and oil from Vincenzo in the car. We will go unload that, and I can show her Coccocino.

Then we need to sleep." Ben cast me a wry smile. "I do. Emily is better rested."

"Mama has your room prepared. She worked hard on it."

"That was kind. I got the impression she is not pleased with me."

"She missed a wedding. Her first child to marry and she played no part. You cannot blame her." There was a light reprimand in Lucio's tone. "And be gentle. This is hard." Lucio tapped his fingers to his chest.

"Papa." Ben shook his head as if trying to erase his father's last comment.

"My life has been long and good. No sadness now."

⫸ Chapter 20 ⫷

As Ben led me downstairs, I felt his hand stiffen against the small of my back, pushing me to go faster and faster on the stone steps. At the bottom I twisted to ask, but he strode past me and was in the kitchen before I crossed the hall. Tense Italian whispers reached me long before I reached them.

I stood there a few moments before Donata looked past Ben and locked eyes on me. She turned back to her son and continued. She must have told him I was there, because he fluidly switched to English.

"It was not right."

"La mia fedeltà è quello di tuo padre."

Ben glanced my way. "English, Mama. Emily won't understand."

"My English is not strong," she challenged.

"It will do," he replied flatly.

"As I said . . ." She drew the words long with exasperation. "My loyalty is to him. He asked me not to tell."

Ben pulled his hands through his hair as if yanking out the strands might relieve pressure. "When has that ever stopped you? Who is at the restaurant now, anyway? You should have called me home."

"Francesca." Something tangible filled the air. Donata thrust out her palms. "She can help."

"She can, but she never wants to. She hates it, and you know it."

"We need her." Donata waved her hands, tears in her eyes. "I did what I think right."

Ben folded her into a hug. "I know, Mama. I know."

Donata slumped, as if holding Lucio's secret had kept her upright. "Dario came and thinks Papa had a stroke in the night. His hands shake. He is tired and not eating. We knew we were there; our time borrowed. But he is going and . . ." As she talked the words drifted into a soft, rapid Italian.

Ben rubbed her back and kept up a whispered litany of "I know, Mama, I know. I am sorry."

I tiptoed from the room to hover in the hallway.

Minutes later, Ben found me. "Shall we go? I need to get that wine to Coccocino."

We climbed back into the car. It felt as if a vacuum sealed us in—and we were safe there. Just the two of us. Ben stared ahead, no words, no movement.

After a moment, I ventured an "Are you okay?" When he didn't reply, I continued. "You're very much like your father, which is odd because I would've said you looked like Joseph, but he doesn't look like your dad, if that makes sense. He's lovely . . . not that Joseph isn't . . . And your mother, I *think* I like her, but I suspect the feeling's not mutual. Not yet." I let my voice lilt up, trying to get a reaction—a grin, a sigh, a bark, something.

Nothing.

"When will I meet your sister?"

"He's worse than I expected—in six weeks. What is next?" Ben's voice was flat.

The car grew hot as we sat. I tried to offer something light and lovely for him. "You have a gift for him, though. The pizza. Did you see how his eyes lit up?"

Ben finally faced me.

"Now I know . . . He wanted me to go, learn, because he knew I needed it. Something of my own. Something I could never do here. He believes that is the gift, the bread." Ben's eyes drifted back to the solid front door. "Ask him about it. If you want to know Papa, that is where you start. It is his love story." Ben quirked a smile, and there was that little boy again. He then shook his head as if chasing away a memory and twisted the key in the ignition. "It grows warm in here—not good for the wine."

Driving back down the road, pebbles a-flying, silence lay between us. I broke it as Ben accelerated our tiny rental around a hilltop corner and a quintessential medieval walled village appeared before us.

"Ohh . . . Why didn't you say you lived near one when I was droning on?"

"It was so cute. You pointed to each one as if it were a little present and you would not ever see another. I wanted to surprise you."

He darted through an impossibly narrow archway and drove up a bricked street, hemmed in by tall walls on either side. He ducked down another, even tighter street and pulled into a small courtyard.

"Come on." He popped the car's trunk and grabbed a box.

I grabbed one, too, and followed him through a gate and another smaller archway—this one for people. No car, no matter how small, could fit. We entered a tiny courtyard lined with benches and a large placard set into the wall. *Coccocino.*

We stepped up broad stone steps and entered

the restaurant. The dining space was bright, with huge windows on the far wall looking into another tiny courtyard. The rest of the natural light came from skylights. There was an open fireplace with a waist-high hearth built into the side wall.

"That is where we grill the meats." He pointed to it as he led me through the empty dining room to the kitchen door. "Here we go," he said softly before calling out, *"Buongiorno!"*

Wait? What? People are here? My mind raced with all I needed for a good introduction—composure, less wrinkled clothing, a warning. There was a lot required to make a good first impression, and I'd already failed once today.

The conversation, which had been moving fast like *vivacissimo* music, stopped. There was a beat of silence before a chorus of *"Benito!"* pounded our ears.

Ben was folded into the kitchen, and I stood by the door with my box. Silence returned as eyes found me.

"Everyone meet Emily, my wife."

I shrugged beneath the box. "Hello."

Ben lunged for it. "I am sorry. Let me take that." He pointed to the group. "Noemi, Giada, Alberto, and Nicolo. And over there is Luigi, who just walked through the door."

"La moglie di Benito!" came out of the blurred chaos before Ben asked, "Where's Francesca?"

"She's at the market in Greve-in-Chianti today. Don't tell me you've forgotten?" Noemi's English was smooth and, to my ear, almost accentless.

"I forgot it is Tuesday. I have forgotten my days." He reached for my hand and squeezed as if conveying something important. "I am not here today for prep, but I will be in tomorrow to see how we are doing, and everything returns to normal Thursday."

"Normal might take some time," Noemi commented.

"Not now." Ben shook his head. "I cannot deal with any mess."

"And Francesca?" Noemi asked.

"She can stay if she wants."

"If she hears you're back, she may not return from the market at all," Noemi said with a wry smile.

"Keep it a secret then. We need the produce." Ben waved and pulled me through the door.

"They all speak English too?" I trailed him through the tables and back out to the car.

"Noemi and Luigi do. They will translate for the rest." Ben opened the car door for me. "You will find most people do here. Europe is a small place."

"Still . . . it's impressive. After two weeks, I was only beginning to speak Atlantan."

"Atlantan?"

"You know, when someone says, 'Y'all come

back now,' and it really means 'Don't bother us again.' That took me a few days. And don't even get me started on 'Bless her heart.' "

Ben laughed as he backed the car out of the restaurant's small lot and drove it up the steep single-lane brick road to an open plaza.

"This is Montevello—almost all of it, really. The town was founded as a walled fortress in . . . I forget, but the village started in 1249 when the fortress got sacked by Frederick II." He pointed around the square. "We have the hotel that used to be a private home until about sixty years ago; the theater where the guild holds summer plays; the town hall, which will be renovated next year; and tourism shops. You will meet everyone soon. It is a small town. And Andre . . ." He pointed to the last shop on the right. "He owns that grocery and the *enoteca*, the wine store, next door. You will like him."

Ben pushed the accelerator, circled the plaza, and headed us down another tight street, our side mirrors almost scraping the house walls on either side. Right before he reached an arch, distinctly too small for the car, he zipped to the left into a parking lot.

"Let us go now."

"Go where now?"

"It is lunchtime. Many will be at Tartaruga, and you can meet them."

"All your friends? Now?" My voice squeaked.

"Come on. It is not every day someone brings back a wife from holiday. You are not a typical souvenir."

"How many people are we talking here?"

"Everyone." Ben nodded as if that answered the question.

I grabbed for his hand and pulled. "Slow down one sec. I'm going to need a moment." I smoothed my ponytail and ran my tongue over my teeth.

"You look beautiful."

"You lie, but thank you." I stopped fidgeting and looked around. "This is beautiful."

Ben followed my gaze to the high stone walls, the brick paths sloping up and down the hills. "It is. It is home."

Home. That word again. In my life, it had always been transient, replaceable with each stepfather or with Mom's next job. But there was nothing transient about this place. Lucio had said eight generations. This was the dream—stones warmed from above and roots that gripped deep below.

As we crossed the small road out of the parking lot and walked up the hill, it narrowed to a mere bricked walking path. It was lined with blond stone leading seamlessly up into the walls of the surrounding houses. It felt old and stable, as if you could feel centuries of walkers before you treading these same paths.

Flowers grew in some of the mortar work. I ran my other hand along the mortar lines; some thick and straight, but every now and then my hand caught a patch where the bricks had been replaced with different sizes and shapes and the lines ran curved and irregular. These were the scars, cracks, crevices, and patchwork that told their story, their history.

"Drainage?" I pointed to two deep grooves in the stone at each edge of the walk.

"We quit using them a couple years ago." Ben winked and pulled me up the hill and into a narrow opening. It was cooler in the shade, but twenty steps and we emerged again into the bright sunshine on the next walk over.

"This will not be confusing soon. There are only three streets wide enough for cars. Each goes through the piazza like spokes on a wheel. One drive and you will understand."

"I'm not driving here."

He stopped. "As soon as we get a cappuccino, we must return the rental. Otherwise it will be another whole day before we get it back."

I opened my mouth, but no words emerged.

"Do you drive standard transmission?"

"I do, but you can't be serious."

Ben kissed me as if that solved everything. "You will be fine. Chianti-in-Greve is only twenty minutes away, and there is a place there for a real lunch, a butcher shop and restaurant in one, Macelleria Falorni." He kissed me again.

"Is that your idea of bribery?"

"Is it working?" Ben grinned as we stepped up to a small café with two distinct outside patios. One consisted of four open tables side by side along the walkway, while the other was made of a tight collection of about six tables on a raised wood platform. The upper patio was packed with people and covered with an awning that magnified their noise.

I pulled out a chair at the only empty table on the ground-level patio, but Ben tugged at my waist before I could sit.

"Not here. Come." He led me to the counter and wagged his pointer finger and thumb at a tall woman with short blond hair. She had time only to nod acknowledgment before her attention was pulled back to a monstrous silver machine behind her.

It took only a second before she processed Ben's presence. Her head spun back around and she gave me a quick once-over. Ben caught it too. "Told you. They are curious. That is Sandra. She moved here a few years ago from Rome."

Sandra reached over and gripped Ben's shoulder with affection as she used her other hand to push two china cups on saucers across the counter. "*Non lasciare.*"

"We will not leave." He tilted his head at me. "You need to meet Emily, in English."

Sandra smiled, small and flat. "Anything for you, Ben." Her English was thick and jarring.

"Welcome, Emily. I wish you the luck." She nodded to the raised patio.

She turned back to her work as Ben ushered me toward the upper patio.

"If you order sitting at this lower patio, you are a tourist and Sandra charges you four euro for a cappuccino. At the counter, she charges you only one euro, but you cannot sit. You must pay to sit. Up here, she quit charging us to sit when Andre set up a coffee stand outside his grocery in protest. It took three weeks for her to give in. Now we pay one euro and we sit with friends."

As soon as his foot hit the top step, a chorus of *"Benito!"* again rose into the air, and we were met with a flurry of Italian, hand waving, kisses, backslaps, and hugs. Everything then grew still, as if, just as at Coccocino, they collectively figured out my significance.

Ben pulled out a chair for me and dropped into one beside it as a man in a green shirt stepped forward.

"I'm Andre. Ben texted me about his pizza and you, in that order . . . Don't feel bad, though— he's known the pizza longer."

"She did not come second," Ben weakly protested.

"You did." Andre nodded to me and pulled an empty chair next to mine, on the other side. He reached across me and thumped Ben on the shoulder. "Don't deny it." He then surveyed the group and bellowed across the noise, "*Solo inglese* . . . Baptiste, you're off the hook. You shoulda learned English long ago." He nudged me. "You don't speak French, do you?"

I shook my head.

"No talking to Baptiste then . . . You're not missing much." He looked around the group again. "Same with Monica. She owns the china shop right there. Both of them only speak French and Italian. The rest of the lot speak English; don't let them fool you." He leaned toward me. "How long will it take for you to learn Italian?"

"I have no idea. I catch some words, but . . . Forget it. I get most of those wrong too."

"English then," he announced, "until further notice."

"Thank you."

Ben smiled at me and squeezed my knee under the table. "I told you; you will like Andre."

Two cappuccinos and I was flying. I tried to follow the conversation as it switched back to Italian, but it felt like swatting at flies. I whacked down a few words, but most buzzed past. I knew when Ben said good-bye, as the whole group moaned. I caught all the *arrivedercis* and *ciaos* and repeated them back as we made our way through the tables and off the patio. But rather than return to the narrow passage between the buildings, Ben took my hand and led me up to the town square.

"I don't think two was a good idea." The flying sensation held the distinct possibility of tipping toward a crash landing.

"I will feed you soon. That will help."

We walked up the hill and out of shadow into the bright sunlit square.

I tugged at him. "Explain *tartaruga* to me. It's an odd name for a café."

"Sandra says she came out of her shell and fully alive when she married Paolo. He owned the café and was against the name switch, but I think he feels the same about her, so we quit poking him about it."

"Turtle Café . . . I like that image."

"Here, I want you to see this."

We walked up a few stairs and Ben pulled open the massive front door of a church. Inside was dark and, as my eyes adjusted, I breathed in. You could almost taste the age, incense, and heaviness of paper, wood, and stone. The only light streamed through the stained glass windows in shots of red and blue.

"It's so quiet. Peaceful."

"You will hear the bells even at the house for this evening's Mass, then again tomorrow morning. I come here sometimes if I am at Coccocino and cannot make it to church with my family on Sundays. They go to Santa Maria in the valley to the south, but this . . ." He stepped deeper into the nave. "This is where Joseph worked that summer I told you about."

"Here?" I stepped forward, my soft ballet flats barely making noise on the stones. The pews were ash wood, worn and warm, and the altar hewn from some kind of stone. I couldn't tell from the distance, but by the way it reflected the light, I suspected marble.

A flicker of gold drew my attention to a side wall. There was a series of paintings along the nave, seven on the wall near me, and an equal number on the other side. "The Stations of the Cross," I whispered.

"*Via Cruces*. You know these?"

"Lily showed me pictures of a set she worked on for a Catholic church in Memphis." I stepped closer. "These are oil on wood. Early nineteenth century?" I caught Ben's shrug in my periphery as I moved to the next one. "These could use a little love, but some of this . . ." I noted places of repair that were expertly executed. "I bet Joseph did this."

"He may have."

"There's still more that can be done." I touched the curled edge of a frame. "This moisture damage is fairly new. It should be scraped out and sealed."

Ben chuckled softly. "Are you looking for a project?"

I smiled. "I think I am."

"When we come for services, you can corner Don Matteo and tell him."

"That seems rude, but . . ." I moved to the next and the next, my excitement growing with each warped frame, surface crack, and nick. "Do you think he'd let me help?"

"His predecessor let Joseph." Ben turned and strolled back out, but I lingered, already determining which glues to use and which pigments might work best.

He ducked back inside the door and called, "Are you coming?"

As we walked out of the church's shadow and hit the sun-drenched center of the town square, I slowly spun in a circle, taking in the small grocery, the wine shop—trying to remember the word *enoteca*—the church, the single hotel, the tourist shop, the town concert hall—solidifying each in my memory.

Home.

➳➳ Chapter 21 ➳➳

Boom.

I shot up and shook Ben. "What is that?"

"I forgot to warn you." His eyes remained closed as he waved his hand in the general direction of the window. "See the top of that tower? Over the hill?"

I rolled over, taking the covers with me, and

looked out into the golden morning. The side of the house sat at the base of a hill. Over the rise I could see the tip of a broad bell tower.

"Church bells?"

"Santa Maria. Every morning at six. First Mass of the day. In a few days you won't notice them."

I hauled the pillow over my head and dug deeper into the covers.

Moments later someone or something poked me. I swatted at it.

"Easy. You will spill it." Ben's voice came from . . . above me.

"What time is it?" I crawled out of my cocoon into a brightly lit room and looked out the window again. Blue sky. Quiet.

Ben held out a small white china cup. "Your cappuccino, Sleeping Beauty."

"Oh . . . I could get used to this." I scooted up against the headboard. "I didn't miss a whole day again, did I?"

"No. Drink that and I'll take you to the village. I need to check in at Coccocino, and you can corner Don Matteo."

"Your mother mentioned going to morning Mass yesterday. Is that soon?"

"You did sleep through that."

"You can wake me, you know." I sipped my coffee, suspecting that ruining Donata's plans, again, was not a good thing.

"Enjoy that and come to breakfast. I'm going to

the garden to see if Mama's herbs are ready yet."

I dressed and found my way back to the kitchen. Donata was wiping down the counters.

"You missed breakfast and Mass." Her censure came out thick. She then looked around, as if she couldn't help herself, and pointed to a plate on the table. "There is what is left."

I glanced over. A platter was piled with fresh peach slices, melon, prosciutto, another meat I couldn't name, and a couple cheeses.

"Thank you, and again, I'm sorry I missed dinner last night too. A mixture of little sleep and jet lag is still swamping me . . . I couldn't keep my eyes open."

Her *hmmm* bordered on a *harrumph.*

I walked over to the table. "Am I the only one eating, or should I wait?"

"It is for you alone." She busied herself at the stove, tightening the knob on her stockpot's lid.

"I can set that for you so the screw will never come loose."

She looked at me, softening for a moment, almost as if I were a memory rather than a person. She then shook her head.

"It wouldn't be—" I stopped. There was no use continuing. She'd left the room.

Ben joined me about halfway through my platter of food. "When I left, small shoots; now many are ready."

I tried to hand him a peach slice but it kept

sliding through my fingers. "You've got to try this."

"I had one; that is yours." Ben laughed as another attempt slipped back onto the plate.

"They never taste like this at home."

"You do not tree-ripen most of your fruit. It ripens in transit. That took some getting used to at Piccolo. Have you tried the pecorino?"

At my nod, he continued. "A friend of mine, Alessandro, makes that. You will meet him soon too. He lives a little ways away and does not like Tartaruga."

"He doesn't?"

"He does not like Andre." He tapped my now-empty plate. "Are you ready?"

"Let me brush my teeth, then I am." I dashed up the stairs and halted right before slamming into Lucio.

"Good morning. Will I see more of you today?" He gave me a formal, yet playful, bow.

"I'm sorry I fell asleep and missed dinner."

His face lit with an ear-to-ear grin, much like his son's. "Do not apologize. I did the same and missed it too."

By the time we returned from the village, minus finding Don Matteo and any discussion of possible work, the house was full of family for a celebration. Donata said it was because Ben was home. Lucio said it was to welcome me. Regardless, family had arrived.

The kitchen was packed with women, the patio with men, and kids ran through the vineyards and in and out of open doors. After a seemingly endless round of introductions, cheek kissing, hugging, nodding, and smiling, and a failed attempt to be useful in the kitchen, I snuck off to find a small dark corner to myself. Ben had long since disappeared among the men.

The room I'd spied when we first entered the house was in fact a library and was, at this time, blessedly empty. I dropped into a large armchair covered in a soft floral-patterned fabric.

"Here you are."

I startled and jumped up.

"Don't get up." A young woman with long black hair waved me back down. "We'll hide together."

She curled up in the chair across from me. Raven hair and dark eyes. And if I was right, she was three years younger than me, spoke "American" like a native, and had trailed her older brothers relentlessly as a child.

"You're Francesca," I said. "Ben talks about you a lot. I'm so glad to meet you."

Her face split into that same contagious smile. "And you're Emily, my new sister." She looked around the room. "We'll hug and kiss later." She laughed as if she knew how uncomfortable I might find that. "It's nice and quiet here. Did they all scare you?"

"Maybe a little, but it wasn't that. After meeting

everyone, I couldn't understand anything that was being said and I was bothering your mom." I held my hand out. "Justifiably so . . . They've got a lot going on and I've never made pasta, don't speak Italian, dropped my wineglass, was standing everywhere I shouldn't have been . . . It was better I retreated."

"Aunt Sophia said Mama barked at you."

"Nobody could blame her. I really was in the way—I couldn't understand what she wanted me to do." I tried to smile.

"Often Mama doesn't require translation."

I smiled. Ben was right. Francesca sported a perfect American accent—one that stretched flawlessly from Chicago to Seattle, dipping down through Colorado rather than passing up near the Canadian border.

"You were a big hit with Aunt Sophia, though."

"How so? I think she's the one who stepped away when I tried to hug her."

Francesca burst out laughing. "Don't take that personally. She's not Italian. She hates hugs and despises the double cheek kissing. She loves that you don't fit in, 'cause she says she still doesn't and no one lets her forget it." Francesca waved her hand again. "It's not true, of course, but she plays it up."

"She'll love me forever then . . . I don't make pasta, cook, sing arias, speak ten languages, or anything else you all do around here."

"That's how we look?" Her eyes narrowed. "Let me assure you that's not the case. I, for one, can't carry a tune, hate to cook, speak only three languages, and . . . pasta is a sticking point."

She twisted deeper into her chair and tucked a leg under her. "It's the greatest sin for an only daughter not to cook—and especially, not to make pasta. In my mom's family, it's the responsibility of the youngest daughter. Very old-school traditional. Mama was the youngest of four girls and has made pasta every day for the past fifty years." Francesca cast me a sideways smile. "According to her, I should've taken over long ago. But I didn't—so she's kept on, annoyed with me on a daily basis. She doesn't like it when things, or people, step out of line."

"Be fair, *Passerotta*." A soft voice drifted to us.

"Papa calls me his sparrow," Francesca whispered before I saw him entering through a paneled door I hadn't noted. Ben followed him.

Lucio continued as they came toward us. "She wanted to share it with you and has fully respected that you don't wish to continue the tradition."

"Fully, Papa?"

"Perhaps not completely and perfectly fully." His voice tripped into laughter.

Francesca smiled at this qualification as I stood to offer Lucio my seat. He greeted me with a quick kiss on each cheek and motioned for me to sit back in the chair.

"I'll be fine here, if you don't mind us joining you. I'm tired tonight and, although family is wonderful, it can be overwhelming too." He lowered himself onto a small love seat.

Ben perched beside me on the chair's arm and ran his fingers through my hair. "You two look comfortable."

"We are. Please don't make us move," Francesca whined.

Lucio held up both hands. "We plan to hide too." He then settled back into the corner of the love seat. "It was the pasta that made Donata fall in love with me."

I could almost hear Ben relax as his father continued.

"She walked into Coccocino one day looking or a job. It was not yet five in the morning and there she was, so young and beautiful. I don't know if you can tell"—he winked at me—"but I am older than she is. I hired her that first moment, and every morning she was there. In the quiet, magic time between night and dawn, I wooed her as I made the bread and she the pasta." He raised his finger. "All by hand, with care, each and every day. It's work, it's life, a sensual pleasure, and I won her."

"You are such a romantic, Papa."

He smiled at Francesca. "As I always say, my girls make it easy."

I, too, folded one leg beneath me and tucked

into the chair as they shared family stories. Ben left my armrest and sat next to his father. His tall frame looked strong and sturdy next to his father's thinner one. The contrast made me sad, as if I were seeing the beginning and the end of a beautiful story.

Gradually Ben and Francesca grew quiet, content to let Lucio wend through time and share his best moments with me. It was the most comfortable, the most welcome I'd felt since walking into the house—far better than all the hugs and double, even triple, cheek kissing Aunt Sophia so despised.

Suddenly Lucio stopped midsentence and pointed out the double doors with a smile. "Watch," he whispered.

I threw a glance to Ben. He nodded confirmation, then focused his gaze out the window. Francesca twisted in her seat as well, and the four of us looked over the fields as the last sunbeams touched the hills. They ignited in a golden orange, fire against the darkening shadows. None of us moved or drew a breath until the blaze disappeared.

The instant it did, the front door banged shut.

Lucio stood and stretched. "And that, my children, was our last moment of peace. Shall we join the others? I suspect dinner is about to begin."

⟫ Chapter 22 ⟪

The next morning I made sure I was awake to accompany Ben downstairs to breakfast. One, I didn't want to be rude again. Two, I didn't want to face Donata alone. I even wondered whether I could accompany Ben to work, each and every day.

"You are up and dressed early." Lucio was already seated at the huge farm table with a book and an espresso. "You just missed Mama. She is out in the garden."

"That may be best." Ben pulled out a chair for me. "I need to go to Coccocino. I did not like the mess I found yesterday."

Lucio laid down his book. "That is my fault."

"I should not have left. Six weeks was too much."

"You thought I was there and I didn't tell you otherwise. And Francesca? She's never worked in the restaurant before. It was unfair to put her in that position." Lucio held up a hand. "But time is racing fast now; you needed that trip."

"Papa." Ben reached across the table and squeezed his father's hand.

"Not unusual at eighty-three, Benito, but I didn't want to believe. It is what it is." Lucio scrunched his eyes shut as if putting a stopper in his emotions. "I am sorry about last night too. I can't believe I slipped. I never told Mama that Joseph lives near Maria and Vito or about Piccolo. That was my fault too. "

I sat back, remembering the evening. The family, so large we were spread across the dining room, kitchen, and patio to eat, was loud, boisterous, and fun—until I heard Lucio call across the table.

"Joseph said Piccolo is twice as busy since your work, Benito. You have the magic touch, you and Emily."

"What's Piccolo?" someone asked in English.

I was so delighted to understand the question; I jumped in without thinking. "Ben's Aunt Maria and Uncle Vito own a wonderful restaurant in Atlanta. Joseph took me there my first night and already Ben had revamped the menu, but together, we—" I stopped, finally noting the absence of all noise and movement across the three rooms.

My eyes shot around the dining room. Every face stone-still. I glanced at Ben. He watched Donata. I glanced at Lucio. He watched his plate.

After a few seconds Lucio looked up and whispered, "Donata . . ."

She raised a hand to him and looked to Ben. "I thought you worked on your pizza at Joseph's home. You went to see your brother. That is what you told me. Maria lives there? She owns a restaurant and knows Joseph? She knows my son? How?" She turned to Lucio. "And this does not shock you?"

"No. Joseph contacted Maria years ago. From Naples. I didn't know he went to Atlanta because she was there until . . . until I visited."

"*Egli fa questo a male di me.*" Donata spoke quietly.

Lucio reached for her hand. "I don't think he's trying to hurt you. I choose to believe he is finding his way back. To family."

"And now you?" She faced Ben.

Ben's lips parted, but no sound came out. His eyes flashed confusion, and I realized he didn't know what to say.

"Please. We'll discuss this later." Lucio squeezed her hand, lifting it within his. "Francesca, please bring me a napkin. I spilled some wine on the table."

It started slowly, but the cacophony soon resumed, though I noted that Donata did not engage again.

Now Ben's voice drew me back to the present. "Are we ever going to talk about that?"

Lucio shook his head, checked the motion for a second as he caught my eye, then resumed, and I wondered if I'd imagined the hesitation. Then he straightened his back and looked at me. "What are you doing today?"

"I-I'm not sure. I . . . ." I glanced at Ben, hoping he might have some great insight or invitation.

"You can paint my portrait."

I scooted my chair back. "I'm not that good. And besides, I don't have my paints with me."

"Oh, but you do," Ben announced. "I got them from Joseph when I went to say good-bye. He said you would want them."

"He did? I told Amy to grab them on her way out of town." I envisioned Joseph's tall figure, so like Ben's, but less open, less thoughtful—arms usually crossed. "That was kind of him, of both of you."

Lucio nodded as if all were settled. "You will fix Coccocino," he said to Ben, "and we will be together." He stretched across the table to pat my hand with each word.

He then gave his attention to Ben. "Last night was all wrong, and it meant you did not tell about your pizza. Tell me before you go."

Ben leaned across the table. "It seems silly now, packing flour, traveling across the world to cook. I should have been here."

"It wasn't." Lucio matched his posture. "You needed to see Joseph. He needed to see you. We are family and we've been fractured too long. I always thought it was the bread—that if I fed you, made something so elemental and basic, like the air we breathe, I could keep us whole. I have been the silly one, hiding my head in Coccocino, books, my own imagination." The hand covering mine now slid to Ben's. "And you could not have done that here. Pizza? I might have stopped you. I resist change, and Mama hates it." He offered a small smile. "You wanted to make something new. Coccocino needs new. You needed new."

"I made a crust I am proud of, Papa. I want to add it to Coccocino's menu. And I want to keep in touch with Maria and Vito, more with Joseph too. I loved my time there and may even visit them again someday. The States is Emily's home."

"I know. All that is right." Lucio sent me a warm smile before facing Ben again. "Make your pizza. Keep Joseph close, and Maria and Vito. I'll figure this out. I promise." He reached up and laid his palm on Ben's cheek, and I noticed how thin his hand truly was. The veins lifted out of the almost translucent skin. The nails were tinged yellow, purple at the bases. He wasn't well, and it was far more than being tired.

Lucio continued. "You will make some for me. I can taste it now."

"Tomorrow. No, give me a few days. I want to play with the water and yeast here; it needs to be perfect."

"Nothing is perfect, son."

"It needs to be my best effort."

"I will wait then." Lucio pursed his lips, his eyes alight with laughter. "Don't tell your mother yet."

"Not after last night. She did not look at me or speak to me again." Ben pushed up from the table and kissed his father's cheek. "I need to go." He squeezed my shoulder. "You will be okay?" he asked softly, as if he'd known all along that I feared being left behind.

I smiled and glanced to Lucio. "I'll be just fine."

"*Bene. Ti amo.*" Ben bent down and kissed me before leaving the room.

"Espresso?" Lucio pointed to the hand-pull machine on the counter.

"Ah . . . of course." The La Pavoni matched my own. "Don't get up. Ben and I refurbished one of these in Atlanta and I know how to use it. I think your son was preparing me for just this moment. May I make you another too?"

Coffees made and cups in hand, I followed Lucio out of the kitchen.

"Look up." He stepped into the small hallway outside the library door. "This house was purchased from a monastery in 1693, and those are the family crests and the shields of the bishops. Then here . . ." He pointed to each corner in turn. "These are depictions of the known continents at the time—no Antarctica. See the grains and green of that one—that's your home, North America.

"But that corner? Ben flooded the hall bathroom as a boy and we fixed the water damage, but the paint, the red changed, and that flaking has bothered me for years. And here . . ." He trailed his finger above my head. "That crack has grown."

He looked straight at me. "Could you help?"

I squinted to see the mural more clearly. "I see the flaking, and maybe some discoloration. The varnish is most likely animal based. But until I get up there I won't know." It was my turn to drop my head and look him in the eyes. "You should ask Joseph. He's the true conservator, and this is his home."

Lucio blinked several times before replying. "He is not here, and it's now your home too."

I nodded. "If you have a ladder, I can examine it."

"Wonderful. Let us go to the shed and get one. It's at the edge of the orchard." He headed through the hall and back to the kitchen at a much faster pace. I set the coffee cups down on a table in the library and hurried to catch up.

I spent the morning in the library with Lucio. While I sketched him, we chatted about books, Ben, and life. Ben had been right about his father. While he may have been an excellent chef, he certainly was a natural-born teacher.

As we'd entered the library, he had asked, "Where do you want me to sit?"

"Right there is fine." I then settled across from him and nodded at the book pile next to his chair. "You can read if you want. I'm only going to sketch you now, to get a feel for the lines of your face."

He picked up the top book and flashed me the cover.

"*Don Quixote*. I remember that one," I said.

"I like him. He reminds me of myself lately, tilting at windmills as if I could change things too."

Lucio paused and looked out the doors through which we'd watched the sun set the evening before. "Sometimes, before I fall asleep or when I catch a piece of music that lifts my soul, I envision another way to live, like that moment last night when the setting sun hit the top of that rise and the leaves glowed. They were alight with life, and it lasted only a moment. That's when I suspect I've gotten it wrong and I've wasted my time, tilting at windmills—not anticipating the unexpected or being present enough to recognize it." He waved his hand again. "Musings of an old man . . ."

I noticed something about the cover. "Do you read it in Spanish?"

Lucio twisted the book as if he'd forgotten he held it in his hands. "This? Yes. If I can, I like to read books in their original languages. I can read five languages. Portuguese, I can only speak."

"Ah . . . only." I settled my sketch pad on my lap and selected a charcoal pencil from my toolbox.

"I feel you gain the author's original intent in his or her own language. I only switch if I need a different perspective."

At my befuddlement, he continued. "Words

don't always translate, and I'm a different man in different languages. I interpret things differently, I think differently. A story changes for me like something alive and growing."

He laid down the book, warming to his subject. He needed his hands. "In general, I read, watch television, do math, and make plans in English. In Italian I sing, cook, work in the garden, and make love to my wife. In German, at least in my head, I form debates and arguments . . . I often reprimanded my children in German." He grinned. "I also used to clean Coccocino's kitchen in German. It sparkled."

"It astounds me how many languages you all know."

"They're all around you here. German and Spanish I solidified working in Berlin and Barcelona for years before I took over Coccocino. The restaurant was my mother's place, passed down from her father. She was chef for many years before me. I had only taken over the year before Donata arrived."

It wasn't long after that he'd drifted away in memory, then into sleep.

Shortly after Lucio drifted off, I crept out of the library and climbed the ladder in the entry way to have a look at the fresco.

Donata's voice startled me.

"Emily, what are you doing?"

The ladder shook, and it rattled worse as I flew down its few rungs.

"Lucio asked me to examine the ceiling. There are some things I can do to help it."

"It is not your concern."

"I . . ."

She pushed past me and entered the library.

I crouched down on the ladder to peek through a crack in the door. Lucio wasn't asleep anymore.

Donata started in a quiet voice, but soon the words flew up, both in speed and in volume—in Italian. But I didn't need to be fluent to understand that something was wrong. Me.

Lucio's calm voice interjected at first, then died away in the torrent.

I climbed off the ladder and stepped away from the door, but within two steps I realized I had nowhere to go. Ben and I lived here. *Do I go to my room?*

The library door flew open.

"Fine. Lucio wants you to do the work." Donata ground out the words as she stalked past me.

Lucio smiled from his armchair and waved me inside. "As I told you, she does not like change. She fears what is to come."

I dropped into the seat across from him. "I don't have to do this."

"Don't you want to?"

I couldn't help nodding. I needed something to

do, something to fix. Forty-eight hours and I was already feeling lost. I had secured Donata's pot handle the day before. I couldn't help it.

"That was not about the painting. She knows it needs to be fixed. It is about my timing. Have you ever noticed how much that matters?" He continued without waiting for a reply. "She would have been pleased if I'd asked you to do that years ago, but now she feels I'm 'putting my affairs in order,' as the English say. That she does not like."

"Is she right?"

Lucio studied me so long I thought he wasn't going to answer. He hadn't been forthcoming with Ben; what made me think he'd tell me the truth? What business had I to ask?

He nodded, once. He could not have been more clear, more decisive.

"I'm sorry."

"I have lived a good and long life, full of love." He shifted. "Now, will you continue to draw my picture?"

I looked out the library door, feeling again like an intruder and wondering if Donata should be sitting with her husband, not me.

Lucio followed my gaze. "She has gone to her garden. Again, it is about timing. She needs to get out."

I lifted my toolbox off the floor, grabbed a few pencils, and reopened my sketch pad.

"Tell me what you've seen since you arrived. Have you been to the church? San Biagio?"

"The church in the square? Yes, Ben took me there on Tuesday."

"You need to go back. I will take you." Lucio's eyes drifted shut, then popped open. "You need my eyes open, don't you?" He glanced to my lap. There was no hiding the five deep brown pencils.

"I'm working on your nose," I lied. "Actually, I'm not drawing anything. I make a bunch of little lines on the sides of the charcoal drawings to capture color; I don't actually color my drawings."

He wrinkled his nose. "May I see it?"

"Soon." I smiled and went back to our conversation. "I thought you and Donata went to Santa Maria."

"We do, but I want you to talk to Don Matteo. There is work at San Biagio we must discuss."

I laid down the pencil. "Did Ben tell you that?"

Lucio's eyes flashed something I couldn't name. "How does Ben know?"

"How do you know? That's the first thing I noticed. The paintings. He thought Joseph worked on them when he was there his last summer, but there's more to be done. There is definitely moisture in the framing, if not the artwork. I thought I'd ask."

"I was talking about the mural."

"I didn't see any mural." I mentally retraced my steps through the church.

"It's there. Covered. On the south side of the transept, across from the small altar . . . It's a job for someone who fixes broken things."

⫸ Chapter 23 ⫷

The bells woke me again. Despite Ben's assurances, they were not fading away.

I lay awake and revisited the previous day. After lunch, I'd climbed the ladder again to examine the ceiling paintings. At first it was uncomfortable as Donata huffed and puffed her way around me, going to and from the library. But she finally calmed down, sat and chatted with Lucio, and I was able to focus. I could catch notes of their conversation and bits of laughter. Donata's voice surprised me. It was soft and coaxing, like a lullaby.

But I was certain that wasn't the Donata I would encounter today. Every time she looked at me the music stopped.

I whispered into the lightening room, "Are you awake?"

Ben grabbed me around the waist and pulled me close. "No. Are you awake?"

"Can I go with you this morning? To Coccocino?"

"Why would you want to do that?"

"To be with you." That sounded much better than *To get out of here*. And it was true. I loved watching Ben work and come alive as he made his pizza dough or his bread starters or even as he peeled vegetables. He often forgot others were around and sang. It was enough to be near him.

"Of course you can. It is time I got up, though." He leaned over and kissed me. "Things are a mess."

I sat up. "What's a mess?"

He shook his head as he pulled on jeans and stepped into the bathroom. "It is our busiest time. We make 75 percent of the year's income in the summer, and our farmers have not been delivering, the books have been left unmanaged, the kitchen is in shambles. We do not have enough produce, and the meat and fish orders are wrong."

"How did all that happen?"

"Francesca." He smiled, small and flat.

We headed downstairs, and once again there was a beautiful platter of fruits and meats on the table.

"*Sei in anticipo*," Donata called from across the kitchen.

"I need to be at the restaurant early. We are behind on prep and . . ." Ben stopped as if he decided it was news best not shared. "There is much to do."

He crossed to the espresso machine and began to pull us both shots. "Mama?" He gestured to a small cup.

"*Sì.*" She nodded with a smile—which completely disappeared as she glanced my direction. "You are up too. To paint?"

"I thought I'd go to Coccocino with Ben. See if I can help him."

Donata merely raised an eyebrow. I had to give her credit; not one word spoken, and she said plenty.

I dropped into a chair, accepted my espresso with a tolerably fluid "*Grazie,*" and ate a little breakfast. Ben joined me, but Donata kissed him on the top of the head and carried her coffee out of the room.

I caught his eye.

"She just wants to see Papa."

"I'm sure that's it." I smiled.

Within minutes, we, too, were out the door. Ben tossed me the keys.

"You're kidding?"

"You cannot spend all day and night in Montevello. You will have to get back somehow. You have already driven it."

I dropped into the driver's seat, remembering our trip to return the rental car. I had lurched along behind him in this very car, stripping its gears and stalling at every intersection.

Ben sat very still as I ground around within the gears and finally got his car going the right direction. At the first intersection he sat silent.

"You aren't going to tell me where to go?"

225

"You have driven this way before. You will remember better if you figure it out."

"Don't blame me if you're late." I turned the car left. He flinched. "Ha!" I drove to a roundabout a few meters away, circled it, then doubled back the way I'd come and straight up the hill beyond.

Ben grinned. "Told you."

Once I got out of the valley and could see Montevello perched above me, it was easy to find my way. I wove carefully through the narrow archway, up to the town square, then back down the one artery I knew—the one to the car park near Coccocino.

"Are there other parking lots?"

"This is the best. There is one more on the other side, but getting through the arch there is tough, even for me, and the spots are smaller."

"This is the one for me then. I can't imagine any parking spaces smaller than these."

We hopped out and wove our way through the narrow walking passages to Tartaruga Café.

"Have you ever thought about living here, in the town?"

Ben looked around and shrugged. "When Francesca moved here, she asked that too. I never thought about it."

"Francesca lives here?" I hadn't thought about where Francesca lived. "We should . . ."

Ben waggled his thumb and finger at Sandra in greeting. "We should what?"

Something told me now was not the time . . .
"Nothing. Nothing at all."

We carried our cups to Coccocino. No one else
had arrived.

"I have the *soffritto* to make. Do you want to
help?"

"What is it?"

"The cut vegetables, the dressings, that form the
base of sauces, risotto, much of what we make."
While he spoke, he laid down bunches of carrots
and celery and a bowlful of onions. Soon his
knife was flying.

I started in beside him, cutting more slowly, and
in larger pieces.

He glanced over. I could see his brows furrow
and could barely resist touching between my
own as he'd done to me many times.

"It's not my forte, is it?"

"You can help in other ways."

I wiped off my hands and looked around. "I'll
find something." I walked over to a side counter.
There were about twenty knives resting next to the
sharpening stone. Those I knew how to handle.

About an hour later Ben came over. "You are
so quiet."

"I enjoy this work. Do you want a new knife?"

"Yes. Mine felt dull. That is another thing; no
one sharpened knives the entire time I was gone."

I handed him one and followed him back to

collect his. The next moment brought a scream and a flash of red across his white coat as Ben held his hand tight.

"What did you do?" he demanded.

"I sharpened it. What?"

He crossed to the sink and rinsed his hand. "It is not bad." He spoke more to himself than to me. He then walked to a side cabinet and pulled down ointment and gauze.

"Let me help." I reached for his hand. The cut wasn't deep, a tiny thin slice across the pads of all four fingers. "What happened?"

"I . . ." Ben's voice lifted in question as he pulled away and walked back to the knife. He lifted it to the light. "These are only beveled on one edge of this side of the blade. You never sharpen both. I sometimes use this flat edge for leverage."

"I didn't know." As he laid it down, I reached for his hand and quickly cleaned it before wrapping it in the gauze.

"It is not your fault, but—"

"I should've asked. I thought I could . . ." My voice drifted away as Ben closed his eyes. I knew that look, not because I'd seen it on him before, but because I'd felt it on my own face—usually when dealing with Amy.

"I am worried, Emily." His voice was low and tight. "There is too much going on. This is too important."

"I know. I'm sorry."

"Come here." He opened his eyes and waved me over with his good hand. The other was clenched in a fist at his side. He draped his arm around my shoulders and pulled me close. "I do want you here. Is there something else you can do?"

"As much as I'd like to say yes, we both know you don't need me here right now. Let me head back home and work on your dad's ceiling. He would like that, and it is something I know how to do."

Ben's face cleared, then clouded. "I am not trying—"

I laid a hand on his chest. "I know you're not, but you're busy and now you're hurt." I pushed back and pulled the strings of my apron loose. "I will go, you get stuff done here and I'll see you back at home tonight." I reached up and kissed him.

"This is not how I wanted your first days to be." He shook his head.

"There's a lot going on, and none of it is your fault . . . I'll see you tonight. Okay?"

"*Bene.*" Ben returned to his vegetables, and I slipped out Coccocino's back door.

I wandered up the walk, not ready to return home quite yet.

"Good morning."

"Lucio? What are you doing here?"

"Donata had some errands, and I came along. I have had a robust coffee at Tartaruga and visited with Sandra. I like her."

"Me too." I fell into step beside him.

"Are you going to help Ben?"

I looked back toward Coccocino. "I've already done enough there. I was in the way. I was actually heading home to your ceiling."

Lucio linked his arm through mine and stopped. "Then you have a moment."

"I do."

"Let me catch my breath. I'm so tired."

"Do you want me to get Ben's car?" I looked down the narrow road. This was not one on which the car could fit. "Tell me what to do."

"I'll be fine. Just move slowly . . . Come with me." Leaning heavily on my arm, he led us to the church.

I pulled open the heavy door. Two steps and we were engulfed in a cool quiet—the only sound the tapping of Lucio's cane in between our brief moments of rest.

He turned at the altar and headed into one of the transepts. There was a small altar on one wall and a few pews facing it. He walked to the plain back wall and spread his hand flat against it, much the way I did when trying to feel moisture within a wall.

"It's here, the mural I told you about."

"It's covered? I can't just start stripping the

paint." I stopped talking as the sound of a door shutting echoed through the church.

A man, a priest by his black clothes and white collar, rounded the corner.

"Lucio?" He paused. "*È bello vederti.*"

Lucio stepped forward, kissed him on both cheeks, and ended it all with a hug. "Good to see you too," he said in English. "Emily, let me introduce Don Matteo. Don, please welcome Ben's wife, Emily."

"Ah . . ." Don Matteo smiled and spread his arms wide. After a double kiss, ending with another hug, he, too, continued in English. "I had heard Ben married. It is so nice to meet you."

"It's nice to meet you too." I nodded, wondering how quickly I could ask about the Stations of the Cross paintings.

But Lucio had another job in mind.

"I need to talk to you, Don Matteo." Lucio stepped back to the wall. "Joseph painted a mural here many years ago, while working for Don Pietro. He spent an entire summer on it. I would consider it a great favor to allow Emily to uncover it. It is her work, restoration."

"A mural? I have never heard of this."

"It was long before your time. He worked for Don Pietro in the summer of 2000, doing repairs, restoration, and odd jobs in the church. Then he started the painting, and it . . . it consumed him for three months."

"Where is it?" Don Matteo looked at the blank wall.

"Under here." Lucio tapped the wall. "I need to see it again . . ."

Before I die finished his sentence even if he didn't say the words.

Don Matteo pulled his neck back in surprise, then nodded in understanding. He'd heard the unspoken ending as well.

"I will look through our records and see if I can find any notes. Will you come back in a few days? We can discuss it then."

"*Bene.* I thank you." Lucio clasped the priest's hand within both of his own as if it were a done deal.

⋙ Chapter 24 ⋘

The next day I stayed home. And after another fairly silent lunch, I climbed back up the ladder to finish washing the second half of the mural. Ben had spent almost an hour the previous night rubbing out the neck crick the first half gave me —with his one good hand. I'd spent that hour apologizing that he had only one.

Donata and Lucio again sat in the library. I liked seeing them like this. He was the same no matter where he was or with whom he was chatting, but she was transformed. Around me she was lines and angles, stiff words and clenched fists. Peeking through the door, I saw the fluid movements of a dancer, a curving neck and hands rising and dipping as if telling a slow and beautiful story. I heard soft laughter fill the room.

They were talking of books. I caught titles here and there and words I knew connected to stories.

Lucio was telling her what he'd read, how it felt, and what it meant to him. She didn't answer back, as if her stories didn't come from books, but she kept asking questions. *"Dimmi di più."*

Tell me more.

Soon I noticed the lack of all sound, and moments later the door opened fully.

"He is asleep," Donata noted as she passed by my ladder. I peeked in the open doorway to find Lucio, head to chest in his favorite armchair.

I worked on, dropping my saturated cotton balls into a bucket with a soft *plink* every few minutes.

Much later I heard another voice somewhere below me.

"Anybody home?"

I looked down and had to grab the back of my neck with the motion. The 180-degree shift sent shooting pain down my spine. I stepped down to ease the angle.

"Your father is sleeping in the library, and your mom . . ." I had no idea how much time had passed. "I think she left the house. I heard the front door shut a while ago."

"Her car isn't here. I came in the back." Francesca stepped toward the kitchen. "Come meet a friend." I followed, trying to fix my hair and straighten my T-shirt as I went.

Anne had been right that first day. Francesca was a beauty, delicate and quiet. She had the raven hair of her mother, but a more delicate jawline and nose. It made her feel like a whisper, while Donata, to me, personified a scream.

A small yelp stopped my attempts at grooming and dropped me to the floor. "Who is this?"

The dog immediately climbed on me as if trying to dig into my lap, its tongue darting up to capture my face. "Oh . . . okay . . . We're going to tip . . . We're tipping now."

"Natale, get off her. *Via*."

"I like it." I righted myself as the dog settled into my lap and offered up her belly. "Natale?"

"It means Christmas. Ben gave her to me last Christmas. Silly, huh?"

"Not at all." I rubbed Natale's silky ears. She was white with light brown spots. "You are so cute." I rubbed her all over. "Is she a spaniel?"

"Probably a mix of several spaniels . . . She's never going to leave you alone now."

"That's a good thing. I might keep you," I said in the singsong voice globally reserved for dogs and babies. I dropped my voice and looked up to Francesca. "What are you up to today?"

"I was finishing up end-of-year cleaning at

234

school. Tomorrow I start setting up for summer camp." She gestured to the dog, still wrapped within my arms. "Do you want to see her work?"

"What does she do?"

"She's a truffle dog." At my expression, she continued. "You know . . . truffles. You serve them in restaurants, shave them over pasta."

"I know what they are, but I thought they used pigs for that."

"In France. Here we use dogs, and she's the best. Aren't you, girl?"

My doting dog immediately left my lap and leapt to Francesca. "Traitor," I called after her.

"She knows who feeds her." Francesca rubbed Natale behind her ears, and the dog's left hind leg started an *allegro* tap on the floor. "Come with me tomorrow. It'll be the last time I can go until camp ends. Alessandro and I will head out around nine."

"Alessandro? Ben mentioned him."

"You haven't met him yet? He's one of Ben's best friends. You'll like him."

"That's what everyone says about all Ben's friends."

"And?"

"I do."

Ben climbed into bed beside me. "What are you reading?"

"Your father gave me this."

Ben tilted the cover toward himself. "*The Taming of the Shrew?*"

"He and your mom were talking all morning, and when they came out for lunch he reached up and laid this on the ladder. Not a word. Just a wink. What's up with that?"

"You'd have to ask. He loves his books." Ben tapped my nose. "Almost as much as you love yours."

"Not exactly the same books." I laid the book in my lap. "I met Natale today."

"Was Mama here?"

Speaking of shrews. I bit my tongue and simply shook my head.

"That is a good thing. She hates dogs. Francesca sometimes brings Natale to annoy her. Now is not the time for that."

I began to get a fuller picture of why Francesca didn't live at home. "She invited us truffle hunting."

"Ah . . ." Ben leaned back. "I forgot to mention that. She texted me today, too, and I accepted. Is that okay?"

"Sure. When she asked me, I did the same."

Ben closed his eyes.

It gave me a chance to study him unobserved. The lines around his eyes dug a little deeper tonight. "Good night?"

"Busy. Too many bumps."

"Would it be easier if we lived closer? In the village? Maybe near Francesca?"

236

Ben cracked open one eye and stared at me. "I . . . Are you okay here? I caught that before, but . . . now is not the time for that. Are you unhappy?"

I reached over and clicked off the light.

Hiding my emotions, my expressions, was easier in the dark. "Of course not. Forget I said anything."

After a deep exhale, he pulled me close. "This cannot be easy. I know that. But I need . . . I need your patience. I wanted to bring you home and I envisioned how it would be, how it would feel. This is nothing like my vision."

My heart dropped as every fear rose before me. "Is it me?" He had discovered the truth. He saw the real me. I was not *that girl*. I was . . . me . . . and that wasn't enough.

He squeezed me tight. "Never you. Other than the knives." I could hear a smile on his lips. "But Mama and Papa . . . Life will never be the same again, and I should be here. But instead, I am there even more than usual because it is a mess. Coccocino was his life's work, Papa's family legacy, and I cannot let that slip. Not now."

I curled into him because, while I might not know much about his family, I understood pressure, fear, the need to fix things, and the black hole that opened within you when you realized nothing could fix all that was broken.

⋙ Chapter 25 ⋘

"What are we doing again?" I pulled on a pair of jeans and a long-sleeved T-shirt. "Won't we be hot?"

"You dig through brambles up there. You will want to be covered, and we will be home before it gets too hot. I need to be at Coccocino by noon." Ben tapped my back, urging me to go faster down the stairs. "Alessandro, if we are lucky, will feed us."

At the bottom I turned to the kitchen. He opened the front door.

"No breakfast?"

"No time. We are late. Francesca promised me all Natale's truffles. I do not want them to leave without us."

I followed, but not without a sense of dread. Somehow not showing up at breakfast was going to be my fault, and somehow Donata was going to make it very clear.

Ben circled the house rather than hop in his car. "It is a rough ride up the mountain. We will drive the truck."

I caught up as he hopped into an old pickup truck, like 1950s old. "Why'd Joseph tease me about my station wagon? This is much older."

"Joseph hated this truck, but it runs well. Papa would never sell it."

Soon I understood the truck's necessity as we bounced along a rugged country road, climbing higher and higher up the side of a mountain. Ben's tiny tin-can car was much too delicate for such an adventure.

"Explain to me dogs versus pigs. Francesca said Italy is dogs; France, pigs."

"And therein lies our national superiority." Ben winked. "Dogs are as effective in sniffing the truffles, but they do not eat them. A pig you have to pull off quickly or no truffle. A dog will dig it up and bring it back."

The switchback turns grew tighter and tighter as we reached the top.

"Aren't those olive trees? . . . They're different," I commented.

"They are, but the leaves are smaller and sparser up here. These are the last until we dip back below six hundred meters. They will not grow above that altitude." Ben looked out the window. "And those only produce about five kilos of olives per tree. My parents' trees will give twenty to twenty-five kilos. More oil, but more subtle flavors than what those trees give. I use both at Coccocino."

He leaned forward and pointed out my window as we crested the top and began a rapid descent. "All this land, from that hill"—he swept his hand across the full expanse of the horizon—"has been in my family since the thirteenth century."

"All this land is yours?"

"With seven other families. It is private land the church sold to us in the mid-1600s. All direct descendants can hunt on it—no one else. For us, it is through Nonna. But the land around it is all fair game, even though it, too, is private. Different designations. We can hunt that land, but it is best not to get caught. A standing agreement about no daytime hunting on someone else's land exists. It is impolite. Night is another story."

"And I'm betting you took full advantage of that." I shook my head at Ben's mischievous smile.

"After we stripped the truffles from close by, we took Alessandro's dog to a few select farms. She was so quiet, no one knew. We earned our spending money. Here truffles do not bring much, but back then was the beginning of shipping them to the States. We were paid a few hundred euros from a couple restaurant buyers, and they then sold them abroad, probably earning thousands."

"That hardly seems fair."

"That is the way of the world. And we would not turn down a few hundred euros."

Without slowing, Ben pulled a sharp right and drove us into a narrow lane. "Alessandro caught on, though. He has expanded his family's farm to host truffle hunts, lunches, and full-day experiences for tourists. *Agriturismo* at its finest. Today will only be us, though."

The truck lurched into a compound—more accurately, a random collection of farmhouses built around a central courtyard. There didn't seem to be any sense of planning, as though another structure was simply built when and wherever there was need.

Francesca waved from a side yard filled with dogs. "You're late." She bounded toward the car and hugged Ben.

"Stop whining." He laughed. He then bent and picked up Natale, who covered him with kisses.

"Don't try to steal her. You can have the truffles, but she hunts for me today."

"She knows who loves her. Yes you do, *cucciola*. I knew you had the nose. Yes you do, yes you do." He lowered Natale to the ground, but she kept trying to jump back into his arms.

"*Benvenuto!*"

A short, broad man strode from between the buildings and hugged Ben tight, slapping him on the back.

When they separated, Ben gestured to me. "Alessandro. Emily."

"Ah . . ." Alessandro nodded. "*La moglie del pizzaiolo.*"

The pizza maker's wife. Andre had started calling me that too. It was new, being called not by name, but in relation to someone else. At first it scraped up my spine. Now . . . I was beginning to enjoy it. It gave me a sense of place, in a place where everyone else already belonged.

Ben glanced at me before correcting Alessandro. "Emily."

I shifted my eyes away, a little embarrassed at what he may have seen in them during Andre's first teasing.

Alessandro pounded Ben's back. "Come grab an espresso and we'll be off."

Ben followed Alessandro back to the squat house. Francesca watched them both and kept patting Natale. I watched Francesca.

Ben emerged minutes later holding two small china espresso cups. He handed one to me, then threw his back like a shot. I tried to do the same and ended up coughing. Alessandro laughed. Ben winked. Francesca said nothing.

"Let's go." Alessandro waved his arm in the air and barked out a quick command that all the dogs understood. We set our cups on the stone wall and followed. Ben caught up with him quickly, while I hung back with Francesca. Within five steps, Alessandro and Ben veered to the right and headed up a steep footpath. The dogs raced after them, passed them, dove through the brush, and were gone.

"Here we go." Francesca spread her arm out, inviting me to climb the path first. "I love these mornings. When we were kids they never let me come, especially on their night raids. I was probably too young, but I hated being left behind."

"Is this why he gave you the dog? To truffle hunt?"

Francesca's eyes followed her brother. "He simply said I needed one. He even had Natale trained for me."

Within minutes the dogs started pawing at the ground, tails wagging. Some squealed and danced. Others remained quiet and focused. They would dig a small hole, nip at it, then scurry to either Francesca or Alessandro and drop a small black rock into their hands, then nose their pockets.

"They're only interested in the treats." Francesca held her palm out with a small kibble in it for Natale.

"That's it?" I laughed.

"She's very easy to please." When Natale dashed away again, Francesca held the truffle out to me. "Want to see one?"

"Sure." I expected my hand to drop with the weight when she tossed it into my palm, but it didn't. The truffle was hard, wrinkly, and brown, but light. "I thought truffles were white. And it's so hard." I scraped at it with my nail.

We walked on.

"These are summer black. You're thinking of winter white." Francesca gestured to a string bag hanging from Alessandro's waist. "What we've collected so far today will bring in about a thousand euros. If they were winter white, it'd be twenty thousand. But you'd never find so many white at one time. Very rare. And they're all hard. Haven't you seen them shaved in restaurants?"

I handed it back to her. "Not the restaurants I frequent."

"You'll get to taste these. They're wonderful." Francesca carefully put the truffle in a bag hanging from her waist. "A gentler taste than the whites. Probably gauche to say, but I like them better."

We followed the dogs around a path with which they were clearly familiar, pushing in and through brambles. Ben had been right, long clothing was needed, as every exposed inch was soon covered in small scratches. Within about an hour we arrived at the farmhouse.

"We're back? Was it a circle?" I looked back up the path.

Ben joined us. "It was. We have four routes, as truffles tend to be in certain places and return again and again. We walk the same paths many times a season." He thumped Alessandro's shoulder. "Are you feeding us today?"

"*Certamente.* Come on." Alessandro led us into the small building from which Ben had emerged with the coffees. It was a beautiful kitchen, almost rivaling Donata's, with countertops a mixture of stainless steel, marble, and wood. "We cook the lunches in here when we lead the tours." He glanced back to Ben. "Eggs?"

"Whatever you want to serve. You are the chef."

Alessandro grumbled and pulled over a basket of eggs. He flipped on the gas burner under an iron pan and started cracking the eggs into it.

My jaw dropped slightly. This man knew his way around a kitchen. One hand to crack eggs. Knife flying over a variety of herbs. He whisked a fork faster than my hand mixer. And minutes later he scooped eggs out onto plates, drizzled them with olive oil, and shaved a good portion of one of our truffles over them. He pushed the plates across the counter.

The first bite melted in my mouth. "I splurged on a tiny bottle of truffle oil last year for salads, but this is so much better."

"Bella! You did not." Ben slapped his forehead. "You were swindled."

"How?"

Francesca smiled. "Because there's no such thing. It's only olive oil and synthetic flavoring. Truffles have no oil."

"I paid thirty bucks for that bottle."

Alessandro scooped another helping onto my plate. "Happens to us all. I got swindled once too."

Ben and I left a few minutes later, happily full and carrying a good-sized bag of truffles for Coccocino. Francesca stayed to help Alessandro clean the kitchen.

As we bumped along home, I turned to Ben. "Does Francesca like Alessandro?"

"Yes." Ben offered nothing more.

"And?"

"There is nothing more to say. I know she does."

"Have you mentioned it to him?"

This caught Ben's attention. "Why would I?"

"Eyes over there." I flapped my hand back toward the road. "Because maybe he hasn't noticed. He seems really shy."

"He is, and we need to leave him be."

"Why?" I saw a project emerging.

"My sister and my best friend do not need me digging into their lives, especially their love lives. Got it?"

"Got it." I laughed at his tone. It veered toward repulsion. "No brother and best friend digging into their love lives."

Ben chuckled softly. "That includes my wife."

He drifted away in thought, which was fine with me. I had a plan to develop.

"You are too quiet. It worries me."

I glanced over at him and thought up a quick distraction. "Do you want to get a dog?"

"Hmm . . . You are making me think, Bella, that you are not happy here. Are you?"

Something in his tone made the hair on the back of my neck prickle. "Why would you ask that?"

"First an apartment. Now a dog."

My mind instantly recalled Ben's statement.

Mama hates dogs. Another statement of his smacked me simultaneously. *Now is not the time for that.*

I looked out the window and wondered how long I'd get things wrong. A month ago, life made sense. Now I was sitting in a pickup truck, in Italy, next to my husband, who had a bandaged hand, living with his parents. And I'd just insulted every-thing he held dear . . . again.

I felt a tap on the back of my head.

Ben was watching me; his eyes held a simul-taneously sad and loving look. "This is different from your world. It is different even from mine. I hope you understand."

I shrugged—to answer would bring tears. I took a deep breath and thought of something I could do.

"Do you think Francesca would let me help her set up for camp?"

"She certainly would." Ben reached over and rubbed the back of my neck. I leaned into his hand; my neck still hurt from working on the ceiling.

Ben took the final sloping left off the mountain and headed to his parents' house. He glanced at me. "It is not so bad, is it?"

The hitch in his voice caught me. I twisted fully to him. "Not at all. I love your dad. And the ceiling is looking wonderful, isn't it? Even your mom has stopped grumbling about it."

"*Bene.*"

I reached over and laid both my hands on his arm. Sometimes you need to feel someone to know they're with you, completely with you. "I am fine, Ben. Please don't worry about me."

"I do worry. I love you. I worry about Francesca too. And Mama. It will not be easy. What is to come."

Lucio.

He continued. "Thank you for going to Francesca's camp. She will need a sister right now."

"I'll go tomorrow. I might also offer to help out at camp when the kids arrive. Bring my paints in or something."

"She will like that too."

⇛ Chapter 26 ⇚

I walked up the short path to the school. It was a low building and I entered at ground level, but I could see the hill drop away behind it. I suspected it was built into the hill like Anne's castle and that its floors extended many levels down. It took a few minutes of wandering the bright and fully decorated hallways before I found Francesca's classroom.

"Hey." I knocked on the doorjamb. "Are you busy?"

"Just finishing up. What are you doing here?" She was sitting on a tiny chair filling white plastic bins with crayons, scissors, and other supplies.

"I came to see if I could help and show you something I thought the kids might enjoy." I propped a white canvas against her desk and dug through my toolbox for a bottle of my gentlest solvent. I didn't need to be too careful, so I soaked a cotton ball and dabbed it against the white. Red burst through at my first touch.

"You painted over a painting?"

"I thought they might think it fun to discover a painting rather than make one."

"They will." Francesca leaned against her desk and smiled. "You remind me of Joseph. He used to get excited by stuff like that too. Even as a kid, I remember him repairing things, uncovering things. He used to help out at the church a lot and even worked at a small gallery here in Greve, touching up damaged pieces."

"He doesn't come home much, does he?"

"It's been several years now. Papa went to Atlanta a few years ago to visit, probably five now. As you gathered, Mama didn't go." She shook her head. "Papa didn't invite me, but I don't know that I would've gone if he had. I'm tired of chasing my brother."

"I got the impression something happened." I heard my line hit the water before I could stop it. I shook my head. "It's none of my business."

"It kind of is now, isn't it?" Francesca quirked a smile, lifting one side of her mouth. "And if you can find out what it was, you're a better detective than I am, because I've asked. Papa says Joseph chose to leave, but prays he'll find his way home. Mama won't discuss it at all. And if Ben knows, he's never said. He and Joseph were close once, but that's gone too."

"I'm sorry." I understood fractured families and the glue we dabbed on to try to repair them. It never stuck, never held fast. "Families are complicated. My dad was furious that I got married."

"Why?" Francesca barked.

I wanted to hug her. Loyalty spread through every aspect of her being. She clearly couldn't understand why anyone would be upset about his daughter marrying her brother.

I laughed. "It had nothing to do with Ben. I don't think it even bothered him that he hadn't met Ben. It had to do with me being impulsive and rash and dropping the ball with my sister, shirking responsibility. As I said, families are complicated."

Francesca nodded but didn't ask any more questions.

I gestured to the white canvas. "The solvent is a specialized soap, completely safe. The kids can use it themselves if you think they'd like to do this. I could bring several small canvases."

"They'll love it. Do you want to come present it

to them?" At my eager nod, she walked to her desk and flipped open a calendar. "I keep the mornings fairly free for self-directed activities. You can come any day you like."

"Perfect. I don't even have a calendar to check. I'm wide open." I picked up the painting and propped it beside the table.

"Ben's busy right now, isn't he?" She laid down the calendar and returned to the small table. "I messed up at Coccocino. Noemi should have been in charge, but Mama forced me and, it being my family's place, no one had the guts to tell me what I didn't know. And I knew nothing."

"He's busy, but I can't help either. Actually, I'm doing the opposite. The bandage on Ben's hand? I did that by sharpening all his knives. I had no idea that some knives have blades with only one beveled edge."

"They do?"

"See? Who knew?" Whether she knew about the knives or not, she got my humor, played along, and with a single question made me feel at home. I almost hugged her for it.

My biggest struggle with Italy was not the language. Ben was right, most people spoke English, and I understood enough Italian to misinterpret almost every conversation. But nuance, humor, sarcasm, and reversals—all that was lost. Everything was heavy and literal and lonely. And Ben couldn't help me. I was alone.

I'd even called Amy a couple times, just to spar.

We sat quietly for a few minutes, filling the plastic boxes, and I finally felt at ease.

Francesca broke the silence. "What'd you think of the hunt?"

"I loved it. Something about it made me feel a part of this land and your family like I hadn't before." I quirked a small smile. "Sitting here comes a close second."

"I'm glad . . . I won't be able to go for a few weeks because camps run on the weekends, too, but Ben can take you back up to hunt. Or wait, and I promise, you, me, and Natale will go once camp ends."

"Deal." I moved on to another box. "Alessandro's a handsome guy." I was back to fishing.

Francesca slid me a glance. "What did Ben say?"

"Nothing, I promise. In fact, when I asked him about you two, he very clearly told me to keep away."

Francesca blushed a beautiful rose color. It was warm against the black of her hair. A blush on me was more of a blotchy oil-mixed-with-water affair, a discordant clash of color. I envied the whole cream-and-roses look.

"You can report back that there's nothing to tell." Francesca dropped her voice.

"I'm not reporting anything to Ben. I've already treaded on dangerous ground asking. But . . . I'm not so sure. I saw the way Alessandro looked at you. He watches you, and guys don't do that with friends or sisters of friends."

Even yesterday morning when he'd been annoyed, Ben had looked at me like nothing could or would change his love. Never consciously noting it before, I recognized it now. There was a look. It was special and it needed to be savored, protected, cherished.

I rested there a minute, and the giddiness of discovery passed as a flutter of guilt wafted in. I was not protecting it now—Ben had asked me not to interfere.

But I didn't retreat. "I think if Alessandro thought one day that he couldn't look at you like that—he'd miss it."

"What do you mean?" Francesca's hands stilled.

"You can't miss what's always in front of you."

She lifted both brows. "You remind me of Emma."

"Who?"

"A character in a book. A matchmaker." Francesca sat back in the tiny chair, tipping it onto its back legs. "Mama isn't demonstrative, instructive, I guess, and Papa . . . You know him. He's a storyteller. If he can't put a lesson into a story, he'll give you a book and hope you learn it from there. He's not very direct."

I thought back to all the books Lucio was stacking next to my chair. I'd been sure there was a plan.

Francesca continued. "Anyway, Emma's a matchmaker. Papa made me read her story when I was about ten to teach me humility; at least that's what I think I was to learn. Then before I could go on a date, at sixteen by the way, he made me read *Vanity Fair*. That was supposed to teach me about the hypocrisy of humans, the games we play and the ways we use each other. Open my eyes and all that. But I haven't dated anyone . . . I've been in love with Alessandro since I was eleven, fifteen long years. Talk about a humbling experience."

"Maybe you need a plan."

"It isn't that I haven't been trying to come up with one, you know. Do you think it's fun waiting on the sidelines hoping you'll get noticed?"

"I know it isn't."

"Did Ben keep you waiting?"

I barked out a quick laugh. "Two weeks from meet to marry? No. Ben was the dream that swept me off the sidelines. He sees something in me I still don't see, and I pray every day he won't realize he imagined it all along."

"What do you see in him?"

"In Ben . . ." I, too, leaned back in my chair. "He's bright and true and cares about all the right things. The world is better with him near, and the idea of his leaving was like the thought of losing an arm or a leg, or some part of me I'm not sure I could live without."

"I've never heard love described that way, but

it makes sense. That's how I feel, even about Alessandro's friendship. To risk that feels foolish."

"I get that." I dropped a pair of scissors into the last box. "But you're still on the sidelines."

⋙ Chapter 27 ⋘

Bees buzzed. Something heavy held me down. I tried to wriggle away, certain I'd be stung and that I'd done something wrong. *Did I swat the nest?*

Garbled words met my ears. I opened one eye to find Ben reaching across me to grab his phone. He shifted himself upright as he listened.

"What's wrong?" I whispered.

He held up one finger, asking me to wait. *"Bene, bene, Mama."* He said the phrase over and over until he hung up.

"What's up?"

"Francesca didn't show up at camp this morning, and the director got worried and called Mama."

"It's only eight in the morning. She probably overslept." I sat up. "Why's your mom calling? Isn't she downstairs?"

"She took Papa to Assisi today."

Lucio had talked about it during dinner. Donata was against it. Ben was against it. Francesca was against it. I was silent. And Lucio was determined to go.

"I need to see the Basilica again. Assisi is very

special to me. Or you could take me to Roma? To see San Pietro . . ." He'd even laid his hand on his heart.

"Papa. You can't go to Rome. It's a long drive. You're not up for that." Francesca rested her hand on his arm.

"Good. Assisi is only an hour away. We will leave in the morning. I am best then."

Donata had been silent the rest of the meal.

Ben climbed out of bed and pulled on a pair of pants and a gray T-shirt. "I told Mama I will check Francesca's apartment. Do you want to come?"

"Sure." I scampered off the other side.

We left the car outside the outer wall of Montevello this time and walked through a pedestrian arch. We followed the wall across two "spokes" to what appeared to be an old aqueduct collection area. Ben knocked on a door built into the wall.

"This is the coolest place ever."

"Her roommate, Caterina, inherited it from her aunt. And it is literally the coolest place also. Her top floor looks out over the wall; otherwise all her windows are on this side, and because of the few windows and the thick walls, it stays very cool. I store overflow wine here."

"Only you would think of that."

"I'm not the only one. Osteria Acquacheta does it too."

"Michel's place? She shouldn't help him; he's the competition," I teased.

"Bah . . . What helps one helps all. Besides, he taught me most of what I know. Coccocino's kitchen was too intimidating at times."

"Ah . . . Mama." I nodded with meaning.

Ben bobbed his head in time with mine. "Yes, Mama." He banged on the door. After several good thwacks, he lifted a flowerpot and grabbed a key.

"You can't do that. What about the roommate?"

"Caterina should be at work, too, and if not . . ." He opened the door and called inside. "*Ciao*, Caterina!"

There was no answer.

The door opened into a small dark kitchen, as wooden shutters blocked the window. I placed my hand against an interior wall. Ben was right. The stones were cool. While I stood looking around, Ben flipped a light switch, then walked straight to a small glass table and picked up a piece of paper.

I peered over his shoulder, but I couldn't read the cramped script. Cramped Italian script. I craned closer and saw Francesca's name at the top. "So?"

No reply.

"What's it say?"

"It says Caterina would like to know where my sister slept last night, that she has not seen her since yesterday afternoon, and that she is angry she cannot reach her." He put the note down and pulled out his phone. He tapped it for a call. No answer. He tapped out a text.

"Could she have slept at Alessandro's?"

Ben spun around. "Why would you ask that?"

"Because she's in love with him. He's in love with her, too, you know."

He narrowed his eyes, thinking. He whispered to himself in Italian, but *stupid* translates.

"Wait a minute. What's so—"

He held up the same finger he had in our room, asking me to wait. But it was not a gentle request this time. His stiff posture made it a demand. He tapped his phone again.

I stood there as a torrent of fast-flowing Italian spewed into the phone and back out. Standing three feet from Ben, I could hear Alessandro's tense raised voice as clearly as if he stood beside us.

Ben tapped off the phone and sank into one of the kitchen chairs.

I pulled out another, scraping the legs across the stone floor, and sat across from him. "So? What's up?

"Francesca went up there last night and told him she would not be around this summer. Some nonsense about time, space, moving on or maybe forward. It made no sense." Ben lifted a brow, annoyed. "He was yelling."

"I heard . . . So he got angry and convinced her to stay?"

Ben sat perfectly still, his eyes on the table-top.

I snapped my fingers in front of his nose. "Why was he angry?"

"He was angry because he felt she was manipulating him. He told her to be gone already."

"I don't—"

Ben raked his hands through his hair, pulling at the short ends, his nails white with tension. "Alessandro was married for a couple months about six years ago. No one talks about it, because it was annulled and we spread the rumor that it was no big deal. He had met her in Rome and she wanted to go home; she was young and regretted it. End of story."

"And . . ."

"The truth, which only I know, is that his wife 'moved on' with a wine buyer from Germany. And he was destroyed. Alessandro never trusts easily, but when he does it is firm and he is a solid friend. It takes long to get that trust. Francesca had it, and now . . . it is finished."

"You said you didn't even know if they were interested in each other, and you knew all this?"

"I am not blind. Why do you think I gave her Natale? It gave her a reason to be up there."

"You gave her the dog as a matchmaking tool?" *And she called* me *Emma?*

"Francesca needed to grow up, and Alessandro needed time. It felt right."

"Could you have clued me in?"

Ben looked sharply at me. "Why? It was not our business. I told you it was not." He leaned back in the chair, all sharpness draining away. "He is a good man, Emily. But this is not good."

I reached out and touched Ben's hand, then withdrew mine. This was going to be easier with no contact. "I need to tell you something, but you can't get mad."

"Why not?" he asked with curious sincerity.

I stifled a groan. It wasn't literal!

I took a deep breath and tried again. "I mean I'd rather you didn't. Because I think this will make you mad and . . . I pushed Francesca to talk to Alessandro. No, that's not true. No pushing, but seed planting. I definitely planted a seed about talking to him. Not a big seed. Very small. Mustard-seed size. Tiny. Tiny seed." I rushed out the final words.

"Those can be powerful seeds." Ben's jaw flexed.

"Are you mad?"

"Disappointed. I thought we understood each other. This . . . this is my family, Emily."

I cringed. There were no extra *e*'s in my name. There was no soft look. In fact, he avoided my eyes as he stood and walked to the door. He gestured for me to go through it first before silently locking it and returning the key under the flowerpot.

"What are you going to do?"

"If Alessandro said half the things he said he did, Francesca is devastated, and I need to find her. It is my job."

"Why—"

"I am her brother, Emily. Papa cannot do it, and Mama is the wrong person. So it lands on me, as it should. That is what brothers do." He headed down the walk. "I need to take you home. If my parents get back before I do, tell them I have gone to Florence, to Martine's apartment."

"Why not call?"

"If Francesca will not answer, Martine will not. Loyalty. This will require more door banging."

"I'll come with you."

"I . . . I need to handle this alone."

I trudged along beside him, fully convinced *mad* would've been better.

Ben pulled up to the house but didn't get out with me. I dropped back into the car. "I want to help. What can I do?"

"*Niente.*"

Niente. The very word hollowed out my chest. *Nothing.* And not said in English. Ben was so faithful, so careful to use English around me, to include me in every conversation, to make sure, even when I wasn't part of the discussion, that I

261

could understand, follow along, feel connected. *Niente.*

I tried again. "What about the restaurant? It's so busy. I . . . I could go there to help."

He held up his hand to stop the *worst idea ever.* "This will take only a few hours. I texted Noemi. She will start prep early. I need to go, Emily. Please."

I reached up and kissed his cheek. "I'm sorry."

I unlatched the door and walked into the silent house as he drove away. At home and at work, I'd often walked into unoccupied, silent spaces. Houses that weren't ready for their families yet; work spaces not approved through final inspections; my own apartment, where I'd set up a workshop in the dining room area for small items. Silence had never bothered me.

Until now.

It didn't belong here. This house was meant for warmth, hugs, kisses, crowds of family, and yelling. Its thick stone walls were meant to keep the family close and force the impact of their passion and love to spill out the windows and doorways into the countryside.

Not today.

Today it was silent. I walked the few steps to the short hallway into the library and looked up at the ceiling mural, knowing I should work on it. I should climb the ladder and work on the only thing I had permission to touch and the skills to fix.

Instead, I headed into the library and plopped into my favorite armchair. I plucked at a loose thread, considering the irony that it was Donata's favorite chair too. I knew that much from peeking into the room from the ladder. I should find a new favorite spot—I certainly didn't need to give her any more ammunition for disliking me. But I couldn't bring myself to move. Since I'd dropped into it on my first day, it had felt like my only safe place in the house—if I didn't want to spend all day hiding in my room.

I reached for the sketch pad I'd propped against the chair's skirt and pulled a few colored pencils from my toolbox resting under the side table. I could see him so clearly. Lucio, off to his beloved Assisi this morning. I closed my eyes to picture the tones of his face, then chose soft beiges and browns for his cheeks, sun-worn and time-weathered, grays and whites for his hair and brows.

I then dug out darker tones to capture the stubble across his chin and cheek, turning again to gray down his neck. Ben looked so like his father. Would he, too, be this soft and gentle past eighty? He had such energy, but I could see it mellowing, deepening with wisdom and even more gentleness with time.

I missed him. *How extraordinary!* Ben was only driving a half hour away, but I missed him. I'd created a wall between us, and though it might be small, it existed. Little betrayals mattered, and I ached to make things right.

I grabbed another shade of brown to capture the shadow within Lucio's right cheek, which sank a little more than his left. That was the more interesting side of his face, as though it was the side that had made all the tough choices in his life. That would be the focal point of my next painting. I would capture that side more fully—for one picture couldn't capture even a fraction of Lucio's essence.

When I'd recorded all the shades within his hair and face, I dropped the pencils back into the box and studied the picture. It was time to begin painting. It was my own ritual, to start fully in charcoal—it drew me deeper into the art before I set it in oil. I ran a finger over my interpretation of his eyes, smudging, softening them a touch, and then I stopped. Ben was in them too. There was an expression in those eyes that captivated me; it held regret, memory, love, and loss, even a touch of wistful defiance, but mostly a soft acceptance. They were beautiful. And I'd captured them.

≫ Chapter 28 ≪

By midafternoon the stillness drove me crazy, and I escaped to the paths at the back of the house. They led me past Donata's garden, through an orchard of apple trees, and up through the vineyard, as the hill climbed to the north. At the top I found a field of sunflowers on the downward slope. Every single one faced away from me.

I wandered back, and as I approached the house's back patio, I noticed that the huge doors were now open. Someone was home.

Donata leaned over dough on the wood island.

"*Ciao.*" I stood in the doorway.

She looked up, watched me a moment, then resumed her work. She punched the big ball of dough and worked it back and forth, her full weight and shoulders rocking with the effort.

"Ben's gone to Martine's in Florence. He thinks he may find Francesca there." I mentally calculated time and distance—Ben should be back by now. I pulled my phone from my pocket. Nothing.

Donata didn't lift her eyes from her dough.

"Are you making bread?" As soon as the words came out, I knew they were wrong. Donata made pasta. At first, it seemed a silly distinction to me, but I'd quickly learned identity was

265

wrapped up in bread. For Lucio and Donata, even Ben, it was self-defining.

She confirmed it with one word. "Pasta."

And although the word is the same in English and Italian, her vowels and eyes screamed in Italian. Very distressed Italian.

I leaned against the doorjamb trying to fix what was or wasn't between us. "I do that, too, work with my hands when I'm upset. Fix a clock, put together a shattered china plate, make all the pieces fit back into the puzzle if I can."

"You work on that platter." She pointed to a charger resting on a side table.

"I found that last night, after everyone had gone to bed. I couldn't sleep . . . I should've asked."

She shrugged. "It is good work."

I couldn't help but smile. It was the first concession, warmth, I'd received. "Thank you."

Her eyes shifted to the farm table across the kitchen. Mine followed. I'd left my sketch pad there on my way out the door.

She stretched a flour-dusted finger to it. "May I see?"

"Sure."

She wiped her hands on a dry white towel and circled the island. I opened the book and began to slowly turn the pages. There were several of Lucio, a few landscapes, a couple of Ben, and a small one of her. I froze. I'd forgotten that I had drawn it. Her eyes were tight as they were the first day we'd met—not that they'd softened much in the week since.

It was a striking picture, a beautiful one, because Donata was beautiful, with her square jaw, straight strong nose, and umber eyes that flashed like topaz in delight and darkened to coal in an instant. I'd finished it late one night as I had sat in her kitchen.

I'd focused so fully on her I found myself forgetting time, place, and even myself. At the end I'd been exhausted and finally ready to sleep. I'd reached her somehow—her vulnerability, her strength, her fierce loyalty, her fear—and revealed her. But it was only on paper. In life, I hadn't made that leap.

She touched the edge of the picture as if meeting herself for the first time. "I feel that way." She pulled back and twisted her hands within the dish towel. "Right now. That is what I feel."

Her breath exhaled weariness and disappointment, long held close and tight. Without another look, she flapped her hands, crossed back to the island, and buried them in her dough. "Go . . . Go . . . Lucio is in bed. This morning was too hard, but he will be happy to see you."

I headed up the stairs, tempted to turn left rather than right, and hide in my room. I tapped on Lucio's bedroom door.

"Such an exciting morning!" he called as I entered. "First Assisi, then such tension and drama. It seems she's now back safe and sound." He lifted an old flip phone from his bedside table and then waved it toward the chair opposite him. "Sit."

"I'm glad." I sank into the chair and a sigh emerged, almost as if it pushed out like air from the cushion beneath me. "Where I'm from, no one would've sounded such an alarm. Her boss would've left her a voice mail, maybe fired her, but . . ."

"No Mama calling? No brother chasing her down?" Lucio's voice was laced with laughter. "Probably best not. She is a grown woman."

"No new sister setting her up?" I told him the whole story. It was bound to come out soon.

Lucio smiled. "I didn't know you were such a romantic."

"Meddler." I hated saying the word, but it felt right.

"You wanted to fix something, and that felt good. It always does." Lucio pushed himself up farther against the pillows and templed his long fingers in front of his face, tapping the tips together. "I'm sorry for your sake. But as for Francesca, I'm not entirely sorry it happened. Alessandro has tended to his wounds too long. That isn't a good thing. If he does have feelings for my daughter, she needs to rise within his priorities. This may turn out well in the end."

My phone beeped.

Francesca at work. Behind at Coccocino.
Won't be home until late.

"Ben." I laid my phone back in my lap. Lucio
watched me. "He's headed to the restaurant."

"See? This is all good. Come. Let us tell Donata."
He glanced at me. "Perhaps not everything."

In the time I'd visited with Lucio, the kitchen
had been transformed. Much of Donata's pasta
hung from three wooden racks, and she'd started
an extraordinary-smelling sauce. Garlic, tomatoes,
basil, and something sweet wafted through the
kitchen, mixing with the wild smell of the thyme
growing on the windowsill. And the counters
looked like Christmas, bowls of red tomatoes,
chopped greens, and herbs lying in bunches.

"All is well. Your chicks are where they
belong," Lucio announced.

"*Bene.*" She nodded.

I stopped in the doorway, but Lucio continued
to the stove and stood behind his wife. Donata
didn't turn or move. Rather, her body stiffened in
recognition of his closeness. Yet at his slightest
touch, she spun and melted into his arms. They
stood, no lines of separation between them,
unmoving, one. Her head tucked perfectly beneath
his chin.

When I was upset or unsure, Ben held me the
same way. I shook my head, remembering
Francesca's story about her father. Books told

stories. Books told us about ourselves. I now knew exactly why he had me reading *The Taming of the Shrew.*

Katharina, the main character, wasn't a "shrew" because it was enjoyable or fun, as I first thought. I'd immediately pegged her as a terror, Bianca as a brat, and Petruchio, her suitor, a bully. But as I read deeper into the story, I began to understand that Katharina reacted to those around her—family who constantly overlooked and diminished her. And once someone took her seriously, made an effort to reach her, she responded. At first I'd also thought Petruchio made the effort simply to secure her fortune, but then I figured out that he could have married anyone and worked far less. Something in Katharina, even simply hearing about her, had sparked his interest. From moment one, he felt she was worth pursuing.

Donata wasn't Katharina—I knew that. And even though I'd been ungracious enough in my head to think of her as one, she wasn't a shrew either. But she was someone who seemed to be reacting to everything around her—Lucio, Ben, Francesca, me. Joseph too. Simply because we didn't mention him didn't mean he wasn't ever-present. But to stop, be still, and strive to understand her. That might be something very worthwhile.

A soft laugh drew my focus to them again. Lucio held his wife close and smiled, not at me, but to her, even though she couldn't see it. "Okay now?"

"*Sì*," came the muffled voice lost in his chest. "*Non sarò in grado di respirare presto.*"

He chuckled softly. "If you can't breathe, you can't yell."

She unfolded from his embrace and swatted him, then stepped closer again, eyes fixed on his.

I left them alone and went to work on the ceiling.

I rolled over in bed and stretched my arm into emptiness, glancing at the clock. Something had wakened me. I listened. The front door clicked shut.

Minutes later, Ben entered the room. Like a coward, I pretended to be asleep. Soon he climbed into bed, but he didn't pull me close as he usually did. He didn't whisper good night or kiss my hair.

And the absence of it, of him, was profound.

I whispered into the dark, "Did you get a rest at all today?"

He rolled over and touched my cheek. My gratitude and relief at this simple gesture swamped me. I lost my train of thought for a moment, feeling emptied and humbled—and equal parts humiliated that his rolling over, touching me, and implied willingness to talk meant so much.

I focused my thoughts. "I didn't know, Ben. About Alessandro. His wife. Any of it."

"I did not know to tell you. Part of me had forgotten as well. Francesca needed time to grow up, and Alessandro steadied her. Alessandro needed time too. I had always hoped."

"Don't be mad."

"I am not mad. I am tired and sad, for many reasons." His tone told me the chat was over, and I couldn't blame him.

There *were* many reasons to be both tired and sad.

❧ Chapter 29 ❧

I overslept again.

"You have to wake me up."

Ben stood over me with a cappuccino. "Why?"

"Because it's Sunday and I'll get the stink eye if we miss church."

"We will go to San Biagio. Papa said you met Don Matteo."

"Yes, he . . ." I stalled. Lucio had specifically asked me not to mention the mural. Did that include Ben? Considering the Francesca fiasco, I decided it best to keep my mouth shut. "He introduced us last week."

After Mass, Don Matteo stood at the door

shaking hands with his parishioners. He held on to mine.

"I hoped to see you again. I forgot to call Lucio back. Will you come see me?"

Ben looked between us.

"Of course. Tomorrow?"

He nodded, his glasses sliding down his nose with each dip of his head. "I'll be here all day."

As he walked to the car, Ben asked, "What is that about?"

"Doing some work there." The evasion felt wrong, but I was unsure how to navigate my way through these secrets. My own family held none —we didn't communicate enough to have any. But here? I tripped over them right and left.

Ben threw an arm around my shoulder. "The Stations of the Cross? That is *magnifico*."

"I hope so."

As we walked down the hill to the car, I realized that Sunday Family Dinner loomed ahead of us—an event now worthy of dread and capital letters. Donata had canceled the previous week's, as it was only days after our celebration dinner and the Piccolo disaster. But tonight there'd be talk too. Something about Francesca, Alessandro, and her flight to Florence was bound to come out—and who was responsible.

The dread grew palpable as we drove home. It rose to a choking point when I recognized Francesca's car already parked at the front door.

As we entered the house, Donata barked from the kitchen in stiff, clear English, "You took your time."

"Mama?" Ben strode to the kitchen, clearly surprised.

I rounded the corner to see her pointing a large knife at him. "Papa is in the library with Francesca. Go see your sister, then you help."

Ben raised his brows to me as he ducked back into the hallway. I glanced to Donata and found her eyes now trained on me.

In slow, sure English she said, "You go too. You may have more advice for my daughter?"

"About that . . . I'm sorry I said anything to her. I—"

She returned her gaze to the table before I could finish. Her hands moved back and forth with the knife, cutting the swath of dough in thin, sure strips. She then angled the knife and slid it through the center, as if inserting it into a roll of paper towels, and lifted. Pasta unfolded like Rapunzel's hair down the tower in thin, even strands.

My breath caught. It was beautiful. It was art.

Donata flicked a glance at me, shocked, surprised, almost loving, before she remembered her anger. She tossed her head to the door. "Go find Francesca if your sorries you must say."

I trudged to the library. It was empty. Voices drifted in from the side door. I walked out into the warm afternoon and onto an olive tree–shaded patio. Lucio sat in a reclining chair tucked within a blanket as his children leaned on the stone wall in front of him.

All eyes found mine.

Ben reached out his hand. "Are you okay?"

"She is mad." I pulled *mad* long across several *a*'s.

Francesca laughed. "Of course she is. That's her default emotion."

"*Passerotta*," Lucio gently admonished.

"Papa, it's true and you know it. Emily didn't do anything. I never should have even told her about our conversation." She leaned across her brother to poke me in the arm. "Sorry about that. I wasn't thinking." She then faced Lucio again, her hands outstretched. "This is ridiculous, Papa. I—"

"You disrespect yourself chasing that boy." Donata blew onto the patio. She then narrowed her eyes at Ben. "He is a friend, but he plays with the heart. That is clear."

"Mama," Francesca whispered.

"There will be talk. Do you not care about this? About your family? Your . . . reputation?" She pronounced the final word slowly and carefully as if she had looked up the English translation specifically for this moment.

"I didn't do anything wrong," Francesca moaned. "He made me mad, that's all. Okay? And there's nothing to talk about. It's hardly worth any gossip. I told a friend that I wouldn't be around much. End of story. And now, believe me, I won't. So it's true."

"That is not true." Donata faced Ben. "You know they talk."

"What does she mean?" Francesca bumped her brother. "Who talks?"

"Nobody."

"That is not true," Donata repeated. "At the café, Andre shares all the news. There are no secrets."

"Mama, Andre is the same as he was twenty-five years ago. You know that." Ben lifted his palms as if begging her to understand. "Andre bullies Alessandro. There is nothing to it, and no one cares anymore. You say never to listen to gossip. We do not. Why does this upset you?"

"Talk is a beast easy to feed. Then it devours you." She stalked back into the library.

Francesca groaned. "She's insane. You do know that? This wasn't a big deal. Alessandro was a jerk and I got mad and went to Martine's. It's my business. My assistant covered with the kids at camp, and I apologized. What's her deal?"

Lucio chuckled within a sigh. "Your mother has very few hot buttons, but possibly harming your reputation, creating gossip . . . You hit two big ones."

"Then she's a hypocrite. She moved here alone, Papa—a young woman, showing up in the night, barely twenty. Are you kidding me? Talk about creating gossip. Even Nonna saw the hypocrisy in all her rules. Can't you talk to her?" Francesca pushed off the wall. "I won't come back. I don't need a free meal this badly."

The color drained from Lucio's already pale face. He set his hands on the armrests and pushed forward. "You go too far. You will respect your mother, and if Sunday dinner with your family is only a free meal to you, by all means take time away. It is your choice. But don't you disrespect your mother in our home."

Francesca pressed her lips together as if stifling a protest, but she nodded. She then gave her father a light kiss on the cheek before walking off the patio and into the trees circling the house.

Moments later we heard her car tires crunch on the gravel drive. Lucio sighed and pushed himself up. Ben jumped to assist him. Lucio nodded his thanks, then drifted away. I assumed he was going to find Donata and tell her the news. One less for dinner.

Ben returned to his perch next to me and we sat in silence.

My dread had been pointless. Sunday Family Dinner never materialized. I didn't know if Donata sent word or everyone knew by osmosis, but not one person showed up.

Ben and I cooked a little of Donata's pasta,

coated it in her sauce, and ate at the kitchen table alone.

"What happens now?" I carried our plates to the sink.

"I need to go see Alessandro."

"Now?" I turned off the tap and spun around.

"He hurts, but he also hurt her. It has been days, and as much as I do not want to get involved, I need to talk to him, as a friend." He pulled at his neck.

"It's not so different here, is it? I mean . . . your mom is overreacting, right? This isn't fodder for serious gossip. Does anyone really care?"

Ben leaned against the counter next to me. "Yes and no. It is a small town, traditional. At times, judgmental. People know she went to talk to him. Mama was right; Andre has said as much. Gossip travels through the water." He paused.

I looked up, startled. *Osmosis.* How did he . . . ?

He smiled as if he'd read my thoughts, and I wasn't too sure he hadn't.

I smiled back.

He tugged at my waist, pulling me in front of him. "But no, it will not harm her reputation. Papa was right. Francesca was right. Mama has hot buttons. It will, though, give Andre ammunition. That animosity started when they were seven . . . Nothing new or unusual about that."

I clasped my hands behind his neck and kissed him. "I'll wait up."

278

He looked at me, almost questioning. "It could be late."

"I'll still wait up."

His eyes instantly cleared—as if we were no longer on opposite sides of a chasm. He pulled me tighter, kissed me good-bye, and headed out.

I spent the night painting. I'd set up my easel in Francesca's old bedroom. The posters and corkboards of friends' photos, postcards, and souvenirs still pinned to the walls reminded me of Brooke's room, or of Amy's when we were growing up. With each move, I would help Amy set up her half of our room on day one—pinning the same pictures and the same posters in apartment after apartment. She had teased me about my "blankie." I smiled, having only now recognized hers.

As I worked on Lucio's portrait, I wondered how well or how little I knew my sister. How well or how little I knew Ben. Or Lucio? Francesca? My own parents? Amy had been right. I had carried my "blankie" with me, physically and mentally. I carried my perception of how things worked, how they should work, and how they could be fixed into every aspect of my life, every job and every relationship. And yet the important things held an intangible quality I was only now recognizing. I remembered mentally balking at Rachel's comment, as relayed through Brooke. But now I found a thread of disconcerting truth within it. *She says some things can't be fixed. We just have to endure them.*

. . . And perhaps share in them. Ben wasn't going to Alessandro's to fix things. Loss of trust? Could that be fixed? Certainly not by Ben. I suspected he was going to share it. That was Ben. That was what made him so attractive and also so inscrutable. I didn't fully understand him, yet so desperately wanted to.

I was so deep in thought and in the painting, I didn't see Ben until he stood beside me.

His short intake of breath brought me back to the present.

"How'd it . . ." My question died as I followed his gaze to the painting of his father before me.

Ben stepped forward. "That . . . I will remember him just like that."

I took a step back, stunned at what was before me. It was Lucio. He sat in his beloved library, light spilling around him, highlighting one side of his face. He was so vividly present. And his eyes . . . arresting. They revealed his soul, and tonight I felt the heartbreak within them.

We stared for a moment until Ben sighed and dropped onto the corner of Francesca's bed.

I ran my fingers through his hair.

"How was Alessandro?"

"He feels manipulated and he is very angry. He was not always so angry, but it is his first emotion now too. We talked . . . and I warned him that one can only be a victim for so long before it sinks too deep to rip away."

"You said that."

"He needed to hear it."

Too deep to rip away. His phrase caught my attention and niggled at something I knew or had seen, but couldn't quite grasp.

≫ Chapter 30 ≪

The next morning I hauled an old Vespa out of the shed and headed to Francesca's school.

Her classroom was empty, so I wandered around until I found her watching the kids in a side playground. She was hard to spot at first among the trees and shadows. Kids laughed in bright sunshine atop a slide, then whizzed down into the shaded yard below. Francesca was hidden in this dappled light, eating an apple and frowning.

"Hey." I approached.

"Hi." She took another bite and watched the kids. I dropped next to her. "I wanted to say again—"

She laid a hand on my knee. "Don't. It doesn't matter and it's done. I'm more mad at myself than at you." She shrugged slightly. "I wanted some great declaration; I could've waited or walked. Either would have been more honest." She thumped her fist against her heart. "It was my fault."

"I pushed you." I leaned against the bench's back. "And your mom . . ."

"None of that is new either. I'm only sorry for Papa's sake. I shouldn't have said what I did."

"Will you come over tonight?"

She slid me a glance, a smile playing on her lips. "Are you trying to fix this?"

"Probably," I conceded. "I only meant—"

"That now is not the time for petty family squabbles. Ben said the same thing. You probably come from that—all healthy communication— and I should come home tonight; I know I should." She watched the kids a few moments. "Yes, I'll be there for dinner."

"Good. But so you know, I don't come from any of that."

We sat in silence watching the kids, listening to their laughter.

"Can I come to your classroom today, play detective, like we planned?"

"Please. I've been too distracted to be a very good teacher." She threw me a glance, daring me to apologize again.

"I'll be one for you." I stood. "I strapped a few canvases to the back of a Vespa I found in the shed. I'll go get them and set up."

"You drove that old thing? Walking is faster."

"I loved it! Does no one use it? Because I got to see the countryside on my way here. It was so slow, I could actually smell flowers as I passed them. It was perfect."

Francesca laughed. "It's all yours. No one has driven that thing in years."

"I'm so glad. Now I can get places by myself. That puppy's my little bit of freedom, and you have no idea how much I need that right now."

"You sound just like Mama. She drove that stupid thing for years too."

After an hour and well over a hundred cotton balls, I wandered out of the school yard. It was time to head to the church. Something about Lucio made me worry, feel urgency about his project and a desire to talk with Don Matteo.

Lucio had looked paler this morning, and his fingertips seemed to me more blue and yellow as he'd gripped his cup. And although no one would talk about it, there was something to his trip to Assisi. It all had the markings of a last good-bye.

I entered through a side door and stood, blinded by the darkness.

"Hello?" Don Matteo's voice and footsteps approached. He materialized directly in front of me dressed in black pants and a black shirt, the white of his clerical collar peeking out in the center.

"Ah . . . good, Emily. You've caught me dusting." He shook a white rag, then dropped it on the back of a pew and walked away down the aisle. "Follow me and we'll talk."

I followed. "May I help you?"

"Certainly." He pointed to a small pile of rags near me. I grabbed one, ran it along another pew next to him.

"Dusting helps me think. And call me Father Matt."

I tilted my head, questioning.

He stopped. "Yesterday during Mass, you looked like you needed a bit of home."

"How'd you catch that?"

Father Matt laughed, a deep, booming sound. "Everyone is so surprised when I say things like that, but it's quite natural. I'm looking at you all during the Mass. I see each one of you. It would be more surprising if I did not notice."

"I've never thought of that." I walked down another aisle and stopped at the end before one of the Stations of the Cross. Its frame was warped. Moisture had buckled the wood along the seam lines and cracked the central work. I leaned forward and touched the upper edge. "I know I'm here to talk about the mural, but these pine frames are cracking because moisture got in somehow."

Father Matt came and stood beside me. "They've been on my list this year." He slowly looked around the church, his eyes trailing from the small rose window at the back across the transepts to the central altar. "There's a lot on my list. I've been here only three years, and the list grows rather than shrinks."

"Do you want help?" I tapped the painting's frame. "I can easily rebuild these, clean the paintings, and apply a new varnish. I can get you a portfolio of my work and references."

"Lucio is reference enough." He studied me, then the painting. "My notes say these are from 1914, and I doubt they've seen any refurbishment or care since then."

"I don't know. Joseph Vassallo worked here one summer." I tapped the bottom edge. "See here? Adhesive. Well applied too. I bet he worked on this."

"Yes, I've read all about Joseph this past week. Alberto Rodi kept detailed accounts. He was the caretaker from 1953 until his death last year, and his father held the post before him. They recorded everything around here." He paused and smiled. "In fact, I now know that a redheaded choirboy had a cold in September of '63."

"That's probably when the moisture got in this one." I kept my expression steady.

He looked startled, then chuckled. "You're joking."

"Yes." I smiled.

"The notebooks also told me more about that mural Lucio mentioned." He balled the rag in his hand and walked to the south transept. I followed.

He picked up a thick black book sitting on the

last pew and opened it to a string page marker. "According to this, Don Pietro hired Joseph to refurbish items that summer and do odd jobs around the church. And . . ." He flipped several pages. "On June 23, Joseph asked Don Pietro if he could paint a mural. Alberto wrote here that Joseph was insistent—he used a word that translates close to *beg* in English. There's nothing about the subject, but Alberto recorded the proposed size."

Father Matt looked up at the wall and dragged his finger across the space, almost corner to corner.

"That big?"

He nodded. "It covered this entire wall from about a meter within the window to a meter off the edge." He flipped the pages, scanning. "And he came every day, sometimes asking Alberto if he could work late and lock up the church himself." The priest chuckled. "Alberto didn't like that." He turned more pages, his eyes scanning back and forth. "Then here. Lucio and Donata came to see it on September 8." He shut the book. "And that's the last reference."

"Nothing more?"

"There was one mention that Alberto repainted the wall on September 21 using leftover paint from the 1987 restoration."

"No mention of the subject? Why he painted it or why they covered it?" I ran my hand over the wall and could discern the slightest variance between two cream colors and two textures.

"That wasn't Alberto Rodi or the point of his diaries. The *who* or *why* rarely concerned him. Only the *what*." He waved the book before me. "I enjoyed reading these. It was like spending time with an old friend. I know how much petrol he purchased for his truck on a weekly basis, the cost of candles, and how he fixed the clogged pipes in the sacristy. But I don't know anything about the heart of your brother-in-law or what compelled him to work so hard that summer." Father Matt pulled off his glasses. "Why does Lucio want this? Has he said anything?"

"Just that I'm to uncover it and not discuss it with anyone. I get the impression he's not ready for more questions."

Father Matt nodded as if none of this were a surprise. "I feel uncertain. But I've prayed about this and I do feel we should move forward. I sense Lucio needs this. Very badly."

"I do too."

"Then let us have a few conditions between us. We continue to pray about it, and if either of us feels the need to stop, we do. We can talk to Lucio then. And I ask you to cover it when you are not working on it. I do not want disruptions or talk." He pointed to a small side door. "You will find tarps in the closet off my office."

≫ Chapter 31 ≪

I left the house early the next morning, Ben still sleeping, and arrived at the café before any of his friends had gathered. I stepped to the counter and laid down a euro with a quick *buongiorno* to Sandra. She smiled, nodded approvingly, and handed me my cup. I threw it back, trying not to react as the heat hit my throat, and returned the cup to the counter with a firm tap, mimicking Ben and his friends. Sandra's approving smile kept me grinning as I headed up the hill to the church.

"Hello?" I pulled open the huge wood door and walked the center aisle to the altar. The small door to the right, Father Matt's office door, was cracked open.

He had been hard at work. Upon leaving yesterday, he said he would clear space for me to work on the Stations of the Cross paintings.

And what had been a crowded and chaotic office the day before was now a clutter-free space with a large empty central table and a variety of lamps. I smiled, imagining him scouring the entire church and his rectory for every spare light. I especially appreciated the two mismatched reading lamps that arched over the table.

I laid down my toolbox and returned to the cool stone of the sanctuary. I pulled the first of the fourteen paintings off the wall, carried it back to the office, and began . . .

"Emily?"

I looked up and noted first the light, then Father Matt's drawn expression. "Hi. I hope you don't mind that I let myself in."

"That's fine. I didn't expect you so early." He looked at his watch. "Never mind, it is almost lunchtime. I was at the hospital this morning, and visits took longer than I expected. How are you doing?"

"I'm finishing a difficult seam line. It's got some debris in it, but I don't want to dig too much. The wood is soft. Then I'm using a superglue accelerator so that it'll latch more quickly. This should be stable by tomorrow." I pointed to the other end of the table. "The insides are right there."

He walked to the end of the table. The painting, depicting Jesus' condemnation, surrounded by soldiers and onlookers, rested on a cloth. The edges, protected from air behind the frame, looked bright compared to the yellowed central scene— like skin that'd been protected by a Band-Aid. He touched an outer edge. "Will it all look like this?"

"The tones will be even more clear. That, too, has experienced some discoloration."

"Remarkable." Father Matt walked to his desk and picked up the black leather book he'd shown me the day before. Today torn papers jutted from the pages.

He pulled at one of them. "I found more in here last night about those. They were a gift from the Cathedral of San Rufino in 1972. It does not say here why or what the connection was, but perhaps Alberto didn't know. He wrote that he drove to Assisi and picked them up himself, taking three trips so the paintings wouldn't need to be stacked in the back of his truck. It took him eight hours and twenty-three liters of petrol."

"Nothing about the paintings?"

"No, but there's more about the petrol." He held it out to me. "Here, take this, and the others too. You may find something in them of interest to you." He gestured to the door. "Did you start on the mural?"

"Prep work. I mounted hooks to hang the tarp and tested solvents. I wanted to talk timing with you before I began."

"You can work every day after morning Mass—except Sundays."

That night when Ben came home he found me in the library. "You are up late."

"I got reading these after you went back to the restaurant this evening. They're fascinating."

He reached a hand down to me.

"What time is it?"

"After one." He pulled to draw me close.

"Why are you so late?" I traced a line at the corner of his eye. I thought of these as his laugh lines, but as they cut more deeply into his face, I knew exhaustion, not excessive laughter, to be the culprit.

"I am still catching up. Every night is so busy; there is no time. I feel like I am at Piccolo with our long lists of to-dos, but without you to organize it all."

"Do you want me to come help?"

"Thank you." He exhaled the words as if I'd offered a lifeline. He then squeezed me with what I understood to be a gentle refusal. "I need to do this on my own. This is my work now, and I feel . . ." He looked over my head as if searching for the right word. "I feel I am failing."

I nodded against his chest. "I get that, but I doubt you are."

"How was the church?"

"Exciting. Can I tell you about it?" I pulled back and grabbed the notebook.

"Please. But upstairs?"

I curled into our bedroom's armchair while Ben moved in and out of the bathroom getting ready for bed.

"So I'm starting with the first painting of the Stations of the Cross, and it's got all the usual suspects. Oxidation, moisture, swelling, some warping and cracking. Alberto's diary fills in a little history, but he was more interested in the

291

day-to-day than in the story behind the paintings before he picked them up."

"That does not surprise me."

"You knew him?"

He raised a brow. "Everyone did."

"I know. Small town. Everyone related . . ."

He waved a finger to the book. "You will soon find the incident of the honey in the chalice and the time two choirboys ate Don Pietro's chocolates before one of them, I will not say which, threw up all over the sacristy after rehearsal."

"I read something about honey. Wait—I didn't see your name."

"He called us something else . . . I cannot remember." Ben plopped on the bed.

"Here." I handed him the thick black journal.

He turned back through the pages. "Are you getting all the Italian?"

"More than I expected, or I'm making stuff up. But I've got a translator on my phone that helps too."

He kept turning pages. "Here. Nineteen ninety-two. I was seven." He flipped the corners until he reached May. He dragged his finger down the page, translating far more quickly and smoothly than I had.

" 'The Sons of Thunder ate Don Pietro's birthday chocolate. Two kilos. I saved the silver ribbon for a decoration, but couldn't save the box because the younger'—that's me—'vomited on it. The rug came clean with a mixture of water and vinegar.' "

I laid my hand across the page. "A man after my own heart. That's a good, safe way to clean chocolate."

Ben laughed. "Move your hand." He leaned over the page. "That is what he called us. 'The Sons of Thunder.' We fought all the time." He flipped through the pages. "I bet we are in here a lot. We got very good at the Sacrament of Reconciliation."

"Which is?"

"Confession." Ben grinned. "Do you want me to read you some?"

At my nod, he settled back against the headboard and lifted his arm. "Come here."

I tucked into his side as he started to read. Most of the journal told of daily work in a solid life, but there were glimpses of humor, grace, and care. There were also profound moments of great kindness toward Ben's family or someone else Ben knew that occasionally silenced him. Alberto Rodi may have been primarily concerned with the *what,* but he was most definitely motivated by the *who* and the *why.*

Ben would stall on such passages, sigh, smile down at me, and read on.

It was almost three thirty before we flipped off the light.

⫸ Chapter 32 ⫷

We soon fell into a routine. Breakfast with Donata and Lucio, then Ben and I both headed to work. I climbed onto my slow, lime-green Vespa and followed behind his car down the drive, staying far enough back to avoid the jumping gravel. Soon he outdistanced me and I was left scooting along in the sunshine.

After a few days and several hundred cotton balls, the mural revealed color and texture, a draping of coarse brown fabric, layered facial tones, and one piercing eye. From these few visible glimpses, Father Matt and I could tell it was extraordinary.

"Have you updated Lucio?" The priest studied the one eye.

"He hasn't mentioned it, so I haven't either. Things are good at the house. Maybe because I'm gone most of the day, but I feel like bringing it up would rock our steady boat. He knows I'm here. Wouldn't he ask?"

"When more is uncovered, perhaps we should bring it up . . . but for now, find the other eye."

After work each afternoon I dropped by the Coccocino and stole a kiss and something yummy. I sat in the kitchen's corner and watched everyone work with and around each other. It was like a dance. Everyone knew their place and how to step and when. I understood how things could go wrong within six weeks—the pace was frenetic, and Ben was the leader. Without him, the underlying melody, the backbone to everything, would be gone.

Then I scooted back to the house to paint and read some of Lucio's stories. While I spent mornings at the church, my father-in-law seemed to spend his mornings adding to the book pile next to my armchair.

"I left you a treat." Lucio walked into the room, his cane tapping beside him. He gestured to my pile of books.

"*The Flanders Panel?*" I picked up the new top book.

"Joseph liked that one, and you, like him, enjoy mysteries. That one is by a Spanish author, about a restorer who discovers a mystery in a famous fifteenth-century painting and finds herself in danger."

"Is it in Spanish?" I opened the cover to peer inside.

"English. I bought that on a trip to London."

"Excellent. I'll get to that next. I'm almost finished with *Emma*."

"I didn't suggest that." Lucio sat down across from me.

"Francesca mentioned it."

"Ah . . . And what do you make of it?"

"I'm not sure. Emma is a hard character to like, and yet I do. She is completely the opposite of me, and yet I see myself in her. Actually, I take that back. She's not the opposite; I just don't like our similarities. And yet, I *like* her."

"Good writers do that. They show us ourselves, but in a new light. What did you think of Shakespeare?"

"I've read Shakespeare." I smiled. "You mean specifically *The Taming of the Shrew*, and I'm still not so sure I'm happy with it." I narrowed my eyes at him. "Am I the shrew?" I wasn't about to ask, *Is Donata?*

Lucio sat back and smiled. I knew he was trying to teach me a lesson but didn't want to spoon-feed me. And he knew I knew. Again, a dance. We were each waiting to see who would take the first step.

"Fine." I gave in. "It made me feel like I see things too black and white, jump too fast, and react too strongly—that I'm reactive rather than proactive." A few heated debates with Amy came to mind.

"You are a delight." Lucio laughed. "Literature teaches us empathy. But my children never approached it so willingly." He offered me a gentle smile. "But the lessons aren't so direct. I wasn't positing any theories about you."

"Then why'd you want me to read it?"

"It's fun. Shakespeare wrote bawdy comedy,

and while the play has its problems in a modern context, it is still fun. I doubt he expected to be read four hundred years later, but I suspect he is because he speaks truth. We do push and pull against people. And however it comes about, we recognize when someone takes us to heart and strives to understand us, in here." He pointed to his own heart.

With that, Lucio seemed to drift away into his own thoughts, then into his own book. I picked up *Emma* and continued on with her misplaced matchmaking, all the while suspecting she was missing a match of her own with Mr. Knightley.

Eventually Lucio rose, headed to his shelves, then tapped his way out of the room. As he passed by my chair, he dropped a new book on my pile.

A Portrait of the Artist as a Young Man.

I could only smile and return to my reading.

It was at night Ben and I found each other. He'd crawl into bed beside me and drag me back against his chest, and I'd whisper the same question into the darkness, "How was your day?"

"There was an American family in tonight. They ate well and ordered all the best dishes. Their son reminded me of Joseph. Like the boy tonight, he was so sure of himself." Ben's chest rumbled against my back. "Like that night we first met. He was so arrogant and you were so adorable." He squeezed me tight. "I overheard this boy tell the next table that cholesterol forms in the body because of glass that is mixed with the salt in America."

"Glass?"

"I had to pause to listen as I rounded the tables. I could not believe it. Then he said your companies add it as filler to keep costs low, and then the body heals itself by oozing out cholesterol as a safety coating."

"I highly doubt that."

I felt Ben's chest move again with his chuckle. "I put extra salt in his gnocchi tonight. I could not stop myself."

"Ben."

"He is in Italy. We do not add glass here . . . Besides, the gnocchi was perfection. He devoured it."

"You just missed an American family," Father Matt called across the sanctuary as soon as I entered the next morning.

"Don't tell me. Glass in the salt? In the wine?"

"Glass?" He shook his head. "No. One of the kids scraped back your tarp. I was worried it might have damaged something."

I crossed through the pews. "It can't. The paint underneath is hard. I wipe off the solvent before any color comes up, so it's as tough as it's been for seventeen years." I dragged over the ladder and climbed to unhook the tarp's corners.

The first thing revealed was the man I'd uncovered the day before. The complexity of emotion in his face was breathtaking. There was anger, but also an aching sadness—the conflict fully realized in one clenched fist and the tension in his eyes. *Is that a rock peeking between his knuckles?* His other palm was spread against his breast.

Joseph was a true artist.

"Have you looked at the mural recently?" I called to Father Matt.

"Not for a few days . . . Oh . . ."

I glanced back in time to see his mouth drop open.

He stepped away as if trying to gain a wider view of the whole. "It's powerful, but . . . it's a mob, isn't it?"

I climbed down and stood beside him. "I think so. Look at that child. He's confused, and angry too. Almost like he's been told to be angry. And here . . . Is that a rock? How does he do that? Joseph captured so much conflict."

"He certainly did." Father Matt's voice lilted and lingered as if he were contemplating a different question. With a quick headshake, he brought his attention back to me. "How much more do you have to uncover?"

"If it's as large as we think, there's enough room for at least ten more people. And these are so high I suspect they're in the background, and there's something closer to the viewer down here." I tapped lower, waist level, on the wall. "But I'm working on a grid system, so we'll have to wait."

"I had no idea," was all Father Matt muttered as he walked away.

I stood there thinking the same thing.

That night I twisted slightly within Ben's arms. "I've restored about two-thirds of the hallway ceiling. Your dad is delighted. Have you seen it?"

"I walk through that hallway every day and have not looked up. I am sorry."

"Don't apologize. You've been slammed."

"He was already asleep when I came home this afternoon. Mama was at the kitchen table. She said something about colors?"

I rolled over fully to face him, all the breath leaving my body. "I didn't think she noticed . . . This morning after you left . . . We were sitting in the library and I was putting color to that new drawing I made. I didn't think . . . I just grabbed the colors I saw within him."

"And?"

"They were different. I caught your mom's expression and looked down at the pencils. I'd grabbed chalky colors, paler colors, nothing like the palette I selected even last week . . . She left the room."

"Did Papa see?"

"He didn't say anything, but I think he noticed

before either of us did. He sees so much, Ben, more than any of us. Your mom called his doctor . . ."

"Dr. Salvai. Dario has been a family friend for years. What did he say?"

"I was leaving as he arrived, and your mom doesn't talk to me, not like that. Will you ask her? I want to know too."

"Tomorrow morning . . ." Ben let his words trail away in thought.

I had begun to drift to sleep when he whispered again. "We have been busier than usual. That is also so different this summer. Friends and family are coming by the restaurant. It is normal to stay away in favor of the tourists. We do that for each other in summer. Not now. They come to be close, but not burden Papa or Mama. I find it hard—so many questions in their eyes."

"How do you know they aren't coming for your pizza?"

A snuffled laugh caught the tail end of Ben's sigh. "I doubt it, but making extra now helps, working with the dough helps . . . Come tomorrow morning and cook with me? The rest of the crew can handle prep. No knives, and I will let you go by noon to get to your paintings. I want to be with you."

"I'd love that." I snuggled deeper within his arms.

No lines of separation between us.

☈ Chapter 33 ☈

Despite entering the kitchen well before dawn, upon flipping the light switch we found Donata.

"Mama? What are you doing?"

She stretched her back and pushed up from the table, immediately moving to serve us something to eat and "open" her kitchen for the day.

Ben reached for her. "Wait. We are going early to Coccocino. Go back and rest."

She waved her hands as if trying to find something in the air, something solid she could hold. "I do not sleep. All night."

Ben folded her into a hug. "I am sorry, Mama. How can we help?"

She shook her head. "It is life." She then gently pushed him away. "You go. Go to work. Come home before service. We will eat an early supper."

"Okay. Please do not overdo it."

She raised a single brow.

Ben read the message and pushed out a laugh tinged with frustration. "We are going. Fine. Do what you must."

Ben and I spent the morning together, creating the different styles of breads and fashioning what felt like hundreds of dough balls for the night's pizza orders. We'd arrived early, long before the rest of the staff, and it reminded me of Lucio's stories about wooing Donata—the bread, the pasta, creation, and falling in love.

I almost mentioned it to Ben, but I wasn't sure if the image would bring him joy or pain. Everything felt so fleeting and tender—anything could ruin the illusion that all was well and that this was nothing more than a fun, and oddly romantic, morning.

But it wasn't.

Ben lifted a large tub of pizza dough and bumped into me. "Are you still with me?"

I stepped back from the table, more flour covering me than it. "I was just thinking about your parents, and your mom this morning."

"Me too." He set down the tub, lifted his towel, and wiped my cheek. "Flour." He then looked back to the table. "It is silly in some ways, that bread, this pizza, means so much to me. It is so basic. But it is also like life—built on the elements." He looked around the still-quiet kitchen. "The foundations are all here and when I work with it, I think of them too. I am with them."

He picked up the tub and carried it to a far counter. I began wiping down the wood worktable.

To Ben, it was all one. Life, bread, family, Coccocino, home—there was no commute from work to home, no separation, no fracture between where he went and who he was or what he did.

He was right . . . Simple ingredients. Water. Yeast. Flour. Salt. Love. Made whole and beautiful.

As I pulled the tarp off the hook, still lost in my morning, Father Matt's voice startled me. "I've been reading about your husband."

"Mine?"

"Yes." He raised his brows and held up the diary. " 'Benito Vassallo stole a dozen candles, which he immediately returned after trying to light a passage under the church for exploration. He will polish the candlesticks on Saturday.' I also found the honey-coating-the-chalice prank, which he wiped clean after the service, and there's something about hiding candy in the confessionals. There was barely a day for a while when he wasn't in Alberto's way."

Father Matt dropped into the pew. "But for all his antics, Alberto adored your husband. Joseph too. It's one of the few places in the journals where Alberto says why something was done, not just what was done. *To go exploring. To feed the birds. To make the wine sweeter.* And Ben seems to have cleaned up his act by about fourteen. He isn't mentioned again."

He flicked at the corners of the pages. "In fact, after that mural was painted over in 2000, there isn't another word about either him or Joseph."

"Joseph went to college that fall in Naples. Ben says he never came home after that. Then to the States for graduate school and on to Atlanta." I climbed down and stepped away from the painting. "So?"

Father Matt's head bounced up. "You've moved down your grid."

"You've been gone."

He'd been at the hospital with two elderly parishioners, dear friends, who were suffering.

I jabbed a finger to what I suspected was the painting's focal point. "What do you think this is?"

"It's the color of blood. Could it be a pool of it?"

"I thought so, too, at first, but see here . . ." I walked closer and ran my finger to the splotch's outer edge. "I think that's shadow, as if it's material catching the light. I'll get more uncovered today."

I only had another hour to give to the mural, and I felt Father Matt hover throughout. Both of us were becoming increasingly intrigued. I uncovered more red, which seemed to open to brown. *A cloak? A dress? A cloth over an animal?*

"Is it okay to confess something to you? We priests are unaccustomed to that, but I feel we are in this together." His soft voice crept into our silence.

I slipped the last corner of the tarp over its hook—unsure how to answer yet sure that we were, in fact, *in this together*. "Of course."

The pew creaked under his weight. Father Matt

wasn't a heavy man, but it was old wood and it protested his thick frame. I climbed down the ladder and waited.

"Remember how I asked you to pray about this?"

I closed my eyes. I hadn't. I turned my head, feeling he deserved eye contact with my bit of honesty, when he continued.

"I've been praying, too, and I think I needed this painting, and you. I've been praying for years now, for a revelation. Not something epic. Just something in my heart. I've felt old and tired and joyless for too long."

I sat in the pew in front of him, twisting to face him. "You?" I didn't hide the surprise in my voice. "You're a priest."

He offered a heavy smile. "And I'm human. We all have doubts, fears, and we forget. We forget who we're called to be sometimes, and by whom."

"Isn't that life, though?" I thought back to my moment on the couch in Atlanta with Amy. *Life is hard.* I said it then because it didn't feel like a unique moment; it felt like a continuation of a lifetime of them.

Father Matt's eyes widened in a flash before he could correct his surprise. "It's all there, yes, but that's not what you're to expect each and every day. Who taught you that?"

"Life," I said as if stating the obvious.

He nodded. "She is a convincing teacher."

"The best."

"That's where you're wrong." He waggled a finger at me. "But I've been listening to her, too, and now I'm remembering true life. And this . . ." He pointed to the mural. "Something about this is significant. It's a good thing. It somehow reminds me that joy isn't a feeling, it's a truth."

"Is it ever going to get easier?" I flopped back on the bed, spread my arms wide, and dangled my feet near the floor.

"You are doing great."

I bolted upright. "You liar!"

Ben held his finger to his lips. His parents had come up to their room only moments before. He didn't want them to hear me. I knew he was right, but I also wanted to be heard—by someone.

"Every woman in your family completely ignores me. And the men are no better. They either pretend I don't exist or treat me like a child. One actually patted me on the head tonight."

"Outsiders take some—"

"They need to get used to me? I'm the one alone, I'm the one with no support. They all have each other. Anne implied your mom might be tough, but Sophia, Gemma, Fina, Silvia, and who's that one with the thick glasses? They all shoo me away . . . And they speak so fast I can't understand them. Or, what's worse, they sometimes slow down just so I can catch some of what they say."

Ben dropped beside me. "What do they say?"

"*Inetto.* Your mom said it to that glasses one. I am inept. But I'm not. She just has to show me what she wants done and I'll do it. I'm good at stuff like that. Give me a task and I'll get it done."

"Are you sure she didn't say *onesto*? They sound alike."

"What does that mean?"

"Honesty." Ben brushed a strand of hair behind my ear. "Genuine." He kissed my neck. "Sincere."

I bounced off the bed. "Don't even try that. She did not say that." I thought back and wavered. Had she said that instead? I pressed on. "And *bionda*. She called me that too."

Ben jumped up and reached for the doorknob. "I must go talk to her. That is not right; I draw your line."

"You mean you draw *the* line . . . Why? What does it mean?" I sat down again as my heart dropped. I'd been right the first time. *Inept.* And now . . . to have something truly awful said, to know there was something so wrong about me . . . "Just tell me."

"Blond." Ben crossed his arms and smiled at me.

"What?"

"Blond. You are blond. They were probably either complimenting your hair or they are jealous of it. If you have not noticed, there are no blondes in this family, and you have beautiful hair." He reached for a strand again, but it pulled through his fingers as I lay back on the bed and burst into tears.

"How can that make you cry?"

"Because there's no end. They don't even like my hair color!" It sounded ridiculous to my own ears, but I couldn't stop myself. "And you're laughing about it."

Ben lay next to me and pulled me on top of him, hugging me tight. "I am not laughing. Please, no crying."

I rolled to the side. "And my one ally wasn't there, because I ruined that too."

"I was there."

"You were with your dad, as you should be, but I mean in the kitchen . . . Francesca didn't come. Gemma and Silvia, they talk to me when she's around, but not tonight. No talking to the inept blond one tonight."

"Francesca is still mad at Mama. I gather Mama gave her another earful again about the Alessandro mistake."

"See? My fault again."

Ben rolled onto his side, facing me. "It is over." He kissed my hair. "Francesca and Mama are like oil and water. This is nothing new. Besides, she said Mama was not angry so much at what happened with Alessandro as she was about

Francesca running off to Florence. Mama can be rough when it comes to poor choices."

"That doesn't surprise me. No wonder she hates me. I'm a poor choice."

"Are you done yet?"

I heard a smile in his voice.

"Yes." Even I couldn't keep it up, but I also couldn't smile about it because it was all true. Perhaps it didn't deserve the drama and tears, but the core was true. I was the outsider and, as far as Ben's family was concerned, I was inept. I certainly hadn't proven to be otherwise. Where it mattered, in the relationships, I only fumbled. And, face it, I was blond too.

⫸ Chapter 34 ⫷

"Father Matt! Are you busy?" I called across the church.

He opened his office door. "This is a sanctuary. Shh . . ."

"No one's in here."

"But still . . ."

"You've got to see this," I called in an exaggerated whisper. "Hurry."

"You cannot hurry a sixty-seven-year-old knee. Patience." He walked toward me, smiling. "What?" He stilled upon reaching the first point at which he could glimpse the mural. "It's a face."

"A beautiful one. A woman. I haven't finished it all, but this is a dress. And the red? It's a cloak." I dabbed another cotton ball in solvent. "I can't imagine covering this. Ever."

"It is absolutely stunning." He looked it over. "That young man had talent. Does he still paint?"

"Wouldn't you think? But I never saw that he did. So maybe not."

My comment struck me. Working in his studio, I never saw Joseph work. At all. On anything. He didn't use the worktables, and yet he was going to handle the painting on the Ming vases. And I knew he'd done something spectacular on a Fabergé egg Lily mentioned. Did he work after-hours? Was that when he painted? *If* he painted? Lily said he had a workroom, but I'd never seen it.

Father Matt soon left to run some errands, and I covered the painting. I'd worked long enough and needed a break. Joseph had captured the tension so well it sat hard with me. There was such anger and condemnation in the faces, such vitriol, that I couldn't work on it too long or look at it too closely. Although its beauty was extraordinary, I wondered if Don Pietro had asked Alberto Rodi to paint over it due to its hostility. It was certainly not a welcoming vision.

I calmed my nerves with the fourth of the Stations paintings, the one in which Jesus meets his mother. Mary's face held some of the same characteristics of Lily's triptych back in Atlanta. I texted her a picture, and she replied immediately.

She's lovely. What's the medium?

I replied, Oil on wood. 1914.
She then sent me a picture of her work.

Nice Picasso. Way to make me feel inept.

I typed the word before realizing its significance. It had clearly made an impression on me. She replied again.

The Van Geld estate is proving great fun.
I'll send you more pics later. Talk soon.

"Does Joseph still paint?" I snuggled against Ben in the darkness.

"What makes you ask that?"

I stilled. Ben didn't know about the mural. I felt caught and unsure—and instantly resolved to speak to Lucio, soon.

For now, I told the bare truth. "Father Matt said something today as I was working at the church."

"If he does, he never talks about it. Not that we talk much."

I moved to my next question. "You know those

diaries? You two aren't mentioned after the summer Joseph worked there."

"That does not surprise me. We started going to Santa Maria that fall."

I lay still. It amazed me that I could hear him so well. Not what he said, but how he said it and what he chose not to say. The shades of his voice were becoming as distinct and discernible as the colors I chose for a painting. He had been blue, a soft blue, tired and yearning for peace and sleep, when we started talking. Then it twisted, like color fractured by oxygenation, as if a thread of fear or a dark question inked it.

I wondered myself at what had happened. Was it the mural?

"Are you okay?" I whispered.

"Everything changed that summer. Not just Joseph. When I came home from Anne's house, everything was different and no one talked about it. It is like the way you described last Sunday with the family. Something happened and someone must know, but they keep silent or talk among themselves and I am on the outside. To ask so often . . . It feels like I am beating my head against a wall."

I twisted in his arms to face him. "I'm sorry."

"It is not your fault, *mia bella bionda*." I could feel his smile as he kissed my forehead.

My beautiful blonde.

I kissed his lips.

⫸ Chapter 35 ⫷

"Would you all come to the library when you're finished?" I dried the last espresso cup as Donata put away the knives. Lucio still sat at the long farm table chatting with us as we cleared breakfast.

Ben smiled at me. He knew. "Come. Come, Mama." He bustled her from the kitchen and I hung back, wanting Lucio to follow them first.

As I trailed behind, the light from the library poured into the hallway. It was perfect, soft and yellow. I glanced up at the ceiling mural. That work was complete—I only needed time to varnish it.

A gasp brought my head back down as I reached the threshold to the library.

Donata's hand was clamped across her mouth. I couldn't tell if the portrait before us upset or delighted her.

"What do you think?" Ben asked.

Donata kept her hand on her mouth and then, with a small shake of her head, fled the room.

My eyes flashed to Ben. His widened with no answers. I turned my gaze to Lucio and saw tears in his eyes.

"Is it wrong?"

Lucio took a step and pulled me, first my hands,

then by my shoulders, until I was folded tight against him. "It is perfect. What a gift you have given me. It is exactly how I want to be remembered."

He held me for a long moment, then stepped back and clasped my hands again. He raised them and kissed my knuckles. "You are such a blessing. Thank you. I will now go find my beautiful wife." He walked slowly from the room.

"It's okay?"

Ben stepped to the painting. "More than okay." He scrubbed at his chin, the gesture I recognized as something he did when he couldn't find words.

"I think I upset your mom."

"Because she will lose him. But this . . ." He tapped the edge of the portrait. "He is here. I can feel it in the eyes. You always said they were impossible for you." He faced me. "How did you do it?"

"Something has changed. I . . . I wanted it for him, not for me. I didn't even think, really." I laughed that the one aspect of painting that had always eluded me, eluded me still because I had no idea what I'd done to achieve it or how to replicate it. I'd found the windows to the soul. But had I left a path to follow? "I simply focused on him."

I crossed to the other side of the room, where I'd stacked a few more canvases in the corner. "I was going to show them these as well, but maybe another time." I spun around another portrait of Lucio and one of Donata.

Ben barked out a quick laugh. "You captured her too. There is fire in those eyes. It burns kind, most of the time, but it does burn."

I smiled. He was right. I had captured Donata's essence in her eyes. Again, I hadn't thought about it; I hadn't reached for it. It almost felt as if I'd reached beyond it and landed there.

Ben's voice cut through my thoughts. "Do you have other sketches? Paintings?"

"Lots."

Ben studied his father's portrait. "That show you wanted so much? It could be yours now."

"Do you think? Should I send Olivia Barton the pictures?"

"Right away." He pulled me close. "What have you to lose?"

⫸ Chapter 36 ⫷

Another week passed, and bit by bit the scene became a story. The qualities of hostility, pain, and betrayal that Joseph had conveyed through paint, brushstrokes, and sheer brilliance astounded me. I finally dropped the last of the cotton batting into my bucket.

I stretched and, rather than yell, crossed the church to tap on Father Matt's office door. At his call I pushed it open a crack. "I'm finished."

"I thought it'd be today. I was waiting."

"Come on."

I led him back to the transept. Evening was approaching, and the light only hit the highest windows of the church. I'd twisted my lamp so that it shone directly on the mural's focal point—a woman, staring at the viewer in a three-quarters turn, only one eye visible. But what an eye! What emotion Joseph had captured—deep stress, fear, and even a flash of defiant anger as her body angled to the mob above her.

"You've been so busy the past couple days, we haven't talked about it. I think they're about to kill her." I reached up to touch the faces. "It's so powerful. Look at this man. You can feel his intake of breath after a scream—angry and murderous. Maybe Don Pietro ordered it covered because they're going to kill her. It's horrible in some ways."

"Is this it?" Father Matt scanned the mural from window to corner. "There's nothing more?"

"I cleaned the entire wall. Why?"

"Because it's not finished. This isn't the story. Not the end. It is a mob, yes, but no one dies. They walk away in peace. Calm. No stone thrown."

"They walk away? Is it a Bible story? I think you must have the wrong one."

"There is only one. This is very clear . . . But not

to finish it? What did Joseph mean?" Father Matt stood still, and I couldn't tell if he was speaking to me or to himself. "You find it in the gospel of John. The scribes and Pharisees bring an adulteress to Jesus, to trick him with the law and force him to condemn her. Instead, he stoops down, twice, to write in the sand of the temple floor. The accusers go away, stones and all, without another word. They leave in silence. Jesus then tells the woman to go and sin no more."

"What did he write?"

Father Matt flicked me the smallest glance before returning to the mural. I couldn't blame him; it was mesmerizing. Disturbing, but spectacular.

He continued. "Scholars have debated that for centuries. What matters is that he offered her, and them if they had not walked away, grace. He would have forgiven them as he forgave her. That is the story. The whole story. Grace."

"Where is He then?"

Father Matt pushed up his glasses. "Exactly. He is not there. Joseph has left the story out of the story. He has not painted the true focal point. He has twisted it."

"Were they angry because she was pregnant?"

"She was not pregnant."

"She is here." I stepped to the painting. "Look at the fabric here and her hands. One balances her on the ground, but the other holds her stomach. In art, and in life, that's usually what that signifies."

"I wonder . . ." He didn't finish his sentence. "Cover it with the tarp for now. It is time to talk to Lucio."

"Lucio asked me not to say anything, but I feel I need to tell Ben. There's something about this. We were talking about that summer, the summer Joseph left, and this is part of it. It was a really painful time for their family."

"I can see why." Father Matt's dark tone confused me. "I will call and ask Lucio to come now. Please go see Ben."

I'd meant I'd talk to Ben tonight. But clearly something had upset Father Matt, and he meant right this minute.

He has not painted the true focal point. He has twisted it.

A returning sense of dread engulfed me as I wandered down the hill to Coccocino. It was early, but the restaurant was already bursting with activity. Tourists ate earlier than Italians.

I walked through the courtyard, listening to all the languages bounce off the stone walls. I passed through the dining room and into the kitchen.

"Emily!" Noemi called across the counter.

"You're better?" She had been out with a cold, stretching Ben all the thinner because of it.

"It was horrible; I couldn't shake it. How are you?"

"I'm fine. Is Ben around?"

She tilted her head, confused. "He's at the grill. You passed him."

"I did?" I walked back out. Sure enough, Ben stood at the grill pulling off one of his beloved *bistecca fiorentina*. His brow was furrowed in concentration. Mine felt the same.

I stood and watched a full minute before he glanced up. "Bella? Is all well?"

"I came to talk to you."

After he pulled three steaks from the grill, he stretched over and laid a quick kiss on my lips. "We are busy tonight. I have no time to talk."

"It won't take long. May I sit at the bar?"

That brought a smile and a nod. "Ask Luigi to fix you a Spritz."

A moment later Ben perched on the stool next to me. "Okay. I have *un momento*. Spill your beans."

I couldn't help but smile, and I couldn't bring myself to correct him. "What do you mean?"

"Do you think I can spend all this time at night talking with you and not know your voice? Something is very wrong. Tell me."

In that moment, I didn't feel alone. I was tempted to savor it, linger here . . .

"I haven't just been working on the paintings at the church. I've also been uncovering a mural that Joseph painted that last summer. Your father asked me to do it . . . and to not tell anyone."

"Does Don Matteo know?"

A small laugh escaped. "There's no way he

couldn't. It's about twelve by twelve feet. It's huge."

"Joseph painted it?"

I pulled back, a little surprised. "Do you really know nothing about this? It had to have taken your brother months."

Ben raked his hand through his hair and shrugged. "I told you, I got sent down to Anne's. And then Joseph was gone and . . . When my family is silent, it is not good."

"Well . . . I finished uncovering it today, and it wasn't what I expected. It's a story, from the Bible."

"How is that surprising? It is in a church."

"True, but it's an angry, violent scene. No hope or light in this thing at all. And Father Matt says that the murder—that's what the mob's about to do, kill a woman—doesn't happen. He says Joseph purposely misrepresented the story. Didn't finish it. And he painted the woman pregnant, which was also inaccurate, but that he also—"

"Slow." Ben squeezed my knee. "Slow down. What does Papa say now?"

"I just finished it, not ten minutes ago. He hasn't seen it." I leaned forward. "And, Ben, I'm sorry I didn't tell you. Your father asked me not to and I wanted to honor his trust, but—"

"You did right, I think, if that is what he asked." Ben sighed and pushed himself off the stool. "I must get back to the kitchen."

"But—" I slid off the stool as well. "That's why I'm here. Father Matt is calling your parents now. I expect they're on their way."

Ben's eyes widened.

"Let me tell Noemi. I'm coming with you."

He disappeared into the kitchen briefly, and then we walked through the courtyard and started up the hill together.

"Start again from the beginning . . ."

Father Matt stood waiting for us. "Good. Good. You came." He stretched out his hand to Ben. "Your father was anxious to come too. They are on their way." He led us back into the nave. "He doesn't sound well."

"He is not," Ben whispered in reply before his voice resumed its usual tone. "Where is this picture?"

"Come see."

We rounded the corner and Ben stopped. After a few moments, he stepped deeper into the transept to see the entire mural straight on. I watched him scan every inch of the scene's approximate one hundred and fifty square feet.

"You see?" I said. "It's beautiful, but terrible too—"

Anything I was about to say fled as the huge front door scraped against hinges and stone. The sound magnified as it echoed through the church. Anything Ben was about to say morphed into a slow head shake as his mother's voice filled all the empty spaces.

"Why are we here?" It was sharp and cutting. Too loud, too strident for this place of quiet I'd come to enjoy.

Father Matt rushed out to meet them. Ben and I remained in the transept and, for the moment, out of view.

I peeked around the corner. Donata was paler than usual, almost matching Lucio's tones. Her eyes looked completely black. At first I thought she was holding Lucio up. Their arms were tightly linked. But as I stared it became clear—he was supporting her.

Father Matt led them to us. I glanced to Ben, who hadn't moved a muscle.

"What?" I whispered.

He only had time to glance at me before his parents rounded the corner.

Donata's eyes hit me first. "Why did you bring us here?"

I opened my mouth but no sound came. I looked to Lucio. His eyes were soft, but not focused on me. He was watching his wife.

Without waiting for me to find a reply, Donata faced the mural. She studied it, then stepped toward it. She reached up and touched the woman's face.

"*Dopo tanti anni, non è mai va via.*" Her voice was low and felt heavy, filled with heartbreak and something darker. It took me a moment to name it—despair.

"That's not true." Lucio stepped forward and put his arm around her shoulders. He spoke English, slowly and with great care. "It has gone away. This is in the past."

"Not for him. Or for me." She ground out the words, in English now as well, and withdrew her hand from the mural. She held her fingers to her lips. "Never."

Her spine stiffened, and I could see her shoulder blades drop down her back beneath her white blouse. She seemed to grow before me as she spun around. "How did you find this? How did you know? Why?"

"Donata," Lucio whispered. "This is not her fault. I asked her to do this."

Any remaining color drained from her face as her body slumped away from Lucio. "You told her?"

"No." Lucio reached out, but she stepped away. "I asked her to uncover the mural. You, we, need to see it, to face it. And she is skilled, like Joseph."

"Like Joseph." Donata repeated in a soft whisper, eyes on the stone floor.

We stood in paralyzed silence until she lifted her head and locked eyes on me. "Would you do what my son did? Which stone would you throw?"

"I . . . I don't understand."

She turned to the mural and ran her hand, almost lovingly, across the woman. "You did not see me? How could you not? I am here for all to see."

I heard Ben's sharp intake of breath; it matched my own.

But it was Lucio who spoke. "Father, could you tell Donata what you told me on the phone?"

All eyes turned to Father Matt. His eyes clouded in confusion. "You mean about the story not being over yet?" At Lucio's nod, he sighed, warming to his topic. "Joseph didn't finish—"

"No," Donata called out. "There can be no more. How long must I pay?"

"That's not what—" Father Matt stopped.

There was no reason to continue. Donata had fled, her feet making a soft scuffling noise as she dashed up the center aisle and out the door.

Lucio faced the three of us. After a moment he said, *"Mi dispiace." I'm sorry.* And he followed his wife from the church.

≫ Chapter 37 ≪

Ben and I returned to the restaurant. There was much to say, but neither of us spoke until we reached the turn to Coccocino.

"Do you want to wait for me?" He squeezed me tight.

"Do you mind? I want to give them space. You

can send food out to the bar like you used to in Atlanta."

"Only the best dishes." I could hear his smile.

As we entered Coccocino's small courtyard, I pulled him back. "Are you piecing it together now?"

"It all makes sense. You said it yourself, I look like Joseph and Papa, but they don't look like each other. And her fear makes sense too. I wonder about Maria, Vito, all Mama's family. It must have been . . . significant."

"Will she forgive me?"

"Will you forgive him?" Ben looked to the restaurant. "Papa is at his end, Bella, and I understand wanting to set things right, bring wholeness. But he hurt you. He put you where you should not be and I . . . I am having trouble with that."

I reached up and kissed his cheek.

He nodded and slid his hand down my arm to grasp my hand. "Come inside. I will feed you."

Hours later and well fed, I retreated to the dark stillness of Coccocino's courtyard to check e-mails and wait for Ben to emerge.

Dear Emily,

The photos you sent are staggering. Pictures never convey a piece's full potential, so I'm anxious to see your work firsthand—it is alive, daring, and yet so warm. You have a gift for translating the essence of a soul. The elderly man—touching and markedly different, yet recognizable in each of your three treatments—constitutes your focal point. The woman—I need to meet her. I feel the sting of her lectures in my ears.

A new artist, Ron Stratton, has underdelivered for his upcoming show. I have half a gallery available and no paintings. While I dislike dissipating the power of a solo show, I truly believe your work will complement Stratton's more austere ascetic. The interplay could be both dynamic and quantifiable. I can offer approximately eight hundred square feet of hanging space, the entire right portion of the gallery.

Let me know your color preferences and requests in your reply. We'll need to move quickly. I open Stratton—and you—on August 15.

Talk soon . . .
Olivia

"Hey." Ben laid his hand on my hair. "I would have missed you without your phone light." He looked up to the black sky. "No moon tonight."

I tapped it off and stood. "It was an e-mail from

Olivia Barton. I got a show at her gallery, if I want it."

"Congratulations." He pulled me into a hug, but his voice and heart weren't in it. Neither were mine. "Will you take it?"

"I'd like to, someday." I shrugged. "But as you say, now is not the time."

"I was off all night in there." He glanced back to Coccocino's now dark doorway.

"None of it has left my mind either." I pressed into his side. "Do you think they're asleep?"

We stepped out into the small parking lot.

"I hope so. I want to let this settle before talking more." He glanced to my Vespa and gently nudged me away from it. "Let us leave your Vespa here and go home together. It is late."

As we neared the final feet to the house, Ben lifted his foot from the accelerator. No stone kicked up. No screech of the tires. We crept to the door on a slow roll.

We let ourselves in and shut the front door softly, and were met in the dark by a voice.

"I'm sorry."

I closed my eyes. I was tempted to take two steps to the stairs and let them talk. But before I could move, Ben's arm reached around my shoulders.

"Will you come to the kitchen? I made tea."

"*Sì*." Ben replied for us, but I stepped forward first.

Lucio clearly had been sitting at the kitchen table for a long time. There was a crumpled newspaper, the tin of tea, and the espresso machine's knock box—as if crossing the kitchen to empty the tea strainer for fresh leaves had been too arduous. There was even a small plate of nibbles. He gestured to the two spare cups.

He'd only turned on a small light by the stove, so we sat in semidarkness. The light caught only one side of his face such that every line was visible, the bags under his eye, the sagging around his chin and neck. He'd aged within a single evening.

"Please forgive me. I'm deeply sorry." He poured as we sat, and when he handed me my cup, he wrapped his hands around mine. "I have one great regret in my life, and in my haste, I tried to fix it in the wrong way. I should have told you both about the mural. You, Ben, long ago." He pressed his hands into mine. "And I should have told Donata that I asked you to uncover it."

"It is time to tell us everything. No more secrets." Ben's head dropped forward as if too heavy to hold up.

"I know. It needs to end. Joseph needs to come home. Now."

"Papa . . ." Ben's whispered reply told me, and Lucio, that he understood what wasn't being said.

"Donata's parents disowned her when she became pregnant. It sounds so old-fashioned, but

329

it still happens today in many small villages. It was a shame her family condemned, and they abandoned her." He waved his hand as if rolling time along. "She made her way to Montevello and walked into Coccocino, so clearly alone and lost, and started making pasta. She barely spoke to me beyond telling me she needed a job. We fell into working together that first morning, and I was in love with her by the next. It took time, but she soon told me everything. She was brave, and so wounded . . . Still is in many ways."

Lucio caught himself as if he'd meant to keep the last words inside his head. He continued. "I wooed her, day in and day out, until she agreed to marry me. I suspected she thought I was motivated by pity, but I wasn't. From our first moment, I only ever felt love for your mother."

"How have I never heard this? Here?" Ben flicked his head to the front door. The village was outside that door—the village in which everyone knew everything, almost before it happened.

"They all knew." Lucio gave a short, affectionate laugh. "And marrying silenced much of the talk. The men respected that . . . The women? They respected Nonna. Nonna was formidable and deeply loved. She declared your mama family and made it clear that children are innocents, to be cherished and protected. You remember Nonna."

"She was a force."

"Everyone loved her. Everyone obeyed her."

Lucio chuckled, then sobered. "We were wed before Joseph was born, and that was the end of it. He was my son. He is my son."

Lucio leaned back and rubbed his chin. The gesture so similar to Ben's that I couldn't help glancing to him. Ben's eyes held a sad look of understanding, as if his entire childhood was coming into focus.

"That night at Coccocino, Joseph found a letter from Donata's father. She always kept it close. She had written to him about our marriage and Joseph's birth. And he had replied . . . with great cruelty. I have never asked her why she kept that letter, even keeps it now. Mortification? Penance? And then when her father died, her family reached out, through Maria, and Donata refused them. I think by that time she believed her father, even agreed with him."

"That she could not see her family?"

"That she was beyond forgiveness, receiving it or giving it. She could no longer bend. The wound cut too deep."

Too deep to rip away. Ben's words returned to me. He'd been talking of Alessandro, but even when he'd said them they'd reminded me of someone else, of something else. They'd reminded me of Katharina from *The Taming of the Shrew*; they'd reminded me of Donata and even of myself—reacting in the same ways we'd always reacted because we didn't or couldn't see another way. Perhaps we'd cracked too far or not enough to let in something new, something different and unexpected.

Lucio stopped tracing a line in the wood tables and held his hands still. "Joseph is so like her. That letter, something that did not change his reality, changed everything. I suspect he always sensed her fear, even if he did not understand it, and then the fear became him." He caught Ben's eyes. "Do you remember that night?"

Ben nodded. He remembered.

"He went a little crazy in his anger and was arrested. Don Pietro stepped in and offered to hire him, take him on. If not, Joseph would have gone to jail. So he worked at the church and then he painted the mural, every day. He was like water freezing, clear and hard, beautiful in its strength."

"Why did you send me to Anne's house?"

"I wanted to protect you and your mother. Her shame was so deep." Lucio shook his head. "And no one knew what Joseph was painting."

"How could you not know?" Ben whispered.

"We gave him the privacy he requested. He painted at night, and we were delighted that he was working. Don Pietro believed creative work was good work, forgiving work." Lucio spread his palms across the table. "But you've seen it. A masterpiece of hate. Donata ran away."

Ben's head shot up again. "I remember that.

You asked Uncle Vincenzo to keep me longer."

"Mama went to Florence to stay with friends, just as Francesca did with Martine." Lucio offered a small smile. "That was why she became so angry with her . . . We don't change, do we, son? Even across the generations."

Before Ben could reply, Lucio continued. "While she was gone, I asked Don Pietro and Alberto to cover it. I wanted her to forget it ever existed. I wanted Joseph to forget too. I denied him his pain. It was as if I told him that it didn't matter; he didn't matter. And I denied Donata her healing, as if that didn't matter either."

"And here we are," Ben whispered.

"Yes, here we are."

"How is Donata now?" I asked the question.

"As I said, she is like her firstborn son." He let a rueful sigh escape. "Sensitive. I asked her for forgiveness, and I expect she will get back to me soon." Lucio sat back and fixed his gaze on Ben. "I need to tell you something else. I called Joseph tonight. He's coming home."

Ben shook his head.

"It is time, and somehow, in some way, he needs to stay." Lucio tapped at his heart. "In here, he needs to stay."

"Papa . . ." Again, Ben's one word encompassed all that needed to be said.

⇒ Chapter 38 ⇐

Joseph exited the airport in a linen shirt and twill pants. He'd traveled ten hours. Me? One. And he looked more cool and fresh. But perhaps I'd had less sleep and the more frenetic morning.

I'd insisted Ben let me come alone. Francesca had obligations at camp, but as soon as those ended she wanted to be with her father. Ben wanted the same. Although Noemi said she could handle Coccocino, Ben started the day racing back and forth.

This was the only way I could help—and stay out of the way. So I'd woken early, climbed into Ben's tiny car, scraped across the gears, lurched down the road, and merged onto the freeway. The most terrifying part had been exiting on the edge of Florence and making my way through the chaos of winding roads and traffic to the airport. I almost died twice and got yelled at three times before I finally pulled the car up to the arrivals curb, drenched and shredded.

I jumped out of the car at Joseph's approach.

After looking around and confirming that I was alone, he lifted his chin in greeting and kissed both my cheeks. "You're my advance team?"

"Everyone wanted to come, but Lucio . . . your father . . . They wanted to be with him too."

Joseph didn't reply. He simply dropped his leather duffel into the trunk and circled to the passenger door.

I chased after him. "Oh no you don't. You're driving."

He laughed and backpedaled. "Ben is as bad as you. Where do you people buy these dreadful cars?"

I heard myself defending the little beast. "It's a perfectly fine car; it does exactly what it needs to. It's the roads that are terrifying."

As we drove out of the airport, Joseph took a detour. The morning sun still cast a rose haze over the city, made all the more distinct as it bounced off the terra-cotta tiled roofs. In the near distance I could see the Duomo tower above us—nothing could touch it in presence or splendor.

Joseph tapped his window as we passed the Basilica di San Lorezo.

"I had no idea . . ." The Basilica was huge, a massive, heavy structure of brick and stone that spread across a city block.

He slammed on the brakes and pulled to the curb. "You haven't been here? How is that possible?"

"We've been busy."

He lifted a brow. "Yes, I've heard."

"Don't start."

His eyes softened as he gestured back out his window. "It's not as delicate as Il Duomo, but it's my favorite. Consecrated in 393; I find comfort in that longevity, that solidity. And Michelangelo's Laurentian Library is in there— an absolute marvel." He pulled away from the curb and darted back into traffic. "Come on. Let's take a tour. If you think this is good . . ." He zipped down a side street, which opened into a plaza and . . .

"Cattedrale di Santa Maria del Fiore." I let the words roll off my tongue, savoring the sight.

Joseph sent me a smile. "Il Duomo di Firenze. Nine hundred years old and remains the city's crowning jewel. Giotto's bell tower, to your left, is worth the climb. A friend handles restoration for the cathedral; I'll give you his name, he can take you up after-hours." I felt him glance my way. "And show you the restoration labs."

"I'd love that. It's all exquisite." I craned my neck to keep the cathedral and her bell tower in sight as Joseph darted around the next corner.

"Now over here, you'll—"

I gripped his forearm. "I can't tell you how much I want to see all this, but I was given one job—to bring you home."

"That's the Ponte Vecchio." He pointed out my window. The sun cast a perfect replica of the bridge's shops upon the mirror-smooth surface of the Arno below it. "Don't worry; this is the way out of the city."

"Thank you." I sank into my seat.

"I can't believe Ben hasn't brought you to Florence yet or you haven't stolen away yourself. There really is no excuse."

"If you'd been around these past weeks, you'd understand." I absorbed my own words and their biting delivery. "I didn't mean it like that. I just meant it's been a busy, tense time."

Joseph sped up a hill, took a sharp right, and we were on the highway. I turned my head to my window and focused on the scenery. It seemed the safest plan.

It took a good thirty minutes for him to break the silence. "Your questions are deafening."

"I haven't asked one."

"I noticed. At first I think you were scared, but about ten kilometers ago you grew angry, and you're remarkably loud about it, so just ask." He glanced over at me and smirked. "You've huffed three times and sighed five."

I obeyed. "Why'd you paint it?"

"The truth?"

"Please. Because I can't figure it out. I get anger, believe me, but that was more than anger. Your father—your real father, Lucio—fell in love with your mother. You had, have, a wonderful family. You found a letter. I understand being upset, they lied to you, but you have a family that loves you—even I sensed that within days of being with them. Your absence is like an open wound. And that painting—which is spectacular, by the way—and an almost twenty-year exile—it's extreme. How long are you going to punish her?" I watched him, a new idea forming. "Or are you punishing yourself?"

"So you know, then?"

"Know what?"

"How I feel? How I *should* feel?" His voice had arced; now it dropped with disdain. "How I should have absorbed the realization that my mother's sadness, anger, depression, gripping fears—they are all about me. I am the embodiment of all she hates, about herself and her life. Looking at me each and every day kept her shame and her family's betrayal fresh, salt to that wound. And Papa? He chose to pretend and return to his bread and his books, his quiet comforts, rather than help me. You would know how to handle that? Each lie? Each daily deceit?"

"But hasn't it all gone on long enough?"

"Don't, Emily. Don't act like there was a whole that somehow broke, that I'm some object that merely needs a little glue, some drying time, and heat to cure before you can set me back on the shelf. Some things do not get restored, because they were never whole."

"But they can be if . . ." My next words evaporated. Lucio was right, it did feel good to fix things. But not here, not now. I had nothing to offer. "Fair enough."

Joseph exited the highway in a sharp turn and climbed the hill to Panzano.

I sat silent for a minute, thinking of Lucio and all he was trying to fix too. I couldn't help but appreciate the irony. Despite many members treating me like an outsider, I really did fit well within this family.

"What?" Joseph flicked me a glance.

"Nothing."

"You snorted."

"Sorry. I was just . . . It doesn't matter." I took a breath and started over. "Your father's dying, Joseph."

"That's why I'm here." The words came with the soft finality of a sigh.

As he navigated our way through the tiny hilltop town, minus a good wall, we remained silent, but as the road opened before us with a smooth, winding, downhill expanse, he glanced toward me again. "How is Mama?"

"Hurt. Scared, I think. I look in her eyes and I think disliking me helps her right now. Anger is the easiest of all emotions, really."

"True. But I'm sorry, for your sake."

He drove the final slope around the base of Montevello and into the valley beyond, turning at his parents' gravel road. He slid to a quick stop at the front door and, without another word, pulled the keys from the ignition, tossed them to me, and grabbed his bag from the trunk.

Joseph's homecoming was a full village affair. Everyone wanted to know what he'd been up to, how long he was staying, how he had stayed so young and handsome, when he was coming home for good . . .

The questions went on and on, and soon that slightly warm Joseph I'd seen glimpses of in Atlanta completely disappeared and a hard, fixed mask dropped firmly in place—as if each question, touch, and hug stung him. Rather than embrace them or even endure them, he retreated.

"Warm Joseph" reappeared slowly, late in the night. Only when extended family left did his eyes soften and a hint of a smile return to his lips. Ben and I cleared plates and glasses from throughout the house, enjoying the bits of laughter we caught from Joseph and Francesca as they cleaned the kitchen. Donata, hovering about him, but rarely in sight, soon went upstairs to be with Lucio. The four of us found our way to the back patio.

There the siblings began their stories. They started with tales of early childhood, then, as the candles burned low, moved to the lessons and memories of their teenage years.

"Do you remember when Papa took your door off its hinges to teach you not to slam it?" Ben poked Joseph's arm.

"How could I forget? He lost the bolts and Tito had to forge new ones. I grew so tired of that . . . All those lessons, then he'd forget what he wanted to teach and start something new."

"I always thought he did that on purpose." Francesca sighed. "He'd give me some book and then leave it, as if I was supposed to figure it out on my own. Usually I got it wrong, so I'd have to begin again."

Joseph reached out to his sister and whispered, "He got it wrong sometimes, too, Francesca. Don't take it all on."

"But he listened, you know? I'm going to miss that." Francesca hugged her arms around her shoulders.

"Me too." Ben rubbed at his chin.

"But then he'd try to fix it. How can you two not remember that?" Joseph faced his sister. "It didn't matter if you understood his lesson if you disagreed with him. If you missed his point, you got another. Again and again, until he fixed your thinking and you saw things the way he did, whether you wanted to or not. I don't think he ever listened, really listened. He used the time to prepare his next lesson."

"Joseph . . . ," Ben warned softly.

"I'm not saying it was bad. I love him. I'm simply saying to see him clearly." Joseph shook his head slowly. "That's all." He tilted his head up and watched the stars.

"What makes you think *you* see him clearly?"

It was the first time I'd ever heard true challenge in Ben's voice.

"I'm sure I don't," Joseph conceded.

Francesca stood, and I got the impression she wanted to cry. "I should head home." She glanced at Ben. "Will you call me if . . . I mean, he was waiting, right? And now that Joseph is home . . ." Her voice dwindled.

Ben nodded. Joseph looked away.

"Do you want to stay, Francesca?" I reached up to touch her hand. "I cleared my paints from your room. I thought maybe you'd want to."

"Yes." She squeezed my hand. "I'll bring some stuff by tomorrow. Thank you."

The next three days passed in a kind of half light, half world. The house was quiet. We were waiting and we knew it, but we couldn't discuss it. It would make it too real.

In the mornings I finished the Stations of the Cross paintings at the church, walking by the covered mural without glancing its direction or ever lifting the tarp. I noticed Father Matt did the same. We, too, were waiting, but for what we couldn't say.

I met Ben every afternoon at Coccocino. He'd hop on my Vespa and drive us home for his few hours' break between prep and service. We'd sit with his father or, if he was sleeping, with any family who happened to be around.

We chatted in soft voices. They told stories. I listened. But Ben had quit insisting on the family speaking English. Some moments required Italian.

Then he'd drive us back to Coccocino. I'd sit behind him with my arms wrapped around his waist and, in that warm, short drive, I could almost imagine this was the Italian paradise of my dreams. Almost.

"Are you okay?" I lowered my feet as Ben climbed off the Vespa.

"No." He stood next to me but looked over my head, beyond me, toward Coccocino's arched doorway. "Nothing feels right. It feels . . . it feels like it never will be."

I didn't reply; I couldn't. He was right. It felt like the world had tipped and nothing could right it, fix it, again.

I turned the Vespa around and headed out of the town's arch and onto the winding road down into the valley. I drove even more slowly than usual, but it was quieter than usual, as though everyone else was slowing down and waiting too. The height of tourist season, yet not a single car passed me.

Not ready to return home, I kept on, past the driveway up a new and unexplored road. I breathed in the evening sights and smells—sunbaked earth and stone, the dust kicking up on the dirt road, the bumps of rocks that had probably sat there since some Roman had found himself too tired to clear them—and let them soothe my soul. There was something about the land that did that to me. It invited me to stop struggling and rest.

A flash of black dancing in yellow caught my eye, and I pulled the Vespa over. *How . . . ?* The field of sunflowers faced me. Every single yellow-petaled, black-centered, stiff-stalked flower stared right at me—for the very first time.

"Aren't you all pretty? Finally decided to share yourselves, huh?" I sat for a few minutes, snapped a few pictures, then slowly turned the Vespa around.

When I entered the house I heard a soft "Emily?" drift down.

I trudged up the steps to the landing and poked my head into Lucio's room. He was propped up in bed—just as we'd left him not an hour before.

He flapped his hand at me, as if he had only the energy to move the wrist, and the rest swung on momentum. "Is Ben back at work?"

"He is, but he's not happy about it." I sat on the corner of the bed. "He'd rather be here."

"Work is good. We're just waiting, aren't we?"

"Don't say that."

Lucio fixed his gaze on the window. "I have a favor to ask." He let his sentence sit, and the silence gave it weight.

I began to dread what might come next.

"Don't paint over the mural."

I wrapped my arms around my shoulders and pulled at my shoulder blades as if trying to split myself apart, or make myself tight and small. I wasn't sure which. I just knew I couldn't grant this favor. "I need to paint over it, and soon. Uncovering it only brought pain. You must see that, and now is not the time—"

He cut me off. "Emily, no. Covering it in the first place was the mistake. Donata never needed me to fix her pain. She needed me to share it. I never . . . I never did that well. You . . . you can let the story unfold."

"It's taken a turn for the worse."

"Don't all stories do that, before the beautiful ending?"

I slumped. "But it's not a story, Lucio. You must see that; it's your lives."

"That is where you are wrong. They are one and the same. I missed that they are meant to be shared." He reached for my hand, which was resting on the quilt between us. "Wait six months. If you and Don Matteo agree to paint over it then, you may."

"And if you disagree?"

"My darling daughter, I won't be here to protest."

≫ Chapter 39 ≪

I sat in the library reading. I had long since finished *The Flanders Panel* and, other than being thoroughly annoyed that the conservator smoked like a chimney while trying to restore a painting, in a dust-filled room no less, I loved it.

I was now on to Lucio's latest selection, Joyce's *A Portrait of the Artist as a Young Man*. This one was hard for me. I had nothing in common with this young boy, becoming a man. It was a chaotic narrative that I failed to grasp, jumping through time and full of angst, religion, nannies, and prostitutes. And yet, I had to concede, my own thoughts, efforts, and concerns often felt as tortuous and weighted. The need to reach wholeness and clarity overwhelmed young Stephen Dedalus. It overwhelmed me.

Francesca, who had moved back into her room a few days before, opened the door and interrupted me.

"You need to call Ben."

That was all she said, but nothing more was needed. I nodded and tapped my phone. He answered on the first ring.

"I'm sorry to call."

"I am on my way."

I laid down my book, unsure what to do. I

knew where everyone was, upstairs in Lucio and Donata's bedroom. When Lucio hadn't woken that afternoon during Ben's break, we knew. He had slept all yesterday. All night. His face was paler, his breathing more shallow.

Dario, their family doctor and distant cousin, had been in and out of the house more times than I could count in the past two days. Ben dashed back and forth between his father and his father's life's work. Joseph hovered. Francesca read in the chair by his bed. Donata cooked. I hid in the library.

We were prepared to be completely unprepared.

I walked outside and waited on the gravel drive for Ben. Soon dust flew up along the tree line.

He leapt from the car and, rather than walk straight into the house, pulled me into a hug and stood there for a few heartbeats. Then he nodded into my shoulder, and we walked hand in hand into the house and up the stairs.

Donata sat at the side of the bed, Francesca next to her with an arm draped around her mother's shoulders. Aunt Sophia and her husband, Lucio's youngest brother, whose name I still didn't know, sat in the armchairs. Joseph perched on the windowsill. His face was perfectly still, a mask, and I knew that even if he wanted to, Joseph had no idea how to cross that room—physically or figuratively.

I reached my hand out to draw him over, one

outsider to another. He shook his head and dug his fingers into the sill.

Ben immediately dropped next to Francesca and reached a hand out to touch his father's leg, a small bump under several blankets.

Donata glanced at him and then returned her gaze to Lucio. She rested her hand on his forehead. *"Ora puoi andare. Siamo tutti qui e ti vogliamo bene."*

I understood, and her words brought tears to my eyes. She loved him and we were here and he could go. She said more, but I could no longer catch her words as she lowered her face to his and whispered against his lips.

Within moments his shallow, rasping breath quieted. Donata tipped over and rested across his now-still chest.

⫸ Chapter 40 ⫷

The next morning I woke early to bring coffee back to Ben. He'd barely slept. Neither of us had.

Considering I'd crept down the stairs before dawn, I expected the kitchen to be empty. Instead, I found myself in a sea of black. Already there was no room to breathe. Women in long skirts, thin cotton shawls over black blouses, loose and light in preparation for a hot day, filled all the space between the dining room to the back patio.

Men in black pants and dark shirts, T-shirts, broadcloth, or oxfords—all black—filled every other room. I hadn't known. I'd thrown on a printed blouse and simple beige cotton skirt because I thought we'd be alone, that the day would move slowly and we'd all have a moment to adjust.

I pulled two espresso shots and raced back upstairs. Ben was pulling on a black shirt. Without saying a word, I put the cups on the dresser and pulled him into a tight hug.

As we stepped apart, I gave him the lay of the land. "The house is full down there already and everyone's in black."

"*Sì.*"

I pulled the covers over the bed, hastily making it. "What am I to do? I don't have any black. I don't want to embarrass your family."

"It does not matter." He looked me over without expression. "Ask Mama or Francesca if you want something, but you look fine." He squeezed my arm and gave me a quick kiss on the top of my head. "You do, I promise."

"Okay." I nodded simply to end the conversation, not because I agreed.

Ben downed his espresso, then twisted the doorknob. "Are you ready?"

Again I only nodded.

I couldn't bring myself to ask Donata or Francesca for something black. This was not the time for them to worry about my wardrobe. So I skirted the gathering, as I usually did, and hoped no one would notice me.

It was clear that all the details had already been arranged. From snippets of conversation I learned the funeral had a time and location, a hearse ordered, flowers organized. It felt as if not only details had been arranged in advance, but everyone knew their role and fulfilled it before anyone thought to ask.

Now it was time to talk, remember, and eat— the dining room and kitchen overflowed with food, and the glorious and colorful display felt almost obscene. Red tomatoes sat against bright white fresh mozzarella, and that lay beneath bold green basil leaves; beef rolls in a thick red *pomodoro* sauce; fresh pasta dishes, some cold, some hot; and bread . . . *Panina gialla aretina, Bozza pratese, Ciaccino,* and *Ficattola.*

Lucio had taught me the names one day while we sat in the library—me sketching his portrait, he telling me stories of baking, Donata, and the trials and tribulations of running Coccocino. Ben had taught me how to recognize all the different varieties, even how to make and mold them. I looked around for him, but he was nowhere to be found. He'd been absorbed by the sea of black.

I soon found myself sneaking off to the library.

The room was cool, shaded and empty. The wood shutters were almost fully pulled across the windows. I already missed the sunshine and my mornings with Lucio.

I shut the door behind me, pulled the shutters open, and sank into my usual chair. Donata's chair. Rather than pick up my sketch pad, I reached for my book. A slam brought me to my feet.

Donata raced across the room and yanked the shutters closed. One squealed on its hinges and another splintered with the force. The sound bounced off all the hard surfaces, even the soft ones.

"I shut these. There is no light now. It is gone." Her English was thick and slow, each consonant getting full attention and all the room's available oxygen.

I certainly wasn't getting any. I slid from the chair and backed away. "I . . . I'm sorry."

"No. I do not want that from you. He is gone and I am where I began. Alone." She looked around the room. "All I had . . . All my life . . ." She dropped into his chair and covered her face with her hands. There was no sobbing, no sound at all. Perfect stillness, and then she raised her head slowly. "I have lost . . . *ogni cosa*."

Everything. I understood. I had ruined everything.

Her voice dropped and her gaze trailed to her fingers. She was kneading them together, her knuckles white with the force. "What did he say? He asked for you. There is more I do not know."

It took only a moment to understand. "I'm not to paint over the mural for six months, if ever."

"He gives it to you." A single tear ran down her cheek. "And me?"

I stared at her.

"Please go."

I couldn't find Ben in the house. People said he was here, then someone would point to another room. "Over there."

Several minutes of frantic searching didn't produce him, but it did my Vespa. I hopped on and sped down the gravel road with no clue where I was headed.

About an hour later Ben found me. I'd pulled the Vespa off to the side of the road and was sitting on a rock watching the sunflowers turn.

"Give them time and they will face you." He walked up behind me.

"I doubt that. They've only done it once, and I don't think I get a second chance." We both knew my answer was illogical.

Ben sat down. As there wasn't room on my rock, he'd dropped to the ground next to it and looked up, his face several inches below mine.

"She blames me. For the mural. And that your dad asked me to leave it."

"She cannot blame you for all that."

"She does, in English too." I didn't turn my head. "She wants me gone, Ben, and I don't blame her. I don't think an apartment in the village is far enough right now." Suddenly I was sad I'd ever mentioned it. When I'd wanted to leave, it was one thing, but knowing that my presence was wounding Donata was another. Illogically it made me want to stay, help . . . do something.

Ben reached up and touched my knee. "She is grieving. She is angry. She acts like she is strong, stronger than Papa, but she never was. She leaned on him, tucked into him right here." He patted his chest at the base of his neck. The precise place I tucked into him. I couldn't help my small smile because I knew how safe Donata must have felt.

I looked back to the thick green backs of the flowers stretching across the field and hill before me. "That doesn't change who she blames, how she feels."

"All the elements were here, simmering for years, long before you arrived." He laid his elbow on his knee and leaned into me. "I understand her better now, after Papa talked to us. She has always been so afraid, but I could never call it that because I did not know. She reminds me of your poppies, that painting you showed me in Atlanta."

"The stems that couldn't bend?"

"You said the wind would break them." Ben kept his eyes trained across the field. "I think Mama broke."

"We need to help her, Ben. Joseph would call me the salt to her wound now."

"That would be unkind of him."

I only shrugged because that didn't mean it wasn't true.

"Maybe, after the funeral, we could go to Atlanta together, stay a couple weeks for that show Olivia offered you. Give Mama time." Ben's voice dropped to a whisper.

"What?"

"Time may be all she needs."

I knew he was wrong, and it almost frightened me that he even suggested it.

Ben, who worked to bring people together, who went to the US to reach his brother, then stayed to help an aunt and uncle he'd never met. Ben, who'd learned to make spectacular pizza to honor his parents, and his craft and his restaurant . . . Ben felt it was best we go?

I glanced down at him. He wasn't looking at me, but across the field. I realized then that he understood. At least I suspected he did. Time wasn't going to help Donata. He was offering it to me. An out. A chance to breathe.

"Maybe that's a good idea."

≫ Chapter 41 ≪

The funeral was to start at ten o'clock, but Santa Maria was packed by nine. Ben left me in the first pew before going through a small door to my left. I hadn't been in this church before, and I soon found myself assessing the paintings and what work they needed—anything to distract.

My eyes kept darting to Lucio, resting in his open casket before the altar. He looked much the same, yet completely different. It was true what they say, all warmth leaves in death. His face was chalky, white, with an odd transparency to his skin. My eyes pricked. I'd never called him Papa, and yet that was how I'd come to think of him. It now felt like I'd withheld something precious from us both.

As people entered, they kissed his forehead or cheek before finding a seat. Although everyone looked the same, dressed in black, the tone felt markedly different from the house. There people had bustled about, and although a palpable sadness hovered, a sense of celebration over Lucio's life permeated the atmosphere. Not here. Here Lucio's loss felt like a crashing tidal wave. Sniffles and an occasional sob echoed off the stones.

Someone tapped my shoulder, and I spun around

to find Father Matt staring at me. "I didn't see you come in."

"You were lost in thought." He squeezed my shoulder and looked past me to the altar. "Lucio called a couple days ago and asked me not to paint over the mural. I gather he asked the same of you."

"He did and I said I wouldn't, but it's a mistake."

"I'm not so sure. Have you prayed about it?"

"No."

"I wondered. Because if you had, we were hearing very different messages." He leaned closer and dropped his voice to a whisper. "I agree with Lucio and feel a peace about it, though I have no idea why. Donata is formidable when angry." He chuckled softly and pressed his fist against his heart. "But I feel it here. The mural must stay, for now."

Speechless, I swung back around.

He tapped me again. "I'm sorry that upsets you."

"She's not angry so much as devastated, and leaving it there is a cruel reminder of her past. It wasn't only the pregnancy. She lost her family, her parents, siblings . . . everything. And I uncovered it for the world to see and judge all over again. She won't forget it—no one will now."

"You did not remind her of something she had forgotten, Emily. She had never forgotten it, covered or not."

When I didn't turn back to him, he tapped me again. "Will you come see me tomorrow?"

I shrugged. "Now that the paintings are finished, even walking into the church feels like a betrayal."

"Walking into church is never a betrayal." He squeezed my shoulder one last time, then retreated through the same small door to my left.

As the music began, Ben reemerged from it, paused at his father's casket, kissed his cheeks, and shut the lid. He escorted his mother inside and then reached for my hand as he sat between us.

I caught few words as Don Giorgio's deep and aging voice broke across the congregation with heartfelt love. It was a full and formal Mass. The priest swung the thurible full of incense at the crucifix and the paschal candle, and at the final commendation, Father Matt incensed Lucio's coffin as well. I'd studied the practice when I'd restored a thurible for a Catholic church in Chicago.

We soon shuffled down the center aisle and out like a row of ants—dark clothes and dark cars. Following the hearse, we trailed a long line deep into the countryside. I'd never ventured far in the direction we headed and realized that I didn't know what lay beyond the farthest hill. I'd painted that very one from Lucio's bedroom window.

We crossed over it and another, and another, before we finally arrived at a cemetery packed with mausoleums. Tucked within the center, and surrounded by flowers, was one for *Vassallo* and *Gagliardi*, Lucio's mother's family.

Don Giorgio spoke a few words in both Italian and Latin, then everyone filed by, laid a quick kiss on their hand, and touched it to the wood.

Cars dispersed, and Ben and I were among the last standing.

"Home?" I asked.

"This is only the beginning." He clasped my hand. "How are you doing?"

I squeezed his tight. "How are you?"

He shook his head but did not reply.

As soon as we crossed the threshold, Ben was again swept into a sea of black. I skirted the tide and, unthinking, made my way to the library. But what had been my warm yellow sanctuary now held Donata's anger—and it felt as real as a living entity, one I could reach out and touch, but would rather avoid.

Today, even though shutters still covered the windows, the double doors stood wide open. I walked straight through the room, out onto the small patio, and into the trees beyond. I wove in and out until I found a path. A little farther on, I found a bench.

A snapped twig swung me around, and I saw Francesca before she saw me.

"What are you doing out here?"

"Alessandro just arrived." She dropped next to me. "I don't feel like facing him today."

"He may want to say he's sorry or offer support. You were . . . are . . . friends."

She tucked her knees under her skirt. "Let me be immature for a sec, then I'll be a big girl and do my duty."

I laughed. "Don't be mature on my account."

She nudged me. "We've lived in the same house lately and I've barely seen you."

"I've been lurking on the edges. I'm not needed close."

"But you're family." She nudged me harder, and I tipped away.

"Debatable . . . I don't feel like family."

"And what does family feel like?" She shot me a quick smile. She didn't expect an answer. Her tone was slightly sarcastic, bold—American—and spot-on.

"No clue."

She laughed. "We probably exhibit a little more than standard dysfunctionality. Did you know Joseph called for a car and is leaving in about an hour?"

"Today?"

Francesca pressed her lips in a firm, straight line, keeping her criticism tucked safely inside.

"I'm sorry . . . Did you hear about the mural?" I hadn't had the courage or the chance to talk to her about it in the past few days.

"I went to the church and saw it yesterday."

"You did?"

"Yes . . . It's amazing. I remember it, you know." She caught my expression and offered a slight nod. "Yeah. Ben was gone, but I was only eight. I was here . . . I was actually with Mama and Papa that evening. Of course I didn't understand the significance, and until Papa told me the story a few days ago I'd forgotten all about it, even about Mama leaving. Now it's all back."

"I am so sorry."

"Why?" She grabbed my arm. "Everything makes sense now. There was so much that was wrong for so long. Mama is so rigid, always has been, and I understand it now. Everyone talks about how Joseph hasn't forgiven her for years for who knows what, but she never forgave herself. She hasn't finished the story any more than he failed to do. I feel like I finally get why it's so hard to be here. Why I sometimes hate it."

Francesca stopped as if remembering the day, and why she was sitting out on a bench, with me. "I shouldn't say all that. Not now. I just wish I'd known why she was always so angry and afraid. I wouldn't have poked at her so . . . I might've actually tried to understand her, even make pasta if that would've helped." She snorted. "Forget that. I still wouldn't have made the pasta." She dropped her head to her hands. "For all Joseph's criticisms, Papa was our glue. I don't know how we'll be without him. No one expected Joseph to stay, but will he come back? How will we ever be a family now?"

"You will. Ben's kinda glue-like." I nudged her. "I think you all sticking together is very important to him."

"It is." Francesca nudged me back. "I'm glad you married my brother. He's a keeper."

When I didn't reply, she bumped my shoulder again. "Hey . . . I agree." I looked back to the house. "What will happen to you and Alessandro?"

"I'll learn to let him go."

"That's my fault. I tried to fix something that wasn't broken."

"It is now." Francesca tried to laugh, perhaps for my sake. "But it will all be okay. We couldn't have gone on much longer like we were, despite the fact I may have wanted to. You do reach moments, you know? Turning points. We were close to one."

"Speaking of turning points." I stretched my back. "I was offered a show in Atlanta, and Ben suggested we both go. Give your mother a break from me."

Francesca shot straight, genuinely surprised. "He did?"

"She's hurting, and lest anyone forget, I am the one who barged into her home, disrupted everything, and then uncovered the mural."

"You have been busy."

"Very."

"But to leave now?" Francesca shook her head. "It doesn't feel . . . I mean, you'd come back, right?"

Now I pulled up, surprised. It hadn't occurred to me that I wouldn't . . . And yet . . . "Of course. It's just for a gallery show. Ben offered up a couple weeks, but we both know that's not possible."

⫷ Chapter 42 ⫸

The next week held much of the same. Each day the house filled with people, with food, with stories and laughter, with tears and drama. I skirted it all, tired of not fitting in and weary of Aunt Sophia's overt humor at my discomfort and Donata's palpable antipathy.

Ben began working more, finally returning full time for service on the fourth night. And Francesca moved back into her apartment. So rather than escaping into the countryside on my scooter, I hid in her room and painted. Ben and I had decided to accept Olivia Barton's offer, and in a week we planned to head back to the States, him for three days, as that was all he felt he could afford away from Coccocino, and me for ten.

But as the day drew close, a black certainty crept over me. I needed to go alone—for myself and for Ben. Each morning when I came down to breakfast, he was already there chatting with his mom. Each afternoon when he joined us during his quiet time between prep and service, she brightened and offered her only smiles of the day.

Donata was drowning. She was tighter, thinner, angrier, and slowly filling with despair. She needed Ben.

Each night he'd pull me close and it would again, for a moment, feel like magic—like the mornings Lucio described as he fell in love with Donata at Coccocino. Like our own nights in Atlanta when we'd stay up talking, holding hands, flicking paint on each other—not able to say enough, share enough, get close enough. Like the nights only weeks ago, when Ben would hold me close and we'd share our days, laughing about Lucio's latest literary lesson or Donata's best passive-aggressive barb. We were on the same side, and sharing it all made it sweeter and more golden. But not now. I couldn't say if it was me or him—I just knew the magic was gone.

The night before our trip, he still hadn't packed. He came home at one in the morning and, like his father so many nights ago, I stood waiting in the front hall.

"Can we talk?"

"Bella? You scared me. Why are you awake?"

"I couldn't sleep." I led him back to the kitchen.

I smiled when I looked down at the table. So like Lucio and I hadn't realized it—the table now showed evidence of my long waiting night: the tea tin, a small plate of food, a book, and the espresso machine's knock box—because it really was too far to the bin to dump the cold tea leaves.

I sat down and passed a cup between my hands. Ben sat across from me. "Emily?"

"I don't think you should come to Atlanta with me tomorrow."

"Why?"

His tone surprised me. He wasn't questioning the fact, just my reasoning—as if he already had his own.

"Because you're needed here. Even three days, and that's not counting travel, is too long."

"You are my wife."

The declaration almost made me smile. I knew he meant *I go where you go,* but it fell flat to my ears. He might have said *You are a cheese sandwich* and it would've evoked the same emotion. I needed to be out from under the pressure, and taking Ben away from Coccocino and Donata simply added more pressure.

"I'll be back soon." I looked up. "Please let me do this. Let me go, and then I'll be back. You do what you need to do and I'll do the same."

"What does that mean?"

"It means I need a break. I . . . I think I've been trying to pretend I'm someone I'm not—a member of this family." I waved my hands around the kitchen. "But all I do is knock into things, and right now is not the time to be knocking into things. I feel like if I get back to what I know, being who I know, then this will all sort itself out."

Ben reached for my hands and stilled them around the cup. "What are you talking about?"

"I'm talking about being comfortable, understanding how things work, fit together. You say I like puzzles, and I do—but this is not one that fits for me and it clearly doesn't fit for Donata, and she's the more important one right now. Please. I just need to go—"

I stopped. There was an unexpected tinge within my voice, an irritation, a burr—anger. From Ben's expression, I knew it surprised him too. His eyes widened, then softened, then dimmed.

"You have decided."

"Yes."

He wiped a thumb under my eye. "Has it been that bad?"

"Don't ask that. You know it hasn't." I scrunched my nose to stopper my emotions. We were going off script . . . I took a deep breath and said what I'd rehearsed, all that I'd meant to say in the first place. "Let me head back for a few days and see this show through in Atlanta. I committed to it. I'll even get some of my stuff out of storage in Chicago and check in with Amy. It'll be good to take care of all that."

Ben nodded. Up. Down. Up. Down. He agreed, but not because he felt the same. He agreed because I gave him no option. I'd seen Amy do the same thing.

Joseph surprised me outside customs and baggage claim.

"So you're my advance team?"

He caught my tone and grinned. "I am your only team. Ben texted your flight information and asked me to meet you." He grabbed my bag and headed to parking. "He didn't have to ask. I would've come. You're staying with me, by the way."

"I thought I'd get a hotel, now that Ben's not with me."

"What does Ben have to do with anything?" Joseph threw me a glance. "You make me wonder if this trip signifies more. You are my sister. Yes?"

"Yes." I nodded.

"Then don't act like family isn't family."

I smiled. This from the one who hadn't gone home in seventeen years and left the day of his father's funeral.

Joseph pulled into ACI's parking lot before I realized we weren't headed to his apartment.

"We're going to the studio?" I stifled a yawn.

"We've got three days, and you don't get over jet lag by sleeping too soon. Let's get a few of your paintings back into frames."

We entered to find Lily with her face pressed into her scope, scraping at something on a small modernist piece. I leaned against her table and asked, "Anything I can do to help?"

She whacked her eye, jumping up to hug me. "You're here. I figured I wouldn't see you until tomorrow." She waved her hand at my bag. "This is so exciting. Let me see your work. The pictures you sent weren't lit well at all."

"Later. Let me frame them so they look good."

She pointed to my worktable, questioning.

"Not there. We're framing in my workroom." Joseph's voice cut across the room.

Lily raised a brow at me.

"They'll create too much dust, and you don't need the noise. You're under a tight deadline, Lily, remember?"

Lily saluted a "Yes, sir" as Joseph grabbed the duffel and headed to his office.

"I'd better go." I tapped her table. "Dinner tonight? Piccolo?"

"Yes, please. I haven't been there since you and Ben left."

"It's a date." I smiled and followed Joseph, calling to him, "Piccolo tonight?"

"I may be busy, but you go with Lily. I haven't caught up from the trip. The Van Geld estate goes up for auction next week."

Joseph does work. I remembered wondering about it . . . In fact, there was a lot I wondered about Joseph. In the couple weeks I'd spent in Atlanta before, I'd never seen him work, barely stepped into his office, and had no idea where his apartment was, despite the fact that Ben had stayed with him. And I learned little new in Montevello. I read about what he did, mostly from Alberto Rodi's journals, but still knew virtually nothing about who he was, then or now.

Joseph opened the door behind his desk.

"Lily said you had a work—" I froze.

Nothing could have prepared me for the room behind his office. This was no stark and sterile lab. This was a sanctuary. Antique lamps and objets d'art; bookshelves lined with classics; a beautiful Italian Renaissance table stretching three feet by six feet, with huge thick legs and detailed carvings along its flanks; a reading chair covered in bright red velvet, worn on the arms, pillows pushed deep within its corners; and the most beautiful rug I'd ever seen, boasting a cacophony of color in swirling patterns. And yellow. The walls were the exact yellow of Lucio's library.

He followed my gaze, which rested again on the rug. "And they say all the quality is out of Persia. I bought that in Milan a few years ago, woven in Lombardy."

His voice was light, playful, and rather than tilting his accent for his advantage, he seemed lost in his country's culture, heritage, and beauty.

I scanned the room again, absorbing my first glimpse of the true man. My gaze settled on an easel with tubes of paint filling its tray. "You still paint."

"Could you stop? Would you want to?"

I laughed and shook my head. I loved painting, and there was no way I would stop. It was there I felt most alive. *Not only there.* I mentally conceded that I felt that way with Ben too. Rachel's words over coffee that long ago day flowed through me. *You can feel just that alive every day—as long as you don't forget.*

Joseph crossed over to the easel. "Olivia has actually hosted several shows of mine. I paint under the name Luca Bellotto and I'm quite popular with Russian buyers."

"Why hide it? I even asked Ben if you still painted. He said he didn't know."

"No one does. Hence Luca." He spread his palm across his chest. "It's too raw for me. I paint from here."

I envisioned the mural and realized, again, how truly remarkable it was, how devastating— made all the more powerful when I recalled he was eighteen when he painted it.

"Someday, if you'll let me, I'd like to see your work."

"Someday." Joseph rolled a freestanding tool chest over to the table. "Time to get to *your* work. Spread them out and let's see what we're dealing with."

I pulled over some cloth-covered weights to

hold down the edges and started unrolling each canvas, now embarrassed. I knew how talented he was, but to learn he still painted, sold works, and had a Russian following—it was intimidating.

I glanced up as I spread out the first, the second, the third . . . He said nothing.

"Say it. No good?"

He didn't lift his eyes from his father's face. "*Magnifico*."

⋙ Chapter 43 ⋘

The next morning I dropped Joseph at ACI and headed across town to Gallery Barton. I hauled in the three paintings we'd already framed and found Olivia pacing.

"Good. You're finally here."

"Am I late?" I set them down and kissed both her cheeks, wondering when I'd appropriated the custom.

"Not at all, but until I actually have something in hand, I don't trust it." She tipped through the three paintings. "Such aching beauty." She then threw her arms out. "What do you think of the space? Is this what you imagined?"

I walked around. I'd sent her a color number for the walls, a deep Tuscan yellow. I called it Lucio's yellow. "It's brighter than I expected."

"The color you picked was deeper, so I

lightened it a touch. I wanted that sweet spot between taxicabs and Tuscany." She ran one jet-black nail along the wall. "A designer out of Chicago swears by taxicab-yellow walls and I can't say I disagree, especially with your work."

She crossed the gallery, her heels clicking like gunshots. "You've captured the Tuscan sensibility in such a short time. Unbelievable, really; it's like your heart was looking for a home." She spread her hand as if presenting a marquee sign. "Let me show you how I envision this, but feel free to disagree. It's your show. Dune—what a name—will be here tomorrow. He's working as handler, but he's not your caliber, so you may find your-self hanging your own pieces." She glanced back at me. "You're the talent and the crew. I've got a good feeling about this collaboration."

She flicked her finger here and there, pointing out the lighting and other details of the space—all of which would need to be taken into account when installing the show.

"And here is the dividing line between you and Stratton. He gets fully black walls. His work is an entirely white-on-white experience. I think you'll play well off each other. Possibly to your advantage, but don't tell him that."

"I won't." I circled my portion again. "And if I won't get in the way of your painters, I'll hang first thing tomorrow."

"This was supposed to be done by last week,

but that's the way it always goes. The painters should wrap up Stratton's side today."

"Good. I'll walk the space, then get back to Joseph's and finish framing."

"Glad to have you here, darling." She waved her hand and disappeared. Just. That. Fast.

I took my three paintings—one of Lucio, one of Donata, and one of my sunflower field, and positioned them side by side. I pulled out my phone and took a picture of the sunflower painting. And as Ben's voice echoed in my memory, I stored it as my home screen. *My own girasole. Please, Bella, only turn toward me.* I missed him.

I then stared at Donata. Joseph had framed her picture alone. Without even discussing it with me, he'd moved it to his side of the table and set to work. He'd chosen birch and a clean framing style, simple and unconventional, and then added a wash to the finish, laying on a subtle white patina. It was incongruent with the classic style of the picture, but highlighted the deep tones and broader strokes I'd used to form the background. It captured the painting as well as the painting had captured Donata.

I felt a sense of loss looking at her now—one I hadn't expected. I reached for my phone to e-mail Ben. I'd already called three times and sent a couple texts, but hadn't gotten through or received a reply. Cellular service within

Coccocino's kitchen was sketchy at best. An e-mail seemed my next-best option.

Dear Ben,

I'm standing in the gallery right now. Olivia painted the walls "taxicab yellow." You might not know that color, since your cabs are white. But you were here awhile; you must have seen a few. Anyway, it's a shocking, wonderful color.

I sent her my interpretation of a Tuscan yellow, but I have to admit, hers is better. It will play well against my work. The sunflowers will pop, and the glint on the bookshelves behind your father will come to life. There is no yellow to call out within the painting of your mother, but I think its absence will be striking too.

I guess that's it for now. Please call. I've tried a couple times but can't get a connection. You're probably in the kitchen.

I love you.
Emily

I walked the space, measured the walls, and made a thorough list of dimensions, lighting changes, mounting requirements, and placement. And one last time, before heading back to the studio, I tapped my phone to check messages. No missed calls. No missed texts. I tapped on e-mails. There was one—from Ben.

Dear Emily,

I am sorry I missed your calls.

I filleted an *orate* today. It is a tender whitefish; I am not certain if you have it in the States or what you call it. I envied that fish. One flick of the knife, one swipe of my hand, and it was clean. I wish life were that easy.

Alessandro came by the café this morning. Andre teased him so badly that he asked me to take a walk rather than sit. Andre will never let that go, but I doubt Alessandro cares. He came to ask my permission to court Francesca. Our word, *corteggiamento*, feels more active than your words—it is a wooing, enfolding, and embracing. Think of our nights in Atlanta. If you did not know, that was what I was about.

It was sad he had to ask me. A father should grant that honor. I did not tell Francesca. There is no need until he comes to ask for her hand in marriage, and I know that will be soon. He comes to see her every day since Papa died, wanting to be near.

I brought Mama a pizza during my break yesterday. She laughed and grumbled, as is her way. We ate in silence, but she looks better. I helped her move some of Papa's things and I put away your book pile. I hope you do not mind. As I slid yours away, I pulled down one of Papa's favorites. He loved Dante. I borrowed his *Vita Nuova* and read too late into the night. My dreams were full of dark halls and endless tunnels.

I must go back in the kitchen. *Caio*, Bella.

Vita Nuova? His dream bothered me. *Dark halls and endless tunnels?* Lucio never read anything by accident, and I suspected Ben was the same. I Googled the title. It was a mix of poetry and verse, one of Dante's few Italian rather than Latin works, and was his reconstruction of courtly love. A romance, autobiographical in nature, of his unrequited love for Beatrice Portinari—a woman he desperately loved but never "caught." A work of beauty, of longing, of letting go . . .

Ah . . . Lucio . . . Did he never understand and truly find Donata? And . . . Ben . . . What have I done?

I tapped my phone again.

"Emily?"

My heart glowed at the long trail of *e*'s, then

dimmed with its next beat. Ben's tone did not hold the notes of expectant surprise, but rather the sorrow of longing.

"Hi. I've been calling. I just read your e-mail."

"I miss you." His voice was still, without lilt or inflection.

"I miss you too. Are you busy?"

"We are. Two freezers broke. We are hurrying meats to Andre's freezers."

"Oh no, that's not good. I . . . I wish I could help."

He didn't reply.

"You need to go, don't you?"

He hesitated, and I loved him the more for it.

"I do. I wish I did not. I miss your voice."

"I will call later. I love you."

"*Ciao.*"

I tapped another number and listened to the ring.

"Hey, Emily. Why are you calling?" Amy's voice sounded harried. Everyone seemed to have something pressing.

"Does something have to be up for me to call you?"

She didn't answer for a beat. Two beats. "Well . . . yes."

"That's probably true . . . I'm in Atlanta for a couple weeks."

"Why are you in Atlanta?" I heard a shuffling noise, as if she was pulling out a chair.

"Remember that gallery we drove by? They're

having a show of my work, oils on canvas, opening tomorrow."

Her brief pause ended with a happy squeal. "Congratulations! How could you not tell me this? You should have texted; I could've come."

"Don't worry about it."

"Hey . . . I'm sorry about Ben's dad. Is he with you? Ben. Not his dad."

"No." I smiled. Amy always had a quick and easy way about her. "He stayed in Italy. Ben. Not his dad. Well, actually . . ." I stopped. It didn't feel funny. "You never texted me, by the way. What job did you take?"

"I got the job with that party planner."

"And?" I cringed and closed my eyes. My tone was too harsh. What had Amy called it? Patronizing?

"Ems, please. I'm not five."

"Yeah, I caught that too. Sorry. Tell me about the job."

"I'm good at it. Really good. In the past month I've managed three weddings and taken on more new projects than anyone here. It's a staff of seven. And I love it. Listen . . ." Her voice came soft, coaxing, across the line. "I'm doing well, Emily. Be happy for me. I shouldn't have blamed you; I never stuck up for myself. It was easier, you always making everything right, and that was on me. But I'm okay now."

She sounded as if she'd rehearsed that speech a

few times, maybe over a few years. I shook my head, as if she could see me, and so much became clear with each shake. "I *am* happy for you, and I think I got more in your way than I ever should have. That was my fault." I swiped at my eyes, surprised to find the back of my hand come away wet. "I need to go, Amy. I have a bunch of paintings left to frame today. I'll call in a few days when things are quieter. Okay?"

"When do you go home?" When I failed to give a quick reply, she called out, "Italy? Hello?"

"In a couple weeks, when the show winds down."

"Can you come up here before you go?"

"I thought about it. It'd be good to clear out the storage locker." I stood and looked around the empty gallery. "I really do need to go now."

"Okay. We'll talk soon . . . I love you, sis." Her voice sounded like she was throwing out a line. Fishing.

Maybe for the first time ever, I caught it. "I love you too."

⫸ Chapter 44 ⫷

I hoisted Lucio's portrait above my head and aimed for the three hooks I'd secured moments before. Dune, Olivia's handler, had offered to help, but as I felt he'd hung the entire Stratton show at least five inches too high, I politely refused. Besides, there was something comfortable, elemental and tactile, about doing it myself.

Olivia was right. Stratton's austere white-on-white works played well off mine. I disagreed that mine shone brighter—not like at some art shows when the velvet dogs next door make one's painting look like newly discovered Rembrandts —but we certainly didn't cheapen each other.

A soft shuffling noise turned me. Joseph approached, his eyes fixed on my centerpiece. Lucio standing in his beloved library.

"There's a red dot. Have you already sold it?"

"It's not for sale. It's for your mother." I stepped back, assessed it, and then straightened it.

"I didn't get the impression you two were close."

"True, but it's still hers. The first time I showed it to her she ran from the room. I thought she hated it, but then your father said he wanted to be remembered that way, and I figured maybe she saw that too."

"I expect she did." Joseph nodded, still fixated on the painting. "Will you take it or ship it?"

His question surprised me. And yet it didn't. I knew what he was really asking, and I had no ready answer. I loved Ben. But I hadn't found my place within Montevello, within Ben's family, and I wasn't sure I would or could. The way I viewed the world and how things worked didn't come close to the swirling sense of life there. I felt displaced and didn't know if I could survive that for ten, twenty, fifty years . . .

Joseph left the gallery before I answered his question—before I even tried. I watched as his car rounded the corner before I pulled my phone from my back pocket and slid down the wall to the floor. The *girasole* picture on my home screen didn't generate its usual smile.

I tapped Ben's picture. No answer. I waited for voice mail. "Hey, Ben—just calling to say hi. You're probably starting service right now. I'll try later."

I tapped off the call and onto e-mail.

Hey Ben,

I just left you a message. I miss you. More than you know. I've attached a picture of your father's portrait. It's the show's centerpiece. You can see the yellow wall behind it and the red dot on the card, lower left. Joseph thought it strange I was saving it for your mother. But it belongs to her. I know Lucio would want that.

I've been staring at it all morning. You have his eyes. His heart too. You and he are the two best men I've ever known. Please call.

I love you.
Emily

A few hours later, with still no call from Ben, I cleaned the last of the debris and mess from Joseph's worktable and headed toward ACI's front door.

"Wear something beautiful tonight." Joseph saw me leaving and called out. "Tonight is about art, but art is about beauty and desire. The art and the artist are both on display."

With only an answering nod, I pushed out the studio doors. As much as I didn't want to be on display, even chafed that I would be, he was right. Artist and art, in many ways, became one. That was one reason Joseph used an alias, and the reason my own paintings almost brought me to tears. I still felt as if every time I looked at them—Ben, Lucio, Donata—I was trying to reach them, and failing.

As I drove to the gallery, I realized that Joseph had pegged only part of the equation. Art is about beauty and desire, yes, but it's also about truth. That's what pricked my eyes, not the paintings, but what they conveyed. Truth.

And when art touched the soul, it was because it spoke to something beyond ourselves and the temporal; it called out to our deepest understandings and dreams. It reached higher. It meant more. I saw that in Ben's, Lucio's, and Donata's portraits—in their eyes. I saw them.

With a head full of musings and questions, but no answers, I pulled up to the gallery. I caught

Olivia in the window, looking pristine in white linen. She'd dressed with cool confidence, but her quick steps betrayed serious nerves.

Soon I was as jumpy as she was—especially when her seemingly disembodied head popped out from Stratton's white-on-white world and barked at Dune.

"Did you do that on purpose?" I flicked my finger to the painting behind her.

She looked back at Stratton's ten-by-ten-foot "blizzard" behind her and laughed. "I like to share in the experience, but this isn't working, is it?"

I shook my head.

"I should've dressed for your show. I have just the blouse to get lost in those flowers your husband sent."

"What flowers?" I spun, searching.

She pointed to a table just on the edge of Stratton's black walls.

Girasoli.

The massive crystal vase was filled with over twenty large sunflowers standing at least thirty-six inches high. I fingered one and tried to gently twist it. Packed too tight, it wouldn't turn. "They're gorgeous."

"They are. They set just the right tone." She swayed side to side, taking in the gallery. "I love this moment. Right before flight. Can you feel it?"

Flight. I released the flower and stepped back.

"Olivia, I . . . I'm all set up, but I need to go. I'll be back before opening . . . but . . . I'll see you soon." I backed toward the door.

A Portrait of the Artist as a Young Man.

I finally knew why Lucio had laid it on my stack of books.

And it broke my heart . . .

I drove back to Joseph's apartment, refusing to think, refusing to feel. I needed to be alone and motionless to work through this one. I pulled into the parking space in front of his town house and froze. *Amy?*

She saw me before I turned off the engine and was by the door as I opened it. "Surprise!"

I climbed out and hugged her. "What are you doing here?"

"I came to celebrate with you. Ben's not here; you need family to share with. Joseph knows, obviously. He gave me his address." She trailed me up the walk and through the front door. "This is your big moment. Are you okay?"

I dropped my bag on the floor and flopped on Joseph's couch. "I read this book and I finally get it, but now you're here." I looked up at her. "You came."

Amy said nothing. She shot me a strange look but stayed silent and dropped next to me.

"It was a puzzle, a collage of emotion and turmoil along with musings on art, religion, politics, and the nature of true beauty. The hero, Stephen Dedalus, was trying to figure out how to be a man and, in the end, an artist." I leaned back and took a long, deep breath. "Maybe that's why I hated it. He kept trying to define himself. I do that too. I mean, isn't that what *The Way Things Work* is all about? Even when you teased me about it, I didn't see it. We both know what I'm trying to fix."

Rather than reply, Amy simply reached for my hand. I covered it with my other one and kept on.

"But it was harder than Stephen Dedalus thought. It's harder than I thought. He had to leave everything behind, like that Greek myth of Daedalus where he makes his beautiful wings and flies away. That was his name, too, in the book. And that's what he was telling me. He knew I'd need to leave, that I'd never fit in and understand. He was giving me permission to leave."

"The author?" Amy tilted her head, clearly not following me. I couldn't blame her. I wasn't following me.

"Lucio."

"Lucio wrote the book?"

"You're not listening." I moaned and covered my face.

Amy pulled my hands away and held them in my lap. "I'm listening; you're not making sense."

"I'm saying I fell in love with Ben and I thought it'd be enough. He was the dream. And, like you said, marriage is for life and I thought once I married him, that's how it would work. Not for Mom and Dad, but for me. It would all be fixed, finished. But when I got into it . . . I can't fix all I got wrong, and Lucio knew that. He knew I would need to get back to a place I understood and was comfortable. He knew I'd have to stop trying to be something I'm not."

"But I was here, Ems. I saw you . . . You were the best *you* I've ever known. You weren't pretending anything." She flopped back against the cushion next to me. "Do you remember the night Dad left?"

"No."

"I do. It's actually my first memory. I was six, so I should have some before that, but I can't dig any up . . . Anyway, Mom and Dad were yelling, and we both woke up. I said I was scared, and do you remember what you did?"

"Gave you a lecture? Built you headphones from Barbie hair and paper clips?"

"No. You climbed down from your bunk and crawled into bed beside me and held my hand. You didn't say anything. I woke the next morning still holding your hand."

"Why are you telling me this now?"

"Because that's the sister I saw when I was last here. That's the sister who shared the longest night of my life with me and the sister who brought me down here today. And I don't believe she got it all wrong then, and I don't believe she is trying to be something she's not now."

"You don't?" I swung my head toward her. "Then what went wrong?"

"Nothing. You just don't want to get hurt anymore."

⫸ Chapter 45 ⫷

She says some things can't be fixed. We just have to endure them. Wisdom relayed by a fourteen-year-old girl, but I hadn't listened.

My taxi pulled into the airport as my phone rang. *Joseph.* I'd completely forgotten about him. I was tempted not to answer, but I tapped the phone anyway.

"Where are you?" came across the line in a furious faux-whisper.

"I'm going home." I rustled through my bag for my credit card and handed it to the driver. "My cab is pulling up to the airport right now, and Amy is headed to the gallery to meet you."

"You're leaving your sister with me?"

"You can handle her." I smiled at his dry tone. "And it's pretty incredible that she came, so be nice to her. Can you believe she did that?"

"I'm having less trouble believing that than the fact that you're at the airport and not on your way here. What are you doing? Are you trying to end your career before it starts?"

"I'm not. Sincerely. Amy can handle all the details. You said yourself art is about beauty and desire. Amy's gorgeous and poised; she'll handle it all perfectly."

"She's not the artist."

"True." I got my card back and rolled my bag into the airport. "Hang on . . ." I stepped into a quiet corner by the door. Planes passed overhead. I was about to be on one of those.

"Are you still there?" Joseph barked.

"Yes, sorry. I was getting out of the cab . . . Listen, I am the artist, Joseph, I do know that, but my art doesn't come from a place like yours. You've found a home in Atlanta and it works for you, but my art came from screwing up on a daily basis within your family. Mine came from not knowing most of the conversations swirling around me and getting slighted by your aunt Sophia; from every story your father told and every book, good or bad, he passed my way; and from every nasty look your mother sent me. It came from watching her dote on your father, adore Ben, and even send you achingly painful looks whenever you crossed her line of sight a couple weeks ago."

I heard a slight intake of breath, but I couldn't stop. I couldn't risk his opinion, his advice, or his disdain. I needed to finish this.

"It came from sharing their lives, Joseph, when I forgot about trying to fix them. I don't need to fly away to be free and find my art; I need to tuck in and let go of trying to control it. If I don't go home right now, I'll lose it all—everything that matters to me. And for once I have no plan, nothing to do or fix. I just need to be there and . . . I don't know how else to say it, but I need their mess and to accept and forgive my own. And in the end, I think that's what your father was trying to do, too, but he couldn't see it clearly. Just like you said, he got it wrong sometimes."

I waited, expecting Joseph to launch at me. He didn't.

"Joseph? Are you still there?"

"You're so dramatic I was afraid to interrupt. Are you finished yet?" He added an Italian lilt to his dry sarcasm.

"You're such a jerk." I laughed. "I want the show to be a success tonight, Joseph, but I can't come back . . . Will you help?"

"Of course." He sighed. "I'll even escort Amy around the gallery and weave a sense of mystery and romance around your absence. Olivia will eat it up."

"Good, 'cause I've got a surprise for you someday soon."

"What?"

"Nothing yet. Just an idea. I've got a plane to catch. *Arrivederci*, Joseph."

"Wait, Em—"

I clicked off my phone and headed to the ticket counter. It was time to catch a plane; Joseph's questions could wait.

❧ Chapter 46 ☙

The plane touched down, and I grabbed my phone to call Ben. No answer. Again.

I vacillated between hurt, annoyance, pure anger, fright, and anticipation—emotions overlapping, crashing into one another, and churning in my stomach.

I grabbed my chocolate, hurried my way through customs, seized my bag, ran to *Autonoleggio*, and rented my own tiny car. I set my GPS to Montevello and was on my way home like a true Italian—darting in and out of traffic like a crazy woman, too tired to be scared.

I accelerated as I merged onto the highway leaving Florence and sped down the hill, racing in and out of shadow into the valley below, buildings soon giving way to piney woods, olive trees, and cultivated fields and farmhouses. Outside Panzano, I waved hello to the small trattorias, the *emporio* where Clara the shopkeeper ordered my cleaners, solvents, and a few hard-to-find glues, and drove past my favorite field of sunflowers. My *girasoli*.

I slowed to take them in. At present they faced away from me, but they'd turn. They were smarter than I'd been. They always followed the light.

I stomped the accelerator again and turned onto the Vassallos's gravel drive. The quarter mile gave me time to form words . . . any words. None came.

I slowed at the front door and, setting one foot down, realized that none of the words I imagined could quite work. I wasn't sure what I was chasing myself; I just had a feeling about it. There was something wonderful, expectant, and glorious ahead. *Joy*. But I had no idea how to articulate it.

The door opened, and there she stood. "I heard noise" were Donata's only words, but at least she said them in English so I could understand.

"*Buongiorno*," I offered.

She raised an eyebrow and left it arched high. "Why are you here?"

"*Sono a casa*." *I'm home.*

"He is not here."

I'd imagined our chat over coffee, maybe even a bite of pasta, but it was going to take place here, standing face-to-face in the late-morning sun on a gravel drive, without Ben's support.

"I'll find him at Coccocino, but first I wanted to talk to you. I'm sorry it needs to be in English, but I don't know how to say it in Italian."

Donata nodded.

I tried to take a deep breath, but my chest was

too tight. "I never meant to bring you pain, in so many ways, and I hope you will forgive me. And I want to share something with you . . . Would you let me . . ."

My pulse filled my head and ears. This was going to be either the start or the end of us. Donata didn't seem to allow for much waffling in the middle.

"Would you . . . let me finish the mural? In the church? Joseph didn't finish the story, and we need it. We, all of us, need the fact and the reminder of grace and forgiveness. Maybe that's what Lucio wanted, but even he didn't understand how to tell us . . . And maybe I don't either, but this feels like the place to start. The only place to start." I noticed my hands flapping in front of me and I clasped them together to quiet them, to quiet me.

I continued more slowly, hoping she could understand. "I need to stop feeling like if I don't put it back together, I'll never be whole. And I need Ben and I need you. And Joseph too. I need him as a brother, but he needs us. Maybe he never knew, or he forgot. But I think, through the mural, we can reach him too."

Donata didn't speak, but she wasn't yelling either, and that gave me courage.

"If we finish the story, as it is supposed to end, we'll better understand. I know we will . . . And I thought together, you and I might . . ."

I dropped my hands. I didn't know how to say it in English. How could I possibly expect her to understand it? I simply knew that to stay and share life, we needed to finish that story because, unlike all the others, that one was ours. Life and story were, in fact, one.

"*Sì.*"

"Yes," I repeated. "Yes? Are you sure? I mean, did you understand? Because I was asking—"

She held up a hand, and I noticed her knuckles were just beginning to bend with age. "I understand and I agree. It is not right to leave out the vital part, but"—she tapped her heart with a bent finger—"for so many years, it has hurt. I am tired of hurting so. I am weak with it." She used that same finger to point within the house. "Come. I am making the pasta."

"I . . ." My lips parted. "I would love that, but I need to go find Ben. I don't think he thought I was coming back and . . ." I shrugged. "I wasn't sure myself, until yesterday, but I am. I mean, I'm sure, not that I'm back. You can see I'm back. I mean I'm sure I'm staying."

I stopped talking, way too late.

Donata stared at me like I wasn't making sense—and I wasn't. She repeated her first words. "He is not here."

"I know. I'll go to Coccocino now." I pointed down the drive as if that clarified everything.

She shook her head. "He left yesterday, to go

for you. He said he would move there, for you."

"But I'm here!"

"*Sì*. I see that." Her eyes lit with a beautiful smile. It was her first to me and I reciprocated with, probably, my first to her. "Call him."

"I've tried. He doesn't answer."

She waved me to follow her into the house. "He had three stops. Maybe he is not landed."

"I had four." I laughed and pressed my lips together. Tears were next.

I followed her through the hallway and back to the kitchen. It smelled of tomatoes and basil. Not cooked, but clean and raw and infinitely Italian.

"When he lands, he will call."

I smiled, because of course he would. A good Italian boy will always call his mama. Donata's smile told me she knew it too.

She pointed to the huge wood island, dusted with flour. "Wash your hands and I will show you."

Hours later, I washed my hands again and walked out onto the patio. The sun had warmed the flagstones and heat came from above and below— it warmed my skin and bones on its way to my soul. But the sun wasn't high now; it was moving toward the hills and would soon set. Day was ending, and I still hadn't heard from Ben.

I tapped his smiling face on my phone and prayed he would answer.

On the third ring . . . "Emily?" One word, filled with a few *e*'s and endless hope.

I felt my eyes prick again. "I'm—I'm home and you're not."

"I missed your show last night. But I am here, and Joseph is not home. Are you close? Can you let me in?"

Donata stepped next to me and angled her face to my phone. "Tell him he wastes good money." As she pulled away, a smile curled the tiniest corner of her lip. She was so like her elder son—light with the compliments. At least I thought it was a compliment.

Ben's shout brought me back. "Is that Mama?"

I nodded and then realized he couldn't see me. "She said to tell you—Oh, never mind. I'm standing on the back patio having just ruined an entire batch of pasta, but your mother's not yelling, so there's hope, but you're not here and—"

"Bella. Shhh . . ."

I sucked in a deep breath and whispered, "I know what you thought, and I'm sorry." Silence met me. The sun crept behind the hill, taking the heat with it. "Ben?"

"Do not move," he whispered in reply. "Not a muscle."

I smiled because he was so unlike his mother and brother in that way. Ben savored moments, brought them forward to recapture and linger over them. He also laid on the compliments thick, like his *Bistecca alla pizzaiola*—a sauce so thick it could almost stand. I heard his promise, his love, and I understood him. I barely contained my excitement. Barely.

"Can I get a bite to eat? I ruined mine, but your mother's pasta came out really well. She might give me some. And perhaps I could take a short nap?"

He chuckled as a breeze sent the olive leaves dancing. "Only because it will take me some time. I *am* coming for you."

"Good, because I love you."

"That is all I need to know. *Ciao, Bella. Ti amo.*" He sighed across the line. "I will be home soon."

⫸ Chapter 47 ⫷

Six months later

It took Ben sixteen hours . . .

It took Joseph . . . until today . . .

"What are you doing out here?" Ben whispered as his arms slid around my waist.

I kept my eyes on the farthest hill. "I came to see the sunset. It's different now. Winter doesn't shoot off the same colors." I snuggled deeper into his sweater that I'd grabbed from the back of a chair.

"They'll be back." Ben pulled me against him and rested his chin on the top of my head.

"Are you watching?"

"*Sì*. It's the most beautiful moment of the day. It reminds me of Papa."

"Is he here?"

"Dust just kicked up on the drive. It will be any minute. Do you want to come up and say hello?"

"Not yet." I shook my head. "Your mother asked everyone to wait until at least nine to come over tonight. She's nervous. Let's give them a moment. This has been a long time coming."

Eighteen years and six months.

And the last six months alone had been staggering . . .

After Father Matt's first exclamation of surprise, he welcomed me into the church each morning and read aloud as I painted. Each and every day. He said I needed to better know this man I was about to add to the church walls. And he was right. It took me time to understand even the smallest fraction of the grace, wisdom, and unconditional love I sought to convey through the mural.

Some I learned from Donata. We were changing together, and although we scraped and bumped occasionally, she no longer shooed me from her kitchen. She didn't purse her lips when she spoke English. And she even slowed her words, inviting me to understand and learn her Italian.

And when Olivia finally sent Lucio's portrait

back, Donata had reached for my hand with both her own and clasped it tight. Now the portrait hung above the fireplace in the library and often, when I looked up from working on a painting or reading a book, I found Donata curled in Lucio's chair across from me, reading or simply staring at her husband.

Some I learned from Francesca. No longer trying to manage or "fix" her, I listened to her—as she planned her wedding, whined about Alessandro's taciturn nature, or daydreamed about married life. Those last musings always made me smile. Rachel's words came back to me often as Francesca chatted. *You can feel just that alive every day . . . After all, you get to be with that one guy who lights up your world and shares it with you.* Francesca was going to have a wonderful time. I was having a wonderful time.

Those "sisterly" moments also made me realize what I'd missed with my own sister. We were only now beginning to share like that, and as Amy would say, it was "on me" that we'd missed so much.

I felt Ben smile against the top of my head. "Look."

We watched as the sun's last rays ignited the white underbellies of the olive leaves. It looked like silver flashing within gold. It was beautiful and never failed to thrill me. Within seconds, it was gone and the hillside shaded and cooled.

I turned in Ben's arms. "We should go now."

"Are you going to be okay?"

I loved the hint of concern in his voice and kissed him. His eyes widened in surprise.

"You once told me that Piccolo was never about the restaurant. It was always about Maria and Vito. I won't be sad about the mural either, even if Joseph scrubs the wall, paints over my work, and starts afresh. I truly don't believe it all could've happened any other way."

I'd sent Joseph a picture of the completed mural only days before. Within seconds, I received a five-word text.

You lack the necessary skill.

My next text was from Lily asking me what I'd done to get Joseph on a plane home so fast. He was leaving ACI in her care to "restore a ruined beauty" back home.

"Okay, forget all that." I shook my head. "I'm not as mature as you. It'll kill me. It was some of my best work."

"I disagree." Ben chuckled. "I think the eyes ended up a little freaky." His tone captured my Midwestern notes perfectly.

Sarcasm. I smiled, kissed him again, and pulled him up the hill.

The kitchen lights spilled into the darkening evening. Candles lit the farm table on the patio, and Ben had lit a fire in the stone fireplace at the patio's edge.

Ten places were set, but I knew Donata had planned and cooked for at least sixty. Her son was home. And laughter from the kitchen confirmed it. No one had obeyed her—family had arrived early.

Ben reached his arm around me and kissed my temple. "And that, my dear, was our last moment of peace. Shall we join the others? I suspect dinner is about to begin."

A Peek Behind the Curtain . . .

This page is great fun. Yes, there is the risk of forgetting someone who has helped shaped the journey, the story, and that would be bad . . . But there is also the joy of remembering—and the delight of introducing them to you . . .

I'll begin by introducing the fiction within my fiction. First, Montevello. It's the one and only fictional town I've created and I hope you enjoyed it. Think Montepulciano meets Montefalco meets Vitigliano and you're getting close. Throw in a bit of my "research trip" truffle hunting, wine tasting, olive oil tasting, eating, walking, and more eating, and you are there. I hope you savored Montevello's steep, narrow streets and sunbaked walls—and the espresso. Second, my Italian. It was important to me to use, in many ways, "incorrect" Italian—a learner's Italian with words, verbs, and conjugations occasionally wrong as it is what Emily heard and interpreted. I hope these constructions didn't prove too jarring to my fluent Italian-speaking friends.

Now you must meet some extraordinary people. Daisy Hutton, editor, publisher, and friend, is a daily inspiration. She gives the best of herself to every project and every writer—with an amazingly contagious smile. I hope never to take her faith in me, or in these stories, for granted. Thank you, Daisy.

The incredible team at HCCP is next—Jodi Hughes, Kristen Ingebretson, Paul Fisher, Becky Monds, Stephen Tindal, and the amazing Sales Team who work tirelessly to make these stories beautiful and get them into your hands. Kristen Golden gets a special shout-out and introduction. She shares her publicist acumen, excellent taste in books, and extraordinary glow and glitter with me—and I'm the better for it.

And now meet The Home Team:

Claudia Cross brings literary knowledge, diplomacy, my kind of humor, and great generosity as my agent, mentor, and friend. Elizabeth Lane dreams up the "events" with me, and is my first, last, and all-stages-in-the-middle reader. She is also my beloved sister. The three MMRs always play an important role . . . Three generations of Joy Seekers: Meet my mother, my cousin, and my younger daughter.

And though you've met them before . . . the entirety of Team Reay is ever-present and deserves mention. The kids are growing older, but we parents have decided to stop *all* growing for a time. We'd like to savor these last years before they're out of the house and not weighing in on stories or dinner plans and fighting us for control of the music.

Last, but never least . . . meet you. You are a vast set of wonderfulness full of readers, bloggers, reviewers, and now friends who have generously read these novels, joined in this journey, and reached out, meeting me on social media or in person. Thank you.

Again and again, *thank you* to everyone in this beloved cast. I'm beyond grateful to share *A Portrait of Emily Price* with you. Let's join together for something new this time next year . . .

Discussion Questions

1. Emily believes all can be fixed at the beginning of her story. Whether you believe it's true or not, can you see yourself acting in this way or have you seen others doing so? Is it a common belief? Do we have control over anything/everything or is Emily deceiving herself?

2. At Ammazza, Emily looks at Ben and realizes he might "find a sense of wonder, a sense of wholeness or delight" in her. Why do you think she finds that disconcerting? Would you?

3. Everything Emily touches she tries to fix. What drives that? Have you ever felt such compulsion? Are we naturally wired that way or is it fairly unique?

4. Emily wonders, *What if I'm trying to be someone I can be?* Have you ever felt like that? More comfortable in a new aspect of you, while afraid it may not be real?

5. At her wedding, fears plague Emily. Do you feel she's stepped too far too fast? How

realistic is it that someone could find something so special she is ready to leap that fast? Have you ever done something so bold?

6. Amy tells Emily that marriage within two weeks is "for lust, not love." She then withdraws the statement. Was she right the first or the second time? Can someone find "true love" in only a matter of weeks? What does "true love" even mean?

7. Francesca calls Emily an "Emma." Is Emily meddling or innocently helping a friend? Or asked another way . . . Is she helping Francesca or herself?

8. We all have a lens through which we see the world. What are some of them you see in these characters? Do you see any within yourself?

9. In watching Donata, how easy or hard is it to become trapped in one's mistakes or what others tell us about ourselves?

10. Lucio teaches and shares through books. Do you think he was trying to teach Emily about herself through his choices or simply sharing something about himself?

11. The changes in Emily's art surprise her as it develops from "freaky" eyes to capturing the

essence of the person she paints. What does she discover within her art, and what brought about that change?

12. Why did Emily ask Ben not to come with her to Atlanta? Was she running to or away from something? Can they be the same thing?

13. Do you think Lucio gave Emily *A Portrait of the Artist as a Young Man* as an escape hatch like Emily thought, or could he have had another purpose in mind? Or no purpose at all?

14. The author brings Emily and Donata together before Emily finds Ben. Why do you think that was important to her?

15. In finishing the mural, what was Emily chasing? Did she find it?

16. Do you think Joseph will "stay," emotionally if not physically? Why or why not?

About the Author

Katherine Reay has enjoyed a lifelong affair with the works of Jane Austen and her contemporaries. After earning degrees in history and marketing from Northwestern University, she worked in not-for-profit development before returning to school to pursue her MTS. Katherine lives with her husband and three children in Chicago, Illinois.

Visit her website at www.katherinereay.com
Twitter: @Katherine_Reay
Facebook: katherinereaybooks

Center Point Large Print
600 Brooks Road / PO Box 1
Thorndike, ME 04986-0001 USA

(207) 568-3717

US & Canada:
1 800 929-9108
www.centerpointlargeprint.com